A
THRONE OF
WINGS & EMBERS

THE FORBIDDEN HEIR TRILOGY | BOOK THREE

EMILIA JAE

EMILIA JAE
FANTASY AUTHOR
EM'S BOOKISH REALM

A Throne of Wings and Embers | The Forbidden Heir Trilogy: Book Three.

Front Cover Art: Celia Driscoll

The Map of Velyra: Andres Aguirre | @aaguirreart

Interior Art in Order: Celia Driscoll, Dakota @bookishkoda, & Lena @l.moon_art, @pandacapuccino

Editor: Makenna Albert | www.onthesamepageediting.com

Proof Reader: Tabitha Chandler | www.tabithadoesediting.com

First Edition | September 2024.

Paperback ISBN: 979-8-9888968-4-5 | Hardcover ISBN: 979-8-9888968-5-2

Content Warning

Please note that this book is not intended for readers below the age of 18, and may also contain content that some readers might find triggering. This warning is due to explicit language, descriptive violence/gore, mass executions, PTSD, mentions of past child abuse, and mentions of sexual assault.

This series has multiple POVs, including the villains. Please note that these villains are true in their nature. They are wicked to their core and you will see inside of their minds, which can be disturbing to some readers.
Reader's discretion is advised.

VELYRA

VAYR SEA

ANERYS

ALAIA VALLEY

EZRANIAN MOUNTAIN RANGE

ELLECASTER

CELAN VILLAGE

VAYR SEA

THE ELORA ISLES

THE SYLIS FOREST

CETO BAY

TORTUNELL

ISLA

DORAELI

VAYR SEA

to the eldest daughters who carry
the weight of their own realm on
their shoulders.

to the quiet girls who are dreamers
with stories in their heads and
endless love in their hearts.

& to all the women who have ever
felt the need to prove themselves in
a man's world.

this is for you.
this is for all of us.

PRONUNCIATION GUIDE

Elianna (Lia) Solus: Ellie-Ana (Leah) Soul-iss
Jace Cadoria: Jayce Ka-door-ia
Kellan Adler: Kell-an Add-ler
Avery Valderre: Ay-ver-ee Val-dare
Finnian: Finn-ee-an
Zaela: Zay-lah
Veli Elora: Vel-ee El-or-ah
Nyra: Near-ah
Nox: Nocks
Idina: Eh-deena
Callius: Kal-ee-us
Kai: K-eye
Azenna: Az-enn-ah
Empri: Em-pree
Madalae: Mad-a-lay
Sylvae: Sil-vay
Matthias: Math-thigh-as
Bruhn: Broon
Agdronis: Ag-dron-iss
Euphoroot: You-for-root

Places:

Kingdom of Velyra: Vel-ear-ah
City of Isla: Eye-la
Ezranian Mountains: Ehz-rain-ian
Sylis Forest: Sigh-liss
Alaia Valley: Al-eye-ah
City of Anerys: An-air-iss
Elora Isles: El-or-ah
Vayr Sea: Vay-er
Doraeli: Door-aye-lee
Tortunele: Tor-tune-elle

Spells & Language of the Gods:

Ignystae: Ig-nee-stay
Tinaebris Malifisc: Tin-aye-bree Mal-if-isc
Malifisc Venitian: Mal-if-isc Ven-ee-shun
Venifikas Sussorae: Ven-if-ik-us Suss-or-aye
(The Witch's Whisper)
Umbra Selair: Um-bra Soul-air
(Shadow Summoning)
Impyrum Kortyus: Imp-ear-iam Court-ee-ous
(Mind Control)
Odium Embulae: Oh-dee-um Em-boo-lay
(Rift Walking/Portal)
Meritsas Lokoi: Mer-it-sass Low-koi
(Truth Speaking)

Prologue

The Heir

EVERYTHING THAT I AM and everything that I have yet to become, I owe to the family I have made—for what is a queen without her court? Who would I be, or who would my rage reshape me into without my court of rebels and mate at my side to ground me?

The realm was my birthright by blood and claim, and since the moment I took my first breath in this unforgiving world, its malevolent beings have done everything in their power to rip it from my grasp.

Too long had I been forced to lurk in the shadows of the castle, never allowed to know the true love of kin. Too long had the realm been forced to bear the wrath of the wicked queen and her scorned hatred for my father. And too fucking long had I endured manipulation, trickery, and abuse from those I should have been able to trust.

The Kingdom of Velyra would be mine if it were the last thing I ever did, for the realm itself would not rest as long as my lungs breathed air.

Heir of the Realm.

Descendant of the First of the Fae.

True Heir of the Mother Goddess, Terra.

The One Who Was Promised.

Lia Solus, Captain of the Velyran army, a hidden orphan raised by the castle staff, and secret daughter of the king, was no more—for she has been mended and reforged into what she was always meant to be.

Elianna Valderre—Queen of the Realm.

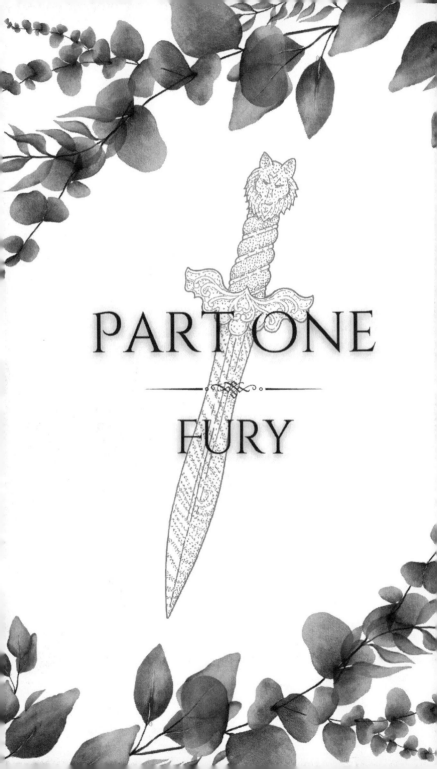

PART ONE

FURY

ONE

Jace

I STOOD TEN PACES behind my queen, watching as she took her reforged blade and slit Vincent's throat. I had seen her wield weapons in battle and hold her own against multiple men twice her size, but something about her finally taking a sliver of her revenge had unleashed the primal beast beneath my skin.

Lia released her prisoner's blood-soaked, lifeless body and left him slumped in the chair he was bound to as she approached the three of us.

Gage stood at attention beside me, face hard as stone, and it was one of the few times in my life where I couldn't read him. Zaela, on the other hand, wore her concern like a heavy cloak, her furrowed brow and tense shoulders giving her away. I couldn't take my eyes off my mate, feeling a wave of pride wash over me, knowing how much she craved the taste of revenge—needing it more than the air she breathed.

Lia re-sheathed her dagger at her side and halted before us. "We leave *now*," she announced, turning to move toward the entrance.

I took a step forward to follow, but Zaela rushed past me and caught up to her instantly. "Is this wise, Lia? I understand you are upset, rightfully so, but—"

Lia stopped in her tracks. "But?" She tilted her head to the side, and Zae physically tensed beneath her stare.

For the first time in my life, I witnessed Zaela gulp. "But," she hesitated. "We should come up with a plan before we make our move. It could be a trap. You never know at this point."

"It isn't a trap. They are *fleeing*. I watched the fear slither into Vincent's eyes when he realized I put it all together. If we don't move now, we could miss them," she said and went to turn, but then stopped herself. "And besides... I have a wyvern."

Lia pushed past her, and I took a step closer to Zaela. "Now is not the time to question her," I breathed as I moved to guide her with me to the door.

"Lia knows what she's doing," Gage chimed in from my other side, not sounding entirely convinced of his own statement.

"Let's hope so, for our sake," she whispered as we followed Lia into the gloomy, mud-slicked streets.

Lia burst through the townhouse's door, and Avery and Veli were instantly on their feet, jumping up from where they sat and waited for our return. Nyra was also now alert where she sat next to Avery; her once blood-stained coat was now washed and clean.

"Where have you been?!" Avery shrieked as she stared at us with eyes full of worry.

My mate didn't answer her as she stormed up the stairs, her heavy footsteps echoing throughout the townhouse.

I turned to Avery. "We have...business to attend to," I said as gently as possible.

"Business?" she erupted as she crossed her arms and stared at me. "What kind of business? You all need rest! It is nearly the middle of the day, and none of you have slept. Where did you even go?"

I smirked as she tried to mother the warriors among her.

"Avery, will you please, for the love of the gods, just *shut up* and let them do what they need to?" Veli hissed from the corner where she stood.

Avery whipped around to her. "No, I won't. Not if my sister is about to go on a *death* spree and possibly get herself killed."

"She will be okay. Nothing will happen to her, I promise you," I said as I gently placed my hand on her shoulder.

She looked up at me, eyes clouded with judgment. "You? Who just lied to us all? Some mate you are to her." Avery ripped her shoulder from my grasp.

My jaw popped open, and I tried to reel in my temper before it was accidentally unleashed on her when she had only voiced her feelings. "I thought I was doing the right thing. You were all drinking, and I refused to have her out there if she wasn't sober and battle-ready. It was to *protect* her. All of you."

Her glare softened as she continued to stare at me. "You should've been honest," she whispered. "You should've known she would come after you."

I gave her a curt nod. "You're absolutely right. I made a bad call. It won't happen again. That I can assure you."

As if it wasn't bad enough that I had to deal with Lia being upset with me, but now her sister, too, and my cousin.

Gods, Cadoria, what the fuck did you do?

"Promise?" she breathed as she held out her dainty pinky finger.

I chuckled, feeling the room shift into something lighter—thank the gods. I held up my pinky, but she ripped hers away.

"I take these incredibly seriously," she stated sternly.

The corner of my lip lifted. "I would hope so. These are currency around here," I joked, and she reluctantly wrapped her pinky around mine. Her intense stare and features slowly softened, and I stopped myself from blowing out a breath of relief.

A loud crash sounded from upstairs, followed by a guttural scream of frustration, forcing our gazes to the ceiling.

"What the hell is she even doing?" Veli asked from where she remained in the corner.

"I assumed getting supplies, but now I'm not so sure," I answered as my heart raced.

"You all reek of death. Who did you kill?" she hissed.

Avery's eyes flared, and she sniffed the air, which earned her a look from Zae. She turned to Veli. "That nose of yours is terrifying. What exactly does death smell like?"

Veli rolled her eyes and ignored her as she turned to me. "Well?"

I cleared my throat. "We took a prisoner captive, and he is...no longer."

"Kellan?!" Avery shrieked hopefully.

"His second. Vincent, I believe his name was."

Her brows furrowed. "I don't think I know that one."

Gage took a step closer to her, and her eyes lit up. "He was the one who stabbed Landon."

Her face twisted with both sadness and fury. "Then I am glad you killed him." She then smiled up at him, and the sudden change was a little alarming, but so was the past twenty-four hours. We were all out of our minds with grief and shock.

"Lia killed him. We just captured him," Zaela said as another loud crash sounded.

Avery's eyes flared. "You know," she gulped. "I always used to ask her what it was like to kill someone, and she would refuse to talk about it. Perhaps it bothers her more than she lets on."

I hadn't known that. In fact, I *hated* that I was unaware of that little bit of information.

As I delved into our bond that still burned with her fury, I tried to push my own emotions aside to get a better sense of any other sensations my Lia might have been harboring, but I felt nothing.

"I'm going to go check on her," I announced, then bolted up the stairs as fast as my legs would carry me.

The wooden floor creaked beneath my boots as I rounded the corner at the top of the staircase. Peering down the hall, I could see the door to our bedroom was cracked open.

Silently, I made my way through the dimly lit hallway and looked into the room through the narrow opening of the door. When I couldn't see much of anything, my hand instinctively moved to push the door open, and as it swung wide, the sight of the shattered mirror and the mess of objects strewn across the floor made my heart lurch.

"Lia?" My voice was gentle. "Lia, I know you're in here." I took a step in and glanced over to the other side of the bed. She was sitting on the floor, shrinking up against the wall, with tears streaming down her face as her chin rested on her knees.

She slowly met my gaze. "What have I done?"

My eyes widened, and I leapt over the bed and was in front of her instantly. I dropped to my knees and reached over to gently wipe her tears as they continued to pour from her silver-lined eyes. My thumb smudged the dirt and gore that had caked onto her face to find that her tears had stained her cheeks.

"What do you mean?" I asked as tenderly as I could manage, trying to keep her from sensing my concern.

"You need to get as far away from me as possible, if only until I deal with this disaster. The others, too," she choked out.

My brows furrowed. "Lia, I'm not following."

"Do you love me?" she asked, and my heart painfully thudded at her question.

"More than anything," my voice rasped out as my eyes frantically searched hers.

"I cannot understand how." She let out a gut-wrenching sob. "Everyone who has ever cared for me is *dead*. I'm a monster. You need to get as far away from me as possible and take the rebels with you. Please."

I stared at her in silence for a few seconds. "My Lia," I started, but she stopped me instantly.

"Don't you fucking *dare* say it isn't true! I killed my own mother!" she shouted. Her voice lowered to barely above a whisper. "And then my father and Lukas were murdered because of me. Everyone I love is killed. Everything I touch withers." Her stare lifted to meet mine once more. "And if something happens to you, I will never forgive myself. The gods may as well rip my soul from the realm and burn it to ash because I won't survive. This all started because of me, and now I must be the one to end it."

My shaking hand reached out and cupped the back of her head, pulling her closer to me. I pressed my lips to her forehead and held it there as a tear of my own slipped from me.

"I used to think there wasn't a single fucking thing in this realm that I wouldn't do for you," I admitted, and slowly released my hold on her as I pulled back. "But I just realized that there is, and it's that." Our eyes were locked on each other as her bottom lip trembled. "I will *never* leave you. I will follow you to the edge of this world and beyond, no matter what you say or do. I'm not letting you go. I won't. So, please, never ask that of me. You know how much I despise disappointing you."

"What if something happens to you?" she croaked out.

I shrugged one of my shoulders. "And what if something happens to you? You think I could survive without you, either? The risk is always there, but not being at your side will never be an option. The two of us being apart won't protect us. If anything, it would doom us. If loving you means death may greet me early, then I will welcome it wholeheartedly, because a life without you is a life I want no part of. However, I plan to survive...with you as my queen."

A ghost of a smile tilted her lips. "I love you," she whispered shakily as she threw her arms around my neck, burrowing her face into the nape of it.

I wrapped my arms around her, squeezing tightly, as my heart continued to race in my chest. "You just scared the shit out of me."

"I'm still mad at you," she admitted when she leaned back and looked at me, her mouth twisting back into a scowl.

"That's fine," I said, and surprise flashed across her features. "I'm incredibly sorry for lying to you, but I will be honest and admit that if given the chance, I would do it again without hesitation. It's not as if demanding you to sit out during a *battle* would've gone over well. If the suggestion even slipped past my lips, you likely would've locked me in a closet and gone out yourself."

Her temper was rising to the surface once more, tiptoeing along the bond, so I continued. "You were half drunk. I wasn't going to take the risk, and I did it to protect you, and

I *know* you would've pulled some sneaky shit on me if roles were reversed."

Her cheeks flushed, and she sucked in her bottom lip as if trying to suppress a laugh.

I raised a brow at her. "Do you deny it?"

Lia was silent for a few moments, and then her eyes flew to the ceiling as her lips betrayed her, tilting upwards. "No."

"That's what I thought," I huffed out a laugh as I rose to stand. I reached my hand out to help her up when I admitted, "Gods, I thought you were up here upset that you had killed our prisoner." I blew out a breath of relief.

"Absolutely fucking not." Confusion twisted her face as she stared at me beneath furrowed brows.

"There's my Lia," I chuckled as I reached out and pulled her into my arms. I rested my chin on the top of her head and asked, "What's our next move?"

Her eyes lifted to mine, and a mischievous grin appeared on her infuriatingly beautiful face when she said, "I have a plan."

TWO

Elianna

"This is a shitty plan, Lia," Zaela hissed from beside me as we watched Nox soar out from between the mountain peaks, answering his summons from my high-pitched whistle.

"Well, it's the only one we have on such short notice, and I won't risk anyone else. Feel free to stay behind if you're so against it," I snapped back at her. "My original plan was to go entirely alone with Nox, and if I were to fail, Jace would take you all and flee."

Zaela let out a cackle. "As if he would ever agree to such nonsense."

"No sense in not trying," I said with a sigh.

Jace suppressed a laugh from my opposite side as Nox's landing rumbled the ground beneath our feet.

"What is the exact plan again?" Gage asked as I made my way to my wyvern.

"Perhaps if you weren't so enthralled by the princess' eyes, you would've been paying better attention when we spoke of it, Gage," Jace teased.

My lips betrayed me, and I smirked as I continued walking up to Nox.

"Have you seen her eyes? They're like pools of honey that I'm just dying to take a swim in."

"Okay, that's enough out of you," Zaela huffed at him.

"For once, I agree. Keep that for talk amongst the men, please. She's my sister, after all," I called over my shoulder and caught a quick glimpse of Jace playfully punching Gage in the arm for what he had said. The sound of their laughter echoed over to me.

Nox was staring at me as I stood directly below his snout, looking up at him. I covered my eyes from the sun that had finally decided to make an appearance.

"Nox," I greeted him, my voice soft. "I'm truly so sorry about yesterday. Whether you ignored my call because of your fear of thunder or you couldn't hear it over the storm, I will probably never know, but we could've used you out there. However, what matters is that we have you now."

Yesterday felt more like a distant memory. As if it were a lifetime ago when we discovered Nox could scent Kai on Avery and Finnian...but not on me. Proving what Veli had guessed regarding Kai's true sire being Callius instead of King Jameson. And without a true Valderre on the throne, the realm itself would come undone, for we were the only bloodline that stemmed from the Mother Goddess, Terra.

He lowered his enormous, horn-covered head to my eye level and then nuzzled his chin on my shoulder.

I blew out a breath of relief as I lifted my hand to scratch his chin. "Well, I'm glad all seems to be forgiven. Just *don't* try to hurt them anymore, okay?"

He pulled his head back to look at me, and a glimmering golden eye met mine in understanding.

"Good. Now, do you think you can carry the four of us?" I smiled and pointed to the three behind me over my shoulder.

A growl crawled up his throat.

"Nox," I said in a hushed tone. "Behave yourself, please. Now is not the time. Now tell me, is the desire for revenge against Kai still *burning* within you?" My lips twisted into a grin.

Nox stood tall, raising his head high as he let out a deafening roar of agreement that forced us all to cover our ears. Even the birds flew out from the treetops in the distance.

"Well, I'm glad we all agree," I said with a breathy laugh.

"What's the verdict?" Jace asked, peering up at Nox as the three of them stepped up to my side.

I placed my hands on my hips as I stared them all down. "Hope none of you are afraid of heights." My voice dripped with wicked anticipation.

"I hate every single one of you," Zaela grumbled from his side, and I suppressed a laugh.

"Listen," I started as I stared her down. "I'm not risking the soldiers. They're exhausted, and many are already injured from last night. Plus, it will take us a day to get to the forest's edge with an army, and they already have half a day's head start. It will only take us a few hours by flight."

"Four against an army. Brilliant idea," Zaela huffed.

I raised a finger and tilted my head to the side, nostrils flaring. "Actually, no. Four plus *a wyvern*. He counts for at least a thousand soldiers," I tried to convince her, reeling in my temper at her need to question me.

Her eyes roamed back and forth between me and Nox for a few moments before she finally let out a breath. "We're all going to die."

She stepped out from our side and stomped over to the wyvern, who warily watched her as she approached.

"Fuck, this is going to be so fun," Gage said as he followed after her.

Jace stepped up next to me as we watched the two of them try to figure out how to get into the saddle.

"You truly believe he can carry the weight of the four of us?" he asked.

My eyes roamed over my wyvern. He had grown significantly since we escaped the Islan dungeons all those weeks ago. It was as if a proper diet and using the muscles of his wings had allowed him to rapidly grow into the colossal, powerful creature he should have always been.

"Of course. He'll be fine. Besides, I'm praying to the gods it will be a quick victory. None of us are getting off of him," I said as I took a step forward, but he reached out and grabbed my wrist.

"Promise me, Lia." His authoritative tone sent a pool of heat between my thighs.

I turned to face him. "Hmm?"

"That you won't do anything reckless and that you will *actually* stay on Nox and let him do the work."

There was no room for argument in his tone.

I leaned up on my tiptoes and kissed his scar that crossed the bridge of his nose. My hand drifted, and I grabbed my bow that he held in his other hand for me. "Come on, let's go before Nox gets too annoyed with them before we're even in the air."

Jace grumbled a retort I didn't care to listen to as we stalked over to the wyvern. Right after we arrived, Gage had managed to pull himself up using the straps of the saddle that hung down at Nox's sides. He lowered his hand, and Zaela grabbed it, allowing him to heave her up into the saddle with him.

I halted at Nox's back foot as he slowly lowered the front of his body down, allowing me easier access to climb onto him.

"Oh, come on!" Gage yelled.

"He couldn't have done that for us?" Zaela grumbled.

I laughed as I crawled up into the saddle with Jace following behind me. "You should've asked him for help." I shrugged.

"You're kidding me, right?" Zaela sighed.

I pulled my bow over my head and allowed it to rest over my shoulder as I settled myself into my seat.

"I forgot how enormous this saddle is," Gage observed, and I turned back to face him. "What have you guys done on here, huh?" He fluttered his eyebrows as he glanced back and forth between me and Jace.

"You think we've had a chance to do anything? The second I surprised her with it, it's been nothing but absolute fucking chaos," Jace said, annoyed.

"So there *were* intentions of what I insinuated."

A snort slipped from me. "You know that thought never crossed my mind, for some reason. Thank you for the idea, Gage," I said as I turned back to him and winked.

"Anything for you, my lady."

"For the love of the gods, you two," Jace huffed at us. I then felt his arm wrap around me as he secured the saddle's belt for each of us.

"Thank you, Mother Jace," Gage joked.

My mate sighed, and I knew we were pushing our luck with him at this point, but I couldn't help but cackle along with the other two, desperately trying to push my nerves down for what was to come.

"Listen, you have *no idea* how high we are about to be. See those clouds?" He gestured to the sky, and all of our gazes followed. "We are going to be there. Think falling from that is fun?"

Gage went to open his mouth, but Jace cut him off. "On second thought, don't answer that."

I glanced down and admired the intricate designs in the saddle as their bickering continued in the background. With my back turned to them, I allowed the mask I had been wearing the past hour to slip.

I imagined what it would be like to finally destroy Kellan and everyone who had ever harmed my family. My need for revenge slickly worked its way through my veins as if it were oil, and my fingertips ached as they traced over the saddle's stitching, waiting for vengeance to come.

Ignystae.

Veli's word from the tongue of the gods rattled me. Its power radiated through my soul as I readied myself to put it to use for the first time—praying to those very gods that the witch was right and that Nox would answer to its command.

My breathing turned heavy when I felt the weight of Jace's hand bearing down on my shoulder and his evident worry for me through our tether. As I turned toward him, his concerned hazel eyes locked with mine. My mask no longer worked on him because of the mating bond, but I would continue to fake the smile with him all the same.

I moved to face forward once more. "Hold on, everyone." I grinned as I felt all three of their bodies stiffen behind me. "Nox...let's go for a ride."

His enormous wings shot out from his sides, and with three booming flaps, we were in the cerulean midday sky.

THREE

Kellan

I LEAPT FROM MY horse as we arrived back at our camp on the outskirts of the Sylis Forest. I couldn't believe how much of a fucking disaster everything had turned into.

The entire ride back, I was forced to clutch the nape of my neck to prevent my body from bleeding out, thanks to Elianna's little stunt she pulled. I couldn't *believe* I let the bitch slip through my gods-damn fingers—literally. I had never fled from a battle in my life, but it was clear that her blade had nicked a vital vein. It took all my efforts to hold the skin closely together with my bare hand until it worked to heal. I had to survive. Too much was at stake, and I've worked too gods-damn hard to lose it now, *especially* at the hands of Elianna.

How had I missed the dagger strapped to her thigh? And how did she even *have* that?! I fucking snapped the damn thing in half the last time we were in this gods-forsaken place. I knew it was the same dagger, too—I noticed the wolf's head atop the hilt.

Stalking through the camp, we pushed our way through the soldiers that awaited our return, and I ignored the passing looks as they realized how beaten to shit we all were.

"Vincent!" I barked. I hadn't seen him since we were forced to flee. I roared his name over and over as I stumbled through the camp and arrived at my tent.

Where the fuck was he?

I picked up a bucket of water that remained on the ground within my tent from the day prior, splashing some up into my face and onto my wound that had finally begun to stitch itself closed.

As I peered down to try to get a better look, a growl crawled up my throat. That would scar. I would make Elianna pay for that. My gaze drifted down to my thigh, where the commander had slashed my flesh with his blade, and I thanked the wretched gods that it had nearly healed entirely already.

I stalked over to my cot in the far corner of the tent and started rummaging through the bag I had hidden beneath it.

After grabbing hold of the small jar of salve that I had stolen back in Isla, I began to generously apply it to my neck.

I cleared my throat and yelled, "Vin—"

My words were cut off as Callius appeared between the flaps of my tent's door. He looked me up and down carefully as a scowl twisted his face.

"Well," I started. "You're not Vincent."

"What the fuck happened, Adler?!"

"Wonderful to see you too, Callius," I mocked as my head tilted.

He stormed halfway across my tent and stopped abruptly. "Don't try to pull your bullshit on me, Kellan."

I eyed him. "What? Are you pissed about the salve?"

A grin twisted my face as I offered him the jar with one hand as the other continued to spread it onto my wounds.

"I don't give a shit about the salve!" he boomed as he smacked the jar out of my hand and sent it flying across the tent.

My brows flew halfway up my forehead as my gaze followed it through the air, and then slowly moved back to face him. "Woke up on the wrong side of the tent, did we?"

"Enough!" he roared. "Tell me what happened. Now."

"The humans were slightly more prepared than we anticipated. We would've won, but I was injured." I gestured to the side of my throat and the bloodstains that soaked my entire front. "Obviously."

"So, you left? *You* of all males fled?"

The tone of his accusation sent a spark of fury through me.

My jaw ticked as my stare tore away from him. "It was Elianna. She got the upper hand on me, which will *never* happen again. I thought I had completely disarmed her, but she unsheathed a hidden dagger and forced the blade down into the nook of my neck."

"You're gods-damn right it will never happen again. I'm taking over. You're *done.*"

I rose from where I sat and stood in front of him in an instant, hovering over his body. "Come again?" I growled through my teeth as he refused to break my stare or back down.

"Are you fucking deaf, now? You're. *Done*."

He went to turn on his heel away from me, but my arm whipped out, and I clutched his own aggressively between my fingers, yanking him to face me once more.

"Release me, Adler. Don't be foolish," he warned.

"I am *not* going anywhere. These are my soldiers—*my* army. I command them, not you. You don't get to relieve me just because you held my position once upon a time." A grin twitched up the corner of his lips, but he remained silent as he stared into my eyes. "What? You think you hold all this power because you retired from this to occupy the queen's bed? You're nothing but a cock to play with to her," I seethed.

Callius ripped his arm from my grasp and took another step into me. We stood chest to chest in the center of my tent as low growls of challenge rumbled through each of us.

"And what is it you're doing, huh? Oh, I know you much better than you think, Kellan. Do not forget who raised you since you were a mere boy."

"My father raised me."

He scoffed. "Your father was a pitiful excuse of a male who sailed the seas on some insane belief that he ruled them. You were not executed among the rest of his crew because of *me*. I taught you everything you know, boy," he spat at me with venom, but I flashed my teeth at him in response. "And the answer to your question is yes. I do hold this power because of what I am to the queen, and to your dismay, I am significantly more than just a *cock* that awaits in her bed all hours of the night."

Gods, he was really pissing me off.

He took a single step back from me, and his eyes looked me up and down in disgust. "Don't think I don't know what you're up to. The King's Lord? Is that what Kai thinks?"

"It's the truth," I growled.

Callius raised a hand to stop me from continuing. "Save it. You didn't give a fuck about Solus until recently, and now suddenly, you're trying to convince the queen to let you keep her as a little pet? You try to wander off with a small army of *your* choosing to go and fetch her, yet come back empty-handed?" He tsked at me. "You *know*. And I am very well aware that you know who and what she is, and I'm here to tell you that you can take that little dream of yours and ignite it into the flames that you love to play with so much. It's never going to happen."

My eyes flared at the realization he knew what I had been secretly planning since discovering Elianna's true identity. My heart started pounding, and I attempted to maintain a steady breath, hoping to avoid raising any more of his suspicion.

"I don't know what you mean," I lied, and not as smoothly as I was hoping.

"Kellan, this is pathetic." Callius sighed as he rubbed his temples. "She will never be queen. You will never be king. That is certain. *That* I can promise you."

"And why is it that she would be queen in the first place?" I asked through my teeth, still trying to save face as I refused to break eye contact.

"For fuck's sake, Kellan, I—"

A loud horn sounded off in the distance and shouts from our soldiers rang out all around the tent. Echoes of their armor clattered, snagging both of our attentions.

He turned back to face me, a scowl twisting his features, and lifted his finger in front of my face—I wanted to bite it off.

"This isn't over," he hissed at me. "Pull any more shit, and I will tell Kai and the queen of your bullshit plan faster than you can even feel regret...mark my words, Adler."

And with that, he rapidly turned from me and stalked out of my war tent.

Breaking through the tent flaps, I found the camp in a state of utter chaos. Soldiers were frantically running around, grabbing any weapons they could find, as they readied themselves for what appeared to be an oncoming attack.

"Vin!" I bellowed into the air as I stalked around the madness, dodging males as they ran past, ignoring me. "Where the fuck is Vincent?!"

"Captain," a voice called, and I whipped around to see one of our younger recruits, William Carter, standing before me, still covered in gore stains from the night prior.

"William, where is Vincent?" I howled at him as more soldiers slammed into us from each side, their shouts filling the air.

His eyes widened slightly, and he blew out a nervous breath. "Captain, he didn't return with us." He took a hesitant step closer to me.

"*What?*" I demanded.

"A few of the soldiers witnessed him get shot down with arrows. The commander and a few others swarmed him once his body hit the ground. He's either dead or has been taken captive. He was never among us the ride back to camp."

No. No, that was absolutely fucking unacceptable. Vincent? Killed in battle or taken as a captive? I refused to believe it.

My hand shot out, gripping William's throat with a firm hold. His arms went lax at his sides, and he didn't show a hint of fear as I was about to choke the life out of him for being the one to deliver the news to me.

"I don't believe you," I hissed through teeth clenched so hard that I thought they would shatter in my mouth.

"You don't have to believe it, Captain, but it is the truth." He paused for a brief moment as my stare continued to bore into his. "What can I do in his place?" he choked out with the small amount of air I allowed into his lungs.

With my grip tightening on him, my arms started trembling, and I then hurled his body several feet away. It took him a few steps backward until he found his footing. He straightened his armor and re-approached me, unafraid.

"As I said, Captain...what can I do in his place?"

I huffed out in annoyance, rubbing my temples as the madness continued around us. This soldier was young by our standards and appeared to be hungry for power. As I stared into his eyes, holding him by his throat, it was almost as if I was peering into a younger version of myself—that could prove useful.

"You want my trust and respect? Tell me what the fuck is causing all of this madness."

His spine straightened. "Scouts reported a wyvern headed directly for us. The creature was reported to be only a few miles east when the messenger falcon arrived."

"You're shitting me."

"That's not all, Captain," he started, and my eyes bulged as if this could get any worse. "The report stated there were figures atop the beast, essentially...riding it."

My panic disintegrated instantaneously. It appeared that I no longer had to draw Elianna out of her hiding spot once more, after all. No—my little traitor was coming right to me instead. And she was alone.

I dragged William with me through the disorder of the camp as I invited myself into Kai's tent to find that Callius was already with him, preparing him for a possible battle.

"You run, you hide, and as an absolute last resort...you fight. Do you understand me, Prince?" Callius said sternly to him. "I know I have provided a small amount of training for you since you were a boy, and we have revisited this on our journey here, but you do not possess the skills needed for attack."

"You lack belief in your future king?" Kai waved him off as Callius' eyes flared with nerves at his words. "Regardless, if the army we brought does their job correctly, I won't be doing any of those things," he hissed. "And you better ensure they do just that," Kai tacked on threateningly.

"Don't worry, Prince." I took a step forward since neither of them had noticed we had entered yet. "For it is not an army that approaches us."

Callius pivoted to me. "Adler," he growled, and I smirked. "If it's not an unexpected attack, then what has everyone frantic out there? I couldn't get an answer from anyone." His voice rose with each word.

I crossed my arms as my smirk grew from ear to ear. "It isn't an army. It's Elianna."

Kai's face turned lethal. "Your males are afraid of Solus?! A single fucking female?" he barked at me. "What kind of army are you running here, Captain?"

I bit my tongue so hard that I felt blood trickle down my throat as I worked to keep my retort from coming out. "Well, I assume they fear the wyvern she rides and not necessarily her." I watched as they both eyed each other knowingly. "And we know just how to deal with that wyvern, don't we?"

A wicked grin crept up Kai's face, making it clear he was out for her blood.

"I'll have the lines formed," Callius started as he moved past me. He turned back and met my stare. "You want to earn back your rank and my trust? Make yourself useful this time and keep the prince safe. It's all you're tasked with, and so help me gods if anything happens under your watch..." he growled as he made his way through the flaps of the tent built for a king.

A blaze of fury ignited within me as I turned to the prince, who eyed both me and William. "Remove yourselves from my tent immediately. I don't care what he said, Adler. I can handle myself," he snapped, as if I would try to coddle him like his fucking mother.

The clattering and shouts beyond the tent ceased as Callius' voice boomed, demanding they all get in formation beyond the camp.

"Of course you can, Prince. Just stay put and do me a favor... Don't do anything stupid," I demanded of him.

Before he could get out his retort, I exited the tent, forcing William to follow.

FOUR

Elianna

I REVELED IN THE winds as they rushed around my face, whipping my hair around as we soared through the sunlit sky. The four of us kept our eyes peeled for the retreating army, but it appeared they had already marched farther back than we anticipated.

"Do you think they already made it back to their camp?" Zaela shouted over the loudness of the breeze.

I contemplated momentarily as my eyes continued to observe the ground below. "I would be shocked unless they had arrived on horseback and hid them beyond the battlefield."

"I did notice some horses in the distance when we shot that bastard down. It's definitely possible," Gage chimed in as he held his arms out at his sides, just as I had done once I was finally comfortable flying.

I turned to Jace, and he shrugged a shoulder. "Regardless, we will catch up to them. If they made it back to a camp, we will just light up their whole fucking army."

I gave a wicked grin in response to him. "Agreed," I breathed.

A sudden growl rumbled beneath us and up through the saddle as Nox's gaze looked to a dark mass a few miles ahead of us.

My spine instantly straightened, and I crawled halfway up his neck to get a better look.

My eyes squinted from the blinding sun as I noticed the village.

"Nox, that's just Celan Village, it's not—" I cut myself off as my eyes focused in on the giant, moving mass. "Holy shit, it's their camp," I breathed as I whipped around and leapt back down onto the front of the saddle to face them.

"They really made camp there?" Jace asked through a grumble of annoyance.

"It's a little poetic, don't you think? He destroyed the village, and now we get to destroy him in that very spot," I taunted him.

The tiniest smile graced his face. "Well, when you put it that way…"

I blew out a breath. "Are you ready? Things are about to get heated. Literally," I said as I looked at them through furrowed brows.

Gage was the only one who laughed.

I carefully reached over and unslung my bow from my shoulder, ensuring it was within easy reach. My opposite hand gripped the saddle tightly as my gaze fixated on the camp awaiting our arrival.

Every second in the air brought us closer to my revenge. Every breath my lungs took hitched at the thought of obtaining a sliver of my desired vengeance, and what it would feel like to finally bring their deserved karma to them—and that karma was *me*.

Jace's chest pressed against my back as he gently kissed the side of my neck. "Give them hellfire, my Lia," he whispered into my ear, sending a shiver through me.

My grin was infinite as I lifted my bow high and roared a battle cry. It echoed through the clouds we soared through, signaling Nox into a nose-dive directly toward the enemy war camp built on our own terrain.

Our bodies were at the mercy of the relentless winds, forcing us to grip the saddle tightly. The closer we dove to the camp, the clearer our view of what we would be dealing with became.

Their soldiers had already formed the lines that I had drilled into their brains so gods-damn well in another life. A life where I blindly led them to slaughter thousands of innocents. A life that would forever stain my soul and haunt my nightmares for the remainder of my existence. I couldn't change the past, but I would do everything I could now to make it right for a better future—a better and safer realm.

We were barreling straight toward them, and none of the soldiers abandoned their posts.

Out of nowhere, an arrow whizzed by my face.

"Fuck! Lia, look out!" Jace shouted from behind me as I ducked down from another one.

The sudden onslaught of arrows seemed to come from every angle—launched into the air from the back of the lines, raining down on us.

Ignystae was on the tip of my tongue as I prepared myself to give the order.

Straightening my body, I peered down below to see how close we were, and my eyes flared. "Nox, pull left!" I shouted as I forcefully flattened my hand on the left side of his neck. He turned just in time before we would've crash landed directly into the army.

Shouts rang out from the ground, and arrows continued to fly at us from all sides as we circled the masses below.

They didn't deserve to be *immediately* incinerated—that would be a mercy.

They deserved so much worse.

Jace placed his hand on my shoulder behind me, a reminder that he was there, as we soared over the army in taunting circles.

My eyes then locked on the camp itself instead of those before us. I realized that if they had nowhere to flee back to or supplies to replenish their empty sheaths, they were sitting ducks.

I sucked in a sharp breath—it was now or never. My knuckles turned a ghostly white as my grip on the saddle tightened. The word worked its way up my tongue, sizzling my veins like lightning in anticipation.

My nostrils flared as the veins in my neck pulsated, and I screamed, "*IGNYSTAE!*" My voice was unrecognizable as it bellowed the word into the open air.

A blast of scorching heat erupted as Nox shot an enormous wall of fire down onto the camp, answering my command with its fiery force.

The tents and those who had remained inside them were immediately engulfed in flames. They screamed in agony and terror as they desperately tried to put out the blaze.

"Holy gods!" Gage shouted from behind me. "Hell fucking yes, Lia."

"Mother of the gods," Jace breathed.

"It worked." Zaela's words were barely audible.

My lips twisted into a wicked, menacing smile. It had worked. Veli was right—Nox understood the tongue of the gods. A growl of anticipation rumbled beneath us as if the wyvern realized this himself.

"Lia, have Nox eliminate the army before he's out of his flames!" Jace reminded me.

Right. One more fireball at their remaining supplies couldn't hurt, though.

My command rang out once more into the smoke-filled air as my fingers started to ache from gripping the saddle so tightly.

Nox circled and sent another blast of flames down at their supply wagons, which immediately turned to ash.

"YES!" Zaela roared behind me.

"Everyone, hold on!" I screamed as Nox turned quickly to the right and soared above the soldiers below.

My wyvern came to a halt before the army. He beat his wings in perfect unison, the powerful downbeat of them keeping us aloft, hoovering above the soldiers. They continued to shoot their arrows up at him, but they just bounced off his armor of scales.

Nox released a blaze of relentless flame down at the forces who refused to yield to us and his inferno.

Screams of agony and fear rang out between the roar of the flames as he lit up the entire army.

I hoisted myself up and steadied my balance on Nox's shoulder while gripping his neck for support. I felt Jace's body tense behind me as my eyes searched the burning terrain below. Disappointment nearly suffocated me when I couldn't find Kellan among the troops in the flames. I searched every bellowing, terror-filled face. None of them were him.

Thick tendrils of black smoke wafted into the air around us and almost completely blocked out the midday sun.

"Where the fuck is he?!" I screamed right before my jaw ticked.

"Lia, I——" Jace's sentence was cut off by a sharp hiss as an excruciating sting radiated through my own arm.

I whipped around, jaw agape, and beheld my mate as he clutched his arm that an arrow had skimmed through, leaving a gash open in his flesh.

The arrow had cut through his armor. Jace hissed again as his eyes found mine. Blood dripped down the metal.

I was at his side in an instant and pressed my finger to it. My fingertip instantly sizzled from the contact, the skin bubbling as if it were burned.

The arrow's head had been dipped in wyvern's blood.

My eyes flew up and met his once more, but I couldn't see anything. I couldn't comprehend a single thought as my vision darkened completely and enclosed around me, draping me as if it were crafted from Veli's shadows.

"Jace! Are you okay?!" Zaela roared as she joined Gage in unleashing their arrows down into the burning army.

"I'm fine," he lied, as my arm burned from his pain. Jace reached his hand out, cupping my cheek as he attempted to bring me back to reality. "Lia," he breathed. "I'm okay. I promise."

"No," I whispered as my eyes rapidly darted back and forth between his own, but they were unseeing in my rage.

My body pivoted to look below once more, and my eyes finally locked on the source of the blood-dipped arrows.

Kellan stood atop a burning wagon as he reached into his pocket and dumped a blood-filled vial onto another set of arrows as he took aim at us.

"Nox!" I screamed as my stare bore into Kellan's. I watched the tip of his lips twist into a smirk as he released the arrow aimed at us. "*IGNYSTAE!*" I roared, my voice unrecognizable.

My friends yelped, holding onto anything they could as Nox took off at terrifying speeds. We barreled through the smoke-infused air and toward Kellan, a cascading wall of flames erupting from Nox's gaping jaw.

I nocked my arrow into place and released it as we rapidly approached him. Kellan leapt from the wagon, barely escaping my arrow by tucking and rolling, and then took off in a run into the line of tents that were up in flames.

Nox hooked a sharp right turn and swooped down after him once more. We raced through the line of burning tents, so low to the ground that any soldier unfortunate enough to stumble into our path was instantly splattered against Nox's chest.

The screams were slowly dying down as the fire absorbed everything in its path. Tents, wagons, and supplies had been reduced to ash. The soldiers were no longer concerned about fighting us and focused all their attention on surviving the attack.

They wouldn't. I would make sure of it.

The time it took to catch up to Kellan felt as if it were hours when it had been mere seconds. Time slowed as I raised my hand and screamed my command into the burning sky.

Nox unleashed the last of his flames directly at Kellan's back. My sweat-slicked face contorted into a sinister grin, eagerly anticipating the sight of Kellan's body engulfed in the flames—only it never came.

Kellan pivoted to the right and dove out of the way, only half a second before he would've been consumed by the inferno.

My eyes flared with fury as I watched him strain to push to his feet before taking off once more between the burning tents. Nox struggled to turn at such speeds and had to move to circle back.

"*Fuck. This,*" I seethed, my teeth clenched so tightly that I thought they would shatter.

I spun around in the saddle, grabbed Jace by the chest plate of his armor, and pressed my lips to his. "I love you," I said on his mouth.

"Elianna, don't you fucking dare!" he roared at me, but it was too late.

I jumped up onto my feet, glanced down to the ground fifteen feet below us, and leapt from Nox's back.

I tucked my knees tightly to my chest and rolled once I hit the terrain. My body refused to waste even a single second as I sprang to my feet and took off running after my former lover.

The echoes of my mate's shouts of panic were lost in the roaring flames surrounding me.

FIVE

Kellan

I'D GIVE THAT STUPID beast one thing—it certainly had more flame than I anticipated.

My gaze roamed over the burning field, and I took in the sight of my remaining soldiers as they flailed around, their bodies up in flames.

"*Adler!*" Callius' voice boomed through the smoke-filled, suffocating air.

He appeared through the haze and gripped me by the collar of my shirt. His face was barely an inch from my own as he violently shook me. "Where is the prince?!" he roared. "Where is Kai? You had one fucking job!" He released my shirt and shoved me backward, almost causing me to lose my footing.

My back stiffened, and I waltzed back up to him and pointed in his face, mimicking him only an hour prior, before the camp had been set aflame.

"Keep your fucking hands off of me!" I barked at him. "I don't know where the little prince is," I spat. "I left him in his tent."

"Oh, you mean the tent that is now up in flames?!" Callius screamed at me.

"They're all up in flames! Everything is! There's no escaping this." I gestured to our camp. "What would you have me do, Callius?"

He turned in circles frantically as anxiety cloaked his features. "Find him. Alive. Or it's *your* head," he ordered as he took off running back toward where the wyvern continued to circle above, screeching.

"Gods-dammit!" I shouted as I kicked a helmet that lay on the ground at my feet, sending it flying directly into the cinders of a dying fire.

I stormed around the camp, aggravated to no end at this bullshit, as I used my foot to overturn bodies and examine the fallen soldiers.

None of the ones I came across were the prince.

My gaze shifted upward, and I caught sight of three figures jumping off the wyvern and into the camp that held what remained of our army.

Which could only mean one thing—Elianna was on the ground.

Elianna

I crept around the camp, hiding behind the few burning structures that remained standing as I searched for Kellan through the floating embers and ash.

Nox let out a thunderous screech, forcing my neck to snap in the direction of where he was. I watched as Jace, Zaela, and Gage leapt off from him, just as I had only minutes ago, likely to search for me.

"Gods-damn those three," I huffed.

The fires were dying down, and since Nox was out of flame, it meant we would need to finish the rest of the soldiers off with our blades.

I peered around a collapsing supply wagon and noticed horses tied off in the far distance. I was about to turn around to head back deeper into the war camp when one specific war horse caught my attention.

My eyes widened in surprise. "Matthias," I breathed.

I sheathed my sword and took off in a sprint toward my horse that I hadn't seen since before I left for Ceto Bay.

My steps came to a skidding halt as I reached him and threw my hands around his neck, a sob slipping from my throat. I pulled away, and he nuzzled his nose into my soot-stained chest armor.

"I can't believe they brought you here." My eyes roamed down his body and fell upon the dreaded emblem that Kai had seared into my horse's back. "I'm so sorry. I will make him pay for everything." My tone darkened with each word.

I unsheathed my dagger and cut the rope that held him to the post. I pulled on his reins and gestured to the fields in the distance. "Go! Lead them from here. I will try to find you! Go!" I ordered, my voice cracking in desperation as I prayed to the gods he would listen. My heart stuttered as he took off into a gallop.

My feet were moving before I could form a thought as I ran down the lines, cutting the ropes to free the remaining horses. As soon as they were loose, I turned and watched as he led them into the wild fields.

I leaned against the tree the last of them had been tied to and blew out a shuddered breath. Right when I was about to turn back and continue my search for Kellan at the camp, my attention was abruptly drawn to the creak of a branch coming from directly above me.

My body stiffened, instantly going on high alert, and I reached for the pommel of my sword. A shrieking battle cry then sounded from within the tree's branches.

My neck snapped up just in time to see Kai as he leapt from the shadows of leaves, aiming to land directly on top of me.

SIX

Elianna

I DIDN'T HAVE TIME to unsheathe my sword before Kai dropped on top of my body, sending both of us crashing down to the ground with a grunt and rolling through the thick mud left from last night's storm.

"*Finally.*" A cackle left me as I sent my fist directly into his jaw. He roared in pain as his teeth cracked beneath the force of my knuckles.

Our bodies continued to tumble as we both threw punches anywhere we could. The little shit got a few decent ones on me, but I didn't care. I barely felt them as the revenge I craved so deeply consumed me now that it was within my grasp.

The thickness of the mud slowed us down, and he pulled himself atop my body. Kai hovered his face directly over my own, and only madness lingered in his stare. His blood-stained teeth were bared in a menacing smile—but so were mine.

"Any last words, Elianna?" he breathed as he went to reach for his sword.

"Let's start with *fuck you!*" I yelled as I shoved my knee directly into his groin and swung my head upward in tandem, head-butting him so hard that I saw stars myself.

I shoved his body off of mine as he howled in agony. Pulling myself to my feet, I cackled wickedly as he rolled around on the ground, clutching his manhood while blood poured from his nose. It couldn't be more clear that he had never been struck before. The sight of it was pathetic, but I wanted to enjoy this and prolong his misery, just as he had threatened with me in the dungeons.

"Get up," I screamed as I unsheathed my sword. "Get the fuck up, Kai." My feet worked to circle him—a predator trapping its prey.

He sluggishly pulled himself to his feet as his breathing turned heavy. Kai then drew his sword and pointed it at me. "You wish to die, don't you?"

"No, actually. Killing you would be no fun if it was easy." I shot him a grin. "So, let's see what all that royal training gave you, little prince."

I lunged at him, and he lifted his blade as it clashed with mine. We swiped at each other over and over, each blocked by our own swinging blows.

He dove toward me, and I lowered my blade to kick him directly in the chest, sending his body flying backward.

Kai turned to face me once more, desperately trying to catch his breath. "What's it like to be kept a secret because of the *one* person who was supposed to love you?" he spat at me with venom.

I roared into the air as I swung once more. Our swords met, and we held them there in a struggle for power, just as we had figuratively for our entire lives.

"What is it like to abandon your own race and betray your kind and kingdom, all for some pathetic *mortal?*" he hissed as his amber eyes bore into my own.

I slashed my sword down his blade and moved to strike, but he managed to block it as he took three massive steps backward.

"You know *nothing* of love and peace. Your soul was forged of pure poison, just as your mother's was. You are *not* fit to rule, and that is by both blood and temperament," I bellowed at him as we moved to circle each other.

Any hint of amusement on his face dropped, and his eyes flared in confusion at what I had just declared. I took the distraction as an opportunity to strike. My blade sliced down his arm, but to my surprise, he was almost completely unphased and struck right back, using the adrenaline from his rage to push him forward.

Our swords met again, and we held them together in a struggle once more. I looked deep into his eyes as a scowl formed on my face. "King Jameson wasn't even your sire. You are no more fit to rule than the peasants you look down upon within the streets of the slums. You're not even a proper prince. Your dearest mother decided to fuck the *help*," I spat the words I knew would strike him the hardest. "Callius is your true sire and blood. Not the king. You. Are. *Nothing.*"

He stared at me as if he were frozen in disbelief, unsure of how to proceed before his face morphed into a creature of

47

wrath. "You lie!" he finally screeched as he moved to strike again, but his eyes said everything his lips wouldn't. He believed it. "And at least I have a fucking mother, Solus!" he shouted at me between blows.

I screamed in frustration as my amusement at toying with him had abruptly ended. "I'm going to kill you, Kai." I paused for a moment as our stares latched onto each other intensely. "And it's *Valderre* to you!" I bellowed as I felt the fire within me rise to the very surface.

My feet moved, and I twirled around to strike him down, but he took off *running*. The coward was now sprinting away from me.

I bolted after him as he moved as fast as his body would allow with a limp now straining his left leg. He moved further away from the camp and toward the forest that was a mile back in the distance.

"Lia!" My name echoed through the air as it was called out in desperation from behind me by my mate.

I refused to halt, though. No, I couldn't stop. Not when Kai was within my grasp. My neck pivoted, and I glanced back at Jace and watched him as he took off in a run after me, but I moved to face forward once more. If I stopped my chase now, we would risk losing everything we've worked for in this battle. If Kai and Kellan survived, this was all for *nothing*. And that was unacceptable.

Even just that split second of turning around cost me as I lost sight of Kai, who had been fleeing in front of me only a moment ago. I came to a skidding halt a mile from the forest's edge, where clusters of enormous boulders littered the terrain.

I sniffed the air, and through the metallic scent of blood and iron, the aroma of the prince's fear clogged my nostrils. He was near.

I silently crept around the boulders, moving with the blade of my sword stretched out in front of me. As I jumped around a boulder, movement caught my attention near one of the largest rocks in the landmark's center.

A smirk twisted my features. "Caught you," I whispered.

I sprinted to the rock and plastered my body to be flushed with its jagged edges. My neck craned as I searched for him.

I leisurely moved around until I fully circled it, ending exactly where I began beneath a slightly roofed covering formed from the granite itself.

My lungs let out a breath of annoyance, and then I noticed that Jace, Gage, and Zaela were nearly caught up to me.

My arm was throbbing with a lingering burn from Jace's wound, and blinding anger clouded my vision as I realized that Kai had escaped.

He must've made it into the forest. I was cursing myself from within as I went to step out to search for Kellan again when a subtle noise caught my attention.

Before I had time to react, Kai leapt out from the side of the boulder that I was pressed up against and sent his fist flying into the side of my face. My head bounced off the jagged rock, and I felt the flesh of my cheek tear open at the violent contact of it. The hilt of my sword slipped from my grasp and fell to the terrain.

My head pounded with a sharp, aching throb as my blurry gaze fixated on Kai, who stood before me with the tip of his blade pressed against my sternum.

I let out a breathy laugh. "Well played, little prince."

"Shut the fuck up, Elianna!" he shouted through shattered teeth, his eyes nearly swollen shut.

I went to reach for my dagger at my thigh, but he swiped his blade down, the very tip of it catching my hand and slicing a gash across the top of it.

I hissed as blood dripped down past my fingertips. His sword was aimed at my center once more.

"Now, *I'm* the one who will be killing *the great Captain Elianna Solus*. I can't even begin to tell you how long I have waited for this day," he admitted. "I finally know why Father spent so much time with you, why he always appeared to prefer you to his *legitimate* children." Kai continued to ramble as I let out a sharp laugh, drowning out his words. He had completely disregarded what I spoke of earlier regarding the king not being his true sire.

My mind frantically rushed through ideas on how to get out of this as he continued his triumphant speech. I glanced down at my sword on the ground. There would be no way to reach it in time before he gutted me.

"Are you even listening to me?!" he screamed, and my neck snapped up to meet his stare once more.

I was about to make my final move to strike when, out of nowhere, an enormous, looming shadow appeared over Kai. He was so lost in his bloodlust that he didn't realize it himself. Suddenly, tiny pebbles of rocks cracked off the giant boulder I stood beneath and rained down on me, bouncing off my shoulders before falling at my feet.

My lips twitched upward lazily, and I flashed my canines at him in the most menacing grin.

I watched as his smile of assuming victory faded from his features as his gaze hesitantly rose to the top of the boulder's edge.

Kai's skin turned ashen as his eyes widened in absolute terror. He lowered his chin to stare at me, his jaw hanging open in pure shock.

"Fuck you, Kai," I breathed.

An ear-shattering roar of triumph erupted from above before Nox swooped his head down and stretched his maw wide, revealing the numerous rows of his dagger-like teeth as he prepared to sink them into Kai's flesh. The wyvern then effortlessly snatched his entire body into his mouth.

The prince's screams of fear and anguish ripped through the burning fields as Nox tightly snapped his jaw down onto him and lifted his head back up and out of my line of sight. The thunderous crunch of bone rang through my surroundings as Kai's blood rained down on the terrain.

I ran out from under the boulder and looked up to watch Nox as he finished Kai off and swallowed his body whole.

"Holy mother of the gods," I breathed as my jaw fell open.

Stampeding footsteps that sounded off behind me came to a screeching halt as Jace appeared at my side—Zaela and Gage arrived only a second later, and the four of us continued to stare up at the wyvern that had just killed the prince.

"Did he just..." Zaela started.

I nodded slowly. "Kai is dead," I rasped out.

"Holy fuck," Jace breathed.

Nox's eyes narrowed in on the camp behind us, and a ferocious growl rumbled through his chest. Arrows began to land at our feet from the remaining soldiers as they formed lines behind us with their pitiful excuse of what remained of their army.

We all turned to face them, observing the remaining threat—there were nearly a hundred of them left, bravely barreling towards us.

I glanced from side to side. We wouldn't win against that many—not with Nox out of his flame.

"Let's go," I muttered as I turned on my heel and moved to climb up the boulder that my wyvern remained perched on.

I positioned myself in the saddle, and the three of them climbed up behind me.

"What about Kellan?" Gage asked. "We couldn't find him. We weren't sure if you finished him off before we saw you fighting the prince. He could still be out there."

My jaw locked. I didn't know where Kellan was. I wasn't sure if he had actually perished in the flames or if he had escaped once again from my grasp. The unknown threatened to make what barely remained of my inner walls collapse, but I refused to show them that—not when they were counting on me.

Nox had destroyed the false heir. I had to focus on what remained on our side, and now, with Kai dead, we stood a chance at survival and victory.

"His time will come," I said coldly, and I felt Jace place his hand atop my own as it rested on the saddle while the crippled army moved to corner us.

Nox let out a deafening roar in their direction, their charge at us coming to a screeching halt. My wyvern's wings shot out at his sides on command and swiftly propelled us into the air.

The soldiers watched in awe and horror as we took flight, their armor clattering against each other as they collided with those in the front who halted the lines.

"And now the queen will know *exactly* who and what she is dealing with," I announced as I craned my neck to face them. My heart stuttered when the grins on their faces matched my own.

Nox let out a few chirps of approval to the words, the tune of them echoing through the endless fields and the clearing clouds of smoke as he sent us soaring through the sky and headed back home.

SEVEN

Kellan

I STOOD AT THE edge of our camp in what could only be described as horror as I watched the wyvern swallow the prince whole, spraying his blood across everything in sight.

A roar of wrath tore through my throat as I watched the future of everything I had ever worked for evaporate before my very eyes.

I was tasked with ensuring the prince survived the attack, and he very much did *not*. If only he had stayed put and out of sight like he was told, but no. He had to go and run off and then try to fight Elianna himself as if she wasn't one of the most well-trained, fiercest warriors I had ever had the pleasure of battling alongside and now against.

I watched the entire gods-damn thing and never thought she would kill him. She was toying with him. I could tell by her stance. I didn't think she would have it in her to kill her own brother, but I never took the gods-damn beast into consideration.

Now, here I stood atop the embers and ash of what remained of our base, destroyed by the very person we came here to end. I watched as she and the others climbed atop the wyvern's back and flew off into the distance, disappearing between the cover of the clouds.

The ground was scorched—littered with broken weapons, shattered armor, and charred corpses.

I blew out a breath of frustration as pure, utter panic took over me for the first time in my life. The queen would have my head on a spike for this and perch it atop the castle's battlement.

Where the fuck was Callius? Hopefully, among the melted bodies, but I knew I wasn't that gods-damn lucky.

I locked eyes with William a few yards away as I made my way through the burning field—at least *someone* of use survived. I went to stalk over to him when Callius appeared from behind one of the half-disintegrated wagons.

"Adler," he barked. "Here. Now."

Anger lingered in his tone, but it paled when compared to what it would have sounded like if he had become aware of the prince's fate.

I pivoted away from William and aimed toward my predecessor instead. I went to open my mouth to speak as I reached him, but he cut me off.

"Where is the prince, Kellan?" he asked through his teeth. My eyes widened as I refused to break his stare. He reached out and grabbed each of my shoulders, shaking me violently. "Where the fuck is Kai?!" he roared and then threw my body several feet from him.

Without hesitation or a single sensible thought running through my mind, I unsheathed my sword and pointed it at Callius as I found my footing.

"Don't you fucking touch me," I said to him. My eyes searched the area, and I was relieved none of the soldiers were around this end of the camp to witness what was occurring.

Callius' face morphed instantly. What once appeared as anger turned into crippling fear. "Where is he? ...Where is *my son?!*" he bellowed, worry and agony seeping through each word.

My brows lifted in confusion. "I'm sorry?" My head twisted to the side in curiosity.

"Kai," he choked out. "Where is he, Adler?" The lines of his face etched deeper into his features as grief cloaked him.

I slowly lowered my blade to the ground as I stared at him in disbelief. "No. That part I heard. I meant the other part..."

Callius' eyes flared, realizing what he had just revealed, assumedly by mistake.

"Callius, what do you mean your *son?*" I demanded as I lifted my blade slightly to have it at the ready if needed.

His spine straightened, and any sense of the mourning "father" instantly vanished from his features as his gaze fixated on me, calculating his next move as he remained silent.

"Kai is dead, Callius..." I began, and I watched his body jolt as if he had taken a dagger to the chest. "Exactly how long have you been occupying the queen's bed?" I taunted him, making no attempt to hide the amusement slowly crawling up my features.

His face twisted into a scowl made of nightmares and ruin as he finally spoke. "Since before you were even a thought in this realm." He paused, and his eyes roamed over me as I remained in my stance. "And now you know too much." The second the last word left him, he charged at me.

Without hesitation, I lifted my blade and drove it into his gut as I dodged his attack. Everything around me slowed as I plunged the sword deeper into him until the hilt reached his body, and the blade was straight through the other side, dripping with his blood. His expression dropped as shock consumed the both of us. My eyes narrowed in on his as he stared at me, dumbfounded.

"And now you will join him," I said, and I ripped the blade from him.

Callius took a hesitant step toward me before falling to his knees on the charred terrain.

He lifted his already fogging eyes to meet mine as blood dribbled from his lips. "What have you done? I taught you everything you know... You were like a son to me," he rasped out, barely above a whisper as he clutched his wound.

"Apparently not," I grumbled. "I was not raised in a castle and handed everything on a platter of gold, as your *true* son was. I was raised in filthy barracks and kicked down more times than I could count before I was able to climb the ranks and make something of myself. You made sure of that," I hissed, my face twisting into a sneer.

His body swayed to the right as he spit blood at my boots. "I raised you the way any son of mine *should* have been raised. With honor...dignity...*balls,* for gods' sake." He coughed up more blood as it continued to pour from his wound. "I had no say with Kai. He was to be known as the heir to the throne and sired by Jameson Valderre. Kai knew nothing of it. He was never supposed to. Idina never told him, and we never planned to."

His wheezing deepened. "You have now taken my only true son from me, my plans I have worked for longer than you've even breathed, and now you've stolen my life."

I rolled my eyes at his dramatics. "You have enveloped yourself in the queen's secrets for far too many centuries, Callius." I tsked. "I hope her pussy and doting on her every beck and call was worth whatever failing plan you two conjured."

"You will *not* speak of my mate that way," he growled viciously. Callius' lips curled back as if he were an animal.

I barely heard the words as my mind emptied. I couldn't even form words at what he had just admitted, and then he continued. "And as I said, you stupid fuck, I'm significantly more than just a cock that awaits in her bed."

"What in the gods' names did you just say?" I blinked, confusion flooding my every thought.

"Idina is my mate." Callius lifted his chin to greet death in the face as he confessed his lifelong secret. "And *everything* we have done since we were barely older than younglings has been to obtain the crown. Her father? He planned it all. *All of it*. Aside from assuming his infant daughter wouldn't have a mate when he promised her to the Valderres, but I made myself useful to keep her near."

My jaw fell as I lifted my blade once more and aimed it at him.

"Her father's death," he spoke again. "Was obviously not part of the plan, either. When everything unfolded, we needed to conjure something entirely new. A new plan to take over the throne and Elianna's birth made that possible."

I shook my head rapidly from side to side. "I'm not following."

"The queen's war opened the doorway for everything her father wanted!" he spat, and out of the corner of my eye, I noticed William lurking behind the other side of the wagon.

His strength slipped, and he nearly face-planted into the ground, barely catching himself with his hands as they slid through the dirt and ash that surrounded us.

"Get up!" I hissed as I shoved at him with my boot, keeping my blade fixated on him.

He sat up once more on his knees, wheezing with almost every breath. "The plan was to kill Jameson in battle, make it look like an accident, or that he was struck by the enemy, but he rarely left the castle. Between that and Salvinae following him around as if he were a lovesick puppy, it was impossible to get him isolated, so after a while, we left it alone. The king was fixated on Elianna and too busy grieving the death of his love to even notice what was going on around him, the old fool."

Callius huffed out a pitiful excuse of a laugh. "It took over a century to solidify a new plan, and it didn't come until I stumbled upon that wyvern's egg out of pure luck as I searched for more mortal camps at her orders. The king's death couldn't have foul play suspected, and poison wasn't an option. Those things take time, but we finally had our chance to seize the throne and Velyra entirely. The queen did everything in her power to make sure our plan worked, and that included keeping our son in the dark regarding his true lineage. We had to wait until the opportune moment. You have no idea what it's like to be berated by your own child because they believe you are *beneath* them. I have spent over a century dealing with exactly that. Elianna almost once again fucked everything up by being in the king's ear about ending the war."

My eyes roamed over his dying body. "If the queen is truly your mate, then how could you stomach it knowing that she entertained his bed?" I questioned.

He let out a wicked chuckle, but there was nothing but wrath within it. "I *couldn't* stomach it, but we had an image to uphold. Surely, if she fell pregnant without having slept with the king, then that would raise alarms with him. It nearly killed me, and I wanted to kill him. I imagined what it would feel like to strangle the life from him every time I was forced to endure the thought. I spent my entire life preparing for those nights. Her father nearly beat it into me so that I would have to grin and bear the agony of it. Everything I have ever done has been for her. Her father tried to keep us apart, but I wouldn't allow it, so if I wanted Idina, I needed to learn to live with it."

"If she never cared for King Jameson, then why in the realm would she ban healers? To her own fucking armies!"

Callius eyed me. "Idina doesn't take kindly to being disrespected. It was her way of punishing Jameson for believing he had a mate in Elianna's mother and acting out on his feelings about it while she couldn't. And in the end, they weren't even gods-damn mates, for he never felt her pain when we killed her."

I continued to stare at him in disbelief.

"While she never wanted his love, she expected his respect. She even hoped he would occupy himself between the legs of another female one day. We just never expected him to give someone else the firstborn, *true* heir."

He paused and took a few painful breaths. "The wrath of a female scorned could rival that of the gods."

I was silent for a few moments as I watched him. My mind raced at everything he had thrown at me between his dying breaths. The corner of my lip tilted as my new plan formed.

"...And now I will be leaving her without both her son and mate." I leaned down closer to him and whispered, "I wonder how easy it will be for me to infiltrate the castle now."

His eyes flared wide as he moved to stand and make his final move to strike, but instead, I plunged my sword once more down into his sternum, straight through the other side, killing him instantly.

His body went limp and slid down the blade, hitting the ground with a *thud* as I stared down at him, trying to process everything he had admitted to me.

"Captain?"

I twisted my neck to look in William's direction and watched as he eyed Callius' body cautiously and then lifted his stare to mine.

What the young male did next would determine his future—or whether he had one.

"Hmm?" I hummed at him as my jaw ticked.

He cleared his throat. "Do you have orders, Captain? Only eighty-three soldiers remain, and most are wounded. They are working to salvage anything left."

I smirked at him as I pressed the tip of my boot to Callius' shoulder, holding his body in place as I ripped my blade free from his flesh. I then wiped the blood clean on the side of my pants before re-sheathing it on my hip.

My gaze focused back on the male. "Care for a promotion, William?" I asked him as I sucked on my teeth and scratched at my beard, acting as if nothing had just happened.

He answered with a grin that I imagined mimicked my own.

I could've sworn that in the far-off distance across the continent, the agonizing screams of the queen shook the realm.

EIGHT

Jace

I WATCHED LIA CLOSELY as she leaned back on her elbows and stretched across Nox's saddle to take in the late afternoon sun as we journeyed back home.

She was acting as if everything was fine, wearing her mask of bravery that I'd come to recognize all too well with her. However, down the bond, I sensed nothing but dread.

"Lia, that was badass," Gage interrupted the silence that we sat in.

She smirked, but it didn't meet her eyes. "It didn't exactly go according to plan, but I'd say we made a statement."

"You killed the 'heir' to the throne. I'd say that's more than a statement. In fact, I will take that as us winning the war," Zaela said with a victorious laugh.

Lia blinked, and her eyes roamed around the clouds as we passed them in the sky. "It's not over yet."

My heart fluttered painfully, which I assumed mimicked her own, as I felt her concern hanging over me like a looming shadow.

Zaela and Gage began bickering about who had the most kills once we had our feet on the ground back at the war camp. I crept up closer to Lia, pushing aside the burning pain in my arm as my body worked to heal the gash with the wyvern's blood. She sat at the very nape of Nox's neck as if it brought her comfort to sit in her former seat.

"You're upset," I whispered. "That's okay, you know."

She turned to face me. "I'm not upset that he's dead or the nature of how he was killed. In fact, that part is quite poetic..." She let out a sad, breathy chuckle. "When I first met Nox, I told Kai that I hoped the wyvern would eat him." She pursed her lips to hide a tiny smirk I could sense forming.

An involuntary snort left me at her words. Only my Lia would come up with such a threat.

She blew out a breath. "Kai deserved to die. He deserved the death he was dealt, and I stand by that. My concern isn't for me or for that of the kingdom but for Avery and Finnian."

My brows furrowed in thought. I hadn't even considered the prince and princess that we were about to come home to. The past two days had been such a whirlwind that, combined, they felt as if they were a year.

Only four days ago, we found the citizens who fled Isla, led by Avery and Finnian, and then last night was when we fell under attack by Kellan's army.

I looked back at my mate and realized that exhaustion had overtaken her features. The vibrancy of her eyes had dulled significantly, and her shoulders sagged as she forced her body to sit upright. Even as she joked about her threat all those months ago, her gaze was distant. When was the last time either of us slept? I honestly couldn't remember.

"You can just tell them you believe he succumbed to the flames," I suggested.

She met my gaze and shook her head gently. "I'm tired of lies and secrets." My jaw ticked nervously in response, hoping that it wasn't directed at me lying to her the night prior.

Her eyes turned distant again. "My entire life, I have been those very two things. If I'm to be a worthy queen, then I need to be honest and fair. They deserve to know the truth, and if they're upset with me for the outcome of the events, then so be it. I will learn to live with it."

I took her chin between my fingers, lifting her stare to mine. "Just that alone makes you the most worthy queen the realm has ever seen."

The corner of her lips tilted upward, and we turned to face the setting sun as it disappeared below the horizon, watching the sky transform into a melting pot of warm, fiery hues.

The four of us arrived back at the townhouse, groaning as we shook out of our soot and gore-covered armor and dumped it onto the floor at the foot of the staircase.

"They're back!" Avery shrieked from the kitchen as she came barreling through and went to throw her arms around Lia. Once she noticed her attire, she slowly lowered her arms and gaped. "Oh gods, what happened?!" she whispered as her eyes roamed over all of us frantically.

Lia reached out and grabbed Avery's hand, pulling her into a hug at the princess' dismay. "Well, I'd say we won this round," Lia said cheerfully as she held her sister's squirming body tightly to her own.

Avery pulled away from her as Veli stalked into the room and took in the sight of us. "You all look awful," the witch greeted.

"How's Landon?" Lia rushed out. "I should've checked on him earlier. I feel terrible."

Veli sighed. "He'll live. He's lucky, though."

"Thank the gods," Lia breathed. "Is Finn with him?"

She answered with a nod, but then her violet eyes narrowed in on the gash in my arm that was working to slowly heal itself. "You're injured."

She lifted a talon, and a second later, the burning ache in my arm began to fade. We all watched in awe as the wyvern's blood extracted itself from my wound, levitating in the air before falling to the floor. A sizzle echoed through the room as a burn mark appeared on the wooden floorboards.

"Curious thing, wyvern's blood," Veli said as her eyes remained on the mark, her head tilting to the side as she examined it.

"Don't even get me started," Lia hissed, her stare fixed on the gash in my arm.

Sensing her anger growing, I swiftly switched the subject back to what we were previously discussing. "Lia, why don't you go get some rest? I'll check on Landon." Her gaze snapped up then, eyeing me warily. "I want to thank him for the sacrifice he made."

My mate lifted her hands and rubbed aggressively at her eyes as a yawn escaped her. "Okay, fine. I'll see them tomorrow. I'm going to take the longest bath known to fae kind and sleep for, hopefully, a year."

Moving a step closer to her, I pressed a kiss to her forehead as I rubbed away traces of ash across her cheek.

She smiled up at me. "You know I'd ask you to join me, but I'm afraid of what's about to wash off of me." She chuckled.

"Couldn't possibly be worse than when you arrived here all those weeks ago," I teased, and she scoffed as she playfully swatted at me and then ran up the stairs.

Zaela groaned. "Don't take forever in there, Lia! There's only one tub," she mumbled the last few words as she stalked toward the kitchen in the back.

I turned to the sorceress. "Thank you for that, Veli. It'll just be better if we all talk about it tomorrow. She hasn't slept in days."

"Aye, but neither have any of you," she said before following Zae.

I glanced toward Avery, who was standing there pretending not to be sneaking peeks at Gage while he moved to sit on the settee.

I blew out a breath and turned to move upstairs. I was halfway up the flight when I heard Zae yell from the kitchen, "Get *off* the settee, Gage! You're filthy."

I shook my head, chuckling as I continued my ascent.

My hand lifted and knocked softly twice on the bedroom door.

"Come in," Finnian called.

I slowly creaked the door open, and my eyes fell on Landon as he worked to sit up, wincing at the lingering pain.

"Oh, thank the gods, it's you. If Avery checked on us one more time, I was going to lose my mind," Finnian huffed.

I smirked. "Your sisters mean well."

"Well, *one* of them does," he joked, but then his eyes softened. "Actually, you're right. I shouldn't make such comments. Not right now."

I closed the door behind me and took a few steps closer to them. "How are you doing, Landon?"

He laughed softly. "Well, I've been better, but I'm alive. Lia came back with you, right? I would like to talk to her, but mainly thank her. I know I was out of it most of the way, but I was conscious enough to know she carried me on her *back*."

Gods, how had that only been a day ago?

"She's getting some rest, which is much needed for all of us, but I wanted to come in here to say thank you and to apologize," I answered.

His brows flew up his forehead. "You want to apologize? Why?"

"I never should've asked you to leave last night. I wasn't aware of your skill set in battle, yet I was pleasantly surprised when I saw you out there holding your own. Also, for involving you in my lie to her. I never should've done that or felt the need to in the first place, but I also shouldn't have involved you or anyone else, for that matter."

He blinked at me. "It's okay." His words were barely a whisper.

I let out a chuckle. "Actually, it's not. I came here to let you know that I'm aware of that, and I truly am sorry for it." I crossed my arms and nodded to the door behind me with my chin. "She was very worried about you, but she'll be pleased to see you're already well enough to talk."

His gaze narrowed on me, meeting my own with a bit of fire in his eyes. "I told you to make me useful. I meant that."

I smiled. "You're a good soldier, Landon."

I turned to walk out the door when I heard Finnian step toward me as he said, "Avery told us that you came back here before leaving once more. What happened where you all went today? Did you attack them?"

I halted in the doorway and barely threw him a look over my shoulder. "Your sister will need to be the one to tell you all of that."

I quietly moved down the hall once I clicked their door shut behind me and peeked through the crack of the one that led to the bathing chamber down the hall.

Lia was lying in the bath, surrounded by the bubbles that she loved so much, as her arms were stretched out and draped over the edge of the tub.

I pushed the door open with my boot and watched a smile form as she lifted her head to me.

"Hi," she greeted, voice raspy yet filled with mirth. She sucked in the swell of her bottom lip and held it between her teeth as she stared at me.

"Are you okay?" I asked gently.

Her smile dropped, and her lips pressed into a tight line. "I don't want to talk about it right now, but I know lying to you will do neither of us any good. Stupid mating bond," she huffed jokingly. "I just want to focus on today's victory."

"Of course, my Lia."

Her smile returned at the use of my name for her. "Not sure if you noticed, but I'm no longer covered in the carnage of battle," she taunted as she motioned to her body hidden beneath the water.

"Oh, I noticed," I answered as I quickly kicked the door shut and moved toward the tub. "Please allow me to be of use to you. A distraction, if you will." I winked.

Her giggles echoed and bounced off the walls of the bathing chamber as I jumped into the tub with her, not even bothering to remove my clothes, and then claimed her mouth with mine.

NINE

The Queen

MY ENTIRE WORLD HAD suddenly been ripped from beneath my feet, and an ear-shattering scream of agony tore through my throat as the unbearable sensation of hollowness flooded me.

My body shrank against the wall of my bedroom chambers as I desperately pulled on the tether, the bond that tied our very souls together, to be met with *nothing*. There was nothing and no one on the other end of the line that I had become so dependent on since I was just seventeen years of age.

Tears rushed down my flushed cheeks as pain, mighty and unfaltering, erupted through my chest, echoing through every vein as our bond was severed. The world around me instantly lost its vibrancy; the colors of my vision dulled as the realization slammed into me that Callius was truly gone.

Every corner of the castle would now forever echo with his absence. His booming laughter that we only shared in the privacy of my chambers late in the evenings for all these centuries. His constant presence at my back to make sure I was always safe and the comforting rhythm of his breathing as we slept together in secret for nearly the entirety of our lives.

Suffocating loneliness enveloped me. My gaze wandered up to the empty space in my bed, which would now indefinitely remain vast and cold, a constant reminder of what I'd lost—*my mate*. His scent lingered in the chamber, and I found myself desperately searching for any piece of him, clutching them tightly in the need to capture his essence.

My grief was relentless, swarming through me like a sudden, violent storm. The weight of the realm and my father's ancient vision forcefully pressed down on my chest, making me desperate for air that refused to inflate my lungs.

I had shared every aspect of my life with Callius, and now the void of losing him was nothing but a deep, gaping hole in what was left of my decaying heart.

I reluctantly pulled myself to my feet and straightened my gown as I wandered over to my vanity's mirror. I gazed into my own eyes, once pools of warm honey, now darkened by all-consuming rage and grief. Grief for the life I could've had if I had been permitted to.

I had been born for the sole purpose of this responsibility—infiltrating the crown. A duty my father bestowed upon me when I was still an infant in my mother's womb before he knew what the gods had planned for his daughter.

In an instant, my mind transported me back to the pivotal day that changed the trajectory of my life forever.

My fingers twisted in my lap the whole carriage ride to Isla's harbor, where a ship awaited to bring us home to our small city of Doraeli off the coast of the Vayr Sea. Our annual meeting with the king, queen, and Jameson had been delightful, as it was on every annual trip. I could easily see myself being the consort to the kind and handsome male, though we hardly knew each other. But to be queen...it was all my father wished for and the sole purpose of my birth.

I smiled to myself, knowing I would be a doting wife and queen, the kind the realm needed, just as Jameson would be as their king.

The carriage ground to a sudden halt, and my father opened the door, sticking his hand back in to help me out. "Come, Idina."

I took his offered hand, stepped down, and became enchanted as I faced dark brown curls that tousled in the wind as it rolled off of the sea's waves. And suddenly, all thoughts of Jameson escaped my mind.

The male appeared to be a few years older than me, as I just turned fifteen, and he wore the mark of a sailor for the sea trade upon his cloak. I couldn't help but be mesmerized by his appearance. His gaze darkened as it found my own while introducing himself, and immediately, I found myself resenting the life the gods bestowed upon me at birth.

As our ship sailed over the waves, he walked alongside me atop its deck, speaking of his love for life at sea, and as we neared the dock of Doraeli, my heart sank. There was so much more to this male I wished to know—longed and needed to know. The thought of never seeing him again had my lips in a near tremble.

I turned from him and searched for my father, whose back was to me as he spoke with the captain of the ship. My eyes met

Callius' once more as I gently placed my hand atop his own as it rested on the rail. "I do not wish to leave you. Will I ever see you again?"

His eyes softened as he stared down at me. "My duty is to that of the ship. I have signed my life away as a sailor, Miss Idina."

I shook my head as my throat clogged. "No, my father is a lord and a friend of the king. He could easily get you out of a contract and find you work."

He gave me a gentle smile as he combed his fingers through his curls. "I wish I could do that, but I have a duty to uphold. This was my dream. But I do hope to see you every time I make port in Doraeli. I will make time to find you and visit your family's estate."

My smile dropped as I realized that this could never be. "My father would never allow that. If we were to see each other, it would need to be in secret." I couldn't even believe the words as they came out of my mouth—I never lied or went against my father, but something inside me was screaming to do just that.

Callius' lips tilted in a menacing smile as he guided me to a hidden corner of the ship, where no other eyes and ears may lie upon us. He took my hand in his and lifted it to his lips, pressing them against my skin. "Then let this be our first occurrence of secrecy."

Heat rose to my cheeks, and suddenly, the crew was shouting about needing to dock.

When we rushed out from the shadows of where we hid, my father shot me a look and then offered me his arm. I curtsied to Callius and the rest of the crew before he escorted me down the gangplank and into the city. Sneaking peeks back at the ship, I *could feel his eyes on me as I walked away, already longing for our next secret encounter.*

And now, two years later, we were still sneaking around together in the dead of night every time he made port in Doraeli—talking of life, holding hands, and stealing kisses that felt as if one of the gods themselves placed it upon my lips.

My heart raced as my thoughts consumed me. I was now seventeen years of age and expected to see Jameson for our annual meeting in mere weeks. The idea of it made my throat nearly clog, and I knew I would have to tell Callius the truth of why we had to sneak around so carefully behind my father's back. Originally, I had told him it was due to him being a mere sailor, and the lie tasted wretched on my tongue.

"I must tell you something," I said to him as a tear slid down my cheek.

He swiped it away with his thumb as we lay in a field beneath the stars outside of the city. "You can tell me anything, Idina."

With those words from him, I burst into a river of tears and told him everything. Of my duty to the kingdom and my father. The look of devastation on his face would've sent me to my knees if I wasn't already on the ground as he listened to my words of being promised to another at birth—but not just any other—the future king of the realm.

When I was finished, Callius cupped my cheek in his calloused hand, rough from manning the ships in the sea, as he looked me in the eye and said, "Stay. With me."

In that moment, I knew I was doomed to live a life of heartache and regret, knowing my father would kill us both if I were to break my vow.

Before I could answer him, he firmly pressed his lips to mine—it was all-consuming and ignited something inside of me. Without a single rational thought, we made love for the first time beneath the Velyran stars, feeling nothing but pure magic flowing between us.

I was innocent in the ways of males. Was this how it always felt? Or was it my love for Callius that made it so intense and beautiful? All I knew for certain was that I was terrified my father would somehow discover my treachery of his oath to the Valderres.

After another hour of laying together in intimate silence, Callius walked me back to my family's massive estate. My body trembled with fear the entire stroll beneath the moonlight, making him even more on edge and protective.

"I will be fine, this I promise you," I lied to him.

A growl erupted in his chest. "Your fear is palpable. I can feel it."

My eyes flared, unknowing of why he was so certain of this, but I cupped his cheek with my hand and assured him again that he was just being paranoid. I could sense his anger just as he sensed my panic and lies.

Once at the front gate of our estate, he kissed me fiercely with a gleam of what could only be described as pure love in his eyes. "I will find you tomorrow before my ship leaves port." My heart sank in my chest as I realized he would be forced to leave me again for many weeks at sea. With a final kiss goodbye, he turned from me and quietly stalked down the walkway.

Once he was out of sight, I tiptoed through my home's door. My stomach dropped as I was met with the unforgiving faces,

twisted with disgust, of not only my father but my older brother
as well.

"Where have you been?" my father bellowed.

"Her scent is different," my brother announced as he sniffed
the air with a scowl on his face.

"What?" I whispered, sniffing the air in confusion at his
words.

My father's eyes widened as he stormed up to me and gripped
my wrist so tightly that I thought it would surely snap in his
grasp. I hissed in pain as I looked up into his eyes as my own were
overrun with tears of fear.

"Father, I—" I pleaded, but was cut off by the grip of his
other hand, latching onto my long auburn curls as he huffed my
supposedly new scent into his nostrils.

"What have you done?!" he boomed in my face, the veins in
his neck straining.

My mother came running down the stairs at the same moment
Callius burst through the front door, and the five of us now
stood there, staring at each other in tense, unnerving silence. I
swallowed thickly, knowing that chaos was about to ensue.

I thought my kin was going to kill Callius right then and there
until my mother and I jumped between them all, arms stretched
wide to keep them apart, begging for them to stop.

"You cannot interfere with what the gods have planned for
her," my mother pleaded to her husband. "They have accepted
the bond, and if they wish for it to remain, we must allow it. The
Valderres may never notice the scent change, for they have only
met her once annually since her birth."

My father struck my mother then, and I screamed at the sight,
covering my mouth in pure horror.

"Stop it!" I screamed. "What do you mean? What is going on, Father? Please, just tell me!"

My mother's eyes met mine, her cheek red and swollen. "You have locked a mating bond in place, Idina. Your scent has changed, mingling with this male's." She gestured to Callius, who was huffing through his nostrils, the veins in his neck straining in fury. His lips curled back, looking as if he would lunge at my father if he struck me as he had done to his wife.

My eyes widened in absolute disbelief and terror. A mate?! They were so rare—a phenomenon gifted from the gods to find the other half of your soul. And they had gifted one to me. What should've been a beautiful and rare gift had turned into a nightmare before my very eyes. And Callius and I making love had locked this bond of our souls into place.

My father stepped forward, looming over Callius, and gripped him by the collar of his tunic, threatening his life and telling him to stay away from me.

I snarled at his words. "You cannot keep me from him. I love him! I don't care about some oath you made before I was even breathing. This is what I choose."

I thought my father would truly strike me then, but then my mate's hand reached around my waist, tucking me behind him. "I will pledge my life to you and your family. Never again will I set sail away from her if you allow me to stay at her side. I will do anything to remain here, even if that means shattering my heart when she weds the future king."

I sucked in a sharp breath at his words.

And after a screaming argument between everyone that lasted until dawn, my father accepted Callius' proposal, stating he *could always use another set of eyes and ears within the castle walls.*

Snapping out of the memory, my nails dug into the palms of my hands. Everything had changed after that night—and Callius had been at my side ever since. Protecting me, watching over me and my children, and loving me in secret as I was forced to falsely claim that my undying love was, in fact, not for my mate but for the king of the realm.

As the tormenting memories faded, my grief morphed into the purest and most relentless wrath I had ever known. They offered glimpses of the love we shared behind closed doors and curtains for centuries, serving as a painful reminder of what had always been taken from me—my mate. And now, the other half of what remained of my soul had been ripped away from me indefinitely.

As the realization dawned on me once more, I let out a gasp for air, clutching my chest as I continued to blindly stare into the vanity mirror. I suddenly heaved over and vomited onto the floor of my chambers as my stomach twisted in painful knots.

This couldn't be real, it simply just couldn't. *How?!* How could Callius have met his fate on a quest as simple as searching for those who traitorously fled my city? And our son was with him. *Our son.* The son who shared my honey-hued stare and Callius' dark ringlet curls that I hadn't seen since the day we set sail toward Isla for the final time—when he had been forced to cut it as he was officially knighted into the king's guard to remain at my side.

I would now have to sit here in this gods-forsaken castle, stewing in the unknown regarding the whereabouts of my children until Adler returned with the news of how my Callius had been killed. For the first time since I was just seventeen years old, I felt utterly hopeless and alone.

A knock sounded on my bedroom chamber door.

"*What?*" I snapped, tone vicious.

The door creaked open, revealing three castle guards with their hands resting on the pommels of their swords. One of them, Braynon, I believed his name to be, spoke. "My Queen, we heard screaming a few moments ago, and it sounded as if it came from your chamber."

I quickly swiped away the tears of rage that slipped from me. "And you knock instead of barging through to rescue your queen?"

All three of their faces sank in terror as their eyes bulged. My mind raced as they stood before me. I no longer had Callius to assist with inciting fear among the masses, and the city had been divided ever since my own daughter started a rebellion in Elianna's name. Whisperings of treason had made their way to my ears in the castle, and that simply wouldn't do. I had come too fucking far to lose anything more than I already had.

Another went to speak, but I raised my hand and silenced him. "You will gather all that remains of the city guards and soldiers within Isla. No one leaves or enters my city unless it is of those who left to retrieve the traitors. Am I understood?"

"Yes, Your Majesty," they said in unison.

"Excellent," I said as I straightened the front of my gown. "I want around the clock watch in the city streets. No gatherings will be permitted. And there will be a curfew when the moon is highest in the night sky. Anyone who disobeys orders is to be executed. No exceptions."

If the people of Isla thought it was unbearable to live under my rule before, I would make sure they realized how incredibly wrong they had originally been.

All of their eyes flared as they stared at me in disbelief.

Braynon's gaze then drifted to the vomit on the floor. I moved to step around it, blocking the view, and then his eyes met my dagger-like stare.

"Has something happened, Queen Idina?" another whispered.

My eyes shot to the mouthy one that dared question his monarch. "Is a reason necessary?" His mouth parted, and the scent of his fear stung my nostrils. "Every single able-bodied guard and soldier is to work day and night watching over the city, only taking necessary sleeping breaks until I demand otherwise. Now, have I made myself clear?"

"Yes, Your Majesty," echoed off my chamber walls.

"Perfect. Get out of my sight," I seethed, and they all nearly ran out the door.

I stormed over to my window that overlooked the city and its bordering sea. A snarl worked its way across my lips as I stared down at the ungrateful masses while the gaping ache in my chest threatened to make me collapse.

What was once my father's dream had now become my reality. I was the queen of the realm until my son returned, and the Valderre line was now permanently removed from the throne. And not a single one of the males that had ventured alongside me was alive to see the conquest of it.

TEN

Elianna

I STARED AT THE peaceful face of my mate as he slept soundly next to me. The moonlight peeking through our curtains cast the tiniest bit of light onto his features, and my heart ached as the daunting feeling of what was still to come loomed over me.

My eyes traced down the scar that marked his face, and fury bubbled within me once more as not only *that* scene replayed in my memory, but now of just yesterday when Kellan once again struck him with wyvern's blood. Jace was lucky this time since most of the blaze-infused substance caught on his armor, but I felt the moment it touched his flesh—graze or not, Kellan once again harmed my mate.

My body refused to sleep, no matter how desperately I begged for it. My mind constantly raced regarding what our future would hold. I had acted on impulsive rage and put the lives of not only myself and my mate in danger but also our friends. I just couldn't bear the thought of leading our already wounded and exhausted army out to the battlefield once more. Too many lives had been lost the night prior, but this was war.

Zae was right—it was a shitty idea.

All I could focus on at that moment was that the wicked queen had ordered her troops here to harm what's mine—my chosen family. She would take her other two children back and lock them in their own personal prisons for the remainder of their lives if she ever had them in her grasp again.

They came here in the middle of the night and tried to lure me out, but that wasn't what bothered me. The second I rode out of the dungeon's cavern on Nox's back, I knew they would hunt me until the end of my days. The only thought that kept me going, kept me *fighting*, was that my loved ones depended on me and my claim to the throne.

A single tear slipped past my lower lashes. I wished that something as simple as forfeiting my life to the queen would bring the realm peace, but it would only make it worse. Giving up would doom my people, but if I were to not fight for them, the same fate would await. No matter where the journey leads us, death would follow—that was certain.

I pivoted my body to face the window, and my gaze landed on the moon. A memory of my father walking me around the castle gardens as a youngling when I couldn't sleep played in my mind. The tiniest hint of a smile formed as I thought of him, but for the first time in my life, I despised that I shared his kind heart.

The actions I had partaken in the past few days wouldn't have made him proud. That day, all those months ago in his chamber, when he gifted me the dagger, he said he was proud to call me his daughter and that I would be a fair and just ruler.

Had he not seen this inside of me then? The constant brewing of immense anger that rumbled beneath my skin, just itching, no, *clawing* with talons to come out and unleash itself onto those who have turned me into this.

I took pride in knowing that war wounded my heart when I led the queen's armies. When I was the only commanding officer who deemed it necessary to personally inform and thank the families who had lost their loved ones in battle—battles that I blindly led them to. More so than that, I was proud of feeling empathy for the humans who were once on the opposite side of the lines.

Now, here I was, a throneless queen lying in her once-sworn enemy's land, leading them to risk their fragile lives and fight against the fae I once swore to protect.

My heart raced in my chest, which caused Jace to stir next to me as if he could feel it in his sleep. I carefully slid out from under the covers and stood up, careful not to wake him further, and silently tiptoed out of the room.

Once in the hall, my eyes darted back and forth between Avery and Finnian's doors as I sighed.

Their other sibling was killed because of me—would they see me as the monster I felt I was becoming? Or would they see it as being justified? Regardless of the fact that Nox was the one who took Kai's life, I couldn't confidently say to them I wouldn't have killed him if my wyvern hadn't.

Actually, no. I would've. I know I would have.

Whether they would be upset with me for the rest of their lives or not, I had to tell them the truth of it, and I wanted the three of us to be alone.

I moved on silent feet to Avery's room and opened her door a crack. "Psst. Avery," I whispered, and she stirred quietly beneath her sheets. "Avery, are you awake?"

Her fiery curls lifted from her pillow, and her eyes met mine. "Lia?" she asked. "Lia, it's still dark. Is everything okay?"

I felt awful for waking her, but I didn't know when else we would be able to talk without the ears of the others listening in.

"Can you come downstairs? I need to talk to you and Finn about something important."

She sat up instantly. "You're making me nervous..."

My voice was soft when I answered, "I know. I'm sorry."

I shut the door once more to give her privacy and moved to my brother's door. I opened Finn's door a crack to see he was already sitting upright in his bed as he stared down at a sleeping Landon.

I pushed his door open further. "Can't sleep?" I smirked as I crossed my arms.

"I haven't been able to for quite some time now. Although, I suppose the past few days are for an entirely different reason," he answered sadly.

My features softened. "Care to come downstairs? I'll get a fire going. Avery's getting dressed now, and I would like to talk to the two of you."

"Of course, Lia," he answered as his back straightened.

And with that, I made my way to the staircase.

ELEVEN

Avery

FINNIAN AND I SILENTLY walked down the stairs of the townhouse to find Lia tending to the small flames she had lit within the fireplace. She turned around to face us and gave a soft smile as she gestured to the settee. We made our way to it and sat side by side as Lia hesitantly sat across from us next to the fire.

She anxiously rubbed her knees with both hands as she twisted in the chair to reluctantly face us, her eyes lifting to mine as she bit her bottom lip.

"Lia, is everything okay?" I asked nervously.

"No," she whispered.

Finn leaned forward next to me and said, "Lia, you can tell us anything. I would've hoped you'd know that."

"I'm a monster," she answered.

My eyes widened at what she had just called herself. "Lia, you are many things, my sister and best friend being at the very top of the list, but I promise you...a monster is not one of those things."

"Kai is dead."

My jaw popped open from shock while Finn jumped up from the settee next to me, but the whole time, Lia refused to break our stares.

"I'm so sorry," she whispered nervously. "Well, sorry that regardless of everything, he was also your brother, but I can't sit here and lie to you saying that I'm sorry he's dead."

I blinked at her repeatedly as my mind tried to process what she was saying. Kai was dead—the evil, vile, murderous heir was no longer among the living...and she was *sorry?*

"Did you kill him?" Finn cut in before I had a chance to speak, and my head snapped in his direction.

Lia cleared her throat. "Not directly. It was Nox that killed him, but I also won't say to you that I wouldn't have done it if Nox hadn't beaten me to it. He actually saved me. Between being blinded by my rage, feeling the pain of Jace's injury, and exhaustion, Kai managed to corner me."

Finn blew out a breath, and he reached up to nervously scratch the back of his neck as his eyes remained wide.

"And that's why you believe yourself to be a monster?" I cut in before Finn said something else.

"Does it not make me one?" she asked as her gaze leisurely wandered to the flickering flames in the fireplace. "Perhaps if I had been thinking more clearly, I could have captured him as our prisoner instead."

"No," Finn and I said in tandem, and then her eyes lifted back up to us.

"That doesn't make you a monster," Finn added.

"You speak of giving him kindness that he would never warrant to you. Kai would've done his absolute worst to you, Lia," I said. "That's all he's thought and spoken of for months. I can't even believe he traveled all the way here himself. It just proves that whatever he had in store, he wanted to personally make you suffer."

"He has done despicable things," Finn chimed in. "To all sorts of innocent beings. It never would've stopped, Lia. We are here because of that, and you sat there and thought we would think that *you're* the monster in this situation?" He paused for a moment. "I think it's safe to say that both Avery and I hoped that Kai wouldn't survive this war. If he survived, it would mean that you didn't, and neither would we."

I nodded rapidly in agreement as our brother spoke these words to her before adding, "Mother may have tried to save us, but once Kai was crowned, it would sign our death sentences."

Lia's eyes darted back and forth between the two of us, and then she bowed her head. "I, of course, know that you hated him, but he was still your brother, and for that, I am sorry."

"Well, we aren't."

She snorted at that. Thank the gods.

"Tell us what happened," Finn stated. "What prompted you to rush out of here after everything? Did you just want to catch up to them?"

She audibly swallowed. "I knew Lukas was dead. I knew it, but my heart refused to believe it. I couldn't accept it yet—couldn't bear it. He helped me escape the dungeons and sacrificed himself for me. I think this entire time, I was just pretending it wasn't real and that he was fine, and so was our father. My foolish heart denied what our reality has become." She gestured to our surroundings. "I don't regret this, of course. I could never regret seeing what truly lay inside the castle walls and finding my mate, but I do wish I had been smart enough to have done things differently. Including the events of the past few days. I allowed myself to act on impulsive rage."

I stood from the couch and approached her slowly. While lowering myself down onto my knees, I gently placed my hand on hers. I looked up into my sister's haunted green stare and said, "You are still so young in terms of our race. You weren't raised to know the ways of what it takes to rule; you were taught to destroy the enemy. And that's exactly what you did, Lia. That will never make you a monster. You acted appropriately to a viable threat. What you did does not define the kind of queen you will be in a negative light. If anything, it goes to show how much you care for and love your people."

"She's right," Finn announced from where he remained on the settee.

Lia's face softened, as if the entire realm had been lifted off her shoulders. "I thought you were both going to hate me, or at the very least, be upset in some way."

I chuckled. "Well, maybe we're the true monsters, then."

She let out an abrupt laugh, and I smiled as I stood and reached my hand out for hers.

Lia stood up on her own and wrapped her arms around me, embracing me in the tightest hug I had ever received. "Thank you," she said softly as if my words had healed a part of her that she desperately needed.

Once she loosened her grip, I took her hands in mine as we smiled gently at each other.

"There's something I wish to show you. Something I should have the moment we arrived a few days ago, but time has moved so quickly between the madness that I forgot I had it. I will be right back." I turned from her and bolted up the stairs on silent feet.

I ran into my bedroom and dropped to my knees as I searched through my pack I arrived with. Pulling out our father's leather-bound journal, I traced my fingers over its cover and rose to stand.

When I arrived back at the bottom of the stairs, I was met with the curious, concerned eyes of both my siblings, and then Finn dipped his chin in recognition as he noticed the book.

"This was Father's journal. It's how we learned the truth of his past—what he wished for you and what he truly felt for the queen. It's also how we convinced others to flee with us when they hadn't been entirely convinced by Lukas' final words." Extending my arm out to Lia as I approached, I handed her the journal. She took it with trembling hands as her gaze was fixated on it. "I want you to have it."

Her eyes snapped to mine. "This should be for all of us. King Jameson was your father, too."

I shrugged a shoulder in response, but then Finn spoke. "Hold on to it for us all, then." He reached out and rubbed her arm. "We'll know where to find it." He winked.

Lia let out a noise that was half laugh and half sob as she carefully flipped through the pages with her fingers. A smile formed on her face, and I nearly blew out a breath of relief when I saw it meet her eyes. "That I can do." She threw her arms around each of our shoulders. "Thank you both so much," she whispered.

Suddenly, loud footsteps sounded from above, and we all turned toward the staircase to be met with Gage standing there, curiously eyeing the three of us.

"My lady, Avery," he started, and my cheeks flushed as my fingers flew to cover my mouth.

Lia chuckled softly. "Gage, what are you up to so early?"

"Early?!" he gasped. "My queen, dawn is on the horizon. There is much to do to prepare the people to head to Alaia whenever you deem fit."

Lia answered him with a proud smile.

TWELVE

Elianna

ONCE EVERYONE ASIDE FROM Landon was awake, we all
sauntered into the living area of the townhouse to plan
out our next move.

As everyone took their seats, I couldn't help but stare
at my mate's arm, where the gash from the arrow had
thankfully already begun to heal. I reached out and
gently brushed my thumb along it, and he turned his
head to stare down at me.

Jace took my chin between his fingers, lifting my gaze
to his. "It's healing, my Lia. I'm okay." He kissed my
forehead.

"We need to find out how much wyvern blood they
have in Isla. Luckily, we know they cannot replenish
what they have lost, and without Nox in their grasp, it's
highly unlikely they can obtain more," I announced to
the group as my eyes remained on Jace's.

"We wouldn't necessarily have a way of knowing that,
but it's safe to assume that they don't have much left
if they used a significant amount in your most recent
battle. It is possible they traveled with the remainder of
what was left," Veli said from across the room.

The corners of my lips tipped up at that. "Then they are either out or will be soon enough." I turned to face them. "We ignited their supply wagons, so anything they were traveling with was likely incinerated."

Veli blinked, and her face resembled something like satisfaction, which was incredibly rare to see on the sorceress. "Excellent." Her stare then locked in on my own.

Ignystae? She mouthed the word.

I answered her with a dip of my chin, and she crossed her arms as a knowing grin formed on her face.

"This isn't over yet, though. Not even close. Even with Kai dead, the queen still remains, and whether she is of the Valderre line or not, she likely will not inform the kingdom of Kai's death as it would threaten her claim to remain on the throne since she isn't a Valderre by blood. Though I doubt the people would retaliate after everything they've witnessed from the castle in only a few short months."

My eyes flew over to where Avery and Finn sat, making sure that they didn't flinch or shudder in response to the casual mention of Kai's end. To my surprise, they seemed unphased, which meant they were being honest this morning when I told them the truth of it all. Something resembling pride bloomed in my chest.

"We need to move as many as possible beyond the mountains. Things are different now. Adler is still out there, and the queen will be desperate. She may make reckless decisions when she learns of her son's death," Jace announced.

I stiffened at the fact that what I had done was extremely reckless when I was trapped in my own desperate rage and need for revenge. He eyed me warily for a moment, as if sensing my thoughts down our tether, but then focused his attention on the group before us.

"Will they all go?" I asked. "Beyond the mountains."

Jace sighed. "Likely not, and I won't force them. We will make them aware of how the threat has shifted, and they can make their own choices on whether to stay or evacuate. The crown will know that Silcrowe has been rebuilt now, but our other hidden villages should remain safe."

"How do you move people to the valley?" I asked.

Zaela cleared her throat. "There is a passageway through the base of the Ezranian Mountains directly beyond the courthouse, built into the peak. It's hidden within the city. We never originally planned to rebuild it to what it is today, but now Ellecaster serves mainly as a gate to our true home."

"The path is narrow and rocky in most parts and takes about a day to get through on foot before you are out on the other side, but it's safe. Especially since we're the only ones with access," Gage cut in.

My eyes flared. "Is that how Alaia was discovered to begin with?"

Jace let out a chuckle. "It was actually. A few curious boys wandered too far from home one day many decades ago and were missing for almost a week. The people were distraught and unsure if they had been taken by some kind of creature, but they returned speaking of a valley beyond the peaks."

"What happened then?" I asked.

Zaela gave me a knowing smirk. "No one believed them, of course, until they became entirely too irritating regarding what they had seen. Their persistence finally convinced the commander at the time to listen to what they had to say. He secretly sent soldiers beyond the mountains the very next day to find that the children were speaking the truth."

I smiled. "Those boys were heroes."

Zae nodded proudly. "They were. And continued to be for the remainder of their lives. One of them was my father, who, as you know, grew to be the commander of our race before Jace."

My eyes flared as my head flew in my mate's direction. "You said your mother was here, on this side of the mountains, when…"

Sadness radiated down the bond. "She saw it as a cage, even though it was meant to keep everyone safe. By the time there was enough built and ready for citizens to uproot everything and move to Alaia, my mother was an adult. She made her choice even when my uncle begged her to go. After she was attacked, they were finally able to convince her to move and raise me there, but by then, the damage was done."

His pain echoed into my own, and I couldn't bear seeing him like this for a moment longer. I laced my fingers with his and gave them a squeeze. "We'll make them pay. For all our loved ones." My eyes moved to meet Zaela from across the room on the last word, knowing that she had lost her father as well.

Her lips tilted up as she quickly looked away. "My mother will be pleased to have found herself with several new house guests. She's been itching to fill the vacant rooms. Time hasn't exactly allowed us to be home since Jace took command."

"Gods, I miss her cooking," Gage announced.

"I'm sure she's been bullying General Vern into many dinners and chats since we've visited. She doesn't do well with an empty nest."

I remembered that General Vern was the man Jace had told me about when I first arrived in Ellecaster. He handled all affairs and his soldiers beyond the mountain range in their commander's absence.

Jace laughed. "Leon doesn't do well with an empty stomach, so I'm sure she never has to beg."

Zaela smirked. "Perhaps you're right."

"I'll head to the barracks and round everyone up that I can," Gage announced. "We'll move the first bunch of them now, and we can either come back for those who remain once injuries are healed, or they can head there if they choose to later. When do you want to leave, Lia?"

"As soon as we are able to. I don't want even a second wasted. We need to think of a more permanent plan once we bring everyone to safety."

He gave a curt nod. "Absolutely. I will go and take care of it." My brows furrowed slightly as I watched him make his way to the door, but he quickly turned around to face Avery as if he had forgotten something mid-step.

Her cheeks blushed as he took a confident step toward her and lifted her tiny hand in his own, pressing his lips to it.

"I hope to finally see you when I'm through speaking with them, Avery. These days have refused to allow me any time with you, and I dislike that very much."

"Of course," she whispered with a nervous giggle.

Gage flashed her a grin in response right before he continued his trek to the door and made his way into the street.

"Mother of the gods," Jace grumbled with a sigh as he stood beside me.

"That's a battle you're not going to win, handsome." I nudged him playfully with my elbow as I winked at Avery.

Her eyes widened with a hint of fear as Zaela leapt up from where she sat. "While he prepares the soldiers, I'll head into the city and start moving door to door. This shouldn't be a surprise to them at this point, but if they're too reluctant to leave, I will let you know," she announced with an edge to her tone, right before she followed Gage's footsteps out the door and then slammed it shut behind her.

He turned to me then. "I don't know why she cares so much...if she has feelings for Gage, she..."

Jace was cut off by a sharp cackle from Veli, who had remained silent in the corner for the last several minutes, earning a curious head tilt from me.

"You men are moronic," she stated as she pushed herself off the wall and stalked across the space to her bedroom door.

I bit my bottom lip to try to hide my smirk as Jace turned back to me. "Is there something I'm missing? Or is she just always this wonderful?"

"If you would like honesty, it would be a bit of both," I teased. I pivoted my body to face Avery and Finnian, who were the only two left in the room, aside from us. "What do you all say the rest of us follow her lead and make our way through the city to help warn everyone?"

They all nodded silently, and we moved toward the door, Nyra trotting alongside us.

Hours after we set out to inform our citizens of the new plan, Jace had found me and taken my hand, guiding me to one of his new surprises he said he had in store. However, when I reached down into the bond, it wasn't excitement that I sensed, but lingering sorrow and empathy, further intensifying the dread I couldn't seem to shake in recent days.

He cast a fleeting glance back at me as he led me past the city gates, as the vibrant sunset on the horizon ignited the sky in an inferno that stretched as far as the eye could see.

"Are you going to tell me where we are going?" I asked, mockery and the tiniest hint of sass filling my tone.

"Always so nosey, my Lia," he cooed, causing me to blush. "I just have something I want to do for you, but it can't exactly happen within the city."

That piqued my interest.

Past Ellecaster stretched immense waves of boundless fields and meadows. So, when Jace veered right once we were beyond the gates and proceeded alongside the city's wall, my mind raced regarding where he could've been bringing me.

After finally rounding the first bend, my eyes flared as I spotted Nox perched beside the outskirts of the wall, patiently awaiting our arrival. My breath caught as I took notice of what sat at my wyvern's taloned feet—a wooden box adorned with intricate engravings and silver embellishments.

"Jace," I whispered as my steps faltered and my hand slipped from his.

He turned to face me, and as his eyes met mine, the corners of his lips tilted upward. My mate gestured behind him to the box that lay atop a bed of freshly picked wildflowers and said, "A proper resting for a once great male."

I moved past him, my strides slow. When I stood before my wyvern, Nox's gaze fell from me and down to the box before him that beheld what was left of one of the greatest souls the realm had ever been graced with.

A small, sad chuckle of disbelief left me as tears streamed down my cheeks while I took in the sight of what Jace had made for me—for Lukas. A male he had never had the pleasure of knowing, but he took it upon himself to make sure that Lukas had a chance for his soul to rest with the gods.

I crouched down to the ground, and the tips of my fingers traced over the engravings that read *Sir Lukas Salvinae. Beloved male and guardian.*

Jace slowly approached me from behind, and I pivoted to face him. The cast of the setting sun forced me to squint, but the light that shone behind him beautifully framed his figure, giving him an otherworldly aura, as if Lukas was casting the light onto him himself. He carefully reached down, silently asking for my hand, and then pulled me to my feet.

He guided me backward leisurely. "Thank you," I whispered. "This means so much to me."

His hold on my waist tightened, and he craned his neck to kiss my forehead as he spoke the words onto my skin. "Anything for you."

My gaze moved from Jace to my wyvern, who continued to wait in silence as he watched us curiously. I cleared my throat and gently gestured to the box. "Send him home, Nox." I paused, and when I spoke again, the word was barely above a whisper. "*Ignystae.*"

Nox's gaze softened as he let out a chirp that more resembled a whine. His eyes moved from me down to the box before he opened his jaw and sent a small, contained blaze of flame directly at the chest before us. I watched in awe as his fire swallowed what remained of my lifelong guardian, trainer, and dear friend.

"Thank you for saving her," Jace whispered from beside me. I glanced up and observed him as his focus remained on the box that had already been nearly reduced to ash. "Your sacrifice will never be forgotten," he finished.

I reached up and cupped his cheek with my hand. "I wish you could have met him. He would have loved you."

He gave me a soft smile in answer.

I continued to watch him. "Are you ready to finally put an end to all of this?"

A small smirk tilted his lips as his eyes found mine once more. "Always."

Our gazes returned to the embers that lingered on the ground, where nothing else remained but charred terrain and where Lukas was finally put to rest.

A triumphant grin slowly spread across my face as I took in the sight—the time was finally upon us, upon *me*.

I would reclaim the Valderre family name, my rightful throne, and the Kingdom of Velyra if it was the last thing I ever did.

By blade, blood, and flame.

PART TWO

ALLEGIANCE

BOOKISH
KODA

THIRTEEN

Elianna

After nearly a week of tirelessly informing the citizens of Ellecaster about our relocation and assisting them with arrangements, we were finally ready to proceed to their sanctuary beyond the mountains.

Preparations had taken longer than I had originally hoped. However, I reined in my nerves that refused to settle, realizing that I was asking these people, who still barely knew me outside of what they had recently witnessed, to completely uproot their lives once more.

Endless lines of humans, fae, carts, and livestock stretched around the bends of the city, waiting for us to lead them into the passageway hidden between the peaks. Significantly more people had decided to leave their lives here behind and journey to Alaia than we expected, making it clear that their fear of history repeating itself was at the forefront of their minds.

Scouts reported sighting several of the horses I had liberated from our enemy's army all those days ago, including Matthias. Once the scouts had gathered them up, they were swiftly escorted back to Ellecaster.

I followed my mate's lead as we led the army at our backs to the farthest inner edge of the city, where their stone structures met rocky cliffs. Glancing up into the sky, I watched Nox as he circled above in the nearly dawn sky as he waited for us.

We had sent word by falcon to those beyond the peaks, letting them know what was to come. The plan was for Jace and me to fly to Alaia on our own, making sure they were as prepared as possible for the onslaught of new citizens that were about to pour into the valley. It would also allow me a chance to formally meet the generals who watched over Alaia in his absence.

Zaela and Gage would lead my siblings and the rest of those who chose to relocate through the hidden passage.

We moved past the stone courthouse built into the mountain's base, and a glorious chill made its way up my spine, knowing that Vincent's body had been left to rot within it. The male didn't deserve a proper send-off into the afterlife.

Once at the very back edge of the city, we came face-to-face with what appeared to be an enormous boulder molded to the mountain's base—that was until Jace whistled his command to the guards who watched this secret entrance. My gaze lifted to the top of the left tower, where a soldier pulled a lever. Out of nowhere, concealed ropes connected to pulley contraptions sprung to life, deftly maneuvering the boulder by slowly lifting it up the mountainside.

Our necks craned as we watched the enormous, heavy piece of granite climb the jagged edge of the cliff before us.

"Oh my," Avery whispered as she sat atop Matthias, snapping me out of my trance.

My gaze followed hers to see that the passageway carved into the mountains had revealed itself as the dust and debris leisurely settled.

The pathway was by no means wide, and I could already envision some of the carts lined up behind us having a hard time getting pulled through without snagging on some sort of root or crevice.

"You've been through this many times?" Avery asked as Gage stood beside her mount.

"Oh yes, there's nothing in there. Don't worry. The scariest thing will definitely be your witchy friend."

Veli shot him a look of annoyance from where she stood a few paces behind them.

"Children found this passage?" I asked skeptically, as one of my brows lifted. Nyra danced around my feet in circles, letting out a short growl as she watched the dust settle.

"They believe the passage appeared when much of the city and mountainside had been decimated. They discovered it when people returned here to rebuild the city," Zaela answered. "My father was a bit of a...menace when he was young. Exploring areas he shouldn't have been."

"Weren't we all?" Gage chimed in.

"You're not quite out of that phase yet, my friend," Jace said as he took his place at my side. He wrapped his arm around my shoulder. "Are you ready, Lia?"

"This will take a day for them to push through?" I asked, as my gaze wandered behind our friends to the awaiting masses.

"Give or take. The children will remain in the wagons to prevent injuries and wandering. They are prepared to march through, as the passage is too narrow to make a proper camp in," he answered.

"Excellent." I blew out a breath and turned to Avery. "I will see you on the other side." I glanced at Gage and then back at my sister. "Don't do anything I wouldn't do."

She answered with a wink, and when I stepped toward her, I leaned in close to her ear and whispered, "And that's antagonizing Zaela."

Avery scoffed as I turned to Finn and Landon, who had each mounted a horse. "Be safe."

Zaela approached me from behind and clapped my shoulder. "They'll survive. It's just a day, Lia," she huffed before she started shouting out orders down the lines in preparation to leave.

Day or not, the thought of being separated from them all again made my chest tighten.

"Alright, everyone, let's move out!" Jace boomed.

The endless line of citizens took their first step in tandem. The sound of shouts repeating his words, wagons turning wheels, and the click of hooves on the cobblestones echoed throughout the air. And before I could blink, Zaela had disappeared in the passage, followed by Avery and Veli, while the boys all stood at the front of the entrance, guiding the lines through seamlessly.

Our people smiled, and the children waved excitedly at us as they sauntered by, making the corners of my lips twitch up as I returned their gestures.

Nox let out a loud shriek, forcing my eyes up to watch as he landed and perched himself on a looming cliff of one of the peaks, observing them all as they entered the passage as if he were watching over them himself.

We stood there for what seemed to be over an hour until the very last person in line entered. Jace gave the guards the signal to close off the entrance, and we remained until the boulder landed, sealing it shut behind everyone.

FOURTEEN

Jace

WE SOARED THROUGH THE open air on Nox's back as he glided through the clouds above the Ezranian Mountains. Lia sat on her knees at the nape of his neck, at the very front edge of the saddle, as the wind tousled her hair around her face.

Lia glanced back at me. She slid down the saddle and wrapped her arms around her knees, holding them tightly to her chest as our stares remained locked on each other.

"You seem better, lighter. However, I can't help but notice a lingering sense of dread from you. What's going through your mind, my Lia?" I asked.

Her chin tilted upward to the clouds above as she pursed her lips. "Too much."

She looked back at me to see my stare remained on her as I waited for an actual answer.

"I'm excited to finally see the sanctuary that has allowed the mortals to remain as safe as possible. And I'm relieved that Avery and Finnian truly didn't hold any grudge or ill-will toward me for Kai's death. So, luckily, I no longer feel like a complete monster."

My eyes narrowed in on her. "Lia, nothing in this realm could convince any of us that you're a monster. And if it's the title you fear and do not wish to bear, I will gladly hold it for you. Utilize me for all your needs, whether that be your mate and partner or executioner. The only thing I'm longing to see more than you sitting on that throne is to watch our enemy's blood pool at your feet."

She opened her mouth to speak, but I continued. "I know you're more than capable of doing that yourself, but I'm here for you to not carry the weight of it alone. You, my Lia, are the crown, and I will gladly be your sword."

Her lips curved in a soft smile as she watched me speak the words. "I know."

"Even though I can sense that your fear hasn't eased, I still hope this can bring you even the slightest bit of some relief."

"I hate being so scared, Jace. And the fear that consumes me now isn't necessarily that of titles placed upon my name, but for what's to come. Idina should be removed from the throne regardless of an ascension. No other bloodline in all of Velyra is suited for the throne. We ended the false heir, yet she remains. She's clever...powerful, and cruel to her very core. Idina will do anything it takes to remain where she is. And the news of her son's death will make her that much more dangerous. I fear for our people here *and* my people in the southern part of the continent, in and near Isla."

"Perhaps it will remain a few weeks before she gains the knowledge of his death. It could buy us more time in preparation," I offered.

"Not nearly enough," she whispered, barely loud enough for me to hear over the rushing winds.

I peeked over the side of the saddle and was instantly overwhelmed by nausea at how high we were above the peaks. When my eyes lazily wandered back to Lia, I noticed she had an infuriating grin on her face, her dimples deepening as she sensed my hesitance.

"Scared, Commander?" she mocked.

A breathy laugh left me. "There she is."

She scooted to the side of the saddle slightly and patted the space next to where she sat. "Come on, let's have some fun for once."

"Fun?" I repeated through furrowed brows as I crawled my way to her.

"I know deep down you remember what fun is." She winked and leaned into me, her breath a light warmth on my ear. "Hold on tight, handsome."

As if commanded, Nox shot through the sky in an instant, sending a rush of excitement coursing through my veins. I lifted my hand out for balance, but the wind was so strong it forced my hand back down on his neck.

With a powerful flap of his wings, we were lifted higher into the never-ending sky. The sensation of soaring through the open air was unlike anything I had ever experienced, and once I let go of that meddling apprehension that threatened me every time we were up here, I could finally understand why Lia loved it so much.

Her face was adorned with a beaming smile. She turned to meet my stare and laughed—the most magnificent, genuine, and life-filled laugh I had ever heard. If I were standing, it would've brought me to my knees. My laughter joined hers, erupting from deep within my chest.

Beneath us, the world unfurled in a breathtaking scenery of the rugged mountains. Jagged cliffs and ancient forests stretched as far as my mortal eyes could see, and even beyond.

The peaks below were dusted with a layer of the whitest snow, which glittered off the tips of the pine trees. This view...it was a *gift* to receive the sight of this—something that the average being would never witness.

"Hold on!" Lia yelled with a giggle, and my hands instantly gripped the front edge of the saddle.

Nox brought his wings tightly into his body and took a nosedive back down towards the peaks below. A shout or panic was about to tear through my throat when suddenly we spun—circling round and round before Nox tipped his body even further, hurtling us into a full flip. His wings shot out once more before his second nose dive, sending us soaring between the cliffs and their jagged, unforgiving edges.

The wyvern shot up from between the peaks, sending us into open air once more before he finally leveled out his wings and glided on the wind.

We both carefully sat up, and Lia wiggled her way up to the very front of the saddle, now sitting back on her knees as her body was nuzzled between mine and Nox's neck. She leaned her back into my chest and lifted her arms out from her sides as the wind continued to race past us. I followed her lead and lifted my arms up to hers, lacing my fingers between hers.

I peered around her and caught a glimpse of her infuriatingly perfect face. There was nothing but pure love and bliss radiating in her eyes and down our bond.

I closed my eyes and took a deep breath, surrendering to the moment. All that existed was the endless sky unfolding before us, and my queen.

Avery

How many hours had it been since dawn? I had lost count, but judging by how painful my hips felt from rocking back and forth from the horse's steps beneath me, I would say many.

I had overheard Zaela speak to Gage regarding moving too slowly, even with the horses, but not everyone could keep up on their mortal legs—mainly the women and children. The more people that jumped into the wagons, the slower the horses were able to pull them.

Every time I snuck a peek in Gage's direction ahead, I often found that his own eyes were already lingering on me. The adrenaline from it would force me to swiftly move my gaze down to my hands on Matthias's reins, but I could feel the heat rise to my cheeks beneath his stare.

"Gods, you're embarrassing," Finn huffed out from his horse next to me.

"Excuse me?" I asked between furrowed brows.

"Avery, you bat your eyelashes at any male that waltzes by you in the castle, yet this man comes along and you turn into a shy, giddy...*thing*."

I scoffed in response. "I don't know what you mean."

Landon let out a chuckle from behind us, where he remained on his own horse.

I turned to face him. "Do you have something to say, lover-boy?"

He snorted. "You two are ridiculous...but I agree with Finn." His lips twisted into a smirk, but he refused to look me in the eye.

"Well, I'm glad you seem to be healed and normal once again enough to tease me." I paused as I shot him a look. "And I am not a shy, giddy *thing*, you imbeciles."

"Not typically," Finn chimed in. "But this handsome human comes along and suddenly you're just that in his presence. Has the great and beautiful Avery found someone who makes her nervous?"

"No," I rushed out. "I just have never had a chance to...act out on...actually never mind."

The two of them burst into an obnoxious laugh, forcing everyone's stares in our direction, including Gage's.

"I hate you both." My grip tightened on the reins.

Their soft, wicked laughter surrounded me, forcing me into a bravado of false bravery.

I cleared my throat quietly. "Um, Gage!" His neck instantly snapped around to look back at me from where he was several feet ahead, next to Zaela and Veli.

He instantly circled back and approached me and my horse.

116

"My lady, Avery." Gage smiled at me, and my heart raced as my breath caught. I cursed my brother in my mind for antagonizing me into this.

My mind instantly blanked on what to say as he stared up at me with caring, warm eyes.

"Do your feet hurt from our travels?" I whispered.

Finnian instantly barked a laugh, making my jaw tick, but I refused to look at my brother as he teased me.

"What was that?" he asked gently.

The corners of my lips tilted up. "There's room in the saddle. It was built for two." I paused as his smile fully formed. "That is, if your feet begin to ache."

An unbearable silence blanketed us as he continued to gaze up at me, walking alongside our horses.

"My lady, are you asking me to join you atop Matthias?"

"If you wish to...the invitation remains," I answered.

He grinned up at me. "I would be honored to share a mount with you."

In one swift movement, he gripped the front of the saddle with one hand and effortlessly swung his leg up the other side, planting himself directly behind me.

My eyes widened as the heat of his chest pressed into my back. My entire body went stiff.

"Are you comfortable, Avery?" he whispered into my ear, a knowing wickedness lingering in his words.

A shiver ran up my spine. "Yes," I answered softly.

My brother and Landon felt the tension as it shifted around us like a mist and immediately commanded their horses to trot ahead of us, giving us privacy—or as much privacy as possible in our current surroundings.

"You know, Avery..." His words caused a tingling sensation to run through my body. "It's very kind of you to consider my aching feet."

I tried to speak, but words refused to come.

He chuckled in my ear, seeming to sense how incredibly awkward I was around men. "Tell me about you," he said as his arms wrapped around me and took hold of the reins.

I craned my neck to look over my shoulder and was almost left speechless once more as I met his stare. "What do you wish to know?"

"Everything," he answered without hesitation.

My breath caught, and heat rushed to my cheeks. "Well, where should I start?" I let out with a nervous laugh as I leaned into his chest.

Before he could answer, a deafening shriek erupted from the sky above us, forcing us all to snap our gazes up to the tops of the peaks.

Nox was spotted up above, high within the clouds, and then came barreling down toward the ground. We continued staring as he started performing multiple flips and dangerous moves while navigating the sharp, jutting edges above.

The laughter of children and awe-inspiring noises from the adults echoed down the never-ending lines through the path. We all moved forward swiftly once the wyvern left our sight.

I faced forward once more, about to continue telling the handsome man at my back my life story, when Zaela whipped around from the front where she had been with Veli and came storming towards us.

My whole body stiffened against Gage, and he gently squeezed my knee above my dress.

He brought his lips to my ear then, and whispered, "Don't mind her. She's just ridiculously overprotective. And that scary look she wears is also just her face."

A snort left me at his attempt to lighten the sudden shift in the mood. Zaela's eyes narrowed in on me then, and I felt the intensity of her stare as she crossed her arms once she was halfway to us, a scowl adorning her face.

A short chuckle left Gage as she approached, and it both irritated me and left me entirely confused regarding their situation.

"Zae—" he started, but he was cut off.

"What are they doing?! The whole point of them taking Nox was to get a head start," she shouted up at Gage from our side as she began to walk alongside Matthias.

"It seems that they're just having a bit of fun," I said as I continued to look straight ahead. "You should try it sometime. They also likely left a few hours after us once everyone entered the passage."

I felt the weight of her gaze boring into the side of my face.

"I was *not* speaking to you, Princess."

"Zaela. That's enough," Gage interjected, a bit of bite I had never heard from him in his tone.

I didn't even bother trying to hide my smirk, and now Landon and Finn were slowing their horses, falling back to eavesdrop on what was about to unfold.

"I simply stated a fact that I wasn't speaking to her and came here to directly talk to you. The Commander's Second."

Gage let out a laugh, and I hated that it made me upset he was entertaining her.

"You have never referred to me as such. What has gotten into you?" he asked.

"Absolutely nothing. I need to know why they aren't miles ahead of us."

"Well, I would assume what Avery said was correct and that they're having a bit of fun. The two of them deserve it, no?" he replied.

I turned slightly and glanced at her in time to see her eyes soften at his words. Why did she hate me so much when Lia was so sure of her not having feelings for Gage? He said she's just overprotective, but to what extent?

"Fine," she huffed. "I'm just tired, and my feet ache. Must be nice to have a mount," she retorted with a slight sense of teasing. She then waded through the surrounding travelers and aimed for the front.

"Is she truly always like that?" I asked.

Gage was quiet for a moment, and I cursed myself for letting that slip out.

"Zae means well," he said quietly with a sigh.

Suddenly, the warmth at my back was absent, and he swung his leg back over Matthias and leapt down from our saddle, leaving me alone once more.

My heart started racing.

"I should be at the front with her." He looked up at me as he walked alongside. "It will still be many hours before we are out on the other side."

I gave him a short nod in response, fixing my face into neutrality to hide that I wanted to burst into a fit of angry tears for her ruining that moment between us.

He reached up and gripped one of my hands as they rested on my lap. The callouses from his years of sword use and battle training were rough against my palm.

"And Avery..." I reluctantly looked back down at him. "I still wish to know everything."

The corners of my lips tilted upwards as my heart fluttered. Gage pressed his lips to the back of my hand briefly and then stalked forward to join Zaela and Veli at the very front, maneuvering around Landon and Finn.

The warmth of his kiss lingered and I couldn't help but stare down at where his lips met my skin.

I loathed that my brother and Landon were right—I had become a shy, giddy thing. However, I also realized that what I hated even more than what I have become...was the sight of Gage walking away.

FIFTEEN

Elianna

THE WIND ROARED IN my ears as Nox descended upon the endless rolling hills with grass that swayed in hues of green. The heat of the sun was diminishing as it hung low in the sky, setting the valley aflame under its light.

"Alaia is vast, fixed with our main headquarter city, Anerys, and neighboring villages spread through the countryside. It's ever-growing and changing. The city isn't far from here," Jace said as my eyes wandered around the scenery before us.

"It's beautiful," I admitted softly while Nox gently landed.

He reached out and tucked my flowing strands of hair behind the tip of my ear and then moved to guide me down to the earth with him. Jace leapt from Nox's saddle and then effortlessly caught me in his arms after I jumped out from behind him only a moment later—our laughter floating around us.

"Wow," I whispered as my gaze roamed once more.

"It's almost entirely untouched by man. When they began to build, originally, the idea was to have a mirrored city to Ellecaster on the opposite end of the passageway, but it was later decided to push it a few miles from the entrance—gods forbid we were ever discovered or attacked. This way, the city wouldn't be visible upon exiting the path between the mountains."

"That's very smart," I interjected. "I can see why the mortals named it a valley. Does it all truly look like this?"

"Aside from our colonized areas, yes. And there is still much uncovered." He paused for a moment. "There's so much I wish to show you, so much I have been eager to have you experience—with me."

The corners of my lips tilted. "Show it all to me, handsome."

His eyes gleamed with love as he reached for my hand and firmly pressed his lips to the back of it.

Behind him, the endless fields and rolling hills of wildflowers stretched out infinitely, and the scent in the air was intoxicating—a fragrant blend of floral sweetness and the earth beneath us.

Suddenly, shouts were being called out in the distance. My neck snapped in the direction the calls rang out from to see two figures on horseback galloping toward us.

Jace lifted his arms above his head and began waving his hands in the air at them as he marched forward, yelling back in their direction.

I glanced back at Nox. "Be nice, please." He huffed out a breath of hot air through his giant nostrils, and I shook my head with a laugh in response.

I moved to follow my mate as the horses and their riders drew closer. As they approached, I could make out an older gentleman with salt and pepper colored hair and a well-kept beard to match. The other rider was a woman with short blonde hair whipping around her face as she rode with grace at his side.

"It's about gods-damn time, Cadoria," the man called as he brought his horse to a halt before us. A smile formed on my face at their effortless banter beginning so soon.

"Wonderful to see you as well, Leon." Jace crossed his arms and smirked as the man leapt down from his mount.

He reached out his hand to shake Leon's in greeting, but the man laughed in his face as he extended his arm and wrapped it around Jace's back, pulling him into his chest for a hug. "A handshake. How rude of you, lad."

A giggle slipped from me as I watched from a few feet behind them.

The woman then gracefully lowered herself from her mare.

"Nephew," she greeted him then went in for her own hug the moment Leon released him.

Once their embrace ended, they all turned to me, and heat instantly rushed to my cheeks. My heart fluttered as nerves eagerly tried to take over me.

Jace cleared his throat. "Aunt Lynelle, General Vern," he began, and Leon huffed out a shocked breath at the use of his title. "This is Elianna Valderre."

Lynelle's eyes widened as my name left his lips, and Leon's stance went rigid.

"We have much to discuss, but her arrival shouldn't be entirely a surprise," he continued, his voice stern, as if warning them not to react how they typically would have.

"Nephew," Lynelle breathed. "The next time you send a letter by falcon stating that you have found a way to win the war by means of a 'powerful' mortal sympathizer...you may want to include that she holds royal lineage." A nervous chuckle left her.

She took a hesitant step toward me, and my breath caught as I focused on her face. She was the image of Zaela aged by only a few decades' time. Her hair was a sandy blonde and chopped short at her shoulders while Zae's flowed down her back. The only other difference was their eyes—while Zaela possessed the same eyes as Jace and his mother, Lynelle's were a greyish blue. But their facial structures were nearly identical, only apart in the finest of age lines.

"Hello, Lynelle. My name is Elianna, but you can call me Lia."

"Lia." She spoke my name into the air as if trying to get a feel for it on her tongue. "How lovely." A soft smile formed on her lips.

She turned back to my mate. "And she is what exactly to you, nephew?"

"Everything," he answered without hesitation—sending shockwaves of love rippling down our bond.

The general's eyes flared, but Lynelle's smile beamed brightly. "Jace Cadoria—a man in love. I never thought I would see the day. Come now," she demanded gently. "If the others are moving through the passage, we still have hours until they arrive, and there is much to discuss." Her eyes warily lifted to my wyvern behind us, and she took a hesitant step back.

I glanced back at Nox to see he was playfully snapping at the small hummingbirds as they hovered around his head, seeming to forget about me entirely.

Lynelle cleared her throat as if my hesitance of leaving him behind was making my movements too slow for her to bear.

"You know," she began as she mounted the general's horse—he moved to sit behind her in the saddle. "When you wrote that you would arrive by wyvern, I assumed that was a code I didn't understand. No wonder why this one laughed and brushed it off." She gestured to the general behind her with her chin.

Jace chuckled and reached up to scratch the back of his neck. "I didn't know how else to put it."

"Is the beast to be trusted?" Leon asked cautiously.

I tried to hide the scowl that wanted to form on my lips, reminding myself that it was normal for others to be wary of Nox.

Jace answered before I could. "He will be fine, so long as you don't have any cattle in the area."

Lynelle's eyes widened. "Not in this area, no."

"Then he will be fine," I chimed in as I approached the mare she rode in on.

Once Jace and I mounted the horse together, the other two sent theirs into a gallop straight into the horizon, where the day was turning to dusk.

SIXTEEN

Kellan

WHAT REMAINED OF MY army had finally exited the gods-forsaken Sylis Forest two days prior. We forced through the trees, traveling day and night, only resting when our bodies absolutely demanded it—and even then, it frustrated me to no end. We needed to get back.

Back to Isla.

Back to the queen.

And back to *my* fucking kingdom.

With Callius and Kai out of the picture now, it was only a matter of time until I could infiltrate the castle and its ruler's bed.

That was the way of females—as long as you whispered pretty little lies into their ears, they would welcome you wholeheartedly.

I wasn't beneath Callius' tactics for getting what I needed. If occupying that vindictive bitch of a female's bed was what it took to eventually be crowned king, then so be it.

I was desperate to find a nearby village to steal supplies. Elianna's little wyvern stunt had decimated nearly every ounce of supplies we had aside from the shirts on our backs...and even then, some of those were in tatters, nicked by the flames she cast down on our camp. She even freed our gods-damn horses, forcing us to travel across the entire realm on aching, bleeding feet.

"How much farther to Isla, Captain?" William asked as he caught up at my side.

My jaw ticked as my gaze leisurely fell on him. "Did I just somehow pull a map out of my ass, William?"

The little fuck had a smirk tilt the edge of his lips for a second, and I would've made an example of him right then if I had even an ounce of energy left.

"Land is not my strong suit," I grumbled. "I prefer to take to the seas."

"And that's why you have been forcing us to travel southeast, toward the coast."

My brows furrowed. "Indeed."

"The stars, Captain. That's how I knew. The rest of who remain fear they will drop from starvation or exhaustion soon, whichever claims them first. What is your plan once we arrive at the coast?"

I clenched my teeth. This male was too smart for his own good, and I hated that I was forced to trust him, considering Vincent was now assumed dead.

I cleared my throat. "There are cities and ports along the coast. We could barter for, or commandeer, a ship if necessary."

"Commandeer, Captain?"

"I refuse to be told no, so if they don't have an extra ship to supply their queen's captain, we will take it by whatever means necessary."

We walked through the night, undoubtedly losing many exhausted males along the way. I didn't take a moment to look back and take a head count. Their instructions were clear: we stop for no one. We move straight through, aside from a few hours here and there, to let our bodies rest.

If starvation or exhaustion took them before we reached a port, then that was on them. I had no time to deal with pleasantries.

We continued to move for miles in silence when my gaze landed on mirage-like structures in the distance.

A bead of sweat dripped down my brow, and I moved my hand to shield my eyes from the blinding, scorching sun. No matter how many times I blinked my tired, bloodshot eyes, the vision of what lay ahead remained.

A city. And not just any city, but one with the Vayr Sea at its back.

"William!" I barked into the air, voice hoarse.

Hurried, shuffling footsteps sounded behind me, and he appeared at my side a moment later.

"Aye, Captain," he greeted.

I turned to him then. The male's lips were chapped and appeared to be a breath away from chipping off his face. His exhausted, sunken eyes were a stark contrast to his sunburnt skin.

I gestured to the distant city with my chin, and his stare wandered in its direction.

"Holy gods," he breathed, his voice raspy and parched, as if his throat was filled with desert sand.

"Looks like those pesky gods are finally on our side again, young William." I gripped his shoulder and shook him in victory, but he nearly collapsed at the contact.

Turning to face those who remained, my eyes flared as they fixated on significantly fewer standing bodies than I had anticipated.

"Fuck," I muttered.

"I tried to warn you, Captain." He circled back and faced our remaining army with me.

"What...did the rest of you cowards fucking *drop*?!" I boomed at them. A wicked chuckle left me, but it wasn't from amusement. "Just another gods-damn disappointment."

I counted a handful of them out loud.

"We still have enough to man a ship. Follow my lead, and absolutely none of you speak unless I deem it necessary."

SEVENTEEN

Elianna

OUR HORSES GUIDED US to a war camp a few miles from the mountain range, settled apart from the city. The structures were small, and the soldiers were in few numbers, but the moment I saw it, I recognized it for what it was.

"Is this how you knew we had arrived?" I asked neither of them in particular.

"No, we were actually already here. That's how we were able to meet you so quickly. Scouts reported a flying beast, and well...we were definitely hoping your letter was literal at that point," Leon answered.

We all dismounted our horses and trekked through the camp, passing soldiers as they scurried by left and right, tending to their daily tasks. Some smiled as we strode by; others greeted Jace by name and eyed me warily from the side.

Leon led us to a larger wooden structure in the center of the camp, opening the door for us to follow him.

As my eyes adjusted to the light, my gaze fixated on the center of the room, where a small, round table sat adorned with scattered maps, quills, and an array of weapons.

"This is our outpost closest to the mountain range," Jace began. "It acts as our—"

"First line of defense," I finished for him as I crossed my arms behind my back. "Smart. I'm happy you've put such things in place here, even though you're essentially hidden from the rest of the realm."

He gave a dip of his chin as he pivoted and made his way to the table.

"What news do you have?" Leon asked him as he rounded to the other side, gazing at the maps alongside Jace.

I made my way around the room, my eyes tracing over the artwork, additional maps, and weaponry posted up on the walls.

Jace let out a breathy laugh, the one that had always made my knees buckle. "Where do I even begin?

"Well," Lynelle said. "How about we start with how you met this lovely Lia Valderre?"

A smirk tilted my lips.

Jace's face mirrored my own as he answered, "That's a very long story, one filled with my less-than-charming moments, I may add."

The corners of her lips lifted. "You stated that they left Ellecaster just this morning. It appears we have time for such stories." She paused for a moment. "I would love to hear some of your 'less-than-charming' moments, dear nephew."

Leon pulled out a chair for Lynelle, and she sat in it as if commanded. My gaze lingered over to where Jace stood across from them, eyeing them and their caring gestures intently.

Jace mimicked his general's action and pulled a chair out for me. The four of us sat across from each other under the dim candlelight from the few that were around the room.

Jace blew out a breath. "How did we meet again?" he asked jokingly as his head swung in my direction.

I crossed my arms and leaned back in the chair. "Well, to start, you tied me to a willow tree."

He scoffed. *"After* you kidnapped me and your ship was wrecked."

I waved my hand in the air. "Semantics."

We went back and forth like that for hours, telling them the story of how we met and nearly killed each other several times, all leading up to the one reason we couldn't. Leon and Lynelle's heads moved between us as we spoke, listening to just the very beginning of how our love began and how we planned to use it to unite our races and end the war once and for all.

The four of us laughed until we had tears in our eyes, and sometimes, those tears lingered for the more tragic parts of our journey. This continued until we ended with how we traveled to Alaia and how a new plan was to be forged.

Lynelle smiled at my mate—the kind of prideful smile a mother would give her son.

He smirked at her, as if uncomfortable. "Do you have something you'd like to say, Aunt Lynelle?"

"I'm just very proud of you," she answered.

"I have commanded the mortal armies for years, and *now* you're proud of me?"

"Yes, exactly that." Her gaze moved to me. "For accepting this within your heart. Your bond to a fae woman, only gifted to you by your lineage that you wish to never speak of. I never thought anything like this would be possible, but the least believable part to me...is that you love her in return."

My heart fluttered in my chest, but I blinked, realizing that it wasn't my own reaction to her words but my mate's.

He reached for my hand on the table and then admitted, "Lia was worth changing for."

"It appears so," Lynelle said as she moved to pour another cup of tea that a young soldier had brought in for us some time ago.

Jace leaned back casually in his chair and wrapped his arm around my shoulders. "And what exactly is this situation?" He gestured to them. "It appears you two have become...*closer*."

Leon's eyes narrowed in on him. "She is a wonderful cook. It would've been a shame for her to have an empty table all this time."

"Uh-huh," Jace teased as he reached for more tea himself. He raised a single brow. "Have fun telling Zaela. I'm just ecstatic her focus won't be on being aggravated with us any longer."

Or maybe even Avery and Gage, I thought to myself.

Lynelle's eyes flared as she loudly sipped from her cup. "Remind me to remind my daughter where she received those balls of steel she flaunts around so carelessly."

"Certainly not her brave father who led these armies," Jace heckled.

Her lips turned up, but there was a sadness in her eyes. "She is a mix of us both, that is certain."

"Sass and bravery," Leon started as he wrapped his arm around Lynelle. "Although a dangerous mix, it makes for an exceptional woman."

Jace let out a laugh and looked in my direction, earning a grin from me. "I'll say."

A rush of warmth flooded my cheeks, and I playfully punched him in the arm, eliciting laughter from everyone in the room.

"I know we've sent falcons back and forth since I was last on this side of the peaks, but is there any further news about the soldiers?" Jace asked.

Leon blew out a breath. "Each week, our numbers continue to increase. Young men eager to throw themselves into the fight for freedom."

"And many nervous mothers," Lynelle added.

Leon tried to hide his eye roll before adding, "Regardless, these boys certainly have the heart for it. They will be excellent soldiers—we train daily. And they will be honored to finally meet you now that you're home."

Home, I thought to myself. This was Jace's true home, whether he considered it or not.

Suddenly, the door to the front of the room swung open, putting us all on high alert.

All of our hands flew to our hips, reaching for our swords, until Leon spoke to the young soldier who now stood in the doorway. "What is it? What's happened?"

"Apologies for startling you all," he began. "But dawn is on the horizon, and our scouts have spotted the citizens of Ellecaster emerging from the passage. Your horses are ready to bring you back to them."

"Excellent," Jace said, and we all moved toward the doorway.

EIGHTEEN

Avery

GAGE HAD BARELY SPOKEN to me for the remainder of our time in the passage between the peaks, deeming it a constant necessity to remain at the front with Zaela. A lump had formed in my throat, wondering if he regretted riding with me atop my sister's horse, even if it was only for a few moments. Whenever the thought plagued me, I leapt down from Matthias to walk with Nyra as she trotted alongside us in an attempt to distract myself.

Dawn was finally emerging on the horizon, casting the snowcapped peaks in a golden glow.

"We're about near the end!" Gage shouted. "Send it down the line!"

Murmurs erupted, and cheers shouted, echoing through the passage we had been in for an entire day now. I was exhausted, even though at some point in the night, I had fallen asleep in the saddle—how the men who walked on their feet this entire time were still moving, I had no idea. Even on our journey across the continent, we stopped to rest, even if it was for a few hours.

Veli approached me for the first time since we began the trek the day prior. "Is there a particular reason you've been pouting for the last twelve hours?"

I scoffed at her, earning a rare, wicked smile from the witch. "I don't know what you mean."

She cackled under her breath. "I don't think you should deem yourself threatened by the mortal girl."

"And why is it you believe me to feel threatened?"

She circled around Matthias as we continued to move forward. "You wear your jealousy like a cloak, Princess. It is out there for the realm to see."

"I am *not* jealous," I snapped entirely too loud.

Gazes from all around focused in on the two of us, and I cringed beneath their stares, cursing myself for being so reactive.

She raised a single brow at me, giving me a knowing look before her violet gaze drifted to Zaela's back. "Apologies, Princess."

My stare bore into her as she moved between Finn and Landon's horses to make her way toward the front, and Nyra followed.

After traveling for nearly another mile, the sun shone through the passage at the opposite end from which we came. Cheering continued, and we marched faster toward the open end, desperate to get out of the narrow mountain pass.

"They're here!" Gage shouted over his shoulder.

I smiled as my eyes blinked through the blinding sun to see Lia, Jace, and a few others alongside them, waiting for us at the opposite end.

Everyone funneled out from the passage, and when I made it to the front, I leapt off my horse and aimed for my sister—the others following suit.

Lia smiled at me as I ran toward her and she opened her arms right before I crashed into her for a hug.

"How was the journey?" Jace asked.

"Long," I answered.

"Hopefully, you won't be traveling with us to the nearing battles. Those often take weeks at a time, Princess," Zaela stated as she crossed her arms.

"Any journey without rest feels longer than necessary," Gage cut in, giving me a wink.

My cheeks grew warm, and I quickly averted my gaze from him.

Finn and Landon finally caught up and greeted everyone where we stood, waiting for instructions on where to travel next.

Lia's eyes peered over everyone as the last of their people exited the tunnel. "And everyone is safe?"

"No incidents are to be reported," Gage answered.

"Excellent," the man next to Jace responded.

His stare darted back and forth between me and Finn then. "And you two must be Lia's siblings." We both nodded. "Jace and Lia filled us in regarding your relations to the queen and your true thoughts of her. So long as that remains, you are welcome here."

"Thank you," I whispered, my throat tightening at their kindness, even after all our mother had forced them to endure.

"You have nothing to worry about with that, sir," Finn added from where he stood at my side. "This is the side of the war we will remain on—where we always should've been."

He gave us a nod and a look that almost resembled a smile before turning to address the crowd. "Hello, everyone. My name is General Leon Vern." He gestured to the blonde woman at his side. "This is Lynelle Cadoria." She lifted her hand and gave a delicate wave. "We understand we will be having quite the influx of citizens making the move to the valley of both mortals and fae alike."

"Is *that* all you filled them in on?" Zaela gasped. "Hi, Mom." She smirked at the blonde woman.

Her mother chuckled and then opened her arms, and I was surprised to see Zaela rush toward her and embrace her tightly.

When their hugging ceased, Lynelle spoke. "We received quite the story overnight. Much has been built since your last visit to Alaia, and we do have the room, but everyone may not be all together. We have structures within the city, Anerys, and out in the farmlands as well."

"There are also rooms available in the barracks for soldiers," Leon cut in.

"Excellent," Jace breathed. "The people have made it clear that they are willing to work where they are able to."

"It would be wise for you to address the valley as soon as possible. While we have made it known that half of the newcomers are fae, I'm sure the citizens would feel more comfortable hearing this from your own mouth," Lynelle stated.

"Yes, well, we will take care of that," Jace answered.

"Are you ready to see your new home?" Lynelle asked.

"I'm ready for some of your cooking, that's certain," Gage joked, and I giggled from the side where I stood, watching everyone.

"We have a long day ahead of us. Let's get moving then," Lia chimed in.

And with that, we made our way to our new home.

NINETEEN

Kellan

BEFORE WE EVEN ARRIVED at the city's makeshift, shitty gates, I realized I knew exactly where we were—Tortunele—known as the armpit of the Vayr Sea.

Tortunele made the slums look as if it were a luxury wing in Castle Isla itself. Its occupants were as filthy as the rats in the streets that feasted off the leftover scraps. This land, forsaken by the king two generations ago, became a breeding ground for lawlessness, resulting in the port being overrun by pirates and ex-soldiers who had lost their morals—thieving after gold and females in the dead of night.

I would know—my father was one of them. I hadn't returned to this city since I was a boy aboard his ship.

The city emerged on the horizon as a jumble of dilapidated buildings, their timeworn frames weathered and peeling. Tattered banners and flags marked by pirates swayed in the breeze.

Once we reached the entrance, I led my crew and marched through the port city's wide-open gate—its doors hanging narrowly off broken latches.

Out of the corner of my eye, large figures armed to the teeth with weapons moved to approach us.

Here, the guards resembled mercenaries and were often bought and paid for by the highest bidder—justice administered with a blade rather than a gavel.

I pivoted to William on my right. "Not a single fucking word out of anyone but me."

He gave a curt nod in response.

"Aye," one of the brutes called to me as they stopped mere feet away.

"Aye," I grumbled back. It wouldn't be difficult for us to blend in here. We were already filthy, and what remained of our armor was in tatters. The crew would blend in seamlessly so long as inhabitants didn't discover we were employed by the crown.

"What is your purpose here?" the male demanded as he took a step closer to me, his rotting breath hot on my face.

"Just passing through with the possibility of looking for indulgence," I answered.

The other male's eyes narrowed in on me and then scaled down my body, and I almost reached for my sword on instinct.

He then peered around over my shoulder and spoke. "Where did you come from?"

"Doraeli," I answered immediately. "Our ship was wrecked, you see. So what remains of my crew lingers behind me. We seek temporary refuge and pleasure, and then we will be on our way."

He eyed the other male, and my gaze moved with his. "How long have you been walking on land? Are you the captain?"

"Aye," I answered. "And a week we have traveled. A week we haven't come across a single place of harbor and shelter. I have lost more sailors since we washed ashore."

"And what name do you possess, *Captain?*"

"They call me Ravenne," I answered, giving them my father's surname in place of Adler since it was associated with the crown.

Their eyes widened.

"You're Ravenne's boy? I haven't heard that name in over a century," he admitted. "Rumor claimed you met the same fate as the rest of the crew and were sent to the gallows."

"Aye. Now, what say you here...are we welcome, or shall you throw us out adrift once more?" My patience was wearing thin, but my eyes remained on the mercenaries instead of wandering over to my new second-in-command as he stood next to me in silence.

"Tortunele is just the place for you, it seems," the first brute cut in. "You may pass through or stay, but you will mind your business if you know what's good for you here." He gave a wicked, silver-tooth filled grin. "We don't take kindly to washed up, previously assumed dead strangers."

His threat lingered in the air, and I gave him a curt nod as I moved past him, gesturing for my crew to follow.

William blew out a breath next to me.

"Don't even fucking breathe here, William. Just keep your mouth shut until I say so," I demanded as we marched forward.

In the narrow alleys between the decaying buildings, dirty fucks with matted beards and scarred faces wandered. Drunken laughter and the clanking of mugs echoed from the countless taverns that lined the streets. Filth and wreckage covered the alleyways, while the nauseating aroma of spoiled fish, stagnant beer, and piss lingered in the air.

We passed by gambling dens and shadowy brothels as females with painted lips and hollow eyes beckoned us from beneath the shadows of their doorways.

My lips curled in a snarl as we continued to move past the filth that occupied Tortunele.

Once at the docks, my eyes focused on the bay the city sat upon. Vessels of every size clogged the harbor, ranging from dilapidated fishing boats to sizable, clearly stolen ships, their mast tops swaying like gallows in the wind.

"You truly believe that we will be able to navigate a ship out of this bay unseen..." William began.

I turned to him and raised a brow, and as my gaze wandered behind him, I realized that the remaining members accompanying us were already meandering their way into the surrounding brothels and taverns.

"Captain," he said, pulling me from my daze. "How do you plan to commandeer a ship in a town such as this? We're in no state to take on this many...*pirates*."

I grabbed him by the collar of his frayed shirt. "Listen to me. You do not question me. You speak when spoken to. And you do not give advice. Ever." His eyes widened slightly. "Have I made myself clear?"

Once he answered with a stiff nod, I released his shirt, and he stumbled back, almost losing his footing on the dock and falling into the water.

My gaze landed on a ship that floated mid-harbor—its timber bore the scars of past battles at sea, and its masts wore withered sails, but she would have to do.

"Do exactly as I say, and we will be out of here by dawn," I stated, and he continued observing me while I gazed upon the sea's rolling waves.

I glanced down at him and watched as the corners of his mouth twisted in a menacing grin. "Aye, Captain."

After informing the crew of my plan to commandeer one of the grandest ships this piece of shit harbor had to offer, everything was set in motion.

The night was draped in darkness as my crew moved through the looming buildings' shadows. We neared the dock where the ship lay anchored, and the air became infused with the briny aroma of the sea breeze.

The vessel, barely visible in the dark, radiated an irresistible allure, beckoning me to get the fuck out of this place and back to Isla as if the sea itself were calling to me.

As we stealthily approached, I caught sight of more mercenaries and loitering washed-up sailors patrolling the deck—their lanterns flickering light over the wooden planks. The mercenaries at the docks were adorned with weapons at their hips and poking from their boots.

I carefully raised my arm and signaled the crew behind me to spread out, ensuring they remained hidden. Our true target was out at sea, but first, we had to reach the largest fishing boat moored at the far end of the dock.

As the four males pivoted on the dock, I knew now was our chance to make our move. All we needed was to gain the element of surprise. I let out a soft whistle, and two of my soldiers approached from one side. Another three then moved to cut off any escape routes. Silence was our best ally and stealth our greatest weapon.

As the mercenaries reached the end of the dock, my men were at their backs on silent feet in only a moment—any sound their boots made was covered by the noise of the rolling waves. The moment the hired guards moved to pivot, they found the cool touch of blades at their throats.

A second later, their bodies dropped into the water with a splash—a splash that was too fucking loud to go unnoticed in a town full of fae.

Right when I thought we would be clear of any eye-catching chaos, doors creaked open behind us. Males funneled out of taverns left and right with weapons in hand, and a commotion was already underway before I had the chance to blink. My eyes bulged.

No. No. No. Fuck!

"Move. Now!" I commanded as softly as possible to those who remained behind me.

We rushed to the dock, shoving each other violently out of the way to jump into one of the small fishing boats.

It was every male for himself—if they were too slow, that was on them, not me.

"Row, you fools!" I snapped as roars of disapproval echoed from the opposite end of the dock where we had just been.

"Thieves!" The word sounded out in numerous screams, over and over.

I ripped the oar out of one of my sailor's hands after witnessing his pathetic attempt to help us escape.

"You're fucking *useless!*" I snapped as I shoved him off the boat, sending his body into the black abyss beneath us.

We rowed vigorously as angry, screaming, drunken sailors followed suit in their own pinnaces and came after us in the cove.

Once we finally reached the ship, we ascended its side using rope ladders. My fingers deftly gripped the gunwales as I heaved myself over the edge of the deck. What should have been executed with precision came undone almost instantly.

I pushed myself to my feet and quickly inspected the deck of the ship and was surprised no one appeared to be on board.

"Stupid fucks," I muttered with a grin as I shook my head.

I made my way to the stairs that led to the upper deck to man the wheel when I shouted, "To your posts, now! The ship is ours, gents!"

Fuck, that felt good to say. I never wanted to travel across the continent by land again.

I reached for the wheel, feeling the pricks of the splintered wood beneath my calloused hands, and grinned. "Hello, beautiful," I whispered.

Out of nowhere, a shadow appeared from the far corner, startling me as I caught a glimpse of it.

I reached for my sword instantaneously and swiftly moved to block the blow of my assailant's blade. The clouds moved across the sky, and the moon cast its light upon the brute that greeted us when we initially arrived in Tortunele.

Our blades pressed together in a struggle for power, each of us forcing all of our strength into its hold. "I knew you were going to be trouble. The second you said Ravenne, it was clear you couldn't be trusted. And it didn't even take a day."

As he prepared to strike once more, I reacted quickly by entwining my leg around his, using the force to throw him down onto the wooden deck—a trick I had seen Elianna use too many times to count. Maybe the broad knew what she was doing after all.

"Any last words, you ugly prick?" I taunted him between my teeth as I held the tip of my sword to his chest.

He let out a cackle of triumph as if he wasn't staring at the end of his life at the edge of my blade. "You're just like your father."

My smile faltered, and my jaw locked as a tense silence filled the air. A moment later, with a swift, silent strike, I drove my sword through his gut and ripped it clean across. He gurgled on his own blood as his body went limp beneath my stare.

My gaze moved to the ships that were rowing after us in the harbor to see that they were already nearly a half mile behind. I turned to the ship's wheel to see William manning it in my place.

I approached him silently. The only sound was the echo of my boots as it made contact with the deck.

"Apologies, Captain," he began. "We were running out of time."

I scratched at my beard as I peered back at the cove we sailed from for a final time. "Don't you ever fucking disobey me again," I barked. "Now get rid of the body."

He gave me a curt nod and heaved the body up and over the rail.

A thundering splash filled the sea air a few moments later, and my eyes followed him as he stalked down the steps to tend to his post on the ship. William was mouthy, but he was useful.

With the tide on our side, we set sail under the cover of darkness, leaving the cove behind us as we embarked on our journey back to Isla. The sound of waves, as they crashed against the hull, felt as if the sea were welcoming me home.

TWENTY

Elianna

ALAIA WAS EVERYTHING I imagined and more. I couldn't believe how much the mortals had built in just over fifty years, entire cities and towns, farmlands, and ports alike. It was magnificent. My eyes lingered on Jace as he guided us across the land and through the streets of Anerys.

General Vern had sent out a message to alert all soldiers that there would be an influx of citizens that were both mortal and fae once we arrived. While the stares were bothersome, I knew they wouldn't last. The people had every right to be wary of us, and of me. They had three Valderres in their city, for gods-sake. If they weren't cautious, *I* would've questioned *them*.

With soldiers as their escorts, families with children were led to temporary homes, ensuring their comfort as they awaited news about their future living arrangements. In the evening, Commander Cadoria was expected to make an announcement about his long-awaited return to Alaia and the *secret weapon* he had brought with him.

As Leon moved to help the soldiers, we followed Lynelle to her home—Zaela and Jace's old home—on the outskirts of the city.

I wasn't sure what to expect, but it certainly wasn't a massive estate, with sprawling land that extended far beyond the structure in every direction.

My brow raised slightly and Zaela caught it from where she walked at my side. "My father commanded the armies, Lia. We weren't raised in a hut."

I chuckled softly. "I just wasn't sure what to expect, but it certainly wasn't an estate that could fit all of us."

She walked ahead slightly and then turned around, walking backward as she faced me. "Well, I managed to squeeze us all into my townhouse, didn't I? My mother has empty nest syndrome for a reason," she said with a wink, as she turned to face forward once more and caught up with her mother at the front.

Nyra trotted at my side, and I reached down to scratch her ears as we moved up the gray cobblestone walkway and through the wrought-iron gates that marked the entrance.

The Cadoria Estate stretched over acres of rolling hills, surrounded by towering ancient oak trees, creating a natural barrier. The manor itself was stunning, adorned with vines of ivy that climbed the walls, reminding me of the wisteria vines at Castle Isla.

Lynelle opened the front door and guided us into the open foyer, where a staircase rested in its center, with a dining room on its left, and a living space on its right.

"Your home is lovely, Lynelle," I said.

"Thank you, Lia. Now there are plenty of bedrooms upstairs, although I'm sure Zaela will retreat to her old room." She turned to Jace. "You, of course, can move wherever you wish to, nephew. Your mother's home remains untouched." She gave him a soft, sympathetic smile.

He nodded and gripped my hand, pulling me toward the dining room. "Unfortunately, we don't have time, Aunt Lynelle. We will make our way there as soon as possible."

"Of course, I will go make you all a nice, hot meal." She swiftly made her way down the hall.

The silence was deafening as we all funneled around the room to sit at the dining room table. The tension continued to grow as we settled, and I stared down at my hands as they rested atop the aged wood. Nerves took over me as I picked at the edges of my thumbs, desperately searching for words that I owed them—a plan.

A plan that we all needed in this moment that would carry us through to the end of this century-long war.

I nicked the edge of my thumb too hard, and blood pooled where my nail met its bed. I let out an involuntary hiss.

Jace's hand was instantly placed atop my own as he sat beside me, lacing his fingers with mine. My eyes remained on our now interlocking hands, but I felt everyone else's stares as they bore into me.

I slowly lifted my gaze to the seven pairs of eyes that searched my own for answers.

I blew out a breath. "Did you think we would make it this far a month ago?"

The room instantly felt lighter as the corners of their lips graced their faces with knowing smiles.

"We now need to strategize our next move and devise a plan to dethrone the queen," I said. "We have no way of knowing where Kellan and Callius are, or if they have already made it back to Isla. To ensure readiness, we must anticipate the worst—and right now, it is that they have made it back to Castle Isla, and the queen is aware that her son is dead."

Zaela gave a curt nod. "First, we must start with getting an estimated count of warriors on our side."

"I have an idea of what to expect, but Leon will be able to confirm a more accurate number of how many have been training and cleared on this side of the peaks since our last visit," Jace said. "We should have the numbers."

"And I have a wyvern." I gave him a wink.

"We need the logistics of where the war will come to a close. Where and how far do we plan to make our soldiers travel? The majority of us are mortal, after all. Our men would be worn out faster by a journey across the continent than by a battle alone, leaving us weak and disheveled upon arrival. We must be smart about this," Zaela interjected.

My jaw locked. "I don't want the queen's army anywhere near this side of the Sylis Forest ever again. We get as close to Isla as possible."

"Well, if we're moving on foot, we will need to take it slow to avoid exhaustion," Gage chimed in.

"We are running out of time. And the slower we go, the more of a chance they have at closing in on us once again. We can't afford to take it slow," I countered.

"Lia, you have never fought alongside an army of men aside from the Battle of Ellecaster. Humans are different from fae," Zaela stated.

"She knows that, Zae," Jace growled.

"Well, she isn't acting like it," she retorted without removing her stare from me. "Our men are now your men. Don't doom them because of impatience."

I was silent for a few moments, taking in her words. "You're right, and I'm sorry. How many ships do you have here?"

"I would say at least a hundred, ready to go at any given moment, perhaps more," she answered.

"So, traveling by sea is out of the question for the entirety of the army, leaving us once again to travel all the way by foot." Shaking my head in frustration, I desperately tried to come up with a new plan. "I'm not sure what else we can do. If they close in on us, we risk the innocents. If we march south, we exhaust our troops. We're fucked either way."

Finn, Landon, and Veli's eyes moved back and forth between each of us as we spoke of trying to find the best course of action—and survival—for our soldiers.

Avery's stare remained fixated on me from where she sat directly across the table. Her eyes were calculative, as if she was listening to every word spoken in the room, combing through each of them with a fine pick as she searched for an answer to one of our endless unknowns.

"I have an idea," she stated, her eyes remaining on me.

A wicked smile leisurely tilted my lips. "Go on, dear sister."

Her scheming stare moved to the sorceress on her right. "Magic."

Veli let out a hiss as her face contorted into a vicious snarl. "Foolish, girl."

"No," I interrupted her before she could insult Avery further. "You have kept your secrets long enough, Veli." My eyes made their way back to my sister. "Go on."

Avery sucked in her bottom lip as if questioning if she should truly reveal her thoughts. Her honey-hued stare lifted back to mine. "On our journey here, Veli spoke of traveling by portal."

A scoff left the witch, but I leaned forward over the table and lifted my finger in Veli's direction to halt her.

Avery continued, "She is able to teleport her own body effortlessly. She said it's called *wisping*, but she spoke of a way to move a potential army." She glanced over at Veli and mouthed the words, *I'm sorry*.

"No, you're not. And you know nothing of what you speak," Veli hissed, her violet stare illuminating the darkened room.

"There must be some form of truth to it, Veli. Could you truly move an army across the continent?" I asked.

The silence from my mate and the others added to the intensity as the three of us continued to exchange words.

"I could not do that, no," she answered simply.

"But with others, she could," Avery intervened, causing my brow to lift as I watched them each intently. "What we need is more witches."

"Absolutely fucking not," Veli barked, her lips curling back.

"It's the only way!" my sister screeched just as intensely.

I spoke then. "I would love nothing more than to ignite Idina's war in wyvern's flame and watch it burn to ash at her feet. If what my sister states is true, then it is imperative that you reveal your knowledge of traveling by portal."

Jace leaned back in his chair from beside me, his piercing eyes locked on the sorceress as he stated, "You will obey her orders."

Veli huffed through her nostrils. "A single witch cannot open a portal wide enough, nor for a long enough period, for an entire army to travel through. It is a process that demands the contributions of multiple witches—their focus, energy, and power." She crossed her arms over her chest and met my stare with one equally intense, the gold in her eyes flaring.

"And you stated all those weeks ago that the Elora Coven is no longer. Is that true?"

"The coven...ceased to exist as one many centuries ago. For a rogue witch sought to destroy the very thing that was destroying themselves." Veli tapped a single taloned nail on the table before her. "Grief, loathing, and an insatiable hunger for power ripped the coven apart."

"And all this occurred where?" I asked.

"The Elora Isles," she answered. "Three small marsh guarded islands northeast of the continent, but the witches who once occupied it have dispersed across the realm in hiding. The Elora Isles always call to us—beckoning a persistent whisper in our ears, urging us to find our way home."

"But you never returned."

She shook her head and quickly averted her gaze from mine. "I can never return there." Veli clicked her tongue.

"And as you are aware, I hesitantly use strong bursts of my power. For magic calls to its kin."

I pursed my lips, examining her for a moment. "Why did you leave your coven, Veli? Why did you move to Isla and disguise yourself as a healer?"

She was silent for a few moments. "After all that I had been forced to witness at the hand of my kin, I thought it wouldn't hurt to bring the realm a little...*healing*." The words were barely above a whisper, as if she was ashamed.

My eyes drifted over to Zae as she sat next to Veli, and to my surprise, her stare softened at the witch's confession.

"But you can call these witches to a formal meeting?" Jace interjected.

Veli snarled. "I can. But I will do no such thing."

Avery crossed her arms and glared at her beneath furrowed brows. "Interesting to see you fear something, *sorceress*."

"Watch it," she snapped, lifting a taloned nail in her direction. "You once again forget your place, Avery."

"Her place is directly at my side," I said sternly. "And there it shall remain. She isn't speaking anything that the rest of us aren't thinking. You fear your coven, Veli. That much is clear and laid bare now."

Veli leaned back in her chair, causing the front legs to lift from the floor. Her eyes roamed over me lazily, as if assessing me. "You arm yourself with mortals and inexperienced rulers, thinking you will win the great century-old war. I have pegged you for many things, Elianna, but a fool had never been one of them—until now."

The sternness of my face faltered. "I have armed myself with a *wyvern*."

"You have obtained a *pet*," she spat back. "Yes, it wields flame in its breath, but to what end? As time has proven, the wyvern's fire cannot be solely depended upon. Be smarter."

"I'm *trying*!" I bellowed across the table, breath heaving.

The air in the room was thick with tension. Everyone's gazes averted from the two of us as we stared down our noses at one another from across the table.

Veli's stare shifted to Jace. "And you follow your mate to no end. A commander in his own right, taking the knee to his enemy queen—leading his people to slaughter as if they're cattle."

My lips curled into a snarl.

Jace silently placed his elbows on the table, lacing his fingers together as he leaned closer to Veli. "Please continue to speak as if you know me, witch." Veli's intense stare didn't falter. "For you are correct, I *will* follow my mate to no end. Do you wish to know why?"

When Veli didn't answer, he continued. "I have met no one more selfless, caring, or determined than the female that sits before you—before all of us. You see, witch, you have healed her physical wounds, but I have seen and felt what lies and aches in her beating heart—for its beats echo into my own." He tapped his chest softly with a fist as his eyes remained on her.

My breath caught, and my eyes wandered around the room. Everyone remained silent, watching them intently. Avery's mouth popped open in surprise as she listened to

Jace, and when she made eye contact with me, her soft smile conveyed her admiration.

"So, Miss Veli, you asked me if I will take the knee to my enemy queen and lead my people to slaughter—and the answer is absolutely not. However, what I *will* be doing is standing at my mate's side, leading *our* people to victory, and bringing justice to all those who have lost their lives for the false queen's bidding. Elianna was *never* my enemy. If you wish to name someone a fool, then it is I for initially taking so long to see that."

His posture relaxed slightly and my hand fell to his knee, giving it a squeeze of gratitude.

Veli remained speechless in her seat.

I leaned across the table once more, my breath huffing through my nostrils as our stares met.

"You're stating I need to be smarter. That I arm myself with false bravado, weakened bodies, and limited flame. I am trying to do right by my people, both fae and mortal alike. So, Veli, what I ask is that you cooperate and *help* me. Help us. The fate of the realm depends on it."

"You wish to risk the wrath of some of our world's most malevolent beings to aid you in your war?" she asked.

"You are of their blood and race. If one is benevolent, perhaps more are as well," I challenged. "We won't win this war without allies, and if I can offer that to our troops, then I'm willing to take the risk."

When she didn't answer, I continued. "Be honest. With both us and yourself. Do you see us winning this war without additional powerful allies?"

The silence of the room was deafening.

"No," she finally answered, and while everyone else looked solemn at the word, my heart rate picked up in anticipation of what else I could sense was on the tip of her tongue.

A subtle upward tilt appeared at the corner of Veli's lips, barely noticeable. "May the gods be on our side for what I am about to show you. We will certainly need them to be."

TWENTY-ONE

Veli

NIGHT HAD FALLEN BY the time the argument regarding my cooperation ceased. Zaela's mother returned to the room with a feast prepared only moments after I agreed to summon my coven to help Elianna win back her rightful throne. They accused me of fearing my witch-blooded sisters, and I loathed that they were correct—they just hadn't a clue as to the reasoning.

The issue wasn't whether I could summon my kin to our ancient homeland—it was that I didn't know how to tell them it could mean certain death for all who entered The Elora Isles.

They ate as if their stomachs hadn't received the slightest bit of food in days, repeatedly thanking Zaela's mother for her hospitality while I sat in silence, moving around bits of roasted chicken with my fork.

After she left us once more, they pushed their plates away after gorging themselves and returned their attention to me.

Elianna broke the silence first. "When you first arrived in Ellecaster, Avery spoke of a spell book you possess that aided your escape from Isla. Is that here with you now?"

"Indeed," I answered as I pivoted in my seat and reached for my woven bag at my side.

I placed the small satchel on the table, and everyone leaned closer in curiosity.

"The book wouldn't fit in that, Veli. We don't have time for meddling games," Avery hissed, and Elianna raised a brow as she watched me.

My lip curled back in annoyance as I reached into the bag, and when I pulled it out, my hand held *Tinaebris Malifisc.*

Power radiated from it the moment it left the confines of the bag.

"Holy gods," Elianna breathed. "I can...*feel* it. Its presence." Her eyes moved up toward my own. "How did you...?"

I grinned. "Witchcraft. The bag was meticulously crafted to conceal and protect any magical items it contained, camouflaging it from the realm."

The room was cloaked in near darkness as the sun completely set—the only source of light came from the blazing candles scattered about the space. I placed the ancient book atop the table.

I could feel the power humming beneath my fingertips as they grazed the book's leather-like surface. Memories flashed across my vision of how I came into possession of the relic, and what I had done...who I had *betrayed* to obtain it.

Elianna's gaze bore into me, the flickering candlelight reflecting in her haunted stare. "This is the book you spoke of that possesses the forbidden magic?"

Finnian shivered in his chair.

I tapped my chin with my nail as I observed her. "What do you know of sorcery?"

She crossed her arms. "Aside from what you have already revealed? Not much else."

I pivoted to her human mate. "And you, mortal?"

"I would say my knowledge is even less than what she possesses."

My attention moved to his companions. "And the same for each of you?"

"I know nothing of witchcraft," Gage answered, and Zaela nodded in agreement at his side.

My eyes remained on the blonde, who I had found myself unable to resist sneaking peeks at. My next words were solely for her. "Would you like to know more of witchcraft?"

Her eyes flared in response right before I moved my attention back to Elianna.

"As I have explained to your siblings before, there are different elements of magic—this book has the sole purpose of providing dark, malicious sorcery to its wielder. Once a spell is cast, that witch possesses the power to manipulate said spell at any given time without being in possession of the book."

"Forever?" Jace questioned.

"Indeed."

"So you possess the magic it took to sneak everyone out of the city—the shadows that you also wielded back in Ellecaster," Elianna interjected.

My jaw clenched. "Indeed," I echoed.

"What other types of magic does this book contain?" she asked.

164

"Blood magic," Avery chimed in, and my gaze whipped to her.

"Breaking mental shields," Finnian added.

"Don't forget mind control," Landon stated, and I forgot he was even here. He had barely spoken a word since we arrived at the estate.

Each time one of them spoke, the others' attention immediately shifted, and Elianna smirked in amusement at her siblings and their usual irritating banter.

"Well, that settles that, then," I huffed out as I sat back in my seat, gesturing to the three of them.

"And you can use these in battle?" Elianna asked.

"I have no desire to ever utilize any material from this book again, aside from my shadows." I sighed. "Dark magic has a cost, starting with our youth, and should never be freely wielded. What happened in Isla shouldn't have occurred in the first place."

"Your coven," Zaela interjected. "You stated you are from where? The Elora Isles? Where is it located, and how do we get there?" Whenever she spoke to me, her voice had a slight tremor, revealing an unseen nervousness that she didn't display with anyone else.

A wicked smile crept up my face. "It is both near and far from anywhere in the realm, only traceable by those who know where it is. It lays hidden in a pocket of the Vayr Sea northeast of our continent."

"So we can travel by ship," Gage added.

"No males may enter there. It is forbidden," I warned.

"We will be accompanying you," Jace growled. "We cannot be sure you won't just run off, leaving us behind to rot. As our only source of power, it is crucial that you remain with us for the foreseeable future. In fact, how about before any of this, you take a knee before her now and pledge your allegiance?"

"If my loyalty has yet to be proven, then I do not know why I am still here, Commander. Now, since you refuse to heed my warnings, it appears you wish to put your mate in danger and have her wander into The Elora Isles." I raised a brow.

His features softened as he glanced over at the future queen at his side.

"I live for danger." She winked at him, and he let out an irritated growl in response. Elianna turned to me. "However, why are men forbidden?"

"They are not welcome there; they never have been, and the land itself would work to dispose of them if they were to get too close."

"Define too close."

"I would recommend they do not set foot on the earth," I retorted.

"And what is the plan once we arrive at the isles? How do you summon the witches if the land has been abandoned?" Zaela asked.

The thought of being in the presence of my lost sisters sent a shiver through me—the hairs on my arms stood at attention, and my skin erupted into goosebumps.

"Once we arrive, not only will we be sensed, but my blood will call to them—a mere drop into the cursed soil will beckon them to return immediately."

Elianna's eyes widened, and she quickly averted her gaze from me. She pursed her lips while examining me. "So, that's it then? We sail to your little islands that only you can trace, spill a few drops of your blood, and then your coven will return in that very moment?"

"Essentially," I answered after a few seconds of silence.

"Let's say this doesn't go as planned," she started. "Say they're as cruel as you believe them to still be, and things go awry. How do we kill them?"

I lifted a brow in her direction. "I have told your siblings this as well, but witches are immortal, Elianna. All we require is the essence of a beating heart."

"You and your riddles." She let out a soft laugh and shot her child-like smirk at me. "So, stab them in the heart. Got it."

"No, no, Heir of the Realm. A mere stab wouldn't do. It would need to be removed or destroyed."

Suddenly, the front door to the estate swung open, revealing the general who had escorted us away from the mountains earlier today.

"Gods, you're still here?!" he boomed, eyes boring into his own commander.

"We were just finishing up here," Jace answered.

"Well, thank the gods for that then, Cadoria. I have funneled every soul within a ten-mile radius into the streets, awaiting your return. And you're here doing what exactly?"

"Eating!" Lynelle shouted from the kitchen where she had remained.

The general blew out a breath and focused his gaze back on his commander. "Well, I won't be arguing with her."

"Wise man," Jace responded. "The time has come, my Lia." He reached for her hand.

"Excellent," she said as she placed her hand in his and stood from her chair. Her gaze landed back on me once more while I silently remained in my seat at the opposite end of the table. "If possible, we leave tomorrow."

There was no room for argument in her tone, though every fiber of my being was lashing out beneath my skin.

The thought of having to return to my kin loomed over me—suffocating me with each breath I inhaled. I was thankful that the fae's senses paled in comparison to those of a witch, or else she would've detected the sudden halt of my heart as it stopped in my chest, realizing that the time had come to face what I had done.

TWENTY-TWO

Jace

THE EIGHT OF US rode horses through the city, lit by endless lines of torches and moonlight. The awaiting crowds greeted us with equal amounts of cheers and looks of puzzlement as we galloped through them, aiming for the center of the city. So much had changed since I had last been to Anerys. The outskirts of our headquarter city had expanded substantially.

Each of us dismounted our horses once we arrived at the newly constructed stone courthouse. Leon had already arrived and was atop the rise, waiting for us to climb the steps to greet the city and its citizens. Once we turned to face the masses, a smile formed on Lia's face.

I took a single step forward, half blocking her from view. She had already given this speech to those who had been in Ellecaster with us, but for me, it would be the first time to those who weren't directly under my command.

These were my people, and I was about to tell them the unthinkable. Although I was certain that most of them were already aware of the rumors, it was still difficult to inform them that their commander, the man who had led their armies in the fight against the fae, had fallen in love with one. And not just any fae—the rightful queen and heir of the realm.

Would they believe me or think I had sold us out? I knew in my heart that they would accept Lia; it was impossible not to, but time wasn't on our side. All I could hope for was that they trusted me enough to lead them to her.

My hands hung down at my sides as I looked out over the silent crowd, and just as I went to speak, I felt a warm, familiar touch as she laced her fingers with mine. I glanced over my shoulder to meet my favorite emerald gaze, instantly calming my nerves.

She gave a small nod, and my eyes shifted through the rest of her court standing behind us.

Clearing my throat, I opened my mouth to finally speak. "It has been some time since I have spoken before you all—some of your faces are familiar, while others are new. Regardless of when you joined us, you must know that I plan to lead us to victory, granting us freedom from the wicked queen that rests upon the throne in Isla."

Murmurs erupted through the city, becoming an instant roaring in my ears.

"While I realize that my absence has been substantial as of late, I'm still your commander and expect your attention and respect. Yes, to start, there are fae among us and standing here with me before you now," I stated with authority as my eyes shifted through the crowd beneath the moonlight.

After fifty or so feet, I couldn't make out a single face—just endless rows of bodies and torches lining the streets before me.

"I haven't been entirely honest with you all, and for that, I'm truly sorry." The murmurs of the crowd instantly ceased, casting an eerie silence. "My mother was attacked and left for dead at the hands of the fae thirty years ago during an ambush on one of our villages. I am the result of her assault."

I expected the crowd to erupt once more, but they remained silent.

"My hate for the fae had poisoned my heart and mind, turning me into a vengeful leader who, until recently, would've stopped at nothing to end the entirety of the fae. On a mission we had set out on to lure and trap their leaders, everything I thought I knew about myself and our war had changed."

I took a step to the side and pivoted to face Lia. Extending my hand toward her, she placed hers in mine without hesitation as she stepped up to stand at my side.

"I met an extraordinary female, and she also stands before you today. Everyone, I would like you to meet Elianna Valderre—the *rightful* heir to the Velyran throne."

We were met with wide-eyed stares and audible gasps of disbelief, but surprisingly, the eruption of anger we had prepared for never came.

"She is the daughter of the late King Jameson Valderre, someone we as a race had believed to be responsible for this war, but we are here to tell you that...that was *not* the case."

I went on with the speech Lia had given in Ellecaster and how our goal was no longer to remove the fae from the realm but to remove Idina Valderre from its throne.

"Who's to say Elianna won't turn on us? She is a *Valderre!* And those two red-heads look exactly like the queen you wish to overthrow! They could all be spies!" a shout came from the darkness of the crowd, causing more vicious whispers to ensue.

My body stiffened, just as I thought we were in the clear from angry outbursts. I glanced over my shoulder in time to watch Avery flinch. Lia was used to hateful comments and having to prove who she was, but the others weren't.

"I will vouch for both her and them with my life. For Elianna is *everything* to me and more..." I glanced at her as she remained poised at my side. She stared out at the masses completely unphased, appearing as the fearless warrior she was and the queen she's yet to become. "For she is my mate. My equal in every way."

The crowd went silent at my words. My only assumption was that they were at a loss for them.

"Us humans are not accustomed to fae traditions and lore. However, what I speak of is a phenomenon blessed upon us by the gods. It is decided by their fates, and the bond connects our souls to one another. Her very presence has forced me to come to terms with what I am, and that is a halfling. Both of fae and mortal descent. And as I stand here before you all today, you need to know that if you refuse to trust their kind due to their blood alone, then you will need to condemn me with them as well."

A man stepped forward then, setting himself apart from the very front of the crowd. We stared down at him as he cleared his throat. "Commander, you have done everything you can to ensure we stay safe since you were a mere boy.

Something as insignificant as a sire shouldn't determine how you are judged. If Elianna has your sword, then she also has mine."

My heart raced as he took a step back into his place in the crowd, echoes of agreement sounding from them. "Thank you, soldier," I said, trying to shake the shock.

My gaze moved to Lia. "I know what lies in her heart. She wishes to bring peace to the realm but cannot do this alone. A target has been placed on her back, and she has been attacked, hunted, *taken*..."

My throat tightened with fury, and my hands trembled at my sides as I forced out the words I despised beyond measure—all she had been forced to endure.

Lia lifted my shaking fist and pressed it to her lips as she took a small step forward, her toes reaching the very edge of the step we stood on.

"What Jace is trying to say is that I have also suffered at the hand of my own kind. Males I once trusted and soldiers I once commanded myself. Your commander and I have defied the odds stacked against us so far, and we intend for that to continue. We *will* take the realm back. But you should all know that the current queen's fury will know no bounds, and she will do anything to remain where she is."

Once my anger settled, I stepped up to her side and stood before the masses once more.

"We don't know what lies ahead, but we *do* know it won't be easy," I began. "We are seeking out more alliances and possible routes to help us win this war."

Lia gave a curt nod to the crowd. "Fae are now among you here. They will live alongside you—shopping, working, and mingling in the streets with their younglings. Please show them kindness, for their journey here has been anything but easy. They risked being trialed for treason just by fleeing here—seeking shelter and sanctuary away from the crown. Among them are also males and females who intend to bleed alongside you in these looming battles to come."

"Magic is alive and well throughout Velyra, and creatures we once assumed to be extremely rare, extinct, or just a story to frighten our children in the night have presented themselves to us frequently in recent days," I said once she paused. "Not only are fae now among us but also a witch who assisted in their escape."

"And a wyvern who assisted in my own," Lia announced with a menacing lilt in her voice. I peeked over and observed her smirk while she witnessed the crowd's simultaneous reactions of awe and horror.

When the shock of everything settled, questions began to ring out from them, and we answered truthfully. We told them stories of our journey. Lia spoke of her father's kindness and how that benevolence extended not only to her but to her two red-headed siblings who stood behind us in solidarity.

And when the moon was at its highest point in the sky, the crowd finally dispersed.

Our court stepped up at our sides as we watched everyone funnel through the streets and back to their homes.

"I can't believe you told the realm," Zaela whispered. "I know Lia briefly referred to you as her mate in Ellecaster...but this was different. This *felt* different."

"It was time," I answered.

Gage clapped me on the shoulder. "I'm proud of you, brother."

"As am I," Lia cooed, resting her head on my chest.

And as the last of our people disappeared into the shadows of the streets, we said our goodbyes to Leon and made our way back home.

TWENTY-THREE

Elianna

I STOOD BEFORE THE small cottage that was set an acre behind the manor of the Cadoria Estate, staring at my mate as he moved toward the house that built him. He rarely spoke of his mother, but anytime he did, I was paralyzed by an overwhelming sense of grief as his emotions consumed both of us.

He took another hesitant step toward the adorably crafted home that was set off to the far side of the backyard, surrounded by trees for a sense of privacy. I watched from a small distance behind him as he took in the sight of it all.

I closed the gap between us and laced my fingers with his as I pressed my lips to his shoulder. He took in a shuddering breath at the contact.

"It never gets easier. Returning here. I think it's the main reason I rarely ever do," Jace admitted.

I pivoted my body and wrapped my arms around his front, our chests pressed together. "I'm very proud of you for what you did today." He answered with a low hum. "And we don't have to stay here, Jace. We can go back to your aunt's house and find a room, just as Zae and Gage had with the others."

He let out a breathy laugh as he pulled me even tighter to him and rested his chin on my forehead. "I know. I was hoping for some alone time with you. We've had so little of it."

"I know," I whispered into his chest.

I tilted my head up to look at him as his gaze remained ahead. His hazel eyes sparkled beneath the moonlight, but his jaw was tense—locked, as if every ounce of pain he had ever felt for his mother came crashing back into him.

My gaze wandered past the cottage, where a small, woodsy area marked the boundary of his family's land. A private forest hidden within the valley, all to ourselves. A menacing smile curved my lips, and I was grateful he couldn't see it from where he stood.

His body stiffened. "What are you up to?" he asked, his voice heavy with anticipation, causing a rush of heat to pool between my thighs.

I hummed softly. "I don't know what you mean."

His wicked laugh nearly brought me to my knees as his grip on me loosened slightly. "My darling Lia, you are up to no good." I took a step away, looking up at him with a grin. He took a matching step toward me as he watched me beneath furrowed brows.

"What makes you think that?" I asked as I continued to move backward, toward the trees.

"You forget, I can now sense everything about you. As each day passes, I learn how to decipher it—how to decipher *you*. And you, my love, are absolutely up to something."

"Something..." I drew out the word.

"Something wicked," he answered, and my nipples tightened beneath my shirt. I watched his mouth as he spoke these words, and all I could think about was how I longed for his lips to be on me instead, putting them to far better use.

"Wicked indeed," I answered with a wink right before I took off in a sprint, darting directly for the woods.

I expected him to chase after me immediately, but when I glanced over my shoulder as I ran toward the trees, I was surprised to find him watching me intently—his dimple on display as his face was graced with the most alluring smile.

I came to a halt at the forest's edge and turned to face him.

"Not going to see what wickedness lies in my thoughts, Commander?" I called to him, triggering him to take a single step forward.

My heart raced in anticipation.

"Is it a chase you want, Elianna?" he cooed as his stride continued in my direction. "Because, *my Lia*, I will chase you to the ends of the world and beyond. Until there isn't another step to be taken, for then I plan to freefall together into the vale. It's just you and me, sweetheart—destined to relive our descent over the waterfall."

His promise sent a chilling shiver up my spine. As his steps moved toward me, I continued our little dance and matched them backward once more until I was hidden within the shadows of the trees.

Jace's pace quickened slightly as he lost sight of me. "So I will ask you once more, my queen. Do you wish for me to chase you to the edge of the realm?" His tone had darkened, and my knees nearly buckled beneath me. "I'm waiting, Elianna..."

"Always," I spoke so softly I was almost certain he couldn't have heard it until he suddenly charged at me.

I let out a noise that was equal parts giggle and squeal as I bolted further into the trees. I sprinted through narrow gaps of towering pines, leapt over jagged-edged boulders, and ducked beneath low-hanging branches, refusing to look back as I sensed him right on my tail.

Suddenly, it went quiet behind me, and my steps instantly halted. I listened to the wind as it whistled through the treetops and whipped around, assuming to come face-to-face with him, but was met with nothing but the woods' shadows.

My eyes peered through the darkness of the foggy haze that glided between the trees. Crickets sounded, but there wasn't an echo of footsteps or the sound of a gasping breath. It appeared I was completely alone, but I knew better.

Our bond throbbed beneath my skin, and I felt the steadiness of his beating heart and his deep, pulsing arousal.

On silent feet, I swiftly moved through the brush, carefully stepping over the roots, and pressed my back against the trunk of the oak tree to my right.

Steadying my breathing, I went to peek around once more, when suddenly, the touch of a calloused hand wrapped itself around my throat. A second later, I was enveloped in his scent of embers and cedarwood, fueling a menacing grin to spread across my face as I met my false attacker's eyes.

His grip on my throat was light but put enough pressure to have me slightly straining for air. "What are your plans now that you've caught me, Commander?" I asked, my voice sultry.

A growl rumbled deep in his chest, and in one swift movement, his grip went from my throat to picking me up and pinning me against a tree.

He brought his lips to my ear, and the feeling of his breath sent a shudder through my body. "I've been dreaming of what I could do to you since I had you last."

I inhaled a staggered breath at his words. He started kissing down my neck slowly, his teeth grazing my skin as he took his time teasing me.

I let out an involuntary moan. "Jace," I breathed.

He lowered my legs back down to the ground while taking his hands and moving them over every inch of me, every curve. Our breaths became heavier, our pace getting more chaotic and rushed. My eyes closed under the weight of his touch as my heart pounded with anticipation and the need for him.

Once his hands met my hips, he gripped the buckle of my pants and tore them open, shoving them down my legs before ripping them off completely and throwing them to the side.

I glanced down at my ruined pants and raised a brow, to which he replied, "I prefer them this way."

Before I could respond, his mouth was on mine once more, hoisting me up in his arms again as I wrapped my thighs around his waist, pulling myself closer...tighter...deeper into him.

Jace buried his face in the nape of my neck, kissing and nibbling on every inch of my skin he could find.

He tore the fabric of my shirt with ease, exposing my bare breasts. With my entire naked body on display for him, I knew there wasn't anything I wouldn't do for him. The thought alone sent a pulse of rushing heat between my thighs until I felt myself growing wetter beneath his ravenous stare. A moment later, his mouth was on my nipples, securing one between his teeth—licking, sucking, and biting in the most torturous movements.

The feeling of his hands traveled down my body and a growl left him as his fingertips reached my soaking wet center.

His touch sent a jolt of pleasure through me. Holding me up against the tree, he brought his fingers to my mouth, and I sucked on them, closing my eyes while I let out a moan at the taste of me on him.

"Jace, please. I *need* you." My words were barely audible. He gripped his cock and lined himself up with my throbbing center, and his restraint finally snapped as he slowly inserted himself and started spreading me open.

His muscular arms caught me effortlessly as my body bucked against his. Jace held me in place as his hands gripped my ass while he moved me up and down his cock, his movements never faltering.

My mate's growls of pleasure and ragged breaths filled the forest air, and as his pace sped up, our bodies were reaching their climax together.

Nothing would ever feel as good as him—*nothing*. I felt as if my body would erupt from the intensity of it all.

He tugged me to him, pulling my back away from where it rested on the tree as our mouths collided. I caught his lower lip with my canines, biting down until I earned a moan from him.

Gently lowering our entwined bodies to the forest floor, he laid my back against the terrain. I wrapped my legs around his middle, pushing him deeper into me as I begged for more. His lips kissed my neck as he continued to thrust in and out of me while I grabbed his hair, running my fingers through it.

Our tether was on fire—burning in the intense blaze of our love and absolute need for one another. A surge of energy coursed through our linked souls, igniting a flickering flame that blazed within me, its heat so intense it felt as if I was being engulfed in a scorching inferno.

I peered down and was met with a gold-flecked hazel gaze and heaved my hips upwards as his cock remained inside me. Pushing my thighs over his body, I rolled us over and climbed on top of him to take charge. I sat up on his length and rolled my hips, earning a needy groan from him, which had me instantly going faster and deeper, circling my hips so I could feel every inch of him.

"Lia." My name was a wicked curse on his tongue.

My fingers threaded through his tousled hair as I continued to ride his cock. He lifted his hand to my face and pressed his thumb into the swell of my bottom lip. "Such a good girl," he cooed. "So fucking perfect."

And with that, we both came undone—the linked blaze between us erupted as we surrendered ourselves completely to one another.

With the rush of pleasure sizzling out in our veins, the sounds of rustling leaves transformed the forest floor into a tranquil sanctuary. Breaths heaving, I collapsed against his chest. Our limbs intertwined, we nuzzled into each other, watching the stars gleam through the trees' canopy before sleep claimed us both.

TWENTY-FOUR

Kellan

IT HAD TAKEN ONLY a few days to arrive back in Isla once we left the cove of Tortunele. The Vayr Sea had been kind to us—a small blessing for our weakened, battered crew.

As I stared out at the sea's waves, I berated myself for not having a set plan on how to behave once I faced the queen. If what Callius spoke of was true, and they were indeed mates, then Idina, by now, was well aware that his soul had moved beyond to the vale. But what of her son? Delivering the news of this would have to be handled carefully, and that was something I simply never fucking had the patience for.

As we floated into the Islan harbor, I noticed it was nearly empty. Not a single vessel in sight. Where the fuck were all my ships?!

Once our ship docked, I stormed down the gangplank, and my irritation flared when I noticed the dock's guards were rushing towards me, hands on the pommels of their swords.

"Gentlemen," I greeted.

"Where have you been, Adler?" one of the males barked.

A growl rumbled through me. "Excuse me? Who the fuck are you to question me, Braynon?" I demanded.

"Callius left me in charge of guarding the queen in his absence, which you are well aware of," he spat.

My jaw locked, and my hand moved to my sword as I took a few steps closer to him. We stood chest to chest—the sound of our heavy breathing filled the air as the rest of my crew caught up to me. Maintaining their position behind him, his own entourage of guards edged closer to us.

"It appears you aren't doing such a great job guarding the queen currently, Braynon. What brings you to my docks?"

"Things have changed around here, Adler," the other male spoke.

A growl left me. "Is that so?"

"Yes," Braynon interrupted. "I have orders from the queen to bring you in at once if you are to return with her son." His eyes flared as they moved behind me, appearing to realize that the prince was not in our company.

His stare made its way back to me. "Where is the prince?"

"There is much I need to discuss with the *queen*, Braynon. Not some lazily recruited guard left in charge of the female for mere weeks."

"Arrest him," Braynon shot over his shoulder, and the queen's guards rushed the dock.

I drew my sword, along with those who remained behind me. "What the fuck is the meaning of this?! I am your captain!" I shouted.

Braynon reached into the pocket of his cloak and presented me with a piece of rolled-up parchment. I reached out and ripped the page from his grasp, waving it in the wind to open the roll.

My eyes traced over the words, and I barked a laugh that echoed through the sea air. I cleared my throat and read the note aloud. "'By direct order of the queen, if Captain Adler shall return with my son, Prince Kai, they are to be escorted to Castle Isla. If Adler shall return alone, he is to be...'" My words trailed off.

"He is to be arrested on sight and immediately brought to the queen directly for questioning," Braynon finished for me.

"You're fucking joking," I hissed, as other guards, males that should be under *my* gods-damn command, maneuvered around me and placed my wrists in cuffs faster than I could blink.

"Hardly," he responded as they shoved me down the dock while a carriage arrived at the foot of it.

"And what of the crew?!" I bellowed as my eyes locked with William's. I sent him a look that said, *keep your fucking mouth shut*, and he gave a barely noticeable nod in return.

"They are to remain free males until the queen is fully informed of what occurred on this journey. She is... Rage doesn't even begin to uncover what she has felt and placed upon her citizens."

Fuck. Fuck. Fuck.

I struggled against the chains and lashed out with every step they forced me to take, but they surrounded me, shoving me toward the city's streets.

I stood before the dais of the throne room in Castle Isla as I awaited the arrival of Queen Idina.

How the fuck was I going to get out of this? Why would she assume there was a possibility that Kai wouldn't be with me? She even sent out direct orders for my arrest, if that were the case. Something was off. I knew she would sense something had happened with Callius, but her son, too?

The click of the door sounded, echoing in the empty chamber. My gaze shot to the queen as I remained where I stood, weighed down by the heavy chains that chimed together with every minuscule move I made.

Her eyes were bloodshot, the red hue matching her hair that cascaded down to her waist. Her jaw appeared to be clenched, the hollows of her cheekbones more than apparent as the sunlight peered in through the high, stained-glass windows.

It was so odd to see her walking up the dais alone, without the constant crutch of Callius escorting her. The more I thought about it all, all the signs that had been right under our noses from the moment I was taken under his wing, the more I had to fight back a laugh.

They almost fucking got away with it too, but now this cunt of a queen would be forced to rule without her mate and their son at her side—at least until I could come up with a new plan.

She sat upon the late king's throne, eyes boring into me as a scowl stretched across her face. My stare leisurely wandered to either side of her, noticing that her throne from when King Jameson reigned had disappeared, and all that remained was his.

"Kellan Adler," she began, completely forgoing my title of captain. "You come back to Isla alone, without your army you left with, without Callius, and without my son." Rage surged through every syllable that escaped her lips.

"My queen, perhaps if you would have allowed me to explain what had happened during our quest instead of demanding I be cuffed and dragged to be sentenced before your throne, you would already be well aware of what happened to your son and guard."

"Watch your tongue, Adler," she hissed as she pointed a dainty finger in my direction. "Perhaps you have somehow already forgotten the position you have found yourself in. You are chained and cuffed before the queen of the realm, facing charges. You will do well to behave yourself if you wish to see another day."

I bit down on my tongue to avoid the snarl that was working its way up my throat.

"I can sense it, you know," she said as she snapped her fingers, summoning a handmaiden to deliver a glass of wine. She swirled the ruby drink in her glass as her eyes remained fixated on me.

"Sense?" I questioned.

"Your rage—you wear it like a cloak. It is constantly with you, a reaper leaching off your back. Feeding upon you and every motif you've ever had. It's what drives you, thrills you. In fact..." She paused as she sipped from the glass. A bead of the wine trailed down her perfectly painted lips, and she swiped it away with her tongue as her eyes remained on me.

"I'm willing to bet you wouldn't know who you are or what to do without it."

My eyes darted back and forth between hers. "And what makes you sense this?"

She huffed out a vicious laugh that would've had any other male cowering before her. Something had changed in her, and fortunately, I knew exactly what it was. Perhaps I could make that work to my advantage.

"I recognize this in you, for it is a mirror of myself." She took another sip. "What happened to my son, Adler? Why have you arrived with such little numbers and not a single prisoner in tow?"

Interesting that she would ask about her son before her mate, but she didn't know the extent of the knowledge I held.

"We were ambushed."

"*HOW?!*" she screeched as she lunged forward in her throne, the word violently bouncing off the walls, jostling the wine in her glass.

My eyes flared. "Elianna..."

Before I could get another word out, she cut me off once more. "Your job was to bring my children back to me and be rid of her! I did not give a single fuck about those pathetic fae that felt they might find a better-suited life outside of Isla. They were *not* the priority." Her brows knitted together as she pinched them between her thumb and forefinger. "Does she still breathe?"

I swallowed. "She does."

The queen's stare snapped back to me. "And my son does not?"

Silence blanketed the room, but it was deafening.

"Many do not. Your son being one of them."

She let out a shuddering breath and sipped her wine. "How."

A demand.

I chose to omit the scene of our initial attack on the mortals and cut to the moment of the answer she sought.

"Somehow, Elianna received word of our arrival once beyond the Sylis Forest. She arrived on the back of your wyvern that she initially escaped on, and many were lost in the blaze, including the prince," I lied. "There was nothing that could be done."

"And Callius was among them?" she asked, but her amber eyes shone with a fiery intensity.

She was silently testing me. While I lacked a mate, I knew of their legends. Everything was felt between the two bonded souls—even physical pain. She was trying to bait me into a lie, but she didn't know that I knew better.

The look on Callius' face, as I plunged my sword through his gut, flashed across my memory, and I knew that if the queen were to believe me, I had only one chance to get this right.

"He was not, my queen." Her eyes softened the tiniest amount. "You see, the wyvern burned through its flame, as it had many times before, beneath this very castle. When that happened, both Elianna and her few companions stepped foot on the soil of our camp."

Her breath hitched, and what could only be described as pure, hate-infused dread etched itself into her features.

"Queen Idina," I started. "No, Callius was not lost in the blaze as your son had been. Elianna gutted him where he stood and fled on the back of her wyvern once she realized they were still outnumbered."

I waited for her to speak, but no words found her, so I continued the lies. "I was across the camp when I watched her and a few others ride the wyvern into the smoke-hazed sky they had created. I was forced to listen to my soldiers' agony-filled screams as their flesh melted from their bones. By the time I had reached Callius, his breaths had turned staggered, and his wound beyond repair without the assistance of a healer." Both her eyes and nostrils flared. "But he did ask something of me."

Her head tilted to the side in confusion. "And what was that, Adler?"

I dramatically looked to each of my sides, to the guards that stood at attention next to me, and then met her stare once more.

"I don't believe it's something that you would want others to hear."

Braynon's eyes whipped to me, nearly burning a hole in the side of my face.

"Everybody out," she demanded, barely above a whisper. When no one moved, she screeched, "Get *out!*"

As if they were startled rats in the castle's dungeons, the guards and handmaidens posted throughout the room scattered, fleeing the chamber instantly.

Once the doors to the throne room were completely closed, the two of us were sealed off from the rest of the realm. Taking a single step toward the dais, my chains rattled against the floor, the cool touch of them biting into my skin.

"You have the floor, Kellan Adler." She gestured to the empty room. "And my undivided attention. Now tell me before I lose what very little patience I have left—what did my guard have to say to you that no others could be privy to?"

"My queen, it's not what your personal guard demanded of me...but what your *mate* requested of me."

The veins bulged from her neck as her eyes widened in horror. Her grip on the wine she held in her hand shattered the glass, raining tiny shards down atop her gown and floor.

It took every ounce of self-control I had mastered throughout my life to hide the smirk that was aching to spread across my face.

"What did you just say?" she asked in a hushed, desperate tone.

"Your—"

"No." She held up a hand to halt my answer. "Do not repeat yourself. What I should have asked was *why*. Why would Callius tell you what I am to him?" she snapped, but then her eyes softened slightly. "What I *was* to him," she corrected herself, her voice barely audible.

"Callius feared for you, Queen Idina. For he knew you would rule with an iron fist, but with who to protect you at your side? He told me everything between his dying breaths." Her lips curled back. "Your mate begged me to protect you when his soul entered the vale. To guard you and see that you remained upon the throne that you *both* worked tirelessly to attain."

Her lip trembled for a fraction of a second, and if I had blinked, I would have missed it.

I took another step toward her. "Callius watched his son die." Her eyes flared once more. "He knew he was entering the vale in the same moment as his son, leaving his mate and queen alone in the realm. Your Majesty, Callius wished for me to watch over you in his place. I swore to him that I would guard and protect you from any threat that presents itself to you or your claim to remain on this throne."

Her dagger-like gaze remained fixated on me as she stood from her seat, her heels stepping on the glass she had destroyed, shattering the pieces further.

"Braynon!" she boomed, and the main entrance doors to the throne room burst open.

He rushed in. "Yes, my queen?"

Her eyes roamed over me as if looking for the lies that effortlessly rolled off my tongue. "Remove the shackles from Captain Adler's wrists."

"But, Your Maj—"

"Now," she demanded, the word clattering through the chamber.

He huffed out a breath and shot me a look of pure hatred, but all I could do was grin. It was too gods-damn easy.

The key turned in my cuffs, and they clanked down to the marble floor beneath my boots.

Queen Idina lifted the front of her maroon gown and gracefully took the steps down the dais, unaccompanied.

"Braynon, you are relieved of your duties as head guard now that the captain has returned. Your last assignment is to inform him of the structural changes set in place for the citizens. After that, you are dismissed to return to your previous assignments."

Our gazes lingered on her as she exited the room.

"You're a real fucking prick; you know that, Adler?" he growled at my side.

I rubbed my wrist in my opposite hand as a sharp smirk inched its way up my face. "Braynon, it has always been a pleasure dealing with you, as well. Now tell me...what does the future hold for Velyra under the reign of our queen?"

TWENTY-FIVE

Elianna

My eyes fluttered open as the song of birds filtered through the crisp morning air. The air that escaped my lips with each breath was accompanied by a slight fog from the chilled wind. I lifted my head from Jace's chest and snorted, realizing we had fallen asleep in the middle of the small woodland area set back from his family's estate.

I poked his chest. "Oh, Commander," I half sang to him. "It's time to wake up, handsome."

He answered with a groan, his hands lifting to rub his eyes as sleep lazily left him. "What happened?"

"I was chased through the woods and seduced against a tree by a primal predator and then fell asleep atop his chest beneath the moonlight. And well...here we are," I joked.

His eyes shot open, and he was staring right at me. He chuckled as he scratched his beard. "Oh, shit."

"My thoughts exactly."

He rose to his feet and offered his hand to lift me up. I stood beneath his towering stature, clutching the front of my torn shirt to me as my gaze wandered to where my ripped pants remained.

I huffed out a breath that was a half laugh. "Shall we go face the music?"

"If by music you mean an annoying amount of teasing and mockery, then, of course. We have a lot to plan for when we leave for The Elora Isles."

After everything that happened yesterday, I had somehow forgotten what Veli had unveiled and how our arrival in Anerys would be short-lived. After we had only just arrived, we now had to embark on a quest across the sea.

I picked up what remained of my pants and tugged them on. Jace laughed as he wrapped his cloak around me, and we set off towards the house.

We strolled through the back entrance of the estate to find Lynelle in the kitchen, cooking endless piles of bacon, eggs, and fresh bread.

"Thank the gods, I'm starving," I announced.

"Is that Lia I hear?!" Avery called from the other room, and I chuckled as I moved to stalk in the direction of her voice.

"Now, now, breakfast is almost ready," Lynelle said as she turned to us. She stopped in her tracks as her eyes wandered over the two of us and the state we were in. "Mother of the gods, was the house locked?! You appear as if you slept in the grass last night."

My cheeks burned with heat as I halted in the room's archway.

Gage appeared in front of me then, wrapping his arm around my shoulder as he shot Jace a knowing look. "Good morning, lovebirds," he cooed. "I know you absolutely behaved yourselves in your mother's old house. Right, brother?"

"Behaving was not achieved, and we also were *not* in his mother's house," I admitted as I grabbed his hand that rested on my shoulder and twirled beneath it. His booming laugh sounded through the kitchen as Lynelle waved us all away.

We found the rest of our rebel court in the living area as they waited for breakfast.

"Good morning everyone!" I chirped.

Avery suppressed a laugh. "Lia, you have leaves in your hair."

"Ah, yes, it's all the new fashion," I said as I sat beside her on the settee, moving to rub my dirt and leaf-crusted hair onto her. She tried to shoo me away, but I wrapped my arms around her in a hug that she eventually reciprocated.

Lynelle appeared in the room then with piles of plates in her hands that the boys jumped up to assist her with, placing them all atop the tea table. We moved to help ourselves to the early morning feast.

As we were finishing up in near silence, the front door opened, and Leon appeared in the foyer a moment later.

He gave Jace a curt nod. "That was quite the speech last night, Commander. I'm equally shocked as I am proud. I only wish your mother could see you now."

Instant sorrow threatened to suffocate me, and my eyes flared in response as they shot to the general. "She is," I said to him, and his gaze moved to me as he tilted his head in confusion. "She's proud of him from where she watches in the vale."

Leon gave me a tight-lipped smile, and something that resembled pride beamed in his eyes. "Of course she is. I apologize, Miss Lia."

I returned his smile and moved my attention back to my plate.

Jace cleared his throat. "We need a ship. Is there one ready to sail in our most eastern harbor?"

"Indeed, there is. I can summon a crew, of course. Where are you setting sail off to so soon?" he asked as he helped himself to a cup of tea.

"The Elora Isles," my mate answered, causing the general to choke on his first sip.

"I'm sorry?" he asked through a few subtle coughs as he tried to clear his throat.

"You heard me correctly," Jace stated.

"The men won't be too keen on sailing there, even if they are just legends of myth."

"They are not legends, nor are they myths," Veli spoke from where she sat upon the windowsill. She hopped off and took a few steps toward him. "Your sailors will not set foot on the land. So long as they listen to my demands, they will remain unharmed." She paused for a moment. "Hopefully."

Leon looked at her through furrowed brows.

"The men will just assist us in sailing the ship the far distance. They will remain aboard the ship, and we will take a pinnace to get to the land itself," Jace offered.

Leon nodded. "I will set this up immediately and send a falcon. How many of you are attending the journey? And may I ask...why you're going there?"

"Trust me, you don't want to know the details, but we're hoping to find potential allies. It will just be myself, Lia, our co-seconds, and the sorceress," Jace answered, and Avery shot up from her seat.

Anger crawled across her features. "Oh, I don't think so! This was *my* idea. I'm coming." She crossed her arms.

"Avery, it may not be safe," I whispered.

"As if I give a damn," she spat. "You're not the only one who traveled across the realm, Lia. I'm coming with you whether you want me to or not."

I couldn't help but grin. "Well, it's settled then."

"You can't be serious..." Zaela huffed.

"Let her come, Zae. She'll be fine," Gage chimed in as he smiled at my sister.

"What of us?" Finn asked as he sat on the opposite settee with Landon, who still had a mouth full of food as he observed us all.

"The fewer males, the better," Veli growled.

"I can put them to use around here," Leon answered. "We could always use an extra set of hands, whether that be with training or building."

"Excellent. Is that okay with you both?" I asked, eyes pleading for them to cooperate.

They nodded in unison, and then Landon added, "Now that I'm healed, I would like to train with the soldiers, anyway."

I answered him with a soft, approving smile.

"Anything else I should be aware of?" the general asked.

"Ah, yes. Nox will be coming with us."

"Is it really necessary to bring Nox? We will be on a ship." Zaela sighed.

"Ah, yes. Speaking of which, we will need the biggest ship you have." I offered an apologetic smile to the general. "His wings may need to rest at times."

His face paled. "Well, I will cross the wyvern and its possible feeding issue off my list of issues to deal with for the time being. I'll have our largest ship ready by the end of the day."

"Thank you, Leon."

He showed himself out of the room and into the kitchen, where Lynelle had retreated to earlier.

Jace raised a brow at me. "Really?" His tone was teasing.

"I would rather be prepared for anything, and you can't expect him to fly for weeks straight!"

He shook his head but failed at hiding his amused smile.

"We must be careful," Veli called. "When we arrive at the isles, it would be wise not to have my sisters see that there is a wyvern among us. Only the gods know what would go through their minds if they laid eyes on him."

I audibly swallowed.

"Just remember..." she continued. "You asked for this."

TWENTY-SIX

Elianna

THE FOLLOWING DAY, WE stood before the readied ship in Alaia's most eastern cove. Nox flew high above us in the cloudless sky, circling the bustling docks below him as we all prepared to board for the journey ahead.

Jace parted from us, his footsteps echoing down the dock as he stalked forward with Leon and Gage. They greeted the crew members who had bravely volunteered to accompany us, reminding them where we were going and what was to come.

"You girls better keep your wits about you," Lynelle said as she watched us all intently, acting fearful as if she was a mother to all of us.

My heart skipped a beat as the words left her, reminding me so much of what Lukas used to say to me anytime he sensed I was about to run straight into chaos.

"We'll be fine, Mom." Zaela placed her elbow on Lynelle's shoulder, earning a scoff from her.

She threw up her hands in surrender. "Well, forgive me for being wary when you just returned to me, dearest daughter."

I huffed out a laugh at their interaction—it was so foreign to me. While I never had a mother of my own growing up, it wasn't as if the queen was like this with her own children. Well, aside from Kai. It was such a stark contrast to what I was used to witnessing.

"I'm surprised we were able to get an entire crew to volunteer to sail with us," I said as the wind blew off the sea.

"The true question would be, is bravery or stupidity what drives these men?" Veli said flatly from where she stood to my left.

"A bit of both," Zaela answered with a grin.

"I don't know how you walk in these so easily," Avery huffed out as she approached us from behind. Leon had sent her into one of the shops near the docks to retrieve new clothing for the trip since she didn't have much else aside from dresses and tunics.

"Pants?" Zae said with an arched brow.

"The leathers are gods-awful! And...stiff."

I chuckled as I watched her waddle up to us, getting used to the feel of her new fighting leathers. "You get used to it."

"Why do I not believe you?" Avery rolled her eyes.

"Those men are not taking these threats seriously," Veli grumbled, bringing our attention back to the crew, who were now dispersing and making their way up the gangplank to board the ship.

Leon moved in our direction as I met Jace's stare, giving us a nod of approval to approach.

"Do they truly know where we're headed?" I asked him, as he halted before me.

He pressed his lips together firmly. "Not all believe in bedtime stories for children, Lia. They have been warned and are excited to sail to a land that they have never set foot."

"Stupidity, then," Veli hissed and then stalked toward the awaiting ship. Avery and Zaela moved to follow.

Leon blew out a breath as he observed her. "She seems fearful."

"She does," I answered.

"And you, Miss Lia?"

My brows furrowed as my stare remained on the sorceress. "I no longer fear any fae, man, or creature in my realm. I can't afford to. They will take the knee to me, or they will be dealt with. A being of magic, or no."

Nox let out an ear-shattering screech in the sky above, startling the general. "And is that why you bring the wyvern?" he asked curiously.

My gaze found his then. "I have experienced too many instances where failing to establish fallback plans has resulted in tragic outcomes for those I love." His eyes softened, causing me to pause. "You will never find me in that situation again."

The weight of those parting words settled into my heart as I took my first step toward the awaiting ship.

Sitting on the lip of the railing at the ship's bow, I took in the sea's scent as it stung my nostrils with endless salt and tang. Footsteps sounded from behind me, but I didn't need to turn to know who it was.

"I believe the last time I was on a ship with you, I declared that I never wanted to be in such a situation again," Jace teased as he placed his hand atop mine, where it rested on the railing.

I grinned as I faced him. "You had a great time."

He barked out a loud laugh, earning one from me in return. "If you see a darkened sky ahead, be sure to warn me this time."

"No promises." I winked.

We both turned to face the deck, where the crew was hard at work. "They've been keeping to themselves," I observed.

"Yes, well, they are very curious as to where we are truly headed. No mortal has ever set foot upon the sand that awaits in The Elora Isles."

"They *do* know they're staying on the ship, right?" I raised a brow.

He turned to me. "We've told them many times, but I believe they're just excited to leave Alaia and not be en route to battle."

I sighed. "That won't be the case for long."

"They know, my Lia."

I gave him a soft smile as I leapt down from the railing. We stalked across the ship's deck, passing every crew member who was hard at work. When Jace was called away by a deckhand, I continued my waltz forward.

My steps halted as I came across Veli, who stood perfectly motionless at the stern. Her gaze fixed on the sea as if she could still view the land we left behind hours prior.

I warily approached her. "Veli?" I whispered.

"The men that sail this ship have been given specific instructions on where to sail. They are to follow the—"

"Northernmost star," I finished for her. "We know...is everything alright?"

"This is a mistake, Elianna."

"Not if we win the war."

She scoffed. "At what cost? They will not side with you easily just because you carry the blood of the Valderre line."

A loud, whooshing sound echoed through the sea air as the sun began to set on the horizon. Our chins lifted to the sky as Nox continued to circle above.

"I am willing to bargain," I answered as my gaze followed the wyvern.

Her violet stare snapped to me. "A fool's bargain."

"You don't even know what I would plan to barter."

"Anything is too great. Do not be reckless enough to believe that the Elora Coven would abide by your rules just because you plan to wear the realm's crown atop your head. They are notorious for their defiance."

"And that is why you ran?"

Her eyes narrowed in on me as her talon-like nails dug into the wood of the ship's rail. "You know *nothing*."

"Because you won't speak of it," I challenged sternly, the words funneling through my teeth as I tried to hold back my anger.

She turned from me—her gaze now fixated back on the waves. "You will know soon enough."

Before I moved to shove the witch overboard, I decided that turning back around and finding Jace would be the wiser choice.

TWENTY-SEVEN

Avery

In a matter of weeks, I had fled the only home I had ever known, traveled across the continent on foot, survived poisonous berries, reunited with my sister, and now stood on the deck of a ship for the very first time, taking in the foreign sights and sounds of the sea.

I moved across the deck as gracefully as I could in these gods-forsaken *pants*. Why did Lia love these things so much?

My memory flashed back to one of our many sleepovers in my bedchamber back in Isla. *They make my ass look great*, she had said, and I giggled at the memory.

I pivoted my torso around to get a look at my own and shrugged. "Ugh, mine definitely doesn't look like hers," I whispered to myself.

"It looks great to me," a familiar voice called from behind me.

Heat rushed to my cheeks when I noticed Gage leisurely making his way toward me from the opposite side of the deck.

"Gage!" I gasped.

I took in the sight of him, his deep tawny skin and warm brown eyes. He was so handsome, with a ruggedness that the Lords of Velyra would never bear.

"My lady, Avery," he greeted as he gently took my hand and pressed his lips to the back of it. "Apologies for not having the time to find you until now. How has your time aboard been?"

My eyes flared without permission. How could someone so carefree and joking around his friends be this charming?

"It's been lovely," I rasped out. "It's my first time aboard a ship."

Now, his eyes widened in response. "You've never sailed the seas? Surely a princess has seen all the lavish sights the realm has to offer."

Embarrassment washed over me, and I cleared my throat after a few moments. "I was lucky to get a glimpse of what lay past the castle gates."

Something that resembled sorrow flashed across his eyes, perhaps even pity. "Well, Avery..." The way he said my name threatened to force a shiver down my spine. "I would love to show you all the realm has to offer—that is, of course, if a measly second-in-command is suitable enough to accompany a princess."

My gaze remained on his, our eyes boring into each other in the most intense yet familiar way I had ever felt. "You are more suitable than anyone I have ever met," I answered, and his response was a beaming smile that made my heart sing.

Gage extended his arm to me. "Walk with me?" he asked, and I immediately laced my arm through his.

Darkness crept in on us as the sun set. The crew made themselves scarce across the ship, and we appeared to be the only ones near—just the two of us under the endless, twinkling stars.

He led the way as we waltzed around, arm in arm. "Tell me about yourself, Avery."

"What do you wish to know?"

"I already told you," he said as his steps halted briefly. "Everything."

My heart raced in my chest. "I wouldn't even know where to begin," I whispered. "I'm willing to bet all the coin in Isla that your life is far more interesting than my own. I was cooped up within the confines of Castle Isla's battlement, and there I remained until some weeks ago. Rarely allowed to leave and never allowed to explore."

"You're Lia's sister. I'm sure you found ways to explore," he snarked.

I chuckled. "That we did. Trouble often found us, but never in a way where she couldn't find a way out of it for us."

"That sounds like Lia."

I blinked and looked at him. "You seem to know her so well, even as well as I do, yet you have known her for mere months—a second in time in comparison to me."

"Lia is Lia." He let out a laugh. "She's been herself since the moment I met her, which she came in swinging, by the way. I'm sure you're shocked."

I smirked. "That certainly sounds like her."

"Well, Zae was swinging too. Perhaps even more violently."

Any sense of amusement fell from my face at the mention of Zaela.

"Oh, speak of the woman," he said cheerfully, and my anger surged to the very surface as Zaela appeared at the top of the stairs that led down to the crew's quarters.

Lia funneled out after her, followed by Jace.

"We're letting the crew rest for a few hours while we take watch," Jace called over to us.

Lia held up a bottle from her side containing a dark liquid that swished around beneath the torchlight. "I have rum!" she yelled cheerfully.

"Oh, hell yeah," Gage said under his breath as he reached for my hand and tugged me across the deck.

After almost losing my footing many times from being dragged by him, we finally came to a halt in the center of the ship, where everyone was rolling barrels to create makeshift seats to sit upon. Gage and I opted for the floor of the deck.

Veli wandered out from the shadows of the mast and ambled over to be among us, keeping abnormally quiet—even for her.

Lia took a swig from the bottle as she invited herself to sit on Jace's lap from where he sat on a barrel, making me wish I felt comfortable enough to do the same with the handsome man next to me.

Zaela lit a few more torches on the outskirts of the ship, lighting the space up intimately beneath the stars. Her lips curved when she noticed the witch had joined us.

She even liked *Veli*. Yet, she loathed me. Lia and Gage were free to believe whatever they wanted, but I was certain that this was more than just being overprotective.

Jace sipped the amber liquid and made a face as he stared at Lia. "I don't know how you drink this so easily."

"It's not my fault you're a chickenshit," she answered, unphased.

"Oh, so we're back to that. Here I thought we left that at the waterfall."

"Waterfall?" I questioned.

"Ah, so the princess knew you were mates, but doesn't know your story," Zaela sassed as she ripped the bottle from her cousin's hand and took a gulp herself.

My gaze snapped to Lia, who looked the tiniest bit nervous. "When did I have time to tell you anything, Avery? I yelled to you 'I have a mate' while fighting off attackers at Kai's wedding, for gods' sake." She laughed under her breath, and my own mimicked hers as the memory surfaced.

"So much has happened, yet we have barely had time to process much of it," I whispered as the bottle made its way to me. I sipped it carefully and nearly gagged the second the rum touched my lips.

Gage let out a deep laugh and took the bottle from my hands, wrapping his arm around my shoulders as he sipped from it. I leaned into the warmth of his touch, sending butterflies fluttering through me.

"What's the matter, Princess? Never had real liquor before?" Zaela harassed me from the opposite side of our small circle.

My eyes glanced over to Lia and she gave the tiniest nod in my direction.

I ripped the bottle out of Gage's grip and took a long swig of it, sending the burning liquid down my throat. The second it hit my stomach, I felt a blaze of warmth followed by an unusual giddiness.

"Avery," Gage said with a laugh. "Be careful."

"She's fine," Lia said with a smirk, and I matched hers as we made eye contact.

"Yes, well, we'll see if she's fine in about thirty minutes or so," Zaela pestered. "Tell me, Princess Avery, how are you feeling after such a heaping gulp?"

My breathing deepened as I stared at her. Challenge radiated from both of us. Was this my initiation? Lia had made it known that she and Zaela didn't see eye-to-eye at first. Did she want me to give her shit right back to her?

My eyes lazily moved to Gage as his arm remained around me. "I'm feeling as if I wouldn't mind getting to know Gage better." His eyes flared as they met mine. My focus slowly pivoted back to Zaela, who had fury radiating in her stare. "*Much* better."

"Oh gods," Lia breathed as she rubbed at her temples.

Zaela leapt up, and for a moment, I thought she was going to storm across the small distance between us and move to strike me. Gage's body tensed.

She aggressively pointed at me from where I remained sitting on the floor. "Enough! Enough with your claim you think you will have on him! I'm sure that as a princess, you're used to getting whatever and whoever you want, but that stops here and now!"

"You know nothing about me!" I screamed at her as I climbed to my feet. We stood nearly nose to nose, and out of my peripheral vision, Lia shoved out of Jace's lap and moved to circle us as if waiting to step in if needed.

"Zaela, what is your problem?!" Gage barked at her as he stood at my side, a bit of bite in his tone.

"Oh, I know what it is," I hissed with a snarl. Zaela's eyes narrowed in on me. "She's in love with you, and she hates that you've been sweet to me!"

Her teeth clenched, and my eyes moved to Lia for a split second as her hands flew to cover her mouth in disbelief—her eyes frantically moving back and forth between Zaela and me.

Zaela let out a vicious, bone-chilling cackle into the sky as her head flew back. She stormed up to her cousin and ripped the bottle of rum from his grasp.

"Zae," Jace growled.

She held a finger up at him with one hand as she finished the bottle of rum with the other, silencing him.

She threw the bottle overboard—the sound of its splash echoed through the breezy air. She then wiped her lips with her sleeve as she stalked toward me. Gage moved to put a foot in front of me, but I pushed around him. Despite lacking the training that Lia had, I was determined to stand my ground.

Veli silently crept forward as the scene continued to unfold, coming into further view beneath the torchlight. Zaela's gaze landed on her briefly, then quickly shifted elsewhere.

"You think I'm in love with Gage?! He's like family to me, practically my brother!" she shrieked. "I don't want you near him because I refuse to watch him fall in love with someone who will chew him up and shit him out when they're done with him. He is *not* a shiny new trinket for a princess to play with when she's bored!"

"Zaela!" Lia and Jace shouted in tandem.

"This only proves that you know nothing of me because I would never!" I bellowed, my voice carrying across the sea's waves.

"Ladies, ladies…please don't fight over little ole me," Gage joked, placing his hand on his heart.

Jace accidentally laughed with him as he gestured to him with his hand. "Gage, shut the fuck up for a second, please."

"You don't believe me?!" Zaela whispered wildly. She spun slowly, her gaze lingering on each of us as she completed her full turn. "None of you believe that what I speak is true. You all believe me to be jealous of the princess."

Her gaze snapped to me as her jaw locked, and I crossed my arms in response, a rare snarl working its way across my lips.

She turned to Lia then, who had been abnormally quiet considering the circumstances. Zaela cackled as she threw her head back and looked at the sky. "I know at least one of you believes me."

"Lia, what does she mean?" Jace asked.

"It's not my place to say," she answered, and he shot her a look.

"Zae, I think you have had enough to drink," Gage offered. "Why don't we move on to something different? Nobody believes you to be jealous. I was only joking with you."

Her eyes shifted back to Veli, and all of our gazes moved with hers to the witch. "I haven't had nearly enough to drink for what I'm about to do."

Before anyone had time to process her words, her feet moved to swiftly carry her across the deck to where Veli was standing. Her strides were strong and unyielding, as if she couldn't get to the witch fast enough, yet Veli appeared to be unphased as the mortal woman stalked toward her.

Zaela's steps came to a sudden halt directly before her, and she towered over Veli's small stature as they stood barely an inch from each other. The witch's knowing violet stare bore into her.

All of us inched closer, the air thick with confused tension. My face whipped in my sister's direction, but her flared eyes were fixated on the scene.

My attention moved back to them as well, just as Zaela's jaw popped open, searching for words she couldn't seem to find.

Veli's lip tilted into a menacing grin. "I do not have all night, Zaela Cadoria."

What in the realm?!

Zaela's hands trembled as she reached up to touch the witch's face, and then pressed her lips against Veli's as she gently cupped her cheeks.

"Holy gods," Gage breathed. "Hell yeah, Zae!"

"Well, that's one way to tell everyone," Lia said softly, not seeming surprised in the slightest.

"Oh, this just got interesting," Jace joined the chatter.

My heart raced as my eyes remained fixated on the two of them. "Oh gods," I whispered.

Their kiss broke, and Zaela was frozen in Veli's violet stare.

"I–I'm so sorry," she whispered as she took a step back, looking mortified.

"Do you truly believe I would have allowed you to storm up to me without repercussions if I did not desire what just occurred?" the sorceress hissed, but there was an unusual softness in her gaze—an understanding.

"You're not upset?" Zaela asked her, forgetting that the rest of us remained behind them.

Veli lifted a talon-tipped finger to her lips and swiped away the lingering touch of their kiss. "I enjoy the company of both males and females."

"Oh, thank the gods," Lia breathed, earning everyone's attention. "What?! That whole scenario could have ended in a much worse manner."

Her mate looked at her. "You knew?"

She gave him a gentle smile. "Not long. It was her story to tell."

Jace looked at Zaela then. "I'm proud of you, cousin. I'm sorry you felt the need to hide this from us."

"It wasn't that I wanted to hide it. Just wanted to figure it out for myself before involving you two meddling idiots. I could already envision you playing matchmaker," she teased, crossing her arms. "It wasn't always easy being the only woman among men until Lia came along. But I knew you would always support me in this." She gave him a kind smile that I had never witnessed from her before.

I was horrified. I couldn't believe I just accidentally forced Zaela to tell everyone her secret—a secret that her own family members hadn't known, but for some reason, Lia had.

Gage's arm fell to my shoulders once more and pulled me to him, but an unbearable knot had settled into my stomach. I inched out of his touch and felt the weight of his arm leave me and fall to his sides.

"Zaela, I—"

She held up a hand to halt me. "Don't."

My hand flew to cover my mouth to hide my trembling lip.

"The information has been long overdue to tell," she said as she glanced at Lia and gave her a small, tight-lipped smile. "I only wish the circumstances were slightly more...well, fair." She shrugged. "But perhaps I never would've found it necessary to speak aloud without such a situation."

"I'm just very sorry." My voice was soft. "I thought you..."

"You thought I was in love with someone who I consider a brother." She shivered and made a sound resembling being sick. Her eyes then lifted to Gage's, and her features softened before her stare found mine again. "No, Princess. I do not, nor have I ever, loved Gage in that manner. But he deserves someone who will return the love that he gives. You will do well to remember that. Perhaps I have judged you too harshly, so I hope you will indeed prove me wrong."

Leaving those as her parting words, Zaela moved toward the stairs that led below deck without even sparing us a parting glance.

Veli's eyes wandered over all of us as we remained where we stood. The only sounds were the surrounding waves echoing in and out from where they crashed into the sides of the ship. She then moved to follow her down the steps.

"Well, then..." Jace said after a few moments of uncomfortable silence.

"She'll be fine. Just give her a few hours to be alone," Lia stated.

"When did she even tell you this? How? Why?" her mate pestered.

She laughed at him and wrapped her arms around his torso, pulling him close. "Remember boys' night?" His eyes narrowed in on her as he looked down at her through furrowed brows. She shrugged. "It was her attempt to make amends for what happened between us at the village. She handed me her lifelong secret."

Jace chuckled. "Well, I suppose it makes a lot more sense now on why we had never seen her with a man."

"Zaela must hate me," I breathed as my eyes darted back and forth.

"Zae hates everyone at first," Gage announced as he laced his fingers through mine.

My gaze wandered down to our intertwined hands—the rugged, calloused feel to them was at such odds with my own. A male had never held my hand before, aside from Finnian when we were younglings. His touch, unexpected and tender, carried a warmth I never thought I would feel from a man.

Kai had always said I was born to be sold to the highest bidder, and after hearing those words repeated for decades, eventually you believe them.

"It's through this that she determines if she will grow to like you," he finished, and my gaze leisurely made its way back up to his.

"And you didn't let her intimidate you," Lia said as she walked up to us and enthusiastically shook my arm. "I'm so proud of you for standing your ground. And, as unfortunate as it is, that is how you will earn respect from her."

I blew out a breath, not feeling even the tiniest ounce of relief from their words. They knew Zaela best, but I couldn't help but feel awful still.

A loud screech erupted from the sky as the beat of wings pulsed through the air. Nox appeared in brief glimpses, his amethyst-reflective scales the only sign of him soaring through the clouds beneath the moonlight.

Lia lifted her hand to her lips and let out a sharp whistle to summon the wyvern.

He soared down towards us and leveled himself, sending steady beats of his wings to levitate just beyond the ship's rail—each pulse from them sent a wave of wind at us, blowing my hair straight back. The force of it would have knocked me down if Gage wasn't directly behind me.

Lia approached him and reached out her hand, gently placing it on his snout. "I need you to *gently* land on the ship. Can you do that?"

"Gods, he's the size of the ship, Lia," Jace said with an annoyed chuckle. She waved him off teasingly.

The wyvern's golden gaze narrowed in on my sister, and no matter how often I had been around the beast in recent days, I couldn't remove the lingering sense of fear from our previous encounter of him sending a blaze of flame aimed to kill me.

Nox carefully descended upon the deck of the ship, causing each of us to hold our breath in anticipation. The ship rocked as his hind legs touched down, causing us all to nearly lose our footing.

"I said gently!" Lia screeched, and he curled into a ball in the center of the deck, taking up most of its space.

Lia rubbed her temples. "This damn wyvern."

"You're the one who wanted to bring him," Jace teased as he guided her to the stairs while she yawned.

"Listen, he can be useful," she joked back. "Don't kill anyone!" She shot over her shoulder at the beast, and he let out a disapproving huff.

Gage reached out and took my hand. "Now, how about we get back to learning everything?"

Heat rushed to my cheeks once more, and he led me below deck, following the footsteps of the others.

TWENTY-EIGHT

Elianna

As WE SAILED FARTHER away from the main continent of Velyra, the days at sea became a blur. Zaela's tormenting of Avery and Gage had ceased, and it appeared the two of them were getting to know each other...*quite well*. Veli and Zae could also be seen whispering to each other in the shadowy corners of the ship from time to time. The rest of us stayed busy by lending a hand to the crew as we sailed across the Vayr Sea.

I stood at the ship's bow, my eyes narrowing in on The Elora Isles set off in the far distance as the crew lowered the anchor nearly two miles from shore.

"Are you sure we need to remain this far from the land?" I asked Veli with a sigh as I blocked the sun's glare with my hand.

"We are already too close. They must not notice the ship or the wyv—"

"Wyvern, yes. Nox will stay out of sight," I cut her off.

Footsteps echoed from behind us. "We will paddle a pinnace to shore," Jace announced as he joined us and pointed to the small boat.

"Men are not welcome." Veli's voice darkened.

Jace lifted his hands in a defensive gesture, but his eyes looked unamused. "Gage and I will remain on said pinnace…" He paused. "However, if you believe I will willingly sit back here and remain useless while Lia steps foot on those shores…you are out of your mind."

Veli scoffed. "Witches are not the only creatures who roam those isles, *boy*."

I took a step between them as a growl left Jace. Looking at Veli through deeply furrowed brows, I said, "They will not set foot on the land, but they will be accompanying us as far as your shores will allow. Do you understand?"

"Aye," she answered after a few moments as her eyes drifted to the awaiting land. My stare wandered to her hip, where her hand tightly gripped her small woven bag that held her forbidden book. "If you will excuse me, the contents of this must never return from where it came."

I watched her as she stalked to the stairs, shoving past Avery as she made her way to meet us, and then down the stairs that led below deck.

"What was that about?" Avery asked as she made a face at the witch's back right before she disappeared from sight.

"She won't bring the book ashore," I told her. "We will board the pinnace once she returns. Are you ready?"

As the question left me, I realized that while *she* may be ready to experience her first dangerous task under my command, I certainly was not. My eyes brushed over my sister and I took in the sight of her. Her long auburn hair, normally curled down her back and intricately pinned, was braided over her shoulder. The beautiful, flowing gowns and slippers that made up her attire had been replaced by fighting leathers and boots. My stare lifted back to her face, and when our eyes met, I couldn't help my smile.

"Of course I'm ready..." She returned my gesture, but it beamed brighter than the sun as the sea breeze whipped the small hairs around her face that fell from her braid. "I'll go find Gage and let him know we are ready to leave."

She turned on her feet and followed Veli's footsteps below deck.

A pulsing wave of comfort shot down our bond, and I turned to my mate as he stared ahead at what awaited us. Moving to his side, I wrapped my arms around his waist and pressed my forehead to his back.

"She will be fine, my Lia," he said gently. "You worry too much."

"Avery had never experienced a normal day at the market...and within a matter of weeks, she has led a rebellion across the continent, was under attack several times, and is now about to set foot on one of the most dangerous terrains known to fae-kind. How would you expect me not to worry?"

Amusement flooded me, but I knew the feelings weren't my own. "Do you have something you'd like to say?" I mumbled as my grip on him loosened, and I stepped around his side.

He looked down at me with a single raised brow. "Interesting that you wish for me to not worry about *you* stepping on such dangerous soil, yet you worry for your sister who will be *with* you."

A tiny smirk crept up my face. "Well, that isn't fair."

"How is it not?" he asked, amusement slipping away from him.

"Because I have training, *obviously*," I answered with a grin.

He rolled his eyes in the grumpy manner that won my heart and moved toward the pinnace that rested at the side of the ship.

Veli reappeared at the top of the stairs, and Gage came around the corner from the stern of the ship. My brows furrowed as I tilted my head to the side in confusion. Suddenly, a glimpse of fiery hair snagged my attention back to the stairs.

"Avery, Gage is over here! Let's get going," I called over.

Her eyes widened for a second before giving a nod in response.

I shook my head as my stare moved back to Jace. Lifting my fingers to my lips, I let out a whistle to summon Nox.

His wings sounded thunderously through the air as he emerged from the clouds, descending toward the ship's deck, causing it to sway violently as his feet touched down.

"Everyone is to stay aboard this ship. No one leaves. It's not safe for you to step on those lands. Nox will remain here, and to be honest, it may be best to stay out of his way. He gets cranky when I'm out of his sight," I bellowed to them, and each member of the crew's faces paled. "Nox, stay here."

He huffed out a steaming breath through his nostrils at my demand.

"I mean it!" I snapped as I held up my finger.

I turned to face my friends. "Let's go recruit ourselves a coven."

TWENTY-NINE

Veli

THE MEN WORKED TO row us to shore, and with each maneuver of their paddles, a sickly pit of dread dropped further into my gut. The echoes of the splashing waves served as a constant reminder that with each stroke they made, the closer it brought us to our possible doom.

Elianna didn't take my cautions seriously, and I could claw her eyes out for disregarding my many pleadings. The forbidden princess did not understand the workings of magic, let alone that of a dark nature. Even her siblings, who had witnessed it firsthand, barely had a grasp on it, but they knew to fear what lurked within it.

I could not fault the rightful queen for her desire to seek a better life for her people. After all, that was precisely what brought me into the predicament I have now found myself in.

"Shouldn't be long now." Elianna's words snapped me out of my trance.

I blinked through the haze that covered my distant eyes. Our pinnace was now only but a half mile from the shore of the isles, giving the humans aboard a better view of what lay on the enchanted land.

226

"It looks so…" Zaela started.

"Eerie," Avery finished for her.

"If you are afraid of what your sight beholds now, you should paddle back to our awaiting ship while you still can," I warned.

"It's just a bit of fog," Elianna hissed.

I scoffed. "Just a bit of fog, she says."

"While we are well aware of your hesitance to return to your homeland, you will do well to respect Lia's wishes. And to not mock her when she speaks," her mate growled as his arms continued to row us closer to shore.

His words silenced us all.

As we floated into the fog, the air became thick with the scent of moss and earth as we entered the heart of the marsh. The water beneath us morphed from that of the clear sea to a significantly darker hue, reflecting the overhanging canopy of twisted, rotting trees and their vines.

The water became shallower, and soon, we found ourselves navigating through a labyrinth of grassy channels. While those on board remained silent, the bog was lively with the sounds of croaking frogs and the rustle of hidden creatures beneath the underbrush. Sweat beaded on everyone's foreheads as the humidity grew heavier with each passing moment.

Tall grasses stood sentinel along the water's edge; their feathery plumes that once danced on the breeze now remained still as a spear—the land sensed that we were here, and it was watching us.

Memories of my past swarmed me, and my heart raced—a feeling I certainly wasn't accustomed to, but I knew all too well what awaited us in the depths of the isle.

"We shouldn't paddle much deeper into the marsh," I warned them. "For if we need to flee, it would be best to have a quicker escape into the sea."

Elianna gave me a curt nod and turned to her comrades. "You heard her. We'll stop here."

Gage leaned over the side of the small boat, extending his arm out over the water to reach for the shore's edge. Without a second of hesitation, I leapt across the space, and my hand shot out to grip his wrist, rocking the entire boat with the force of the movement.

"Veli!" Avery shrieked, but my focus remained on the human that almost touched the soil of the land.

His brown eyes were fixed on my own, and I could sense a bit of fear lingering beneath the surface of his skin as my grasp on him slowly released.

"You *cannot* touch the terrain. You told me you understood this," I snapped as my gaze then whipped back and forth between his and the commander's.

"Apologies, Veli. I was just trying to get us closer to shore," he admitted.

My jaw locked. "Here will do. Those that are female may either reach for it or step into the marsh to get there." I turned to Elianna. "They *must not* leave this boat."

"Gage, please don't make her say it again." She laughed and then turned to her mate. "You will both need to stay here, and we'll be back as soon as possible." Jace's jaw ticked. "We will be fine."

"The more the witch speaks of what lurks here, the more I'm reconsidering the idea of not coming with you," he admitted.

She huffed out a breath and turned back to me. "Is there no way they may come?"

"Not unless you wish for them to be killed." My talons dug into the palms of my hands in frustration. She wasn't taking me seriously enough—none of them were.

"Fine," she huffed. "Let's get this over with."

With those words, Elianna leapt into the water with her pack of supplies—the splash of it startled the lurking crows that hid in the tree's canopy.

"Trust no one and nothing," I said to everyone as the rest of us followed her lead. I turned back to the men who remained on board as the other three took their first steps onto the land. "Trust nothing you see or hear. The isles already sense we have arrived. Keep your wits about you, or you may lose your life. The wooden pinnace does not guarantee your safety."

"You just make sure they stay safe," Jace demanded as he gestured to Elianna, Zaela, and Avery, who waited for me.

My gaze traveled to the tops of the trees and then leisurely roamed over the surrounding area as I whispered, "None of us are safe, Commander. Not even myself."

THIRTY

Elianna

THE DEAD GRASS CRUNCHED beneath our boots as we marched deeper into the land of The Elora Isles. The weight of Jace's stare dug into my back until we were completely out of their sight. His nerves rattled down the bond, but I knew it wasn't due to him believing we couldn't handle ourselves but more that we were in a foreign land drenched in powerful magic.

We walked between the twisted trees, stepping over their gnarled roots and beneath moss-draped branches.

An uneasiness settled into me, one much more alarming than anything I had felt in the Sylis Forest. What lurked within that enchanted forest was ancient magic, but whatever grew and lurked here felt different—more powerful and *dangerous*.

"How deep into the marshland must we go?" Avery asked Veli.

Zaela stopped short in her tracks, startling me.

"What is it?" I asked as I followed her line of sight through the hazy fog.

"I thought I just saw..." she started.

"You saw nothing if you know what's best for you," Veli warned, tone softer than usual. "And Avery, we will walk until we are greeted by the ancient stone of Elora. It is at the center of this island. That is where I will call to my sisters."

"By your blood..." she breathed.

Veli sighed. "Correct."

The four of us began moving forward once more.

"What is it that you saw?" I asked Zaela in a whisper.

"Eyes. Glowing, crimson eyes. Looking right at us," she answered with a gulp.

A shiver ran up my spine as my hand reached for the hilt of my sword at my hip.

Regardless of whether Veli had to actually summon her sisters, one thing was for certain... *Something* knew we were here.

We walked for miles, quietly following Veli's lead, and in every direction we turned, I could sense that we weren't alone. Animals called to each other from all sides as we passed, and we were each sure to listen to the witch's instructions regarding looking straight ahead and paying no mind to the unsettling sounds.

Once deep into the forest, every single one of my senses went on high alert as the wood went completely silent and still, bringing our legs to a halt. Unease settled into me, and I instinctively stepped around Avery to get in front of her and block any potential threat.

"Veli," I whispered to the back of her silver hair, as she remained looking forward into a dense line of trees.

"Shh," she hushed me. The sorceress slowly turned to face us, her normally pale face somehow now even whiter than the snow that capped the Ezranian Mountains. "We have arrived."

"I see nothing," Avery interjected.

"And they say fae senses were once just as keen as our own," Veli scoffed.

"Never in my life have I wished that I were something other than human until now," Zaela muttered.

"You will all need to be silent for what happens next. Am I understood?" Veli eyed the three of us and I gave her a small nod as my stance remained in front of Avery, who had been unusually quiet since we arrived.

"Are you alright?" I asked my sister softly over my shoulder.

"Yes," she whispered.

Any sign of the terror-stricken Veli disappeared as she took a single step closer to the trees before us and lifted her taloned hand, aiming toward them. "*Malifisc Venitian*," she spoke, her voice radiating a power that I hadn't yet heard from her.

As if commanded by the words, the twisted branches of the trees before us began to *move*. The sounds of their bark as it snapped and creaked filtered through the forest air. The ground beneath our feet rumbled, and Avery took hold of my shoulders as we both worked to balance ourselves to refrain from falling.

"Mother of the gods!" Zaela shrieked as she unsheathed her sword on instinct with one hand and held out her other for balance. Her eyes met mine, and all I saw was panic.

Veli's neck whipped back toward us, and her eyes were glowing just as they had when she healed me in the dungeons all that time ago.

"No weapons!" she hissed, and Zaela immediately re-sheathed her sword and apologized as she worked to remain upright.

Veli's focus went back to the shifting tree line before us. The embedded roots forcefully ripped themselves out of the terrain, causing their connected trunks to be carried away in their wake as we watched in disbelief. My eyes followed one of them, and I had to hold in my gasp as the roots silently coiled back into the soil, relocating the tree to a new area.

Suddenly, the entire forest was silent again. The branches and roots were frozen in place once more, as if they had originally grown where they now stood.

My gaze moved back to the witch before us, whose focus remained forward on what the trees had been guarding.

An entrance resembling a cave materialized before her—an archway of stone with intricate ancient symbols etched into its surface. The arch revealed nothing but the forest's ongoing existence on the opposite side. The woods suddenly darkened, even though we were completely shielded from the sun by the mist and canopy of the trees.

Veli turned to us, her glowing eyes beginning to fade. "There will be no turning back now."

I hesitantly stepped up to her side. "What was that spell you just said to have the trees reveal that arch?"

"It was not a spell. It was an announcement in the tongue of the gods," she answered, as the other two joined us where we stood.

"Well, what did you announce?" Avery asked.

Veli's stare remained on the ancient doorway she conjured. "A witch has arrived."

THIRTY-ONE

Elianna

THE FOUR OF US stood before the stone arch. My eyes wandered leisurely around the unusual carvings that were etched into it—not necessarily a language, but symbols that didn't resemble pictures of anything I recognized.

"May I see your dagger, Elianna?" Veli asked, knocking me out of my trance.

As she extended her hand toward me, I blinked and quickly withdrew my dagger from its sheath on my thigh. The sorceress carefully examined my reforged blade, her gaze tracing the intricate antler carving of Nyra and lingering on the wyvern wings that adorned its hilt.

Her taloned fingers wrapped around the grip, and she instantly moved to slice her palm, letting out a hiss at the contact. The scent of iron clogged my nostrils as violet-hued blood pooled in her hand.

"Gods, Veli," Avery huffed. "A warning would have been nice."

The witch turned to my sister. "You were aware we needed blood to enter and summon my sisters, so I'm not sure why this would come as a surprise."

"She has a point," Zaela said with a harsh chuckle, earning an eye roll from Avery.

Veli looked back at me then. "If I say run...you *run*. Do you understand, Elianna? This will not be a game you can talk yourself out of or a brawl you can fight your way through. This is magic. Ancient and all-knowing. You cannot win against it without owning it in return."

Avery jumped in before I could answer. "She is to be their queen. They should listen to her just as you have...or just as you have attempted to in the least."

Veli's violet stare remained on me, unfaltering, as she answered my sister. "The creatures of the isles do not adhere to the rules of the rest of the realm, Princess."

I sucked on my tongue as I took in her warning. "I understand."

"Good. Now keep that one's mouth shut, and there is a possibility that we may be able to walk out of here alive," she hissed, gesturing to Avery, who let out a huff of annoyance.

Veli took a step closer to the archway and dragged her palm across the jagged edge's surface, leaving a smear of her blood in its wake.

The moment her skin left it, the blood sank into the stone, vanishing before our eyes.

"Gods," Zaela gasped.

The symbols etched into the archway held a faint glow, mimicking the golden hue of Veli's eyes when she channeled her power.

"Follow me, and quickly, before the rip in the realm closes," the witch urged as she stalked through the swirling haze that now lay before us.

I turned to face Avery and Zaela. "Stay behind me while we're in there, okay?"

"Nice try, Lia." Zae laughed as she stepped through the arch after Veli.

Avery and I followed her, and as we walked beneath the stone arch, I blinked repeatedly, astounded by the ethereal vision that replaced the forest in a mirage of magic.

A sacred garden of ruins materialized, and the air hummed with a palpable sense of raw power.

The clearing possessed beautifully carved stone structures that looked as if they had been decaying for centuries and were encircled by towering trees, their branches interlocking. The dense foliage above allowed only shafts of soft, diffused sunlight to peek through, casting a gentle glow on the weathered, moss-covered stones, paving the walkway that seamlessly blended with the forest floor.

Clusters of vibrant, bioluminescent mushrooms sprouted from the ground, illuminating the surrounding soil with a soft turquoise light. Fireflies fluttered all around us, their twinkling blending with the natural luminescence of the darkened garden.

As we cautiously maneuvered throughout the area, I noticed that some of the deteriorating structures bore the same engraved symbols as the archway.

"They are ancient runes carved by the goddess Elora herself," Veli spoke softly from behind me, causing me to nearly jump. "They tell stories of forgotten rituals and magic, so the realm may never forget." She let out a sigh. "But we are far past that."

She stepped away from me and aimed toward the heart of the ruins, where a fountain hewn from granite awaited her, flowing with a brilliant teal liquid that cast its own glow.

"Veli," Zaela breathed from across the space. "This place is...beautiful. I've never seen anything like it. Why would you ever leave?"

Honestly, I was curious myself. The atmosphere was serene, giving me a sense of peace I hadn't felt in ages.

"You are about to find out," the witch answered. "The three of you come here and stand behind me, for I am to now summon my sisters."

"Well, Veli, you already spilled your blood on the arch, and still no one has arrived," I tsked as the three of us met her at the center.

"Well, *Elianna*, that was not where the blood was to call them." Her gaze slowly shifted to the fountain before us. "For the blood is to be dripped into the fountain."

She pricked one of her fingers with a taloned nail, allowing a tiny drop of her blood to pool onto her skin. Her reluctant gaze met mine once more, and for a fraction of a moment, I wondered if what we were doing was right, but it was far too late to second guess now.

Veli flicked the droplet of blood into the fountain and the once glowing blue instantly morphed into a deep scarlet. The ground once again rumbled violently beneath our feet. Avery grabbed hold of my arm, and my eyes flew to

Zaela, who looked terrified. Veli threw her arms back, as if shielding us, and backed us all into a corner of the ruins.

Cackling laughter filled the air, echoing from all sides of us. Our necks craned and whipped in all directions, trying to get a glimpse of who had arrived, but it was no use. The sounds were everywhere, bouncing off the crumbling stone structures and filtering through the space. For a moment, it seemed that the wicked chuckles danced around only in my mind, sending a violent shiver down my spine.

"Lia, what have we done?" Zaela whispered.

I clenched my teeth as my eyes remained on the back of Veli's silver hair while she continued to barricade us behind her outstretched arms.

As the last rays of sunlight that shone through the trees vanished, a mysterious mist wove its way through the ancient branches, creeping down toward the terrain.

Whirling on the wind, four shadowy forms glided into the gardens, resembling wisps of smoke. As the darkness dispersed, wicked figures remained in their wake.

The coven moved to corner us in unison, their cloaks billowing like ghostly spirits. Their faces were obscured by the hoods of their cloaks. With every step they took, their footfalls were hushed yet filled the air with a haunting echo—until they all halted before us.

The four of us remained silent, as Veli had demanded, while a single witch stepped forward from their half-circle. The figure's piercing eyes of crimson were visible through the shadows of her hood. I sucked in a breath as the air thickened with an energy that overwhelmed my senses, leaving a metallic taste on my tongue.

"Well, well, well, do my eyes deceive me, sisters? Or has the traitor returned...?" A voice, dark and wicked, slithered out of the confines of the hood.

"Traitor?" I whispered.

"Veli, what does she mean?" Avery asked nervously. She hushed us instantly.

"Ah, your companions are unaware of what you have done." The hooded witch gestured to us by swirling her taloned hand that matched Veli's. A sniff sounded through the air. "Both fae and mortal accompany you? Interesting. Last we were aware, there was a war happening among them, just as the gods intended all those centuries ago."

"That's why we're here," I spoke, and the red eyes beneath the cloak met mine.

"Elianna," Veli hissed.

"Elianna?" the voice called, radiating a cruel curiosity.

I shoved past Veli's arm and found myself face to hidden face with the mysterious witch.

"Yes, my name is Elianna Valderre, and we are here seeking your help to end the war that plagues our realm," I admitted, hoping it wasn't a mistake to say so soon.

"Valderre," the witch hissed, as if trying to taste my name on her tongue. Her hand extended out to me. "Prove to us that you are who you speak of, and we shall listen to why you have trespassed on our land."

"And how do you suppose I do that?"

A malicious smile shone brightly beneath the shadows of her hood. "Your blood will do."

"No," Veli said sternly, but my eyes remained forward. "She is the heir to the Valderre line. You will take my word for it."

"Aye, but your word means nothing to me, Veli. To none of your sisters since your treachery. If you have not yet noticed, the majority have chosen to not even show."

Rage pulsated through the air.

"Are you their leader?" I asked, gesturing to the surrounding witches with my chin.

"I am indeed High Witch." She lifted her hands and removed the hood of her cloak, and the other three behind her followed suit. "Or I had once been until a single witch worked to tear us apart." Her gaze shot over my shoulder to Veli.

The witch's pale skin illuminated beneath the glow of her crimson eyes, and her skin was that of a middle-aged mortal, not as youthful as Veli's, but nowhere near a crone. The other witches behind her were a mix of a single, wicked crone and two other nearly identical females that were so stunning that they would have brought any male to their knees if it wasn't for their eyes.

"State your name, High Witch," I demanded. Her eyes roamed over me as she contemplated her answer. "You know mine. It's only fair that I know yours as well."

She smirked at me beneath furrowed brows and let out a small chuckle that sent another shiver through me. "Very well then, *Elianna Valderre*, if that is truly your name. I am Azenna Elora," she stated proudly.

"And how much blood of mine do you need, *Azenna?*"

"Lia!" Avery shrieked from behind me, but I ignored her.

"How. Much. Blood."

The witch revealed her teeth in a menacing smile and held out her hand. "Only a drop."

"You will not touch her, Azenna," Veli intervened, stepping up to my side.

Before Veli had time to react, Azenna reached out, taking my hand in hers and pricked my finger, just as Veli had with her own. She then forcefully brought my hand to her lips and swiped her tongue atop the pooling blood right before she tilted my wrist over and let a single droplet fall to the terrain at our feet.

I ripped my hand back in disgust as the sound of rustling leaves filled the air while the branches above us began to dance. The glowing mushrooms at the trunk of their trees hummed in approval. The wind intensified, causing my hair to sway in several directions. However, as I frantically looked around, I noticed it only encircled *me*.

My eyes met Zaela's as they bulged from her face. The rest of the space was eerily still as I was enclosed alone in a storm of breeze. The High Witch lifted her hand and the howling speeds of the wind ceased instantly.

"Holy gods," Avery breathed.

"Yes, that certainly was the work of them." Their leader's eyes moved back to Veli. "It appears you have spoken true."

"I do that quite frequently," Veli grumbled, and if I hadn't been so horrified at what had just occurred, I would have laughed.

"Was that the land responding to my blood, or was it a spell?" I asked.

"Did you witness a single witch here cast a spell, Elianna?"

"No, however, I am not fluent in the terms of magic." I paused for a moment. "So it was the land, then?"

"Indeed."

"It's not the first time that's happened," I admitted.

"What do you mean?" Avery interrupted as she took a few steps closer to me.

I turned to her and then focused my gaze back on the coven before us. "When I escaped the dungeons, and flew—" I stopped myself after realizing I almost revealed we had a wyvern. "I traveled through the Sylis Forest after I fled and was met with danger that caused a bit of my blood to spill. Vines of a willow tree came alive and shot out at my attackers, stopping them from harming me."

"Oh gods, Lia. Who attacked you?" Avery asked.

"Centaurs," I answered. "But don't you worry, we're great friends now." I gave her a wink.

"The soil in the Sylis Forest is similar to what is beneath our feet where we stand—it is ancient and all knowing. The locations remain unaltered by the hands of time and change, retaining their likeness to the era of when the gods traversed their trees."

"Why would her blood matter?" Zaela asked.

"She is heir to the realm, foolish mortal. The Valderre bloodline has always been at the forefront of ruling Velyra, and there it shall always remain. That is, if the realm has anything to do with it," Azenna answered. "That was by Mother Goddess Terra's doing."

"And if the king was murdered in cold blood, and the current malevolent queen was working to crown a false heir, what would the realm do about it?"

"I suppose nothing if an act of violence to the true heir was not occurring in the ancient wood."

"That makes little sense," I interrupted. "I was attacked by a troll months prior to my run in with the centaurs. The forest did nothing to protect me then."

Azenna lifted a single brow. "Exactly how often do you frolic through enchanted woodlands, Elianna?" When I rolled my eyes, she let out a vicious cackle. "Well, I suppose your father was still breathing when that occurred, for the realm had a proper ruler."

I swallowed as I attempted to process the information she assumed, shocked that she guessed so easily. My eyes lifted to meet her stare once more. "Well then, Heir of the Realm to High Witch, I have come here to bargain for your cooperation."

A grin crept over my face as she watched me intently.

THIRTY-TWO

Elianna

"WHAT COULD A THRONELESS queen possibly offer a coven of all-powerful witches?" Azenna spat with a wicked cackle that her sisters echoed behind her.

I took a swaggering step forward. "I am willing to prepare my kingdom and vouch for your acts by allowing you and your kind to roam the realm freely among humans and fae, as you did centuries ago. All creatures will be treated fairly in my reign and without judgement just for existing. There will no longer be a need to hide. However, you will all be expected to abide by Velyran law."

After a moment of uncomfortable silence, an eruption of belly laughter exploded from them all.

"*That* was what you planned to barter?!" Veli hissed in embarrassment at my side.

"Is that not what they want?! They've been in hiding!"

"They already roam the realm freely, Elianna! Just not in plain sight!"

"We're so fucked," Zaela huffed out with a nervous laugh.

"Quiet over there!" I snapped at her, then turned to check on Avery, who was quietly observing the witches before us.

As the coven's laughter ceased, my attention turned back to them as they began to leisurely disperse about the space, breaking the half circle they had remained in. The ones that appeared as twins gathered beneath an oak tree, leaning against its trunk, while the crone moved to sit upon boulders that were spread out through the ruins.

"That is what you offer to barter for our services to aid your war? Elianna, I am insulted." Azenna laughed. "Surely you do not believe we have remained hidden in The Elora Isles all this time...the traitor you keep at your side should have been proof enough of that."

"Why is she a traitor?" I demanded. Veli stiffened at my question.

"Ah, you do not know what she took?" Azenna taunted.

"She stole from the entirety of the coven. Against the wishes of the gods," the crone called.

My eyes shifted to her, and I blinked as recognition took over me.

"*You.*" I took a step toward her while pointing in her direction. "I have seen you before. You're the crone from the village."

"Hello, *one who was promised...*" she hissed with a malicious grin.

"That is what you spoke of when I saw you that day." I took another step in her direction as anger flooded me. "Begging on the streets of a village of mortals. Eyeing them. Watching them. Tell me, *crone*, what were your plans for the villagers if I hadn't scared you off that day?"

"Scared me off? Foolish girl, I simply left to speak to my sisters regarding the message from the gods. And as for your precious mortals...well, they were lucky that day." I sucked in a breath as one hand balled into a fist at my side while the other moved for the hilt of my dagger. "I returned some weeks later to find it had been reduced to ash. Pity."

"So the gods truly spoke this prophecy to each of you individually, then?"

"They did," Avery interjected. "It was in Father's journal. Veli was with him the day it came to her. She said it right to him."

"Avery," Veli hissed.

I lifted my hand and halted her as my eyes roamed over the witches who stood before us, watching us intently.

"So that is where you have been hiding all this time? Did you assume the role of the king's pet following the abandonment of your coven?"

"She is a *healer*," I stated. "She helps people. Veli tried to save my father."

"Interesting that you will do such a thing for another species as you doom your own."

"Enough!" Veli shrieked at the High Witch. "What I did was to save you. Or attempt to." She moved to the heart of the ruins before us and spun as she addressed them. "Everything I did was to save you from yourselves!"

"Lies!" They all began to shout at Veli.

"You wanted the book for yourself," Azenna assumed.

"Look at my eyes, Azenna. My skin. My *youth!* The book had remained untouched for centuries." Veli's stare wandered to Avery and then snapped back to her elder. "That is until a few nosey little fae stumbled into my life one day and refused to leave."

"You had no right to take it from us!" Azenna shouted, the crimson in her stare glowing once more.

"It was destroying you! All of you!" Veli roared.

I took an involuntary step back as power radiated from her.

"Witches were not created to be kind-hearted, Veli!" the crone hissed.

"You took the choice away from us all," the twins voiced in eerie unison from the edges of the tree line.

"Judging by the hue of your stares, I would say your choice had been made back then, Madalae and Empri." Veli crossed her arms at them.

The twin witches' hard stares softened.

"If the cost of all power is our youth, some of us are willing to pay such a price. What use do we have for beauty when we rarely desire the usage of a male? Our choices should not matter to you," Azenna barked.

"Mother of all the gods above, Azenna, you would have led the realm to its doom if I had allowed you to dig your talons into the book any further."

"You are blaming me, little witchling? Be mindful of what you accuse, as my skin has yet to crinkle into ruin alongside some of our sisters. I should rip your heart from your chest for your defiance."

"All those centuries ago, when our coven found the book within this very rift of the realm, you had not dabbled as deeply as those who had brought it to you." Veli's eyes shot over to the crone. "You have not yet held the true power you seek, so you still wear the skin of a benevolent witch. It is your eyes that would give you away."

Azenna's face twisted into a grimace as her gaze roamed over each of us. A cackle left her. "You speak so confidently, Veli."

"I am quite confident. I endangered my life and left the protection of my coven to ensure that none of you would succumb to becoming mindless monsters consumed by power."

Azenna stormed up to Veli—the High Witch and healer now stood chest to chest. "You think you are so much nobler than us because you do not desire the greatest gift the gods gave us? You are not better than us, Veli. You are soft-minded and *weak*."

"Is it the book that you seek?" Avery interrupted their stare-down, and all of our gazes moved to her as she stood on the far side of the ruins. "In exchange for your assistance in our war...is that your price? The book."

My heart started racing as I stared at my sister. Zaela made eye contact with me for a moment and instant panic lit in her stare.

Azenna pivoted away from Veli and took a step toward Avery. "Do not toy with me, girl, for I do not sense the book in our presence. Do not offer something you do not possess."

Avery then removed her pack that had been strapped from her back. She placed it in the soil at her feet and reached into it—when she pulled her hand from within, it held Veli's small, woven bag.

"Avery," I whispered, my eyes bulging in absolute fear.

"You foolish girl, what have you done?!" Veli boomed, jaw gaping.

She reached into the bag and removed the book from it. Power surged in the air, radiating from its pages, even while closed.

"*Tinaebris Malifisc,*" Azenna spoke softly in disbelief, her eyes shining with pure menacing anticipation. "It appears I was wrong, for you do have something worth bargaining for."

Wicked whispers echoed through the space from the coven that worked to surround us once more.

"You will not lay a single taloned finger on this until we come to an agreement of what the use of this entails, and how you will fight in the war," Avery spoke sternly.

"Avery, give me the book. Right. *Now,*" Veli demanded.

"Do as she says, Avery," I ordered as I took a step closer.

The air was charged with a fiery intensity that felt as if it would shatter into chaos at any moment.

"Avery!" Zaela shrieked after a few seconds of silence. "Listen to them!" she pleaded.

"Avery is your name," Azenna said. "Well, Avery, it appears the decision is in your hands, not theirs. Your terms are that we fight in this war? May we use the magic of the book you hold to aid its end?"

My sister swallowed and turned to me as I shook my head rapidly, mouthing the word *no.*

"Do not let your crownless, clueless ruler choose the fate of your war!" Azenna screeched, whipping Avery's attention back to her.

"Don't speak of her that way!" Avery yelled at the witch, but her confidence quickly crumbled, replaced by a surge of nerves that visibly coursed through her body. "I—" she started.

Azenna tsked. "I am afraid I have run out of patience for your lack of assurance, little red one."

"Oh gods," Veli murmured, and my eyes darted back and forth between her and my sister.

I took a few hurried steps toward her, my heart pounding in my chest. Veli matched my urgency, and then we raced to reach Avery, where she stood across the ruins.

Veli reached out her hand as we sprinted to my sister, and her grip on the book loosened as magic began to slowly tug her towards us.

"Let it go, Avery!" Veli shrieked, and she did as commanded.

The book was soaring toward us in the air when, suddenly, it whipped to the left and shot out to Azenna instead.

"No!" Avery screamed, and both of our steps ceased.

Veli vanished from beside me and wisped herself before her High Witch, trying to intercept the book, but she was too late.

Azenna caught the ancient bound pages in her clutches and let out a wicked laugh that rattled the ruins we all stood in. Dark magic swirled and surged in all directions, and a deafening crack of thunder erupted above, the laughter of the coven echoing behind it.

I snapped out of my trance and continued my desperate stride to Avery, throwing my arms around her to protect her in case the witch tried to attack.

One by one, the three other witches shot out into the sky under the cover of their shadowy shields.

"Thank you ever so much, my dear red one. I promise you, we shall hold our end of your precious barter and use our power to end the war," Azenna announced, her voice booming with crackling power as her shadows swirled around her feet.

Veli's eyes glowed with fury-forged intensity as she lunged at the High Witch, conjuring a massive explosion of shadows from her palm.

The blast of hazy-darkness slammed into the fountain right behind Azenna as she disappeared before our very eyes, with *Tinaebris Malifisc* in her grasp.

The ruins fell into a bone-chilling silence. I inhaled, my breath shaking, as I turned to my sister, who had just inadvertently handed a book filled with the realm's most sinister magic to a coven of malevolent witches.

Tears welled in her honey eyes as her lip trembled vigorously.

"Avery." My jaw locked.

"What have you done?" Veli demanded, tone full of wrath as she stared at the fountain. *"What. Have. You. Done?!"* She turned to us then.

"I knew bringing her was a mistake," Zaela murmured from where she stood, and my gaze shot to her as my lips curled back in a snarl.

A sob broke from Avery. "Veli, I—"

"You have no idea what you have done. Not a single *fucking* clue." She moved toward us and my hand shifted to my sword at my hip on instinct. "What I risked centuries ago...what I have *hid* for all that time, was to protect the innocents of this gods-forsaken world from them. And you just destroyed everything."

"How did she even get the book?!" Zaela snapped as she stormed to where we all stood.

I looked at Avery. "Well? How did you get the book?"

"Lia, I'm so sorry."

"This is not a time for apologies." I held up my hand to halt her efforts. "You need to tell us how you got that book and why you even thought to bring it here."

The thought hit me then...of Avery disappearing below deck just after I had told her where Veli was putting the book.

"I brought it in case it was needed. If Veli needed it and we were under attack...I never planned to hand it over. I never knew Veli stole it to begin with or that it was something they desired!" she shrieked as tears ran down her cheeks.

"It never should have been brought here!" Veli boomed.

"You never told us you *stole* it!"

"Little Princess Avery still *never* minding her own business. People are allowed privacy! You are not owed everything just because of the last name you bear."

"Enough!" I shouted. "Everyone calm down."

Veli looked at my sister with disgust. "You have doomed us all."

Avery winced.

"Will it hold?" I asked. "The barter. Will it hold since they took the book? That they will aid us in the war."

"There was no barter made in magic or blood. No true bargain exists now. Just a reclaimed artifact."

"Fuck," I muttered.

"And you!" she hissed at me. "Letting her taste your blood?! She has access to all your recent memories now! At the very least, for the last day. Just as I was about to scold you, the wind picked up, and the chaos ensued."

"My memories?!" I shrieked as I glanced down at my bleeding fingertip she had slithered her tongue across.

"Yes! Which means she knows how we arrived here and what awaits us in the sea," Veli revealed.

"Mother of the gods...Nox!" I gasped, terror taking over me at the thought of those witches on their way to him as we spoke.

Veli's attention moved back to the archway from which we came, her eyes widening in alarm. "We will need to argue about this all another time." Her gaze found mine, and I pressed my lips together tightly, clenching my teeth. "Evil lingers in the marshes."

My eyes slowly widened. "Jace," I breathed.

The four of us took off into a run instantaneously, back through the archway, as I desperately reached down into the bond to get a sense of him. Panic immediately consumed me, making it impossible to distinguish between whether the fear that I felt was his or my own.

THIRTY-THREE

Jace

THE TWISTED TREES, WITH their roots springing from the marsh floor, held my gaze as I stared into their secretive depths. I couldn't feel Lia. It was driving me absolutely insane.

I never felt pain, or panic, or hurt—the bond just felt as if it emptied. To calm my nerves, I told myself that it could have been the work of the magic that lingered in this strange land, but I was losing my last bit of patience that remained.

My foot was bouncing uncontrollably, rocking the pinnace we were forced to wait in.

"Brother," Gage said quietly. "They will be alright."

"I can't feel her, Gage! I can't feel Lia down our bond," I snapped.

He gave me an awkward smile. "I can't pretend I know what that's like, but you know our girls. They're tough." A laugh left him. "A hell of a lot tougher than us sometimes."

I gave him a knowing look as he chuckled at his own joke.

"How much longer do we need to wait? It's been hours. And as the minutes pass, I'm contemplating stepping foot on the land and taking my gods-damn chances."

"I'm all for bravery, but even you know that would be a stupid thing to do. Mating-bond rage or not," Gage joked.

I scoffed. "Mating-bond rage."

"Do you have another word for your territorial behavior?" He raised a brow at me.

My shoulders relaxed as I looked up into the foggy air, taking my time to answer. "Perhaps not."

Silence cloaked the area aside from the occasional buzz of an insect or croak of a frog. Suddenly, my ears picked up a call in the distance. As I looked beyond the marshes, my eyes narrowed and strained, attempting to trace the source of the alluring whisper that seemed to drift from the sea.

My back stiffened, and my stare whirled to Gage. "Do you hear that?"

He sat up straight and surveyed our surroundings through narrowed eyes, his hand instinctively reaching for the hilt of his sword as he gave a slow, small nod.

The distant hum grew louder, evolving into a haunting, feminine melody that seemed to wrap around everything, filling the air with its presence.

The notes turned into a blend of voices that dripped with an alluring honeyed sweetness—a symphony of temptation. I instantly reached down the tether, latching onto it as I searched for any sign of Lia.

The salty breeze carried the song in from the sea that awaited us beyond the bending marsh, and my body suddenly begged to succumb to it.

A splash echoed only feet away from our boat, breaking my trance. My eyes shot to it, and all I could see was a ripple in the murky water beneath us.

"Gage, something isn't right," I whispered.

When I went unanswered, I looked at my best friend and nearly gasped as I noticed his eyes had glazed over and turned a milky hue, seeming to have fallen into a trance-like state.

"Gage?"

When he didn't respond, I leapt across the boat, grabbing him by his shoulders and shaking him vigorously.

"Gage, snap out of it!" Panic overtook me as his eyes remained glazed, but a menacing smirk crept up his face.

"Brother, the sirens call to us." His voice was unrecognizable.

"Sirens?!" My gaze shot back out and whipped in every direction.

The thick water we floated above remained steady, but the calls continued.

His hand dangled over the side of the boat, reaching for the water from where the monsters called to us.

"Gage, no!" I shouted as I reached for him and shoved his body to the center of our small boat.

I smacked his face, but it was no use. There was no reaching him.

Unsheathing my sword, I stood on the benches of the pinnace; my blade held out and ready to strike as I tried to block out the sirens' song.

"Show yourselves!" I bellowed, my voice booming through the twisted trees. "I know you're here. Reveal yourselves, now!"

The sirens' heads emerged from the murky water and the mist that hovered over it. Instinctively, my grip tightened on my blade, and a growl erupted in my chest as two of them effortlessly floated toward the back of the boat. No matter how hard I attempted to block out their songs, I felt an irresistible urge to move toward its seductive pulse.

"A man," a scenic voice called from the front of the pinnace.

My gaze snapped in its direction, and there, perched on the tip of the ship's front, sat a creature from ancient myths and legends.

Her soaked blonde hair was adorned with the bones of her past victims, twisting the top strands away from her face as the rest remained draped over the front of her bare breasts. A tail with shimmering scales black as night splashed in the water below, its fins appearing as sharp as the blade I held.

My eyes lingered on the conch shell embedded in her throat, which legends claimed produced the melodies of their deadly songs. The moment our stares met, an intense sensation of terror gripped me as I was forced to peer into her unseeing, stark-white eyes.

"Mother of the gods," I breathed as I held my blade higher, ready to strike.

"A foolish man," she cooed as she picked a piece of seaweed from her scales. "Your gods are not here. But I am." Her webbed fingers traced the edge of the wood she sat upon as beads of water slid from her hairline and down her haunting face.

"I am no fool," I answered. "I know exactly what you are and what you seek."

She tilted her head to the side curiously, and I desperately tried not to look into her eerie stare.

She leaned toward me, attempting to tease me by exposing her breasts as her hair lifted from them in her bend. "And what is it that I seek…" The creature looked me up and down. "Captain?"

"I am Commander Cadoria, and you will stand down in whatever trickery you are attempting, *siren*."

"Trickery?" she asked. "Commander, I just want to play." A menacing smile tilted the corner of her sharp lips.

"I know what *playing* entails with your kind."

"And what is that?"

"You lure men from their ships with your beautiful songs and false promises, trapping them within the depths of the sea—feasting on their blood and flesh," I answered through furrowed brows. "We were warned of beasts within these marshes; however, creatures like you are not what I was expecting."

A sharp giggle left her, sending a chill down my spine. "You speak of me with disgust, yet you do not know me. Tell me, Commander, what is it you long for most? A beautiful woman on your arm? Or is it power that you seek? A siren's kiss may grant you both." She paused as her eyes roamed over me once more. "Or am I lacking the allure that a commander desires?"

The melody of her sisters' calls continued to fill the air as we stared each other down.

"A siren's kiss is from the pricks of their teeth and always ends in certain death." A smirk formed on my face. "Besides, I have all you offered—the most powerful and beautiful female in the realm. You have nothing I desire...except perhaps having your head on a spike."

A hiss left her, exposing her dagger-like teeth that appeared as if they had been carved into points. Suddenly, the songs that had filled the air ceased, and an abrupt splash sounded behind me.

I whipped around just in time to watch as Gage's body was dragged overboard and beneath the surface of the murky water.

"Fuck! Gage!" I bellowed, and as I went to leap across the boat, the siren whipped her tail out, catching my ankle as I was mid-jump.

My body slammed down into the wood, my head bouncing off the unforgiving edge of the pinnace, causing me to lose hold of my weapon. The sound of my sword clattering as it fell was nearly deafening as an instant headache brewed. I blinked through the blurriness of my vision and was met with icy eyes gazing back at me.

I desperately tried to move my body to strike her as the creature leaned over me, but I had lost all control of myself. As the siren opened her mouth full of razor-sharp fangs, a hymn left her lips.

My eyes glazed over, and a trance took over me simultaneously.

In my mind, Lia's face consumed my thoughts, her panic palpable down our tether that I thought I could suddenly feel once more—yet I couldn't discern if it was her distress or my own dread of losing her forever.

The siren pulled me below the water's surface, and I knew nothing but darkness.

THIRTY-FOUR

Elianna

THE MOMENT OUR STEPS led us beyond the ruin's arch, Jace's panic slammed into me. What had originally started as a slight worry had quickly morphed into pure desperation. My feet couldn't carry me quick enough as I raced between the winding trees. With each step, my feet sank deeper into the spongy ground of the marshy forest floor.

As we hurried back to our men, the coven's cackling laughter filled the air once more. Shadows whipped around us as if the witches traveled within them on the wind. Dark wisps lashed out at us on all sides, and power hummed through the woods as Veli shot her power back at her sisters as they worked to attack us. Loud whooshing noises filled my ears, but all I could focus on was getting back to my mate.

Running through the dense forest, I could hear the trees whispering secrets and the leaves rustling above us as if speaking to one another. With every step, I concentrated on avoiding the menacing roots that reached out to ensnare us. Vines slithered across the path, aiming for our ankles, causing me to occasionally stumble and sway. Ancient magic continued to pulse through the air all around us.

"*Silly little throneless queen.*" The High Witch's voice filled my head as if whispering all around me.

My gaze darted side to side as fear clogged my throat. I unsheathed my sword as I dodged a swinging tree branch.

"Look out!" I screamed as I ducked beneath it, my feet never faltering in my run.

The sound of Avery's screech echoed through the air, forcing me to glance back. I sent up a silent prayer to the gods as I saw Zaela tightly clutching Avery's wrist, desperately pulling her along to keep up with us.

As I pivoted my vision forward once more, the glimmer of strange creatures flitted through the trees—brief visions of phantom figures that seemed to be both part of the forest and yet not.

"I know who you work to save, Elianna Valderre. We are not the only beings that lurk within the wood and marsh." Azenna's voice was sweet with venomous anticipation.

"You will *not* touch them!" I screamed. A branch snapped out in front of me, and I swung my blade just in time to sever it in half, clearing our path.

"What?!" Zaela gasped.

"You can't hear her threats?!" I shouted over my shoulder, nearly out of breath.

"No!" she bellowed.

Mother of the gods. My eyes widened as I realized Azenna had spoken to me in my mind. "Get out of my head, witch!"

"Do not listen to her words, Elianna!" Veli shouted at me as a rush of shadowy smoke erupted from her, crashing into a silhouette that had materialized amidst the trees.

The opening to the marshes appeared before us in the near distance. We were almost there. We were so, so close.

"I can see the opening to the marsh! Hurry!" I screamed as we barreled through the woods that were enchanted to claim our lives.

A wicked laugh cracked through my skull as my breath was suddenly torn from my lungs, feeling as if they had filled with icy water.

"Jace!" I screeched, my voice cracking as panic consumed me.

"What's happening?!" Zaela shouted desperately from behind me, but I couldn't focus on the words to say. Every ounce of my efforts worked to carry me to my mate.

My instincts screamed to keep moving as a soft, haunting melody echoed on a breeze, playing tricks on my senses and distorting my vision until it suddenly faded.

Once my steps finally reached the edge of the forest, I leapt out from the tree line. Avery and Zaela were right on my tail, and they forcefully crashed into my back, sending all three of us collapsing onto the muddy soil.

Veli was there then, emerging from the trees appearing otherworldly, her usual glowing violet eyes gone, now *fuchsia* and gold, as she continued to aim her lashing shadows at the witches' phantom-like figures that glided in the wind.

The witches' cackles faded as they whipped into the open air and shot out toward the sea beyond the marsh.

With pain-induced grunts, the three of us moved to untangle our limbs from each other and worked to stand. I pulled them each to their feet and then my gaze moved to the murky water that awaited us at the edge of the tiny riverbank.

"Mother of the gods," Veli breathed as she took in the same sight that I had. "The pinnace. It's empty."

"No!" Avery yelled.

"Jace!" I jumped into the swamp, storming toward our small boat as fast as the water's resistance would allow.

The sound of Zaela unsheathing her sword ripped through the air.

"Elianna, be careful!" Veli called.

I heaved myself into the empty boat that had remnants of leftover water that had somehow splashed into it.

My eyes turned to the shore where Veli stood, staring at me with nothing but regret written on her features. With each passing second, my lungs burned more ferociously.

"Where are they?" I croaked out through my teeth, my vision turning red from fury and fear.

"They left the boat," Veli whispered. She turned back to gaze into the woods from which we came, as if an answer would lie between the trees.

"They knew not to do that!" Avery shouted.

A snarl danced across Veli's lips. "Just as you knew not to touch my book!"

I tuned out their arguing as my lungs threatened to collapse. Jace's sword was left in the middle of the boat, lodged beneath the center's wooden seat, and I knew with every fiber of my being that he would never willingly leave his weapon behind in uncharted lands. There also wasn't a single sign of Gage.

"Gage!" Zaela shouted into cupped hands as she walked a few steps into the thick, hazy water. "Jace! Where are you?!" Her words echoed and were lost in seconds.

My eyes traced along a line of water droplets that led over the pinnace's edge.

In the distance, the water's surface was disturbed by the sudden appearance of bubbles, which burst immediately upon contact with the dense, humid air.

"Veli," I called in a hushed voice. "Veli, what lurks in these waters?" My eyes shot back to shore to see that the witch's eyes had widened so intensely that it put a pulsating fear in the pit of my stomach.

I stood in the center of the boat, and without a second thought, I sucked in a deep breath and dove overboard.

"Elianna, no!" Veli's plea faded the moment my ears were beneath the surface.

I opened my eyes beneath the murky swamp to realize that the day's setting sun struggled to penetrate the dark depths that lingered beneath it. I frantically swam through the greenish-brown hued water that was filled with fallen leaves and branches, gripping the decaying bark to heave myself deeper into the camouflaged pits.

The swamp floor was adorned with haunting shadows from submerged trees and their gnarled roots coated in slimy algae and moss. Long blades of aquatic grass swayed with the subtle movements of the water, appearing as if they would try to wrap around my ankles.

I kicked my feet and pushed through the murkiness that surrounded me. My eyes glimpsed a sudden movement from the corner of my blurry vision, and I let out a gasp as my attention snagged on Gage.

The thick strands of grass that felt as if they would try to trap me down in their depths were doing just that to my friend, wrapping around his legs and securing him to the swamp's floor. I paddled with all my might as my lungs burned. Once I reached him, I realized he was unconscious, and I immediately unsheathed my dagger and sliced through his nature-made shackles.

Wrapping my arms beneath his, I kicked off the muddy swamp floor and swam as fast as I could to the surface with his extra weight.

My head broke the water, and I let out a desperate gasp for air as my heart pounded in my chest.

"Zaela!" I screamed through coughs as the water filled my mouth and throat. "Zaela, help!"

Splashing sounded, and I turned in its direction to see her racing to me in a sprinting swim.

"Get him on the boat!" I demanded as she reached me, shoving his body in her direction.

"Jace?!" she whispered, horror written all over her face.

I pursed my lips and took another deep breath as soon as she had Gage in her grasp and dove back beneath the surface, praying to every god that I wasn't too late to save him.

Kicking and heaving myself through the hazy water, I frantically searched every space I could as I felt our bond withering away, the tether's beating a faint, fading pulse.

A deep trench appeared, and as I peered over its edge, my eyes landed on Jace in the clutches of not one but *three* vicious sirens.

One held his unconscious body close to hers, while another placed her lips on his, pushing bubbles of air into his mouth—his lungs. I couldn't help but feel a strange sense of relief, tinged with fury, as they worked to keep him alive, if only to prolong his torment.

The third circled around from behind them, her tail moving the water in a rapid current. She opened her mouth, revealing razor-sharp teeth, and sunk them into the flesh of my mate's shoulder.

Pain seared through the crook of my neck the moment her rows of fangs pierced his skin. Rage took over me, and without a second thought, I kicked off the rock and swam as fast as I could to them.

Their attention was caught by the sudden movement, and a strange hissing sound escaped their mouths, echoing through the water.

The sirens matched my movements, and two of them raced toward me while the other continued to hold Jace beneath the surface.

Their sleek tails propelled them effortlessly, creating whirlpools that distorted the surroundings. Suddenly, the haunting notes of the sirens' songs echoed, resonating from the darkest depths of the abyss.

As we rapidly closed in on each other, they soon realized that their hymns had no effect on me, as all of my focus was on saving Jace and bringing him back to the air above.

This quickly heightened their annoyance at my presence for interrupting their feast—on *my mate*.

The first strike from the sharp fins of a tail came at me swiftly. The other siren, her form a distorted blur, lunged at me with bared teeth, emitting a piercing screech. I twisted away, narrowly missing the blow as the water's resistance clung to my movements.

I unsheathed my dagger as quickly as my slowed movements would allow, aggressively swinging in every direction.

Our fight unfolded in a dance of desperation and rage. The sirens moved with a menacing taunt as they circled me with an almost supernatural coordination. I evaded their attacks with a combination of swift kicks and forceful swings of my dagger.

My limited air supply became a constant reminder of the time I was running out of as they relentlessly attacked.

My dagger found purchase deep into one of their stomachs, and in turn, a flowing river of black blood escaped the wound, causing me to do a double take. An ear-shattering scream left the siren as she darted away, and the force of her tail sent me soaring back with the current she made while fleeing.

While the second siren was distracted, I used the opportunity to kick her in her face as forcefully as the water's resistance allowed, crushing her nose beneath my boot, and in turn, she followed the other and fled.

Fading in and out of consciousness, I urgently kicked off the muck ground and propelled myself to the surface. After taking a heaving breath of air, I instantly dove back down.

With a swift motion, the remaining siren whipped her tail through the water, generating large bubbles that she eagerly inhaled—she then once again pressed her foul lips to Jace's and pushed the air into his lungs.

The wicked creature returned her attention to me and released his body, allowing him to sink down to the marsh's floor. I had maybe a minute, if I was lucky, to get him to the surface before he ran out of air, and I lost him forever.

I swam at her in urgency, and her pace toward me matched until we collided in an unfaltering, violent clash. My dagger's blade met its mark over and over, yet so did her fin. Her tail lashed out at me, catching the outside of my ribs, and my body let out a scream from the pain that tore through me, causing me to lose some of my already precious air. Our dance continued in a haze of crimson and black blood that floated around us.

As I made another move to strike, she caught my throat with her webbed hands and coiled her long tail around my legs like a serpent. My eyes bulged as panic consumed me—her piercing, white stare shone brightly through the darkness. I peeled my eyes away from hers and looked at my mate one final time, my heart cracking in my chest. This couldn't be how it would end. I refused.

I turned my attention back to the sea-witch who held me in her grasp, and my eyes wandered down to the center of her throat—where a conch shell was embedded and beginning to glow as she opened her mouth to put me in her trance. With a battle cry, I lost what remained of my air and heaved my dagger as hard as I could at her. The blade plunged into her throat, carving the shell out of her skin.

My hand reached out and ripped the conch from her before she had time to grab it and place it back herself.

The siren screeched so loud that, even beneath the water, I thought I would go deaf, but she released me on impact. The creature shriveled before me, no longer appearing as an alluring monster but now morphing into a decrepit, skeletal form of a husk right before her body floated to the surface.

My eyes followed her for a moment as I pocketed her shell right before I fell out of my daze and dove for Jace's body. My eyes widened in horror at the sight of his beautiful, frozen face. I wrapped my arms beneath his own and pushed off the bottom of the marsh and swam us up to the surface as fast as possible.

The moment my head was above water, I gasped out, desperate for air—but Jace didn't.

"Jace!" I whimpered as I tried to circle around. We had drifted so far from the pinnace. "Jace, baby, I need you to wake up."

My feet kicked violently beneath us as I worked to tread the water for both of us, but the gash in my side from the siren's fin was making me weak.

"VELI!" I screeched. Tears burned my eyes, realizing I couldn't feel Jace's chest moving while I held him. I reached down in the bond, slamming my thoughts onto the bridge that connected us, and felt him fading. "Veli, I need help!" I screamed once more.

"Over here!" Avery's voice called from the edge of the riverbank where she stood. "Veli, they're here!"

I followed her gaze to where Veli was by the boat. She pointed a single taloned finger in our direction, and then closed her fist, pulling it into her chest.

In an instant, our bodies were forcefully dragged through the water, creating a current that surged outward on either side of us, propelled by Veli's magic.

"He mustn't touch the soil!" Veli reminded me as I moved to drag him onto the bend.

"Fuck!" I screeched in panic.

"Brother!" Gage called from aboard the boat where he was recovering. A small bit of relief slammed into me to see that he was alright.

Veli's magic thrust us to the edge of the boat, where Zaela and Gage waited, and the two of them helped me heave my mate into the safety of it.

Once he was aboard, Zaela lent me her hand and helped me into it. I dropped to my knees at Jace's side and frantically looked his body over.

"He's not breathing, Gage. *He's not breathing!*" I bellowed, as tears streamed down my face.

Gage jumped on the opposite side, rocking our small boat at the force of his weight. He looked at me then. The playful appearance his face normally wore was entirely gone. "I'm going to do chest compressions, and I need you to pump air into his lungs. Can you do that, Lia?"

"Yes," I whispered, without removing my stare from Jace's body.

Gage interlocked his fingers and began pushing down onto the center of Jace's chest repeatedly. Zaela watched us, her eyes wide.

"Air, now!" he ordered, and I heaved a deep breath of air between Jace's cold, pale lips.

We repeated this several times, and my breathing came in rapid breaths as I tried to hold my grip on reality.

A sob broke from me, and a scream of agony was working its way up my throat when suddenly a gasp erupted from Jace, followed by him coughing up a horrifying amount of swamp water.

"Oh, gods!" I shouted, right as Zae pushed him onto his side to aid his choking.

"You're okay, you're okay," Zaela said to him, her composure significantly stronger than my own.

Jace worked to catch his breath, and Gage's body sagged with relief as we watched him. My mate's eyes found mine, and the corner of his lips curved. He reached his hand up to cup my cheek, and he swiped my tears away with his thumb.

My eyes darted back and forth between his, but I couldn't find words to speak.

"I'm okay, my Lia. I'm okay," he mimicked the reassurance from his cousin through a few coughs.

A sound left me that was half a sob, half a shuddering breath as I leapt onto him, throwing my arms around his shoulders and gripping him tighter than I ever thought possible.

"I thought I lost you," I whispered into the nook of his neck as I nuzzled my face into it, the chilled drips of water seeping into my skin.

He let out a strained chuckle. "Never."

I leaned back and looked him over meticulously as his coloring slowly crept back into his lips and cheeks.

His eyes locked on me then, a lethal look to them. He pressed his hand to my side, and when he gently lifted his touch, my blood stained his fingers. "They hurt you," he growled.

I laced my fingers with his. "I'll be okay. You should see what I did to them." A knowing grin formed on his lips as I gave him a wink. "What the hell happened while we were gone?"

He leaned up, and Zaela moved to sit on one of the seating boards behind her to get out of his way.

"We were waiting for you, and I was getting...antsy," he started.

"He was ready to risk it all and come after you for taking so long. I was trying to keep his ass in the boat," Gage cut him off.

My eyes shot to Jace, and I looked at him through furrowed brows. "Why would you do that? You knew to stay in the boat!"

"I couldn't feel you." Anger tinged with nerves radiated from him. He swallowed. "I didn't know if you were okay, and enchanted lands or not, I was going to find out for myself."

My eyes widened slightly. "The rift. It blocked out the bond."

"The what?" he asked.

I was about to answer when Veli's voice called to us. "Elianna!"

My gaze found her and Avery still on the riverbank. Veli's talon pointed a few feet away from our boat, where two sets of hate-filled, stark-white eyes stared at us.

I instantly stood, a growl erupting from me as I stalked to the edge of the boat—their tails waded through the murky swamp, aiming for me.

One of them had the audacity to place her webbed fingers onto its ledge and try to pull herself up. My teeth were clenched so tightly that I thought they would shatter as I tried to calm my fury.

"You took something from us. *Someone* from us," she hissed.

Without a second thought, I reached down and grabbed the creature by her soaked, seaweed-crusted hair, heaved her up by it, and then sent my opposite fist into her face. Her cheekbone cracked beneath my knuckles and she let out a shriek of pain as her body splashed back down into the water.

Her counterpart hissed at me but swished her tail to move out of my reach.

The mouthy siren resurfaced and hissed at me.

"*I* took someone from *you?!*" I bellowed, my voice echoing through the marsh. "You held our men beneath the surface, ready to feast on them! I simply rescued them from the fate you nearly gave them, you wicked monsters!"

"You took our sister's conch!" she barked at me, showing her sharpened teeth, and I flashed my canines right back. "She will cease to exist without it, a husk for eternity that you watched her fade into when you carved it from her scales!"

274

"Why would I care that a heartless, murderous creature turns into a husk?!" I snapped at her. "You harmed my *mate*." My gaze whipped back to where Jace, Gage, and Zaela observed us, and then returned to them. I gripped the hilt of my dagger. "You should both receive the same punishment."

"And who are you to deem what a punishable offense is, *fae bitch?*" one taunted.

My back straightened as my stare remained on them. "I am Elianna Valderre, Heir of the Realm." I leaned down closer to them as their brows furrowed with doubt. "And once I take my place upon my throne, I will remember every creature who showed me loyalty, or otherwise."

They eyed each other warily and then met my stare once more. "What do you want from us?"

A thought crossed my mind then. In order to win this war and defeat the false queen, we needed as many allies as possible, no matter how unlikely they seemed.

"What is it that *you* seek?" I turned their question back on them.

"Lia?" Zaela questioned, but I held up a finger behind me to halt her. Concern radiated from Jace, but I worked to block it out.

The twin creatures looked at each other again. "We want our sister's conch returned to us so we may restore her."

"And what do I get in return for resurrecting a murderer?" I shot back, tone steady.

A hiss left the one who barely spoke.

I reached into my pocket and pulled out the shell, rotating it between my fingers leisurely as their eyes steadily followed its movements.

"What are you asking of us?" they asked in unison.

"Your allegiance."

"We do not pledge to, nor concern ourselves, with land walkers."

My lips parted as my eyes darted back and forth between the two sirens before me. A menacing smile formed.

I halted my taunting twirling of the shell and held it between my forefinger and thumb, giving it a small squeeze—a tiny crack splintered through the conch.

"Stop!" one shouted as her webbed fingers reached out toward me. "You claim to be heir to the realm, yet you would doom one of its habitants?"

I flashed her my canines. "I will doom anyone that refuses to take a knee to my claim when offered mercy. If you are not with me, then you are against me."

Pride erupted down the bond.

"Mercy," she mocked.

I pocketed the shell once more. "You attacked our men unprovoked, with no other intention aside from feasting on their flesh and bones. Legends state you are beasts that swam up from the depths of hell. Your reputation precedes you just from this brief encounter. I see no reason to allow any of you to live unless you choose to fight for me in the war that rages on Velyra's soil."

"May be a bit difficult...lacking legs and all." She snickered.

"Not all battles are raged on the land. If we call for you, you will fight. And when the time comes, I will return the conch to you. It is a fair barter."

"A bloody battle in exchange for our sister's life?" the other asked.

"Indeed."

"And what of the fallen?"

I huffed out a breath through my nostrils. "If they are not my men, then you may do with them as you please."

They exchanged feral looks.

"Do we have an agreement?" I demanded. "And if you disobey orders received, I will crush your sister's fragile shell and grind it into dust. Am I understood?"

"And how will we be receiving said orders?"

My back straightened, and I glanced to shore, where Veli and Avery watched us intently.

"My witch will present herself to you when the time comes. You will swim to wherever directed." The remaining bit of patience I had was wearing thin. "Are we in agreement? Vow yourself to my claim to the throne and you shall earn your sister's life back."

The two of them slowly sank back down into the water until only everything above their chins was visible. My jaw ticked as I looked deep into the vengeful, icy eyes that gazed up at me.

"Agreed," they hissed in unison, right before their tails lashed out and sent them soaring beneath the surface and back toward the sea.

THIRTY-FIVE

Elianna

"Do you have any idea what you have done?!" Veli scolded me as she and my sister were pulled into the pinnace. Avery immediately rushed over to Gage and threw her arms around his shoulders.

I scoffed at the witch. "We are now lacking significant allies we were relying on obtaining. An opportunity presented itself and I *took* it."

"At what cost? You truly think those beasts from the deep will listen to your orders as a battle rages in the sea?"

"What does she mean we're lacking allies? What happened in the forest, Lia?" Jace asked.

Gods, I was about to lose my shit.

I turned back to face them. The men wore looks of concern, while those who accompanied me in the woods looked at me in defeat.

"The witches will not be aiding us in the war," I answered and looked to Veli. "Mistakes were made, and I should have listened to her warnings. We shouldn't have come here. I will explain everything, but we need to get back to the ship as soon as possible."

Without a moment of hesitation, our two men posted up on either side of the boat and moved to row us back out to the sea.

"Why won't the coven ally with us? Are they choosing to aid Idina?" Gage asked.

"Gods no, they just...have their own agenda."

"You don't have to protect me, Lia. They will soon know what I have done."

The rowing ceased, and Jace and Gage exchanged a look and then glanced back at Avery before continuing their paddling.

"What do you mean?" Gage asked as Jace's eyes bore into mine. I bit my lower lip to try to stop myself from blurting out what she was struggling to say.

Avery cleared her throat as her eyes darted back and forth between me and the witch. "I stole Veli's book of dark magic, thinking we may need its aid in case we were attacked or lost or...I don't know. It was a foolish mistake."

Jace's eyes bulged, and I nodded slowly, confirming his fear.

"Avery, where is the book now?" he asked as his eyes remained on me.

"They took it," she whispered on a sob.

"That is not all they took!" Veli hissed. "They took Elianna's memories. They could have seen all her lingering secrets and recent plans."

"How?!" Gage gasped.

Jace's stare whipped to Veli. "You were to protect them!" His voice boomed, and he looked as if he would lunge at the witch.

"Aye, but it is difficult to protect those who recklessly offer their blood on a silver platter, and another who exposes our greatest weapon without having the power to hold it."

He turned back to me. "Blood?"

I shrugged. "They needed it to prove that I was the heir...I didn't think she would...*taste* it."

As their oars sliced through the water, we finally emerged from the marshes and entered the open sea. The moon now hung low in the night sky, casting a silvery glow over the dark water.

His body was tense, rigid. "Do you know what they saw?"

A faint, orange glow emerged in the distance, catching our attention. I sprang to my feet and leapt to the very front of the pinnace, eagerly leaning over the edge to get a better view.

My eyes widened. "NOX!" I shrieked.

"Is that the ship on fire?!" Avery asked, jaw gaping.

I turned to Veli. "We need to get there faster. We'll never make it in time." She looked at me hesitantly. "I will *not* let them take Nox!" I screamed. "The coven knows you still live, Veli. Stop being afraid of using your magic!"

"Everyone, hold on," she warned, and her eyes began to glow.

A moment later, her hand lashed out toward the back of the boat, and a wave picked up behind us, thrusting us forward by the powerful current and toward the floating inferno.

I lost my balance from the force of our takeoff and flew backward, stumbling over the bench and falling onto Jace.

He turned me over and wrapped his arms tightly around my chest as we soared over the waves.

We were nearing the burning ship, and as the pinnace drew closer, I could feel its heat intensifying. The scent of burning wood and smoke filled the air, making it difficult to breathe.

Veli's magic brought us to a screeching halt, sending us flying forward. I leapt to my feet and was back at the bow a moment later, staring in horror at the raging flames that were ravaging our way home, and the crew who had stayed behind.

"No," I whispered, as my eyes darted back and forth. I pivoted to face them behind me—their horror-filled, wide-eyed expressions were accentuated by the fiery orange hue cast by the blaze.

"What are we going to do?!" Avery shrieked as Gage held her steady in his grasp.

I let out a loud, ear-piercing whistle, but it was lost in the roar of the fire. "Why didn't he fly away?" I whispered to myself.

A cackle filled the night sky, erupting from the thick, black smoke, followed by a ferocious roar from Nox.

My lips parted as my breathing became heavy. I turned to my mate.

"Don't you dare," he said, his voice filled with desperation. "We are not repeating what happened at the war camp."

I pivoted to the others. "Stay in the boat."

"Lia!" Avery shrieked.

"Veli, can you put the fire out?"

She glanced at the raging blaze and then back at me. "I will try, but the ship will be lost."

I gave her a curt nod before turning back to Jace. I grabbed him by the collar of his shirt and pressed my lips aggressively to his as a tear streamed down my cheek.

"Then come with me," I whispered onto his lips right before I jumped out and dove off the pinnace and into the dark depths.

As soon as my body submerged into the water, I sensed a splash behind me, signaling that Jace had followed my lead. I kicked and paddled my way closer to the ship beneath the cover of the freezing waves, avoiding the embers and ash filling the air.

My face broke the surface, and I gasped for air, only to be choked by the surrounding smoke. Jace popped up next to me then, and we both grabbed onto the side of the ship, circling the outskirts until we came across the side ladder built into the wood.

"Lia, be careful!" he called as I climbed up with him right behind me. "We don't know what we will meet up there!"

Another roar sounded from Nox, and my pace quickened. I would carve the heart out of every last witch that sought to sink their claws into my wyvern.

I pulled myself over the ship's rail, and the intense heat of the flames licked my face. Beads of sweat mixed with the seawater clung to me and dripped down my brows. The crackling of burning timber mixed with the coven's cackles roared in my ears.

"Mother of the gods," Jace breathed as he heaved himself over the edge and stood at my side.

Panic took over both of us as the entire crew lay slain in the center of the ship. The ship groaned under the stress of the fire as the flames became insatiable.

Amidst the madness, a figure emerged from the smoke. Azenna and the other three witches appeared then, all of them shooting a blast of power into the center of Nox's inferno. My eyelids worked to blink through the black smoke, and horror consumed me as I saw Nox cornered by them at the bow of the ship. The power they were shooting at him was making him *shrink*.

"They're hurting him!" I screamed and took off into a sprint, jumping over flames that lashed out at me, ignoring the agony of the burns that formed on my skin.

"Lia, wait!" Jace boomed.

With a swift motion, I unsheathed my dagger and charged at Azenna, her focus entirely on her spell. As my body slammed into hers, the spell they cast on my wyvern shattered, freeing him, and he instantly expanded back into his colossal size once more.

I lifted my dagger high in the air to plunge it into the High Witch's heart when her gaze started glowing once more. Power shot out at me, throwing me from her and across the ship.

"Lia!" Jace bellowed as my body tumbled across the embers of the burning wood. He was at my side in an instant and lifted me from the floor of the ship.

The witches moved to circle us like predators. "Not only are you a throneless queen, but you are a foolish one, Elianna Valderre," Azenna hissed as crimson shone from her eyes, fixated on me. "And now you will pay for it with your life."

"You will not *fucking* touch her." Jace unsheathed his sword as he swiftly maneuvered himself in front of me. He swung his blade through the air, aiming to cleave the High Witch in half, but she vanished and reappeared halfway across the deck.

Her focus returned to my mate then, and her face was riddled with pure rage. She lifted her taloned hand and used her power to rip his sword from his grasp and sent it flying overboard. "You will regret that, *mortal*."

"Lia, we need to jump," Jace whispered as his arm maneuvered around my waist and began pulling me to the ship's rail at our backs.

I was about to lift my hand to whistle for Nox when Veli suddenly appeared behind the coven, levitating in the air over the sea. The powerful wind whipped her silvery hair around as an enormous wave brewed beneath her and her glowing gaze.

With a relentless battle cry, Veli shot her hands out towards us and, in turn, sent the wave she conjured crashing onto the ship's deck.

The witches shrieked as the icy water slammed into them, and they morphed into their shadow-like smoke figures to flee.

A deafening crack sounded through the air as the wave collided with the ship's mainmast and sent it splintering into a thousand pieces as it collapsed. Jace and I braced ourselves as the water rushed towards us a second later and sent us barreling into the wooden rail.

Gasping for air as I choked on the seawater, he yanked me upright while my vision cleared. I frantically looked around and noticed the ship was sinking rapidly from the force of Veli's wave.

"Nox!" I screamed, and I could barely make out his shimmering scales across the ship as the smoke cleared.

Still disorientated, I grabbed my mate's wrist and tugged him along with me as we raced up the deck of the sinking ship. Leaping over and dodging broken, splintered boards, we dashed across the space as fast as our bodies would carry us.

To my horror, Nox was tangled beneath a web of ropes. Once we reached him, I took my dagger and frantically sliced through his restraints, Jace matching my urgency with his own that he pulled from his boot.

"It's okay, Nox, it's okay!" I tried to comfort him as we cut through the ropes, but his growling and thrashing persisted.

I felt the cold seawater on my heels as I sliced through the last cord and turned to find that we were about to be engulfed by the raging waters.

"Elianna!" Veli screamed, and I looked up just as the crone appeared atop Nox, emerging from her shadows.

She gave me a wicked, menacing grin as she reached down and plucked one of Nox's scales from his back, earning a terrifying growl from him as he ferociously snapped at her.

Just as I was about to charge at the crone, Jace swiftly hurled the dagger he held at her face, but she vanished, wisping herself away before his blade struck true.

"I will kill them for what they've done," I said through my teeth as water pooled and swirled around my boots.

"Another time, sweetheart," Jace stated as he hurried me onto Nox's back.

As soon as we settled into our saddle, Nox wasted no time and launched into the air, leaving the sinking ship. He soared out over the vast depths and circled over the boat where our court awaited in disbelief.

With the flames extinguished, the moon's reflection on the waves became our only source of light. As terror filled me, my gaze remained fixated on the bubbles from the remnants of our sunken ship, thinking that in only a day, I may have just doomed us all.

THIRTY-SIX

Avery

WE HAD BEEN SOARING over the Vayr Sea on Nox's back
for two days—we were all starving, sunburnt, and had
barely spoken to one another. The tension in the air was
thick, and it was entirely my fault.

Despite my attempts to explain my intentions to the
men, Lia recommended not talking about the specifics
of what had occurred. It was best to avoid any further
confrontation until it was no longer likely that someone
would be shoved off the cramped saddle.

Following that, Lia and Gage barely spoke to me.
Zaela was back to ignoring my existence, and I was too
terrified to face Veli after the madness of everything had
settled.

When land finally came into view, a sigh of relief
left everyone. Nox flew over the terrain for miles until
Alaia's farmlands were visible, and I had never been
more thankful.

Citizens gawked at us as we landed on the outskirts of
their headquarter city, and the moment my feet touched
the ground, my wobbly legs buckled from not being able
to use them for days.

Three horses and their riders approached us, and as they came into view, I realized it was General Vern, Finn, and Landon.

"You're back!" my brother yelled as he dismounted his horse and pulled me into a hug.

"Hi," I answered softly.

He grabbed my shoulders and pushed away from me while he held me there—his eyes roamed over me curiously and then met my own. "Are you okay? I figured you would be kissing the ground beneath your feet by now," he joked. "How was your week out at sea?!"

I turned and looked back at Gage as he followed Lia and Jace over to speak with the general. "I would prefer not to talk about it right now, Finn."

"That bad?" Landon chimed in, and my gaze whipped to him.

Taking in the sight of them, I nearly did a double take. They were both *filthy*, and Landon was wearing a full suit of armor.

"What the hell happened while we were gone?" I asked with a chuckle that I never thought would come out of me again.

"Training," they answered in unison.

"General Vern put us to work the second your ship sailed away." Finnian laughed. "One of us is clearly much more trusted with a blade than the other." He gestured to Landon and his new attire.

"You'll get there someday, Finn." Landon smiled at my brother, and it warmed my heart, yet an ache followed.

I turned back and observed Gage, whose eyes left the general and wandered to me at the same moment. I quickly looked away, unable to bear the weight of his stare.

"So, are you going to tell us anything that happened? Or do we have to wait for Lia?" Finn asked.

"Well, for starters, I was definitely wrong about Zaela having feelings for Gage."

"And how was that proven? Last I saw, you were ready to claw her eyes out every time she glanced at the man."

"It's not my place to say, but I think you will find that she and Veli have been getting close since we last saw you."

Their eyes flared with surprise, exchanging a quick glance before returning their attention to me.

"Those two banding together sounds terrifying," Finn said.

"It's just as scary as you're thinking." I winked but forgot to muster up the fake smile to make it believable.

"If Zaela doesn't have feelings for Gage, then why do you look so solemn?"

I turned back to where the rest of them stood, where Veli had now joined them as Nox remained between us. As if they felt my stare, they all turned to face us, and their eyes lingered on me for so long that I thought I would faint.

"I believe you're about to find out," I answered in a whisper.

They all approached, the general paying no mind to me as he stormed right past us to mount his horse. "These two have been training with the men since you've left. You can decide where they shall continue their efforts. I will await your orders, Commander," he said to Jace right before his horse took off into a gallop to head into the city.

Lia walked up to us first and threw each of her arms around Finn and Landon's shoulders. "Missed you both! How was it here holding down the valley?"

"Well, *one* of them seems to have passed the general's tests," Zaela joked as she crossed her arms.

"We'll find something for you. Don't you worry, Finn," Lia said as she reached up and gripped his cheeks in her hand, squeezing them together. He shook out of her grasp with a huff of annoyance.

"Are you going to tell us what happened? This one is being strangely vague," he said as he gestured to me.

Lia pressed her lips firmly together as the rest of them joined us. "Yes," she answered. "But not here."

Once back at the Cadoria Estate, Lynelle prepared a welcome home meal—freshly baked bread, roasted chicken, and vegetables from Alaia's farmlands blanketed the table. As the scent of the food reached my nostrils, my stomach growled in agony, aching from days of hunger while flying over the sea. However, the thought of us all needing to form a new plan due to my actions made my stomach churn, leaving me too queasy to eat.

As the food made its way around, Finnian insisted on filling my plate, his concerned gaze fixed on me. Everyone ate in an uncomfortable silence that had been lingering since our flight home.

"We all have much to discuss," Lia broke the quiet as she took her last bite of food.

"What happened?" Landon asked.

My sister's gaze flashed to me and then back to him. "It has become evident to me that I underestimated the true nature of those we sought, and I should have listened to Veli's warnings." She flashed the sorceress an apologetic look.

"So those witches won't be working with us?" Finn realized.

"They will not be," she answered. "The High Witch of the coven has also managed to reclaim the book of dark magic."

"What?!" he gasped. "How?"

My stare moved around the table, and no one would look at me.

"It was my fault," I stated. "I stole the book from where Veli had hidden it and brought it with me. They were able to rip it from our grasp without even touching it." My head bowed in shame.

"Avery," Finn whispered as his stare seemed to see right through me. He turned back to Lia. "Where does this leave us in the war?"

"That is precisely what we need to find out," Zaela cut in. "We no longer have the hope that magic will aid our victory, and we have an army full of mortals that are significantly easier to kill. We need to be smart."

"We have magic," Veli huffed. "But it is that of a single witch. It's still something. Do not count me out entirely."

A wicked smile crept up Zaela's face at Veli's challenging remark, and she placed her hand atop the witch's. I glanced over at Finn, who also took note of their interaction, and he looked at me with a knowing smirk and shrugged.

"I will take the blame for what happened at The Elora Isles," Lia said.

"No. It was my fault." My voice was as firm as I could muster—I wouldn't let her be held responsible for what I had done.

"You shouldn't have come with us," she said sternly, and I flinched. "You weren't ready, and I know that you never had any intention of what happened, but what's done is done. I led us there. The fault is mine."

"Lia," I pleaded softly, but she held up her hand to stop me.

"I've been thinking too much like a captain and not enough like a queen. Commanding and ruling are not one and the same, and I had been a fool to think it would be. I don't just have to worry about soldiers under my command but the innocents who rest in their homes as we fight to protect them. My way of thinking has proven futile, and I'm inclined to believe that I need an adviser if I am to further lead this rebellion to victory."

Jace snorted next to her, and her eyes slowly wandered to him. "Is something funny?" she asked, a hint of amusement in her tone.

"You realize you would need to *listen* to an advisor, right, my Lia?" He winked.

She cackled softly. "As much as it pains me, yes."

Gage stood from the table. "My dearest queen, you may hold your breath for the question you are about to ask. For I accept." He gave her a deep bow, and I suppressed my giggle at his attempt to lighten the mood.

"Gage, sit down," Zaela demanded, but her words ended in a laugh.

"Why would it be you?" Finnian teased, and it surprised me.

"Well, who else would it be?!" He sat down, grinning.

Lia was at the opposite end of the table, leaning back in her chair with her arms crossed as she observed everyone and their fake bickering. She looked at her mate and winked.

"Are the lot of you done?" she asked with a smirk.

Everyone went silent.

"I had a lot of time to think and process everything that has happened in the last few weeks on our flight back to the valley. Even though I remain throneless, I have made the decision to bring back the position of The King's Lord. Only moving forward, it will be referred to as The Queen's Aide."

We all exchanged confused glances but remained quiet as she observed us.

"I have made many mistakes. Too many. Some of these almost resulted in losing those I care about." She glanced at Jace. "My reign will not be based on singular, impulsive decisions. You are all the court of my crown, and matters will be decided together. However, there is one of you who has significantly more experience regarding the inner workings of the realm, and I would be honored if she were to give me a second chance at taking her advice."

Jace crossed his arms as he smiled at the sorceress who sat three seats down from him, and I found my lips doing the same.

Their fuchsia and green eyes were suddenly locked in a fierce gaze, and Veli's nails tapped impatiently on the table, creating a rhythmic clicking sound as they stared each other down.

"I have offered advice to you many times, Elianna, and you did not heed my warnings."

"I know," Lia admitted again. "This is my sincere apology before our court. You know the realm and its people and have served for centuries as a healer. My father trusted you—*I* trust you."

"Why is it you have suddenly deemed that you need an aide?"

"Every great ruler had one," I answered.

"Your father did not. The King's Lord has not been a filled position in over a century," she stated.

The corners of Lia's lips tilted upward. "He had one, just not in title, but he always considered him his aide."

My heart sank as I thought about Lukas and all he had done for our father.

Veli averted her stare from my sister. "And what would this position in your little court of rebels entail, Elianna?"

Lia smiled at her. "Telling me when I'm being foolish, which I know is your favorite."

Veli's eyes softened. "And you will stop acting like a youngling and listen?"

"I will do my very best."

Jace chuckled, placing his hand atop Lia's as it rested on the table. "She makes no promises, but your advice moving forward will not be disregarded."

"He's always had a better way with words," Lia said, gesturing to him with her thumb as he sat at her side. "So what say you, Veli? Will you give this throneless heir one more chance to prove she can rule? For a better realm."

Veli huffed out a breath. "A better realm." Her eerie gaze lifted back to my sister, still swirling with fuchsia from the use of shadows at the isles. "I enjoyed your father's company, and he wore his benevolence on his sleeve, but that cost him his reign."

"We are in agreement there," Lia answered. "That and his concern for my wellbeing."

"You, Elianna..." She paused for a moment. "You are headstrong...impulsive and erratic." Lia's gaze stayed locked on the witch, unblinking, as we all anxiously waited to see how Veli would respond to her proposal.

"However, you are also loyal to any end. More protective and fierce than any ruler I have seen sit upon that throne. The realm as we know it will cease to exist regardless of the outcome of this war. I have been a one-witch rebellion, and we have all witnessed its consequence."

Veli stood from the table as she lifted her glass of wine, and every single pair of eyes in the room lifted with her. "If I am to be remembered as one thing, let it be this—not a traitor or rebel. I accept your offer of The Queen's Aide, Elianna."

We all stood in unison, raising our glasses in a toast alongside Veli.

"To our queen," Jace announced.

"To a better realm," I echoed.

Lia's eyes wandered over each of us. "To my court," she declared, resulting in us all emptying our glasses in tandem.

THIRTY-SEVEN

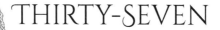

Kellan

I PATROLLED THE STREETS of Isla, making sure a soldier was posted at every street corner and alley alike. No one entered or exited the city without my knowing, and that was by the gates or the sea.

I had been rounding up guards to post scouts throughout Velyra. We had no idea where Elianna was or what her plans were, but it was safe to assume she wouldn't have stayed in the old city of Silcrowe. And with my lies tethered to me under the queen's grasp, I couldn't let her know I knew of it. Everything had to be handled with caution to ensure my web of lies didn't unravel beneath me.

The only thing we truly knew was that the bitch couldn't hide forever. Whether we had to coax her out once more or meticulously scour every corner of the realm, we *would* find her and slaughter her little band of rebels.

"Adler," Braynon called to me as I was stalking toward the seaport.

I pivoted on my heel, not bothering to fix the annoyance on my face. "Braynon, always a pleasure. How can I assist?"

I wanted nothing more than to wipe this lingering weasel off the face of the continent.

"There has been an arrival at the gates," he announced. "No one gets in or out of the city without being vetted by you, Captain." His words had a lingering bite to them, as if he couldn't bear the thought that I was accepted by the queen upon my return.

"Well, who is it?" I barked.

"I'm not sure if I would be able to answer that." He frowned. "It would be best if you follow me." He turned to walk back toward the gates on the opposite side of the city.

After following him through the streets, watching as all the passers avoided eye contact with me, we finally reached the front of the city.

The guards inclined their heads at me as they lifted the gate, allowing me to storm between the two towers.

Two figures hidden within the shadows of their hooded cloaks now stood before me. "Who are you, and why have you come to Isla?" I demanded.

Their gazes lifted to my own, and my eyes flared at what I saw—two pairs of red gazes gleaming at me.

I took a hesitant step toward them as my hand instinctively flew to the hilt of my sword. "I will ask you once more, who are you, and wh—"

One of them lifted her hood and gently placed it to rest on her shoulders, but it wasn't her long onyx hair or sharpened talons that made me feel threatened, but the remaining crimson stare that was locked on me.

"You are the captain, I presume?" she asked, her voice echoing in an otherworldly essence.

"Aye," I offered.

"We have come to speak to your queen."

My eyes quickly darted to the one who had yet to reveal themselves. "We are under strict orders to not allow anyone into the city, and I'm afraid that a meeting with the queen would be out of the question, even for a citizen. Never mind someone who is an..." I looked her up and down. "Outsider."

The second figure removed its hood to reveal a crone beneath it, her appearance vastly different from the other who stood before me, yet she shared the same eerie stare.

"You refuse refuge to two lonely females?" she taunted.

I smirked at her. "It isn't refuge you seek. You demand the queen as an audience for something." Ignoring the hairs that stood up in alarm on the back of my neck, I leaned down toward her. "Now, I must politely ask you to leave the city of Isla, or you will face the wrath of the noose for trespassing."

A sinister grin tilted her lips while her eyes began to glow, and as I quickly moved to unsheathe my sword, my body froze.

What the fuck?!

Suddenly, it felt as if lethal claws were dragging themselves through my skull. And, no matter how hard I strained, my limbs remained immobile, as if they were made of stone.

Sorcery.

"What is the meaning of this?" I attempted to say through my teeth.

"I told you, Captain," she started. "We wish to speak to your queen. And we need *you* to ensure that is possible."

Before I could process a word the witch spoke, my vision became a hazy blur. Talons scraped down my mind, and then my feet marched without my permission. All control of my body vanished, and I unwillingly led them back through the gates, past the guards that stood watch, and up to the castle where the queen awaited.

The Queen

These passing weeks, Adler ensured that every request I made regarding the city was instantly fulfilled, effectively bringing order within the once chaotic streets. The riots and gatherings that had been occurring since my children abandoned me had ceased.

The masses now bowed before me on days I patrolled with guards at my side. Curfews were set, and my captain was working diligently to build up our army with young males as we prepared to march to the mortal lands to destroy them entirely.

Citizens learned quickly that their pitiful pleas for the mercy of their sons fell on deaf ears. I stripped away their freedoms, like petals plucked from a shriveling flower, just as Elianna had from the two that I loved most in the world. Not only that, but she also had managed to turn my other two children against me as well.

I wouldn't let the wyvern-riding rebel bitch steal my kingdom from me, too.

In the dimly lit throne room of the castle, I stood upon the dais, my ebony gown flowing like a river of shadows around the foot of the throne. The room echoed with a sinister silence, broken only by the distant sounds of the newly appointed staff that roamed about the castle, tiptoeing around me as if I would strike them as they passed.

My fingers traced the elaborate armrest of the throne; each touch was imbued with a sense of satisfaction that sent shivers through my icy veins. As my thoughts continued to unfurl, the absence of Callius twisted my heart in agony, and a constant lump in my throat threatened to suffocate me every second of the day without him at my side.

I shoved down the overwhelming anguish, locking it away in the depths of what was left of my soul, and allowed an intense, unyielding rage to take its place.

The doors to the main entrance of the throne room swung open, and Adler stalked through with two females accompanying him. My eyes narrowed in on them beneath furrowed brows.

"Captain, what is the meaning of this?!" I demanded, but no words left him. In fact, his body was rod straight aside from the bending of his knees as his legs carried him toward me. My face twisted into a scowl as I stood from my throne.

"Queen Idina, I presume," the younger of the two spoke. Her voice threatened to send a shiver down my spine, but I ignored the sensation.

"Who are you?"

"Oh, apologies, Your Highness. How rude of me." She snapped her fingers, and the tension in Adler's body instantly eased, earning my curiosity.

"You stupid bitch!" Kellan roared at her, but the female dismissed him with a wave of her hand, sending his body violently flying back into the wall.

My eyes flared, and then my gaze slowly wandered back to the female that approached the dais. I wouldn't show her an ounce of fear. This was *my* kingdom.

"Can I help you ladies with something?" I asked as I tilted my head to the side, ignoring Adler as he pushed himself to his feet and stood at the edge of the room, huffing out in anger.

"Your Majesty," she said with a sly smile. "We have come to offer our services to aid you in your war against the heir of the realm."

My gaze widened. "There is no longer an heir to the realm, for my son is dead."

As she watched me intently, she mimicked my head tilt as her eyes narrowed in curiosity. "You have more than just one child, my queen, but none of those are whom I speak of."

My jaw ticked. "This kingdom doesn't recognize any other heir."

"But it does. The realm always recognizes the blood of a *true* Valderre."

My gaze whipped to the guards that remained at the door and then to Kellan. "Seize them!"

Adler hesitantly stormed toward the females that stood before me, and to my surprise, the one who spoke allowed him to place her hands behind her back without a fight.

"I am Azenna, High Witch of The Elora Coven, and I promise you that I am able to break free from any binding you place me in faster than you can blink."

My jaw throbbed with pain from clenching it tightly as my eyes flickered anxiously between the two of them. "What is it that you seek from me?"

The corners of her lips tilted into a grin. "I want the same as you. To teach those who seek to steal from us that it cannot go unpunished." When I didn't respond, she continued. "You see, Your Highness, I serve no one. I am a queen in my own right. In my own species."

"That is treasonous to say, especially from where you stand, witch."

"Hmm," she hummed. "I am looking to form an alliance. I have no interest in your throne; my only desire is to exact vengeance on those who have wronged me. And you and I share a common enemy."

I cackled. "And what has Elianna Solus done to you, High Witch?"

"Aside from storming into my homelands and attempting to persuade us into aiding her claim to the realm, Elianna *Valderre* has done nothing." I snarled at her for correcting my use of her given name. "Her little spiel was rather moving. My desire for revenge stems from the one who accompanies her."

"Veli," I guessed.

"Indeed, and while Elianna is the rightful heir and shall be recognized by the realm as such, she wishes to rid our world of the evil that lurks in its shadows." She paused for a moment while our eyes bore into each other. "*I* am the evil that lurks in those shadows, Highness."

"And you believe I don't want to protect our realm from harmful creatures?" I questioned.

"I have come to barter with you," she admitted. "I will aid you and your victory in this war, and in turn, I wish to be recognized as Queen of Sylis and claim all the land in the enchanted forest and beyond."

I barked out a laugh. "You think I would barter away a third of my continent? Although we have just met, you did not strike me as a foolish female."

The witch vanished before my eyes and appeared next to me in an instant, materializing from shadows she conjured in seconds.

A moment later, both Kellan and the guards at the doors reached for their swords, but as they went to run toward us, time ceased, halting them mid-sprint.

She then put her lips to the tip of my ear, freezing me where I stood. "We shall work together and against anyone who threatens our rule. You will remain Queen of Velyra. I simply wish to have free rein over the ancient wood and the lands beyond—where the humans reside. My sisters are tired of hiding in the shadows of your world, Idina."

It was the first time she stated my name, and it sent a spark of fury through me, as if her speaking it gave her leverage.

"You wish to harm those who enter the forest?" I questioned.

She barked a laugh as she took a step back from me. "The forest will do that itself, Highness...but if we are to start an alliance, honesty would be a good place to begin. So, to answer your question, I may partake in a bit of fun."

My eyes roamed over her slowly. "I suppose those who matter have been made aware of the threats that linger between those trees."

"Aye," she whispered as she took another step back, but her ruby eyes remained on me. A snap of her taloned fingers had the guards dropping to the floor as she released her hold on them.

Since Callius left the realm, all I craved was power—power that was untainted and feared. The possibility that these witches could provide exactly that was too enticing to ignore.

"You have proven that you can vanish and appear and move objects with a wave of your hand." I gestured to Adler, who let out an annoyed huff. "Prove to me you have further magic to offer, and you may have yourself a bargain."

"Your Majesty?!" Kellan called, but I instantly silenced him as he stared up at me, gawking.

My gaze shot back to the High Witch. "Well?"

A venomous, hushed giggle sounded, as if it were coming from all directions as she disappeared into her shadows once more and appeared where she originally stood.

"I thought you would say that," she said, her figure flickering and transforming into wisps of darkness. Her eyes moved to the crone, who had remained silent.

The crone reached into the fold of her floor-length cloak, her bony, aged fingers grasping an object of shimmering onyx that gleamed amethyst in the candlelight.

"Is this supposed to mean something to me?" I demanded.

Azenna observed me for a moment. "Do you know what your nemesis holds in her possession? What she plans to lead her victory with? For it is not just an army of mortals."

My teeth clenched as I watched her from where she stood at the edge of the dais. "My wyvern," I admitted. "Did you destroy it? Is that all that remains of the beast?" I pointed to the scale in the crone's hand.

"Hardly. We would never seek to destroy a creature as magnificent and destructive as a wyvern. We worked to steal the beast from her but were counterattacked in our siege," she growled. "However, not all was lost during our attempt."

The High Witch took the scale from the crone and approached me once more, slowly making her way up the steps to where I stood before my throne. She handed it to me, the surface of it smooth beneath the touch of my fingers but solid as polished stone.

"What would you have me do with a wyvern's scale, *witch*?" I hissed at her.

A smile formed leisurely across her face as her eyes bore into me. "It is not what *you* can do with it, my queen, but what *I* can."

My eyes flared without permission in response, but the rest of my body remained perfectly composed.

"Tell me, Queen Idina, do you have an unused keep in your fortress?"

My stare darted to Adler—his eyes were fixed on us with unwavering intensity, his initial wariness replaced by an evident curiosity.

"I do not," I answered, as my eyes drifted back to her. "But I *do* have a dungeon."

THIRTY-EIGHT

Kellan

B<small>RAYNON AND TWO GUARDS</small> led the way through the courtyard and down to the dungeons, where the queen had offered the witches a place to put their magic on display. I walked alongside Idina, positioned behind the others, as we followed them.

My body couldn't shake the feeling of being under the High Witch's spell. She effortlessly commanded and steered my body any way she desired with just a movement of her wrist. I had never been a fear-driven male—in fact, I absolutely despised them. However, the suffocating darkness that crept beneath my skin as she took control of me sent an undeniable alarm through me.

This was no longer just a war of fae and mortals. An unknown power had entered unannounced, and it threatened us all. Not only that, but it threatened my fucking plans for it.

The queen was desperate to hold on to the power she obtained through cold-blooded murder. Desperation led to a lack of judgment, and if she believed the High Witch had unlimited power, that meant she could eliminate me from my position. I had no fucking time to be dealing with such nonsense.

"My queen, I feel as though…" I started in a hushed whisper.

"I do not pay you for your opinions, Captain," she cut me off. "You are employed to lead our armada and guards in the direction I demand of you. Nothing more."

"Is it wise to put such trusting fate in a pair of monsters that show up at your city's door unannounced? After they had just been with Elianna? It could be a trap."

Her eyes remained forward as our steps continued. "You truly believe that they would offer to aid our victory in the war if they were working for Elianna?"

No, I fucking didn't. But that didn't mean I wanted them around, either.

"You would barter away a piece of your realm at the first force of power that presented itself to you? My queen, I know I am not a King's Lord, however—"

"Correct, you are not. And I am no king. I am the *queen* and have no need for an advisor, and if there were ever a time I did, it would never be you, Captain."

My jaw locked as my hands balled into fists at my sides. Everything I worked for was gone in an instant and by fucking *females*. I refused to remain just the captain of the queen's guard.

I bit my tongue with so much force that blood trickled to the back of my throat as I worked to choke down my retort.

Her steps slowed, and mine matched on instinct, pushing a farther gap between us and those who led the group to the dungeon's cavern.

"I have been advised by males my entire life, Captain," she admitted softly after a few moments of silence. "I will not be bartering away a single sliver of my land. When the time comes, we will be rid of them, even if I once again have to slit a throat myself."

My steps faltered at what she declared, but hers remained marching forward, leaving me behind in the dark, twisting halls of her dungeons.

Once we arrived at the back of the cavern, my memory flashed back to when Elianna escaped. My eyes darted to the far corner of the space, where the crumbling rocks that fell from the tunneled ceiling remained.

Braynon moved to light the torches that were fastened along the walls, but with a wave of the High Witch's hand, flames ignited at each pillar.

Her focus returned to the queen.

"Queen, is this the space you are able to provide for us?" Her gaze shifted to the chains on the floor. "Ah, this was once the beast's home."

"It was," Idina answered as she took a few steps up to the witch. "Before Elianna stole it from us and rode it out of the city as if it were a warhorse. Now tell me, Azenna, what purpose does this cavern serve you?"

Azenna's gaze met the crone's, who stood by her side, an eerie stillness surrounding her as she watched us all attentively. As she extended her hand, the decrepit woman placed the wyvern scale into her open palm.

The High Witch shot me a wicked grin right before she moved to the center of the open space and placed the scale on the ground before returning to our side.

"The queen asked you a question," I growled. "It would be wise to answer before her patience is lost and your time has run out."

Her eyes began to faintly glow as she turned her attention to where the queen stood. "You asked me what the space was needed for, and I am about to prove to you only a fraction of what our power can do."

Before anyone could respond, the air crackled with a sinister energy, and storm-like winds brewed within the confines of the dungeon.

Azenna stepped forward, her silhouette draped in an elaborate cloak that seemed to absorb the dim torchlight, and raised her arms with deliberate grace. Her eyes, pools of red-rimmed darkness, gleamed with an otherworldly intensity.

As if in answer to her High Witch, a book materialized in the crone's hands, and she then began chanting words I couldn't understand as she read from its pages.

As her spell echoed through the stillness of the cavern, the wyvern scale on the ground began to quiver. Ethereal wisps of smoky essence curled and danced in the air as tiny cracks appeared on its surface.

With each word uttered by the crone, the fractures on the scale widened, revealing a ghostly light that gleamed like liquid moonlight.

"Holy fucking gods," I breathed as my eyes were locked on the scene.

The ground beneath the scale trembled as violent shadows swirled and intertwined with the blazing embers that shot out from its cracks.

Flowing shadows took shape as tendrils of darkness emerged from the fractured scale, twisting and contorting within the confines of the dungeon. A deep, ferocious growl rumbled through the air, putting us all on edge as the tendrils solidified, taking the form of enormous, leather-like wings and a serpentine neck.

My heart raced as I tore my gaze from the madness that was unfolding before us all. My eyes found the queen as she watched—the female was unafraid and completely awe-struck by all that was occurring in front of us. It was in that moment that I knew *everything* regarding this century-old war was about to change.

A fully grown wyvern, conjured from dark magic and the sacrifice of a single scale, now stood before us as it unfurled its wings. Its scales were a shade of obsidian with an otherworldly, blood-red sheen. Eyes that glowed like burning embers replicating that of its maker were fixed upon the queen, radiating both intelligence and an ancient cruelness.

"Your Highness," Azenna spoke once the wyvern's echoing growl ceased. "I present to you my first gift for your war."

The queen moved to take a step toward the wyvern, and I, on instinct, took a step in front of her. "You don't know if that beast will harm you."

I truly didn't give a damn if it did, but if Idina was eliminated, it would pave the way for Elianna to waltz in through the city gates and take the realm that was promised to her by blood. I still needed to climb my way to the top. The queen said I would never move up to be her advisor, but sooner or later, she would miss having a warm body in her bed—I wasn't about to come this fucking far to give up now.

The queen craned her neck to look back at the High Witch. "Will it?" she asked. "Harm me."

"It will not, Highness, for it is under mind control by my dearest Sylvae." She gestured to the crone, who looked at us with glowing eyes.

"So you will control what the wyvern does?"

"Indeed, we can by tapping into the beast's mind. However, the magic he will be under when in use with his rider will link their minds together, giving the rider full control and steer the beast as he wishes."

"Rider?" I barked.

"Do you not wish to ride the wyvern, Captain?" Azenna tilted her head to the side, but a knowing grin tilted her haunting face.

"You stated Elianna rode out of this very dungeon on the back of my lost beast," the queen snapped at me. "You also declared that she rode the wyvern to battle when you were attacked at the foot of the Sylis Forest."

"Aye, but I take to the seas, not the sky," I huffed out.

She took a step toward me, and it took every effort in me to have my gaze not drift over her shoulder to where the eyes of the fire-breathing abomination stared me down.

She put her lips to the tip of my ear, stunning me in shock as she whispered, "Are you stating that your treasonous ex-love is braver than you, Captain?"

A low, wicked laugh left me. "Never."

The queen took a step back and looked into my eyes, but it was as if she saw directly through me—using me as a pawn in her game for the throne.

"Then prove it and consider the sky your new sea," she demanded. "You will bond with this beast just as she has with the one she stole from me. And then you will ride it into battle, engulfing both her and her precious mortals in its flames. Have I made myself clear?"

My eyes gradually wandered away from hers and to the wyvern that stood at attention behind her while the witches stood off to the side, listening to the words spoken between us.

"Crystal," I answered.

"Tell me, High Witch," I started. "What does bonding with this beast entail? Elianna didn't have magic to have hers listen to commands. It just *did*."

She looked me up and down. "I can create a link between the two of you, connecting your minds and allowing you to will the wyvern as you see fit. It will bend at your beck and call if you are in near proximity."

"Show me," Idina demanded. "Show me this link you can create between them."

My eyes flared as the queen offered me up to this stranger's witch magic so freely.

The High Witch held her hand out to me. "Your wrist, Captain, if you wouldn't mind."

"And if I do?" My jaw ticked as my eyes narrowed in on her.

A soft smile graced her lips, but her eyes remained calculative. "I do not believe your queen is giving you a choice in the matter."

"If he wishes to remain in his rank and eventually climb further, he will do this," the queen's voice echoed behind me.

Now the bitch was just playing mind games with me. Not even an hour ago, she stated that this is where I would remain under her reign.

I reluctantly strolled up to Azenna and offered her my hand. She took her taloned finger and swiped it across the top of it, and blood instantly pooled.

"What the fuck!" I barked, and as I was about to lash out at her, my blood started to float into the air, as if they were bubbles from a youngling's bath.

My eyes drifted over to the crone, who held the wyvern in her mind control as she did the same thing to the underside of its stomach.

Azenna fused my blood with that of the wyvern and began mumbling more words in an ancient language, her eyes glowing once again. She held her hands out as our blood spun together at impossible speeds, and as she widened the stance of her arms, the spinning orb of mixing blood separated into two, parting at her will.

My gaze shot to the queen, who continued to watch in malicious awe.

Suddenly, Azenna's arms shot out wide at her sides, and a gust of wind burst from the spinning orbs, making us all instinctively shield our faces.

I blinked through the dust and dirt that was kicked up from the force of the wind she created, and once my eyes were able to focus, they landed on twin cuffs levitating in the air, one significantly larger than the other.

"What are those?" I demanded.

"Your links," she answered and then held her hand out to me once more. "It will also serve as a barrier for exterior magic cast by other creatures."

My lip curled up, but I offered her my wrist. The smaller cuff shot out and clasped around it, locking itself onto me. An unbearable burning radiated from my wrist the moment it locked, and I hissed, vigorously shaking my hand from her grasp.

"What the fuck is this?!" My gaze snapped back to her just as she clasped the other around the beast's neck. The scales beneath its new collar glowed in flames for a moment before fading away.

I lifted my arm towards my face and observed what the witch had done, rotating it as my eyes glimpsed over every inch of my skin. The cuffs resembled metal but were the color of our blended blood. Where the cuff had clasped itself to my body, it left a burn mark on my skin, resembling licks of flames creeping up my forearm.

"Now that you bear its mark, you may test your newfound bond, Captain," Azenna offered as she gestured to the wyvern and took a step to the side.

The crone followed her movements and dropped her control that she had on the beast. I took a step toward it, and it eyed me warily as he sized me up. He puffed his chest out at me, and his jaw cracked open as a growl rumbled through him.

"Command it, Adler," the queen ordered.

"To do what?" I whispered to myself. I was a brave male and would die before I ever admitted otherwise, but what the fuck did they expect me to do with *this*?

Several feet before the wyvern, my steps came to a halt, our eyes locked. I finally ordered it to do what I had always fantasized about commanding the realm itself to do.

"Bow," I demanded, and as if placed into an immediate trance, the beast tucked in its wings and lowered its head to the ground at my feet.

My eyes flared as all sense of concern melted away, a grin now stretching ear-to-ear.

I turned on my heel to face the queen, and she gave me a nod of approval. She then pivoted to face the High Witch, her gown flowing around through the dirt at her feet. "You have yourself a bargain."

THIRTY-NINE

Elianna

A week had passed since we returned from The Elora Isles, and all hands were on deck. The courthouse in the heart of Anerys became our war chamber for devising battle strategies, where we spent most of our time if we weren't out in the fields training with the men.

I stood before the table that lay in the center of our space, which had been expertly carved from stone that served as a map of the realm—a true map—one that included all landmarks on this side of the Ezranian Mountains. My eyes drifted over the crevices engraved into it, representing every mountain, city, and forest that lay between the mortal lands and that of the fae.

Streams of sunlight filtered through the chamber's windows, illuminating the intricate patterns carved before me.

Jace had strategically placed colored markers throughout the replica of the realm, each representing a battalion under our command that was ready to move at a moment's notice. Every point and potential route was meticulously planned, turning the unique table into a chessboard of war where each move held consequences.

My hand reached over the stone, tracing the lines with my fingertips. A flurry of thoughts and strategies raced through my mind as I carefully assessed the cost of each decision we would be forced to make from here on out. My thoughts were a whirlwind of doubt and determination—a constant storm raging within me.

A vivid map materialized in my mind, not of the battlefields, but of the faces of those whose lives rested on the choices we made—the soldiers who placed their trust in both me and my mate to lead them to victory.

My chest rose and fell beneath the weight of guilt and responsibility. I was constantly haunted by the knowledge that, in the end, lives would be lost and families would be broken, no matter how fiercely we fought.

The door behind me creaked open, followed by slow footsteps. His scent enveloped me the moment the air wafted in my direction—a scent I had become addicted to—cedarwood and embers with clashing steel.

"There she is." His voice drifted to me, wrapping around me like a warm embrace.

I turned to face my mate and placed my hands on the table's edge as I leaned into it from behind. "You found me."

"If you were looking to not be caught, somewhere we don't spend hours every day would have been wiser, my Lia."

I chuckled softly. "It's not that." I turned and looked at the stone map once more. "I just want to make sure we go through every possible outcome. I don't want to be in a position we can't get out of. She can't win. Not again. We need to start preparing our troops to march south, even if we need to take it slow to avoid as much exhaustion as possible." My hand balled into a fist as it rested atop the table.

Jace gave me a dip of his chin and approached me slowly. He lifted his hand and gently gripped my chin between two of his fingers, tilting my gaze to his. Hazel eyes locked me in a trance as they bore into my own.

"She won't win." My lips tilted in a soft smile at his words. "This war has only one way it will end, and that is with you sitting on that throne."

He pressed his lips to mine, and it took my breath away. No matter how much time we spent together, it would never be enough. There was nothing my mind or body craved more than *him*.

The moment the warmth of his lips left my own, I was flooded with a sense of emptiness—feeling insatiable by his touch. His warm breath tickled my lips as his mouth hovered dangerously close to mine.

"You're a tease," I hissed, and he let out a breathy chuckle that threatened to make my knees go weak. "What good is a mate if you don't have time to enjoy one another?"

"I will make that time. Always," he stated before he claimed my mouth in a demanding kiss that sent a rush of heat between my thighs.

I wrapped my arms around the back of his neck, and he responded by spinning us impossibly fast and guiding my back down onto the table beneath me—the carved crevices of the mountain peaks dug into my skin, forcing a gasp out of me.

I reached down to unbuckle the belt of his pants, but he caught my wrists, stopping me and leaving me snarling in aggravation.

Our mouths collided once more in a deep, needy kiss as he took my wrists in his hand and secured them above my head. In tandem, his other hand worked to unbutton the front of my shirt, exposing the peaks of my breasts as the fabric fell to the side.

"I stand by the *tease* statement," I growled.

"Who's teasing?"

His tongue trailed up my neck, and he took the tip of my ear gently between his teeth as he captured one of my nipples between two of his fingers, squeezing them in the most delicious taunt.

"Jace!" I gasped as my core liquified from the heat now pulsing through my body.

Hovering over me, he had one knee propped on the table while his other leg remained planted on the ground. He held his bottom lip between his teeth as he stared down at me beneath him.

His eyes desperately roamed over me as our deep panting filled the air. "You are exquisite. And you are *mine*."

"Always," I whispered.

His eyes flared as our word left me—the word I had continuously used with him. Because it was all that would ever matter. He and I together—*always*.

That was all it took to unleash him.

His mouth was all over me—everywhere at once, holding me in place beneath him as he roamed and explored every inch of me with his tongue. Tracing it down my lips, throat, and breasts until it reached my core.

"If I release your hands, you must promise that you will behave," he growled, sending a shiver up my spine.

"You, of all people, should know that I never make such promises."

"That's my girl," he cooed.

Jace released my wrists, and his hand flew to my pants, unbuttoning them in an undeniable, hurried need. He ripped my pants down my legs, dragging my body slightly down the table with it, and I ignored the scraping that dug into my back from the stone beneath me—the pain of it only added to the pleasure.

Before I could grasp what he was up to, his arms spread my legs wide, putting me on display for him as his mouth secured my center in the same breath.

A sound that was half moaning, half gasping left me, as he started to devour me. Sliding a finger into me, his tongue lapped at my pussy, working me like I was the best thing he ever tasted, or as if he were savoring his last meal.

It wasn't enough. It would *never* be enough.

My hands gripped the waves in his thick hair and then moved down to explore his skin. Another flick of his tongue sent my nails digging into his shoulder blades.

More desperate moans escaped me, bouncing off the walls of our war chamber as his touch became more frenzied.

My entire body felt as if it would burst into flames and my arms, on instinct, sprawled out at my sides, wiping away all the markers we had placed for our army.

His movements faltered at the sound of the pieces crashing to the floor.

"Don't you *dare* stop," I panted.

Jace took that as his cue to ravage me, expertly flicking his tongue as he added another finger, drawing out every last bit of pleasure from my body. He curled them perfectly inside of me and my thighs locked around his shoulders, holding him in place.

My breathing turned heavier as my nipples and core tightened. Feeling as if I had no control over my body, I gripped his arms, digging my nails into his skin as release was ravaging every single one of my senses.

One last flick of his tongue sent me in a spiral, and it felt as if my body had ignited in a liquid inferno.

"Oh, gods!" I gasped out as my back arched off the table, riding my orgasm out on his fingers as his movements slowed perfectly. As he touched me, he read my body's reactions as if they were a novel he had memorized every word to—every page turn and scene.

As the feeling of ecstasy slowly subsided, I came to—the only sound that filled the room was my panting as I worked to catch my breath.

Jace pulled himself to his feet and then crawled up the table I remained sprawled out on, lying next to me, and ignoring the fact that we just destroyed our, very strategically placed, battle layout.

My neck pivoted to face him as he watched me intently. His eyes exuded nothing but love, but his grin was wicked.

A smile tilted my lips as I began to giggle. "You denied me what is *mine*," I joked as my eyes flicked down to the bulge in his pants.

"Forgive me, my queen." He kissed the tip of my nose, and it made my heart flutter. "I just wanted to provide you a gift."

He sat up and jumped down from the table, offering his hand to me and heaving me up with him. My spine ached as the feeling of the carved table left my skin. As I moved to button my shirt, he pushed my hands away and carefully did it for me.

I watched him as a smirk crept up my face. "What are you up to?"

Suddenly, the door swung open, and I nearly leapt out of my skin as I quickly worked to pull my pants back on.

By the time I looked up, Veli stood in the doorway, crossing her arms.

"Ever heard of knocking?!" I gasped, but it ended with a laugh. "On second thought, nobody here has, apparently," I huffed as my memory flashed to Gage doing the same to us after my first night in Ellecaster.

Her fuchsia eyes roamed over me, and then Jace. "Last I checked, the war strategy room in the city's courthouse did not require a knock when I am one of the few with a key." She held it up and then pocketed it in her cloak.

My eyes flew to my mate to see that his cheeks had flushed, yet his wicked grin remained.

"Very well," I offered. "Is something wrong?"

"I believe it's time we had a serious discussion regarding your siblings and their roles in the final stages of this war," she answered.

FORTY

Elianna

STANDING AT THE EDGE of the fields, we watched as Finnian took part in training combat with Gage, and other pairings mimicked their stances down the valley. Nox let out a few chirps as he flew overhead, observing the lessons along with us, his enormous shadow looming over the terrain—we were thankful that the soldiers were growing more comfortable in his presence.

"Come to see the show? I just finished my sparring," Landon said as he walked up to us. "Zaela's down at the other end of the field, assigning new pairings."

"This matchup is hardly fair," I huffed.

"It will be significantly less fair on a battlefield, Elianna," Veli hissed.

A horn sounded, and each pair made their moves to strike. The sound of clashing swords echoed through the fields as the combat matches began. The reverberated *tinging* sounds of steel on steel rang through my ears as Gage expertly swung his sword at my brother, slower than he would in an actual battle.

Gage's years of experience and the training I would like to consider I attributed to were evident in the grace with which he moved.

On the other side, Finnian worked to counter each strike, but his movements were slow—*too* slow. My heart thudded as I watched his face. His eyes were focused, determined to prove himself against a seasoned warrior, but it was apparent that he would never last a day fighting in the war.

"His footwork is all over the place," Jace grumbled at my side as my brother tried to recover from rolling his ankle.

"Move your feet, Finn!" I ordered, and he shot me a look of disapproval over his shoulder.

Finn's gaze burned with ambition, but I knew in my heart I would never be able to live with myself if I allowed him to set foot on the battlefield.

The crowd of onlookers watched in hushed silence until Avery approached me. "I don't know who to even root for," she joked, but I could barely muster up a smile.

Gage struck once more, disarming Finn in an instant and sending his sword flying off to the side of him. Our second-in-command then lightly placed the tip of his blade to the center of my brother's armor and gave him a nod.

They both turned to us as they worked to catch their breath. I pressed my lips together as I forced an awkward smile while they moved to approach us.

"What do you suppose we do?" I asked Veli.

"I have a plan," she answered. "But he is not going to like it."

My nostrils flared as I glanced her way and then back to my brother.

"And what might that be, Veli?" Jace asked as his stare remained on the two of them.

"Let me train the boy to be a healer."

Both of our eyes snapped back to her.

"A healer?" I said.

"He would still be close to the battle but not on the fields where death would certainly find him. He wishes to be made useful—this is a way that saves him and helps others," she declared.

"I am inclined to agree," Jace stated.

"You're right. He definitely won't like that," Landon chimed in from where he stood off to the side. "But I also agree."

Gage and Finn reached us then.

"I'm sorry, Lia," Finn started. "I'll do better next time, I promise."

I gave him a soft, tight-lipped smile.

"It's okay, Finny-boy." Gage clapped him on the shoulder. "We'll continue to work on both your sword and footwork."

Finn rolled his eyes in response, but his demeanor quickly changed as Landon stepped up to him and kissed him on the cheek, forcing a blush from him.

"Can we talk, Finn?" I asked quietly.

His eyes wandered over me, and he let out a sad chuckle. "I'm not going to like this, am I?"

I shook my head slowly as I reached my hand out for his.

"No, Lia. Anything you have to say can be said in front of everyone," he grumbled at me. "I don't need to be coddled and scolded for not meeting your standards."

"I would never scold you, Finnian," I snarked. "Coddle, perhaps." A smirk threatened to form on my lips, but I suppressed it.

"You don't think I can do this, do you?" His eyes wandered over each of us as we stood before him. "Even you, Landon?"

"We just want you to be safe," he answered.

Finnian scoffed. "Let's not forget that you were critically injured on the battlefield the last time *you* set foot on it. I could say the same for you," he snapped.

"You're right. *And* I have more training," Landon admitted.

"That is hardly fair!" Finn's voice rose alongside his aggravation.

"But it's the truth," I stated. "We just want you to be safe."

"And I want the same for all of you!" he shouted, making me flinch. "No one will be safe out there! Not a single one of you. We could all die. Not just me. Why is no one else thinking of this?!"

Curious eyes of the nearby soldiers wandered to us as his voice continued to rise. Jace huffed out a sigh as he stepped away from our group while waving his arms to shoo the onlookers away.

"I think of that every second of every gods-damn day, Finnian Valderre." A bite now inched its way into my tone. "I'm sorry that you're upset, but it's for your own good."

"And Avery will be out on the fields when she has just as little training as I?"

"That is yet to be determined, but likely not," I answered. Avery nodded along with my words.

"I just want to be made useful," he said sadly.

"I know, which is why we have a new plan."

Veli stepped up to Finn, her violet stare locking him in a nervous trance. "The world could always use more healers, boy. Your mother banning them over a century ago has made them few and far between."

His eyes flared and then shot back to me. "You want me to learn to be a *healer*? How is there time for such things but not combat training?"

"Look at me, you foolish male," Veli hissed, and he pursed his lips as he did as he was told. "I will teach you the ways of saving lives. You will be provided with as much training and workings as time allows. You will be much more useful there."

"How? You are the realm's most talented healer, Veli. And for good reason."

"She will likely not be in the healers' tents," I cut in. His brows furrowed in response. "Veli will be needed on the fields."

"You mean her magic will be needed," he sassed.

"Precisely," Veli snapped. "We are all playing roles we don't necessarily wish to have. Now it's time to grow up and recognize the areas where your contribution will be most valuable."

Just as I was about to speak again, a strange and unsettling energy filled the air. Power crackled through the sky as dark clouds quickly moved in on the horizon, and the winds picked up, blowing our hair in all directions.

"What's happening?!" Avery shrieked, and Gage moved to cover her, shielding her behind his arms as the winds continued to assault us on all sides.

Nox let out a deafening screech in the air as the power continued to surge.

Jace and Zaela sprinted towards us as the last of the soldiers sought cover from the winds, running back towards the barracks on the far side of the field.

We formed a tight circle, our backs pressed against each other, as we each unsheathed our weapons from our sides.

"Veli!" I barked over the roaring winds. "What's happening?!"

"Someone's here," she announced. "I can feel them."

"The coven?!" Avery shrieked.

Fuck. Fuck. Fuck. How did they find us?!

"Look!" Zaela's voice boomed as she pointed into the distance, her finger aimed at two figures materializing from swirling shadows atop a hill.

Jace's stare flashed to meet mine, and his worry shot down the bond. Worry for us. Worry for our innocent people that rested safely only a mile away in the distance.

"Veli..." My voice dragged out her name as fear slammed into me.

This couldn't be happening. Not before we've had a chance to fight.

My aide's eyes glowed as she stared off at two of her lost sisters. A moment later, the wind ceased, and the skies cleared faster than I could blink. The dark clouds formed by their shadows evaporated from thin air.

"It is Madalae and Empri," Veli announced to us.

The witch twins.

We all remained on high alert, ready to strike if necessary.

"What is it they want? And where is Azenna?" I growled.

Suddenly, their eerie voices echoed all around us in unison, as if it were flowing through the air. "*We wish to speak to the heir of the realm. Alone.*"

"Of course they do," Veli hissed.

"Not going to fucking happen," Jace growled as he tightened his grip on the pommel of his sword.

My gaze drifted to the sky as Nox circled above us. A grin formed on my face then.

"I won't be alone," I stated as his hazel stare locked on mine. I gave him a quick wink as my feet pushed me forward, hand remaining on the hilt of my sword as it now hung at my side.

I swaggered my way across the vast field as the heat of the sun beat down on me. The natural breeze gently tugged at the loose strands of my dark hair as Nox's shadow soared overhead, hovering directly above me.

The twins wore mirrored, stern expressions, revealing no hint of vulnerability as I approached. The atmosphere was charged with tension as their crimson stares were locked on me, unblinking.

When my steps halted at the base of the hill they stood upon, the twins glided down as if they were carried by the breeze. We now stood face-to-face, merely ten feet dividing us.

Empri offered a sly, menacing smile. "I must admit, I'm surprised you listened to instructions and approached us alone. You have a unique reputation for going against what is expected of you, *Elianna Valderre*." She uttered my name in a sinister manner, the sound slithering out with an underlying threat.

"And how have you heard of this?"

"The winds whisper all things," Madalae supplied. "However, I am pleasantly surprised."

My grin returned as my head tilted to the side. "Who said I'm alone?"

A moment later, the ground violently shook beneath our feet. A deep growl rumbled through Nox's chest as I felt his menacing presence at my back. His giant, horn-covered head levitated over my shoulder as he hissed at the witches before me—terror flashed across their features briefly as my wyvern stared them down while guarding me.

A wicked chuckle left Empri. "And I now see that your reputation precedes you."

"My enemy has never played fair when it pertains to the victory in this war, so nor will I."

"Who claims that we come as your enemy, Elianna?" she asked. "Perhaps we come here as a favor."

"And why would such a thing be true? The last I saw you, you were aiming to harm not only those I love but also attempting to *steal* my wyvern." The words left me in a snarl, matching the beat of Nox's growl as it persisted behind me.

"We thought you may say that."

"Because it's the truth. It wouldn't be a difficult guess," I barked. "Now tell me what you're doing in these lands before I have Nox set his blaze upon you."

Neither of them spoke.

My eyes thinned into slits as I stared them down. "One ancient, forgotten word from me, and the both of you will burn."

Their crimson stares flared then.

"You threaten those who work to aid you? Is this not what you originally sought?"

"I threaten those who have threatened me and mine. Why should I trust you?"

The twins exchanged a glance before returning their gazes to me.

"We haven't always agreed with Azenna and what she has sought to do since the discovery of *Tinaebris Malifisc* all those centuries ago. And we have come to heed your warning."

My heart thudded at their words, but my face remained neutral as I observed them.

"What of it then? What have you come here to offer?"

"Azenna spoke of declaring her stance on the war by offering her aid to the current queen who sits upon the Velyran throne," Empri stated.

Panic instantly clogged my throat.

"But she is a creature of the realm. The realm itself will only accept a true Valderre as its ruler," I countered.

"Aye, that is why she plans to get her hands on your blood and intertwine it with the queen's using the book. Blood magic works in mysterious ways and has many uses. This could work to trick the realm itself."

I was going to be sick. "Such a thing is possible?" Gods, I hoped she was exaggerating.

"It is true," Madalae relayed.

"So, Azenna has offered Idina her use of dark magic in the war? What did she seek in exchange?" I demanded.

"The lands within and beyond the Sylis Forest. Free roam to hunt and do whatever she pleases with. She wishes to be a recognized queen in her own right."

"That's foolish. Idina would never offer even a sliver of the realm."

Then I thought it over for a moment. If it secured her victory, she may barter away just that, with no intention of keeping her promise.

"The winds have whispered that what you believe is not necessarily true," the twins relayed in unison, causing a shiver to run up my spine.

I remained silent for a moment as my gaze wandered back to my court as they eagerly waited for orders—their stances declared they were ready to charge at any moment if commanded.

"How is it that you found us? Alaia Valley is hidden from the rest of the world, or so we thought," I stated.

"When Azenna spoke of her plan immediately following our encounter, we rushed to leave and watched as you all soared through the clouds. We have been waiting to hear of what the winds speak before deciding what to do next," Empri answered.

My eyes flared as she spoke of watching us this entire time from a distance and us never knowing it. Shaking that eerie thought, my attention drifted back to the twins. "Is it an alliance you seek? Why would you not follow your High Witch?"

They exchanged another look as if communicating their response telepathically.

"We have experienced firsthand the power of what Azenna now holds. When Veli stole the book and went into hiding, we admired her for it. We were too frightened to ever admit it, but what she did was right. If in the wrong hands, the pages bound within it could doom the realm and every creature within it," Madalae answered.

"For a better realm," Empri added.

I huffed out a sharp laugh as she mimicked the mantra of my rebellion. "For a better realm," I echoed.

"My court is to join me in any further discussion regarding this. And you are to give me your word that no magic will be cast in said meeting. Do you agree?" I asked. "And if you break this vow, make no mistake, I will carve your hearts out myself and turn them to ash."

Twin grins formed. "Agreed," they hissed in unison.

FORTY-ONE

Elianna

A<small>FTER A VERY</small> A<small>GGRESSIVE</small> argument between the eight of us, we all agreed it would be best to discuss this newly offered alliance and its terms in the war chamber. Shielding the twin witches' predatory gazes within the confines of their cloaks, we escorted them to the center of our city, being sure that no wary passerby looked too carefully at them as we stalked up the stone steps of our courthouse.

Once inside, everyone took a seat at our tabled map of the realm. Our gazes roamed over one another, waiting to see who would speak first and see what these two previously wicked witches had to offer us.

"Why are all of our station markers knocked over and on the floor?" Gage asked with a laugh as he looked at Jace with a raised brow.

Jace rolled his eyes at him.

"Brother, you dirty bastard, you," he said, and I noticed Avery's cheeks flush as she sat at his side.

"Accidents happen, Gage," I said with a wink.

"We are here on business, you fools," Veli hissed, bringing all of our attentions back to the situation at hand.

Two blazing stares bore into us as they sat side by side at the opposite end of the table from Jace and me.

"Tell them what you spoke of to me. Also, how you have this knowledge and why you are risking treason against your own High Witch for us."

And they did. They told my court everything they had spoken to me out in the fields.

Jace's concern flared, slamming into my own, and I placed my hand on his knee beneath the cover of the table.

"There are still many reservations that I possess regarding your declared allegiance to Lia," he stated sternly as he glared at them.

"What are your concerns, mortal?" Empri asked.

"Let's start with why you slaughtered all my men aboard our ship, potentially leaving us stranded at your forbidden isles, and trying to capture our greatest asset."

His eyes narrowed in on them, and as he spoke, authority radiating off of him in waves—the voice of the commander protecting his people—the voice of a king.

"Apologies for your men," she answered, tone uncaring. "As for your wyvern, we wanted it for ourselves. There are many things you can do with both its desired flame and blood. It is an undeniable, powerful asset to have."

"What makes you think it would have responded to your orders?" Zaela cut in, every bit of her calculating, cold mask apparent.

"There are spells to incite cooperation, blonde one."

A chill ran up my spine as fury flooded me. My hand balled into a fist on Jace's lap right before I lifted it and slammed it down on the table, bringing everyone's attention to me.

"You will not touch him with your sorcery. Nox has been through enough, just as we all have. You. Will. Not. *Touch*. Him." My lip curled back, exposing my canines.

"Yes, yes, Elianna Valderre. We have agreed to no casting of spells upon members of your side of this rebellion. Your wyvern is included in that," Madalae interjected.

"Why now?" Veli interjected. "Why has it taken you centuries to state your true stance. I had never considered you cowards, yet you let me remain a one-witch rebellion all this time. An outcast and traitor." Her voice was a mix of aggravation and hurt, which was rare for the sorceress.

"We have regrets," they answered together. "Things may have turned out differently if we followed your lead all those years ago, but to go against the High Witch is to go against your monarch and maker—always resulting in execution."

"I remain here before you now."

"Aye," Madalae said. "And you have been in hiding. What is a witch without her magic? Or the full potential of it."

My aide swallowed. "Together, we could have possessed the power to overthrow her."

"It likely would have been a battle lost, with her possessing greater use and access to the dark magic."

My eyes flared then. "The crone."

"Sylvae," Empri added.

"Sure." I huffed out through my nostrils. "Why is she significantly older looking than the rest of you? I understand that dark magic brings this on, but how is it that her appearance is such a stark difference from your own?"

"Sylvae found the book centuries ago. It fell into her possession, and before we knew all it entailed, Azenna had ordered that she cast the spells first as a sort of precaution."

I sat back in my chair, slightly more relaxed, as the anger settled slowly. "So she was willing to sacrifice her?"

"Not necessarily," Veli interjected. "Azenna just didn't want any hidden consequences to fall upon her."

"As far as I'm concerned, that is one and the same. It would be as if I chose one of you to engage in something that I feared was a threat. And I would never do such a thing."

"We know, Lia," Jace whispered, easing the last bit of tension that lingered within me.

Empri's eyes remained on him for a moment before she spoke. "Any other concerns..." She sniffed the air. "Mate of the realm's heir?"

She could scent the mating bond without having known us before? I swallowed thickly. Witches' senses truly were significantly stronger than the fae's.

He hesitated before speaking. "When the ship began to sink, Sylvae plucked one of Nox's scales from his back before you all fled. Why is that?"

The twins' eyes flashed to each other quickly and then back to us.

"After we fled, Azenna spoke of her plan to offer her services to the current false queen. We had no interest in disrupting the natural ways of the realm, so we made ourselves scarce before she disclosed any further plans. She believes we just drifted off to where we had been before, and she took Sylvae with her. You are sure this is what you saw?" Madalae asked.

"It happened right before my eyes. I am sure."

Veli sucked in a sharp breath. "You did not tell me this."

"What can she do with his scale, Veli?" I asked.

"There are many things." She paused for a moment as her stare slowly lifted to meet mine. "The one I am most concerned with is replication."

"Replication?" Avery questioned.

"It is possible that she could use the genetic makings of your wyvern, held within its scale, to conjure an entirely new beast."

"That cannot be possible," I whispered.

"It is magic, Heir of the Realm. Anything is possible if you are willing to barter for its asking price," Empri stated.

Tense, disbelieving silence blanketed the war chamber.

"Say they conjure a wyvern," I started. "Would they be in full control of it in battle? That must take some form of immense power."

"You would be correct. Especially a beast as sizable as the one you possess. It would likely take significant focus to keep the beast within constant control."

"Well, that may help us," I thought out loud.

Zaela scoffed, earning disapproving looks from Avery and Finn. "Lia, how? We had one thing on our side, and that was Nox. If they have one, along with dark magic, we have lost before the battle has even begun."

My eyes wandered over each of their faces leisurely as her words sunk in—defeat written into all of their features.

"I see a slightly more even match now," I admitted. "We each *possibly* have a wyvern. We don't yet know if that was what the scale was for, and we have three witches compared to their two. One of which may be constantly occupied keeping the conjured wyvern under surveillance, so it doesn't attack their own fleet."

"My brilliant queen," Jace praised from my side.

"I haven't lost all hope yet." My gaze lingered on the three witches. "Veli has been appointed as my aide. She has made it known that she isn't comfortable using the dark magic that the book possesses, and I will forever stand by her decision in that. However, I have an inkling that may not also be the case for the two of you. Crimson eyes and all," I said with a small smirk forming.

Two wicked grins formed before me. "What dark magic do you seek to be used?"

"Elianna," Veli cut in. "I refused to use strong bursts of magic in general to prevent my coven from finding the book. Since all that is now considered lost, my last declaration no longer holds true. I will do all it takes to ensure our victory. Including some of the darker aspects if needed."

My eyes flared as a grin formed on my face. "Very well then. And which forms of this magic are you comfortable using?"

As if in answer, dark, swirling wisps emerged from beneath her silver locks as her eyes flashed gold.

"I like the shadows," she said as a soft smile tilted her lips. "They whisper sweet things in my ears while accompanying me. Like little pets that wish to be loved.

Those I plan to put to use in battle." A look to Zaela. "Among other things."

Zae's eyes flared in response.

"You still scare me sometimes," Avery admitted.

Everyone let out quiet chuckles as the last bit of remaining tension fizzled out.

"And what is it that you possess from the book?" I asked the twins.

"While our time between the pages was slim, we were able to dabble and possess more than just shadows," Madalae answered as both of their eyes flashed a quick, glowing effect.

"Excellent," I said. "Regarding your presence in our city, I don't believe it's best for you to remain here. We have many frightened people already."

"We do not wish to stay amongst your mortals," Empri hissed. "But we shall stay near."

"Perfect, then we are in agreement. My concern now is when you will know to come back, when your aid is needed."

Veli let out a huff. "If they stay close, as they claim, I can summon them."

The twins nodded in agreement.

"Looks like we have quite a bit of reorganizing to do," I stated. "Welcome to the rebellion, witches."

I was answered with grinning faces that sat around the table. Their eagerness filled the air, giving me hope that we may have a chance in this after all.

FORTY-TWO

Finnian

INTENSE DISCUSSIONS OF WAR planning filled the days that came after the Elora twins' arrival as we aimed to devise a new plan to bring our mother's war to an end. Once Jace finished clearing enough soldiers, and Veli believed we had knowledgeable healers to minimize casualties, Lia intended to move the troops south.

Lia and Jace's biggest fear was being unprepared. With time running out constantly looming over our heads, we needed to do everything we could to ensure my sister's victory—starting with all these preparations.

The mortal's House of Healers was tucked away in a secluded corner of the city, where my days were now spent. Lia had decided that while Veli worked to teach me, she also may as well bring in as many humans that sought alternate ways to assist in the looming battles.

As the days passed, Veli, along with the other hidden healers that fled Isla, taught us the art of brewing potion remedies, blending salves with herbs, and the proper way to stitch wounds efficiently. Over time, our lessons moved into herbology, where she educated us on healing plants and how to identify their uses by scent, touch, and taste.

As I delved deeper into our studies, I grew to be fascinated by not only the differences within fragrances but also the contrasts between a leaf's smooth and prickled touch.

We each practiced the arts of ailments and stitching, and while none of us could mend broken bones or carved-up skin the way Veli could, aided by her magic, together we could all make a difference and save lives.

Veli approached me after dismissing today's session.

"You are doing significantly well for someone who is only learning. Perhaps you are not such a foolish male after all," she offered.

I lifted a brow at her. "Who are you, and what have you done with Veli?"

She scoffed and jokingly swiped a taloned hand near my face. "I am only speaking the truth. I believe this was a wise choice. You are much better suited here than where you were planning to be."

"Perhaps you're right," I said with a shrug as we both moved to the door. "You also terrify most of your students. So, perhaps, I just stand out," I said with a laugh.

She stared up at me through furrowed brows. "The humans need to get over their stance on magical beings."

"They fear you for good reason," I stated as we walked down the steps and into the bustling streets.

"You and your siblings learned not to fear me—one day, they will as well."

I laughed. "You think we don't fear you?"

Her lips twisted into a full, menacing grin as a small shadow danced around the side of her cheek, popping out from the cover of her silver hair.

"You're learning to control those better, I see," I offered as I suppressed a shiver that threatened to work its way up my spine.

She glanced to her shoulder where the shadow form hovered. "They are not so bad."

"Whatever you say," I said as I focused in on her eyes. They were a constant fuchsia now that she used her preferred dark magic frequently. Although the change wasn't discussed often, we all made an effort to adapt to it.

"If I do not dabble and learn control in times of peace, I will not know how to tame them and their thoughts in times of horror. It is a necessary evil."

I contemplated her words and was inclined to agree.

We turned a street corner to find Landon making his way to us as he moved through the crowd.

"I will see you this evening, Finnian," Veli offered as her steps quickened and she wisped herself away within the masses.

"There he is," Landon greeted as he pulled me into a hug and kissed my forehead. "How's my favorite healer doing?"

I let out a short laugh. "I'm no healer. Not yet, anyway."

"Well, you're a hell of a lot better than I would be," he teased himself, and guided me through the streets.

"That doesn't take much," I joked back. "Did training end early? You're normally down in the fields still."

"Zaela let most of us head home early today for a job well done," he stated.

"Most of you?"

He glanced at me and the corner of his lips tipped up as he huffed out a breath through his nostrils. "It appears that your sister needed a little more...one-on-one training."

My eyes bulged. "I'm assuming it's not the sister who has led armies and is a skilled warrior..."

"You would be correct." His face was riddled with amusement.

A laugh worked its way out of me, even after trying to suppress it. "And she didn't want an audience for such a thing?"

"I think after watching what happened with you, she threw a fit thinking about everyone deciding her role in the war together."

"Classic Avery," I huffed. "How much coin are we betting on how well this goes?" I said with a laugh.

"I'm not brave enough to bet coin against either of those females." We both began chuckling as we walked down the street. "But, needless to say, we're off the hook for the rest of the afternoon." Landon offered me his arm. "Care to join me for dinner?"

Lacing my arm through his, I sent up a silent *thank you* to the gods that Veli was able to save his life the day he almost succumbed to his wounds in Ellecaster. The growth he had shown since only a few months ago, when he was just a stable hand on the castle grounds, was admirable.

"I would be honored," I answered, allowing him to lead the way.

FORTY-THREE

Avery

THE SETTING SUN WAS casting a warm glow on the training platform. My eyes moved with Zaela as she paced on the opposite side of the ring, taunting me.

"Are you ladies ready?" Gage asked from just beyond the combat line, wearing a grin that stretched ear-to-ear.

"Let's do this," I breathed.

"Begin!" he shouted.

Zaela took the offensive first, lunging at me as she unsheathed a wooden dagger from her boot, slicing it through the air. I unsheathed my own on instinct, blocking her strikes as they came at me.

A smile formed on my face. "Ha!" I yelled with a laugh.

"You think you're beating me, Princess?" Zaela hissed.

"I'm merely playing with you." I countered another strike. "Tiring you out before I put in some *real* effort."

Zaela faked a low strike and quickly transitioned into a swinging attack from above—I barely sidestepped before she sent yet another swipe of her wooden blade in my direction.

As we began circling each other, sweat dripped down my brow. A short sense of pride rumbled through me as I thought of the female I was back in Isla. The princess who had never once broken a sweat or allowed to get even a speck of dirt on her finery gowns, yet always dreamed of adventure—and here I was *living* it.

"Avery, pay attention!" Lia boomed, snapping me from my daydream.

My gaze flew to where the sound of her voice came from to see her approach from behind Gage, Jace right beside her.

Gods-dammit.

"This doesn't concern you, Lia!" I screeched as I blocked yet another strike. "I'm training!"

"Yes, I can see that. Now focus!" she shouted.

The muscles in my thighs strained as they worked to carry me, quickly pivoting out of the way from where Zaela struck. With a sudden twist, she spun on her heel, lifting her opposite foot, and kicked the wooden dagger from my hand, disarming me.

"No!" I screeched, as she came at me with a wicked grin on her face.

I lifted my own foot and kicked her in the chest, sending her body tumbling backward across the training space.

My jaw dropped as I pivoted and turned to face the others. Lia stood with her arms crossed, a beaming smile of approval on her face. Gage winked at me, and Jace looked...concerned.

Suddenly, Lia's face dropped. "Avery, look out!" she screeched with a half laugh.

My body crashed into the unforgiving wood beneath our boots as Zaela tackled me to the ground, a battle cry echoing from her. Our bodies became tangled and aggressively rolled across the space as we each threw in a series of punches.

"What's the matter, Zaela? Upset that I beat you?" I taunted her.

"Little princess, it was *I* who disarmed *you*," she breathed.

"Alright, you two, that's enough," Lia called as she stalked over to us.

Zaela rolled off me and pulled herself to her feet, offering me her hand. I eyed her skeptically before taking it, allowing her to pull me up.

"It was a good kick, though," she offered as she rubbed at her chest.

"It sure as hell was!" Lia announced as she pulled me into a hug. "That was badass."

I giggled nervously. "She disarmed me, though."

Lia cupped my cheek in her hand. "That's okay. You're still learning."

"A fight with daggers is different from a battlefield with swords," Jace said as he approached us.

Gage offered me a smile. "She will get there."

A soft smile tilted my lips at his words.

"She still has a long way to go," Zaela huffed, and I rolled my eyes. "The sun will be setting soon, and I promised my mother I would be there for dinner, so let's wrap this up, huh?"

I stuck my tongue out at her back the second she turned from us.

"Gage, will you take Matthias back for us? I want to show Lia something," Jace stated as he gestured to her horse that waited in the distance.

"You got it, brother," he answered as he offered me his hand.

"What are you up to?" Lia asked Jace as she moved to follow him.

I turned to Gage and placed my hand in his as my brows furrowed in confusion.

"Oh, Zaela, darling," Gage joked.

"What?" she huffed.

"Lynelle is expecting me for dinner as well, but do give her my regards." His eyes returned to me. "I have other business to attend to this evening."

Heat rushed to my cheeks as I stood beneath his stare, and my heart was fluttering so fast I thought it would beat out of my chest.

"Yeah, yeah, you two go off and do whatever it is all you couples do. I'll go spend time with Mother Dearest," Zaela said as she stalked off toward the city.

She thought that Gage and I were a couple? The corners of my lips tilted slightly at the thought of it, but things hadn't been the same since the disaster at the isles.

In front of the others, he was always kind and supportive, even occasionally flirty, but we were never alone. He never sought me out in the late evening hours or asked me to accompany him to anything in the daylight. It had been devastating, but I was in no position to say anything regarding it. I knew I was lucky they all still tolerated my presence.

Gage escorted me to Matthias, and when I went to place my foot in the stirrup, he instead effortlessly lifted me by my hips and placed me on the saddle.

I let out a nervous giggle as he then hoisted himself up and sat directly behind me, my back pressed against his chest—just as it had been on our journey through the mountain passage.

He wrapped his muscular arms around me, reaching for the reins, and ordered the horse forward.

The silence was deafening as we trotted towards the city, but when his hand wrapped around mine while it gripped the saddle's pommel, my heart fluttered.

He gently took my hand from it and twisted it in his own, tracing his thumb over the blisters and rough skin forming on the outskirts of my palm.

"Did you ever think you would earn these?" he asked.

My cheeks flushed. "Never, honestly. And I would be lying if I said I didn't hate them and how they looked."

"You should be proud that you have them. You've been working hard—just as hard as anyone else out there."

I pressed myself closer to his chest, enjoying not only the warmth it brought me but also the rapid beats of my heart.

Craning my neck to look back at him, I whispered, "Are you still upset with me?"

He blew out a huff through his nostrils and I felt the heat of it tickle my cheek. His stare shot down at me, but a tiny smile formed, giving me hope.

"No, my lady Avery. It takes a great deal for me to hold grudges, and I find that is especially true with you. So, I will start this with an apology for my absence lately. It has gone on for too long."

I released a shuddering breath at his admission, and I held back the tears of relief as they burned my eyes.

"I thought you would hate me in secret forever. I'm sure some of them do."

"People make mistakes, Avery. We all know that you wouldn't have brought the book with ill intentions. And you didn't hand it over, even when demanded of it. Zaela told me you held on tight, with fear in your eyes, as magic ripped it from you."

"Zaela?" I breathed, confused that she had defended me.

"I've told you many times, she means well. She's just overprotective and stuck in her ways. Her reactions often come on too intense and quickly for her to reel them in before saying something she regrets, but she holds no grudge against you."

When I couldn't find the words to respond, he continued. "In truth, she may carry the burden of believing she caused you to feel the need to prove yourself as part of our circle when, in truth, you have always been a part of us, as you are a part of Lia."

"I just wanted to do something right," I admitted. "I wanted to be brave and smart like Lia. She always has a plan. I guess I just wanted to be more like her and less like...well, me."

He let out a deep laugh that rumbled through me, causing me to turn back and look at him through furrowed brows.

"What?!" I gasped with a half laugh.

"I love how and who you are. Just because I haven't had time or foolishly chose not to be around as much in recent weeks, doesn't mean I haven't taken notice of such things," he admitted, and my cheeks flushed. "Lia is fearless and sharp, just as you said. However, she is also self-sacrificing and reckless. She will be an incredible queen, but it's our job to ensure that she gets there first. The inner workings of her thoughts often bring us into...challenging ordeals."

"Perhaps you're right," I answered.

"Oh, I am." He laughed. "It's funny, though, seeing how much Jace has changed since he met her."

"What was Mr. Serious like before?" I asked as my hips rocked side to side to the beat of the horse's steps, Gage's thighs rubbing against mine.

"If you think he's serious now, you should have seen him before," he started. "Barely laughed, only ever focused on the war. We were losing him before we met Lia."

"Losing him?"

"He wasn't always this way. Yes, of course, he despised the fae, as we all did." My heart strained as I thought about all they must have gone through at the hands of my mother's soldiers. "But his hate stemmed from something deeper, and he was allowing it to consume him and make his decisions for him."

My mind flashed back to the meeting before the city when we first arrived and he explained why his hate for the fae ran so deep.

"And somehow meeting Lia changed all of this?" I wondered aloud.

"She changed everything," he stated proudly. "Not only him but also Zae and me. The whole trajectory of the outcome of a losing war—she has given our people faith in survival once again. And while they sometimes still gawk at you all with fear in their eyes, there is a hopefulness lingering beneath their stares."

"You use your humor as a shield, but you are very wise, Gage," I stated, and his body stiffened behind me. "You should show this side of yourself more often."

"Well, perhaps I hadn't found anyone worthy enough to show this to yet." My breathing quickened at his words. "But I undoubtedly have now. I also have Lia to thank for my own change in stance on the fae, if only for making it so easy for me to fall for you."

My heart was beating so violently, I thought it would burst in my chest. His fingers gently wrapped around my chin and guided it to where his own waited just over my shoulder.

The kindest eyes resembling pools of chocolate gazed into my own, and it took my breath away. Before I could process his intentions, he pressed his lips to mine.

The kiss was gentle and sweet—his touch making me feel guarded and safe. It was then that I realized I didn't need to find a mate to experience profound love; all I needed was a man who could demonstrate its essence.

FORTY-FOUR

Elianna

JACE LED ME THROUGH a sea of wildflowers in Alaia Valley, and I couldn't resist inhaling their sweet scent as the breeze carried it all around us.

Nerves rattled me as I felt his own down the bond, yet he still refused to tell me where he was bringing me.

"Why do I feel as if you're up to something?" I admitted.

He chuckled. "Oh, and what is that like? That's a feeling I have become quite accustomed to with you, my Lia."

He had a point.

"That's hardly fair...I have my reasoning," I teased. He turned to me and continued his walk backwards as he stared down at me through thickly furrowed brows. "That I, *of course*, will never hide from you again, handsome," I added, attempting to save face.

"Uh-huh," he huffed as he turned forward once more. "Well, I suppose this spot is as good as any," he said as he brought his fingers to his lips and let out a shrieking whistle.

A loud chirping sound echoed through the sky, followed by the powerful boom of Nox's wings as he flew in from the distance and landed before us.

"Since when does he listen to you?!"

Jace turned to me with a genuine, radiant smile stretching from ear-to-ear. "We have set aside our differences for the greater good."

"And that would be?"

"You," he breathed as he stepped up to me, wrapping one arm beneath my thighs and the other around my waist as he lifted me into his embrace.

Numerous giggles left me, mixing with his own laughs as he carried me to our wyvern. Once he stepped up to Nox's side, he pressed his lips to my forehead before carefully setting my feet back on the ground.

"I want to bring you somewhere very special, a place I've been meaning to tell you of for months now," he said as he gestured to the saddle atop Nox.

My eyes narrowed in on him as I let out a hum, and he raised a brow in response, as if expecting a retort.

Instead, I turned to Nox and climbed into the saddle as I was told.

"Good girl," he cooed, earning a wicked smirk from me.

He climbed up and positioned himself behind me, ordering Nox to take flight once we were both settled.

"And the others aren't expecting us for dinner as well?"

"No, they won't be. I made sure of it," he admitted, and my eyes flared in surprise.

And with those words, we rode off into the sky, away from the city at our backs, and deeper into the heart of Alaia.

A forest appeared beneath us after flying for nearly a half hour, and Nox landed in a small clearing. My gaze lifted to the tops of the trees, where the sky now displayed vast swirls of orange and purple from the setting sun.

"A forest? And here I thought you had enough of exploring unknown trees with me," I taunted him as we jumped down to the ground.

"These trees are only unknown to you, but I've been exploring them since I was a boy."

Nox let out a growl of annoyance behind us, and we both turned to find him glaring at Jace. I lifted a brow in response and turned to my mate.

"Any idea what that's about?"

"This gods-damn wyvern," he grumbled as he reached into the satchel at his side and pulled out a dead fish, tossing it in Nox's direction. "I said you get it after we're done. You still need to bring us back!"

Nox caught it in his maw and swallowed it whole, letting out a purr-like sound of approval.

I didn't even bother trying to hold in my laugh. "You bribed him. It all makes sense now."

He shook his head at me, his lips pressed together in a thin line, trying to hold back a smile.

Jace reached for my hand, and I placed mine in his as he moved to guide me through the wood.

"Our destination is just beyond these trees," he said, and as the words left him, the air filled with the sound of rushing water.

Recognition instantly flared within me, and I became giddy with excitement—his own tumbled with mine down our tether, making our steps quicken in unison.

My rushed strides turned into a full-on sprint as we raced through the trees together, our laughter filling the crisp forest air.

Our hurried steps halted as a vast opening appeared, and a hidden, serene waterfall emerged as it poured into a tiny pool that awaited only yards from our feet.

"Jace," I breathed, my eyes wandering up and down the falling cascades.

"Surprise, my Lia." He pressed his lips to the back of my head as he wrapped his arms around my waist from behind, holding me close to him.

"This is so beautiful," I whispered.

And it was.

Among the ancient trees of Alaia's foliage, this paradise remained hidden. The air was thick with the sweet fragrance of nearby flowers and the scent of slick, moss-covered stones.

The waterfall was half the size of the one we fell from in the Sylis Forest. It was still framed by vibrant greenery, tumbling calmly over weathered rocks, while fragile ferns sprouted from their crevices. The last bit of light from the setting sun filtered through the dense leaves above, casting mirages on the water's surface.

My heart raced as I took in the sight. Memories of the day that changed everything for us filtered through my mind—of us finding a similar intimate place among the enchanted wood, and what had ensued there and after.

It was the beginning of everything. It was the beginning of *us*.

"Do you like it?" he asked as I remained pressed against his chest. "I stumbled upon this place years ago and have been longing to bring you here since we arrived."

"It's stunning," I answered as I took a step away and turned to face him. "Now please tell me you didn't bring me out here just to look."

My hands reached for the bottom of my shirt and pulled it over my head. When my gaze met his, he captured his bottom lip between his teeth as he watched me. When my fingers aimed to unbutton my pants, his own shot out and handled it for me. He pulled my pants past my thighs and silently assisted as I stepped out of them.

"I will never have intentions of 'just looking' when it comes to anything with you," he breathed.

His eyes roamed over me while I stood before him, wearing only a bandeau fastened around my breasts and the undergarments that were beneath my leathers.

My fingers worked to unbutton his shirt and then pulled it down his arms. Now my own eyes leisurely explored his chest, and the markings from all the previous battles he had fought. My fingers lightly traced over them, working their way down to the muscles that led below his belt.

When my eyes lifted to meet his, my breath caught under his gaze. My touch lifted once more to reach the scar that marked his perfect face—one of our many combined markings that was a testament to everything we had endured together.

Jace took my hand in his and then pressed his lips to the back of it. While he guided me to the water's edge, my gaze drifted towards the hill that led to the falls.

"I should have known," he said knowingly.

"For old times' sake?" I challenged him, while tugging both of his arms to come with me.

"I go where you go." He watched me with a grin.

We each moved to climb the steep, grassy hill that led to the top of the waterfall, his presence a constant support at my back as he followed my lead.

With the moon now ascending and casting its glow, the atmosphere surrounding us became enchantingly beautiful.

At the top of the waterfall, the cascade was a ribbon of liquid silver, shimmering in the moonlight as it fell to the pool below.

It exposed hidden dewdrops on the canopy's leaves, making them shimmer as if they were the stars in the sky above. Bioluminescent fungi emitted a soft, pulsating light on the forest floor. Fireflies danced around us as we neared the small cliff's edge, freely weaving through the air.

It was so eerily similar to the scene in the rift at the isles, yet I felt comforted more than anything.

From the top of the most breathtaking view I had ever seen, a sense of peace washed over me, realizing that this moment would forever be incomparable.

"My Lia," Jace breathed from behind me.

Turning to face him, my heart skipped a beat at what my eyes beheld—Jace on one knee, his hand extended up toward me with a ring delicately held between his fingers. His eyes then locked with mine, filled with adoration.

"Jace." My voice was barely audible. "What is this?"

"Every word I have ever spoken to you regarding where I stand has been true, and that is to be at your side for the remainder of my days—in victory or defeat, in sickness and in health."

My lips parted as I took in his words.

"While I cannot fathom the responsibility you bear on your shoulders, I can still feel it every waking and sleeping moment of the day, and I plan to alleviate any burden from you that you allow. It would never matter to me where we end up after our victory. A cottage on the coast, an estate in the valley, a castle in Isla... I am nothing if you are not with me. And while I plan on us both surviving what is to come, I wish to approach our final stance with you, not only as my mate but as my wife."

A single tear slipped down my cheek at his confession. "You wish to be my King Consort?"

As he stood up, he cradled my hand in his, slipping the ring onto my finger. "I wish to be anything you need me to be, as long as it entails being at your side."

I sucked in a sharp breath.

"What say you, Elianna Valderre? Will you make me the happiest mate in the realm and be my wife?"

My eyes drifted down to the ring now encircling my finger. A silvery sheen sparkled in the starlight, the band carved into two dainty wyvern wings that wrapped tightly around an oval-shaped emerald. My jaw dropped as I observed it, twisting my hand at all angles to view the one-of-a-kind jewelry he had created for me—*his queen*.

"Well, my Lia?" A nervous laugh left him.

A soft smirk crept up my lips as my neck twisted back to peer over my shoulder, where the falls awaited. My hair danced around my face as the night breeze blew around us.

"May the gods help me with you," he said while shaking his head, watching me.

My innocent smirk morphed into a menacing grin as I lowered my hand to my side and took a single step backward towards the cliff's edge—he matched the step forward, mimicking the dance from our first kiss.

"Do I receive an answer from the queen? Or will she keep me guessing as she always has?" he asked with a growl of anticipation.

The edge of the fall's overhang scraped the skin beneath my foot, halting my movements. "You will find my answer at the bottom of the falls, my king." I winked.

Without hesitation, I twisted my body and leapt off the edge of the waterfall, my body descending beside the cascades before diving into the pool that awaited at its floor.

Jace's body landed in the pool only feet from my own, and I floated up to him as we were surrounded by the bubbles rising to the surface. In the depths of the water, I wrapped my legs around his waist, intertwining our bodies, and held his face tenderly in my hands as I pressed my lips against his, savoring their taste.

We sat beneath the cover of the water until our lungs burned for air before swimming to the surface.

"Shall I take your kiss as an answer?" He grinned as he watched me intently.

I swam the short distance between us and wrapped my arms around his neck, nuzzling his nose with my own.

"Always," I breathed.

His hazel gaze roamed over me intently, making my breath catch, and then he claimed my mouth with his. Our bond became saturated with the pulsating rhythm of quickened heartbeats, a love that consumed our very souls, and an insatiable need for each other.

His hands moved to explore my body as we each struggled to tread the water as we succumbed to our constant craving for one another.

I followed his lead as he reluctantly waded towards the waterfall—its deafening roar drowned out the world, intensifying the intimacy, and the mist from the falls kissed my exposed skin.

The water pounded against our shoulders as we moved beneath it—the droplets gleaming on Jace's back.

Upon reaching the other side of the rapid falls, we became wedged between the flowing water and what resembled a small cave carved from the stone. The torrential cascade overhead created a curtain of liquid jewels, glistening in the moonlight.

My mate rested his back against the rock wall beneath the falls, and I silently swam up to him. He instantly reached out beneath the water, cupping the backs of my thighs, and lifted me in his arms. With each shared breath and glance, our desperate, aching desire for one another interlaced down our tether.

Barely able to hold back any longer, I claimed his lips with my own, our tongues knotting in a dance as our hands explored each other slower and more assured than ever before. Beneath the water, I found the top of his pants and slowly began unbuttoning them.

He broke the kiss, leaving me desperate for him, so my lips flew to his neck, where my tongue traced the beads of water that glided down from his soaked hair.

"What is it that you want, *wife*?" he groaned.

I climbed back up his body and pressed our foreheads together. "You," I breathed.

Jace took that as his cue. He flipped our bodies, my back now pressed up against the rock wall, as he forcefully kicked out of his pants that clung to his skin below the surface.

In his need for me, he ripped the bandeau that restrained my breasts, letting them fall freely before him. Jace cupped them with his hands, caressing them with his fingers. He moved that same hand down further, tearing my remaining clothing from my body, and circled my clit as his fingers explored.

"Gods," I gasped, but the echo of it was lost in the raining falls.

His mouth moved up the center of my throat with a mix of teasing kisses and licks, making his way to the sensitive tip of my ear. I felt his hardened length press against my center as his mouth worked to ravish my entire body.

I moved my hand to guide his length down to my entrance, and a gasp escaped me as he thrusted in, filling me. Each thrust felt as if it would be my undoing. I couldn't get enough of him as my thighs tightened around his waist, pulling him in. His mouth was on mine once more, our tongues desperately colliding.

Our hips rocked in tandem, separating and finding each other over and over until we were on the verge of combustion. Caging me against the rock wall, he kissed my neck, running his hands through my hair as I rolled my hips, his cock moving in and out.

Jace maneuvered one of his arms around the back of my neck, cradling it against the jagged edges that protruded from the cliff's cave.

I opened my eyes to be met with an intense hazel gaze fixed on me, and a moan escaped me at the thought of him watching me unravel beneath him. A grunt of approval left him, and there were so many things I wanted to say and act on in the moment, but my entire body burned and ached for him.

I could feel it all around me—both his desire and my own, churning and mingling together, becoming one. He moved in me continually, and I wasn't sure how long it lasted, but all I knew, all my body knew, was that I never wanted it to end.

My eyes peered over his shoulder to where my hand held him for support—the ring he gifted me, what would become our ring of vows, glistening beneath the water droplets.

His lips left my skin, and I instantly felt its loss until he pressed them to my ear and spoke the words that would undoubtedly end me. "You are forever *mine*."

His voice held a mixture of desperation and possession, and if I was standing, it would have brought me to my knees before him.

And with it—I came undone. My entire body unraveled, the heat of my release coursing through every vein within me. A moan escaped me as I shuddered around him in my orgasm, bringing him over the edge in tandem.

His arms gripped me tightly as he steadied us against the cool stone at my back, and my body went completely limp in his arms as I let out a whimper.

I lifted my stare to his and watched as the lagoon water beaded off his thick lashes as he said, "If I meet my end in this, it was all worth it. Every moment of knowing you, every second of being yours...it was all worth it."

I cupped his cheek as our gazes remained locked. "I love you, and I will *never* let that happen. We are seeing this victory through to the end. The *two* of us. King and queen, husband and wife, mates fated by the gods—the title does not matter. What matters is that we will be together. Always."

A whisper of a smile tilted his lips. "Always," he breathed.

FORTY-FIVE

Jace

NO MATTER HOW HARD I tried, I couldn't lift my gaze from Lia the entire flight back from our engagement. She leaned into my chest, pressing random, tender kisses to my jaw every time she caught me staring. I watched as her hair flew in the wind, and her smile beamed ear-to-ear as she kept catching glimpses of the ring that now adorned her finger.

My heart thudded in my chest, pride exuding from my pores as I thought about the fact that I would have a *wife*—an idea that I had given up long ago, never wishing or thinking it would ever exist for me—until her.

I never could have fathomed knowing a love like this before, regardless of the mating bond we shared. I would do anything for her—destroy anyone or anything that stood in her way.

As Nox landed outside the door of my family's estate, the rumbling of the ground gave our arrival away. My eyes flew to the windows to see many curious eyes on us, their faces pressed against the glass as if they were children outside of a toy maker's shop.

"I have a feeling the secret is out," Lia said with a giggle as we leapt down from the wyvern.

"I should've known that a small white lie would have been better suited to tell Gage," I joked.

She patted Nox on the nose, and he nuzzled his snout into her chest as she said her goodbyes right before we began our ascent up the walkway to the front door.

Suddenly, the door burst open, followed by excited squeals from Avery and many knowing grins from the others.

Lia did a few adorable little stomps of her feet as shrieks left her, matching her sister's. They both burst out in excited laughter as they ran towards one another, jumping into an embrace where they swayed side to side.

"Oh my gods, oh my gods, did it happen?!" Avery begged. She pushed out of Lia's hug and instantly reached for her hand, staring at the ring on her finger. "It's so beautiful!"

Lia chuckled as she watched her sister beam. "Thank you." She glanced back at me and smiled softly. "He knows how to make things very special."

My eyes lifted to Gage, whose arms were crossed as he leaned against the doorway, his brows fluttering at me. I moved past the girls and walked up to him.

"Congratulations, brother," he greeted as he clapped me on the shoulder, and then pulled me into a hug. "I can't believe she agreed to spend the rest of her ridiculously long life with you, but it's better to trick her into it now, while you still can."

Laughter boomed from him as I jokingly shoved at his shoulder and walked through the doorway.

Zaela immediately gave me a quick hug and smile, saying her congratulations, as both Landon and Finnian came up to shake my hand. Veli remained in the corner of the living area as she inclined her head at me with a small smile tilting her lips.

"I can't think of a better male for my sister," Finn said. "I know you will take care of her." He smiled at me, and I didn't realize how badly I wanted his and Avery's approval until it had been received.

Lia came in through the doorway, and everyone flocked to her, gushing over the ring while I internally gushed over *her*.

Her beautiful green eyes lifted to mine as they swarmed her, and it threatened to make my heart stop.

Zae was the first to break the circle, and she walked up to my side.

"Where is Lynelle?" I asked, assuming she would have been one of the ones to burst through the doorway in excitement.

Zaela let out a small laugh. "She apparently forgot about our dinner plans and is spending the night at Leon's." She pursed her lips together as she tried to suppress a smirk.

"That is...that is interesting," I said as a sound left me that was half sigh, half chuckle.

"Let them have their fun. They both deserve it," she stated, and I nearly did a double take as the words left her.

As everyone settled into the space, taking their seats on the couches, chairs, and floor, Zaela brought in a few bottles of wine. She handed a poured glass to everyone, and they toasted to us in celebration while Lia sat on my lap in the chair next to the roaring fireplace.

"To the future queen *and* king of Velyra!" Gage boomed.

King. It sounded so strange when spoken aloud.

"So when is the wedding?!" Avery asked as she sipped her wine, her eyes boring into Lia with a mischievous gleam.

Lia sipped her own as her eyes roamed over each of them. "I'm not sure. We don't exactly have time for a wedding. We need to leave soon to get our armies beyond the forest. That alone will take weeks."

"We could do something small here first, though!"

"Avery, it's not *your* wedding. Let Lia and Jace decide," Finn teased.

She stuck her tongue out at him in response.

"Well, I don't hate the idea of celebrating with my court of rebels, in the least." Lia winked at her sister. "However, we still have much to plan. And I don't ever want to be in another situation where we don't know what's happening with one another, and that will be damn near impossible for what lies ahead. The planning of that must come first."

"There may come a time when we will all be separated and unable to guard each other's backs," I announced to them all, and the mood turned somber.

"I refuse to have another situation like with the sirens." Lia craned her neck to look up at me and then moved her gaze back to her court. "All I could sense was an overwhelming panic, which turned into not being able to distinguish his from my own. And if we had returned even seconds later, the two of you may not have survived." Her hand moved to gesture to both Gage and me.

"There may be a workaround for that, Elianna." Veli broke her silence from where she stood in the corner.

Everyone's attention flew to the witch.

"I'm listening," Lia announced as she brought her glass of wine to her lips.

"I told you once before that first night in the city that cradles the mountains—mating bonds are capable of expanding beyond emotions and senses, for that is just the very surface of your link to one another. The practice I'm referring to has been lost for centuries, but I remember a time when politics were not so dire, and mating bonds were more apparent throughout the realm."

"Meaning what exactly?" I asked.

"The use of magic can bring on a further, deeper bond if a mated pair is wed before the gods," she answered.

My eyes flared, and I peered over Lia's shoulder to get a better look at her, but her face was unreadable, and a hesitant confusion exuded from her.

"How can there be a deeper bond than what we already possess? Lore states that nothing could be greater, or even comparable than what this holds," she said.

"Not all knowledge can be passed down between the pages of written books, as texts are often lost." Veli's stare lingered on us for a moment before she continued. "Or stolen." She cleared her throat.

"And what would this entail? I already feel everything she feels," I stated.

"It would be a connection of your minds," she answered.

"What?!" Lia gasped with a half laugh. "As in...he would be able to *hear* my thoughts?" She glanced up at me over her shoulder and gave me a nervous smile, which I responded to with furrowing brows at her hesitance.

"Only the ones you allow to flow through the connection," she answered.

"Oh, thank the gods," Lia said, earning a snort from me.

"It should be as simple as verbally speaking to one another. All it would take is for you to will it into the other's mind," the witch stated. "Although, I'm sure you will need to master it so you are not merely shouting everything at each other."

"Ugh," she let out.

"What's the matter, Lia?" Gage teased from where he sat with Avery on the settee. "Trying to hide your inner-most thoughts from us, hmmm?"

"You all don't need to know everything that goes on in my mind," she huffed.

"Would that be because the self-sacrificial bullshit would need to come to an end?" Zaela questioned, as her eyes remained fixated on her.

"No," Lia growled.

"Such sweet lies," I whispered in her ear. She squirmed in my grasp, but it only made me tighten my hold.

"It's not necessary, but it's an option I wanted to make you aware of," Veli chimed in. "Separation is a guarantee once you are on that battlefield. However, hearing another's thoughts may also serve as a distraction."

"But it could also lead us back to each other," Lia breathed.

"Precisely," the sorceress added. "It is a practice that used to be known amongst both the High Witches and Priests of the realm but was lost once marriages of convenience became the forefront of how the inner workings of the court worked. And if you wish to avoid another siren situation, you would be able to communicate with one another this way. Even see through each other's eyes."

Everyone was silent for a few moments. The only sound to be heard was the crackling of embers as they sparked from the fireplace.

"And you would be able to assist with the practice of these?" I asked.

"It is something you must learn from one another—your bodies and minds working in tandem. Just note that it cannot be undone without severing your bond entirely. However, if there is ever a time where you need to block the bridge or hide your pain, you may temporarily build a wall in your mind if you concentrate hard enough, though you will always be able to sense one another."

Gods, I could already feel the wheels turning in Lia's head at that.

"Wouldn't that defeat the purpose of this? If she's in pain, I would need to know," I grumbled.

The sorceress shrugged. "It is an option if desired. As I said before, this ritual enhances your bond, giving you more access and control. You will still be able to sense one another if one decides to build a shield."

My heart started pounding as I glanced at my mate, and I discovered her gaze was already fixed on me while everyone else watched in silence.

"This is an...intense and irreparable decision. What are you thinking, Lia?"

"That's not fair. You can't leave the decision in my hands alone. It's your life too."

"I would never burden you with the sole responsibility of making this decision, but you should know that I am entirely for it. It's to ensure your safety and that you're never lost to me. I would never be against something as such," I stated.

I then leaned down and breathed into the tip of her ear, "And imagine all the wicked things I could whisper into your mind, my darling Lia."

Her body went rigid while goosebumps formed on her skin. She then cupped my cheek with her palm, a soft, closed-lipped smile forming on her face. "Wicked whispers regardless, it's to ensure your safety as well. Not just my own."

Zaela cleared her throat from across the room. "Well, I believe the decision is made, then."

Avery leapt up from the couch, the wine in her glass nearly tipping over its edge in the process. "It's decided, then! A royal wedding!" she boomed with pure glee.

Gage reached out and grabbed her by the back of her shirt, pulling her back into his arms on the couch, and she fell into him, giggling.

"It's decided," Lia said softly with a smile. "I suppose we can spare one night for a celebration before our departure."

Everyone's face wore a smile as chatter among the eight of us ensued, discussing plans, attire, and the functionality of such an event.

And then the night carried on, the sound of our laughter and the strumming of Gage's gittern filled the air as we allowed ourselves to forget about our endless responsibilities and be a family.

FORTY-SIX

Kellan

My HESITANCE FOR THE witch bitch and her crone had diminished, replaced by a newfound confidence of being able to ride and tame the conjured beast at my will. The wyvern was just as wary and erratic as the previous one we possessed, but under the mind link of the blood-bonded cuffs, it bent to my every demand and call.

And I felt fucking invincible.

Most of my days were now spent patrolling our side of the Sylis Forest, searching for Elianna's potential army from the sky. However, I hadn't seen a gods-damn thing and returned to check on the state of Isla as it was held in the death grip of the queen's iron fist and the High Witch's talons.

I mounted the beast bareback as it was perched atop one of the city's watchtowers. A growl brewed in its chest as it looked out at the crowds passing by, who persistently worked to avoid its gaze. Females and younglings shook in fear whenever they beheld the sight of the crimson-eyed creature beneath me, bringing the sense of power I forever longed for to an entirely new height.

The queen was many things, and while I had deemed her foolish for striking a bargain with the witches, I couldn't help but feel that I was, for once, very wrong. The queen sought power, just as I always had, and she knew that the simplest, and easiest, way to gain such influence derived from inciting fear among the masses.

People wanted to live, and what guaranteed such was abiding by the reigning queen's law. With her constant foot patrol on the streets, and my own in the open air, she swiftly eradicated the possibility of another wave of rebellion forming.

"Captain Adler!" a voice called from the bottom of the watchtower.

I peered over the beast's shoulder and found William on the street below, craning his neck up at me.

"Aye, William?" I grumbled.

"The queen requests your presence in the throne room," he informed me. "The High Witch has presented an idea to her that she wishes for you to be present for."

William had taken over my patrolling at the queen's side while I was tasked with bonding with my mount, which I thought was pointless thanks to our cuffs. However, the witches insisted that forming such a bond would only serve us further in battles.

Elianna's wyvern obeyed her commands without the use of magic, which aggravated me to no end, but false bond or not, my beast submitted to me as demanded.

"And do you have any knowledge of what this is about?" I asked him.

"No, Captain. I was given orders to collect you," he answered as he shielded his eyes from the blinding sun.

I scoffed. *Collect* me.

"Very well, William," I huffed.

Every day, I thought of the use of having William around. While he listened to orders and was a decent replacement for Vincent, I didn't trust him entirely like I had with his predecessor. He was the only one who knew the truth of Callius' fate and had kept it to himself so far. If he knew what was good for him, it would remain that way.

I took my fist and pounded the wyvern's scales on its right side. "Fly, beast!" I ordered, and it let out an ear-shattering shriek into the sky as it beat its wings, sending us shooting upwards. The stones of the tower creaked as his weight shifted and left it.

He landed in one of the side courtyards of Castle Isla, and the staff that were spread out in the mix quivered with fear at our arrival, quickly pivoting in the opposite direction from where we stood.

I climbed down from his back and stalked toward the pillars that led to the side entrance of the castle.

"I would make yourselves busy elsewhere. He may decide he's hungry," I announced with a menacing laugh before waltzing through the doors.

Once I entered the throne room, the queen sat upon her royal seat with the High Witch lingering at her side—the place where Callius had once always been, and a place I intended to be. Both females stared me down, their gazes narrowing in on me with each step I took to approach them.

"You sent for me, Your Majesty?" I interrupted the silence.

"Yes, thank you for joining us, Captain," she answered. "Azenna has informed me of magic that may come of much use to me."

"And what might that entail, Queen Idina?"

A chilling smile leisurely spread across her ruby lips, and my eyes drifted to the witch at her side.

"Captain, you do recall what it felt like when I took control of your body, yes?" she taunted.

My jaw locked at the reminder. "Indeed," I said through my teeth. "How could I forget?" I cocked my head to the side.

"What if I were to tell you that there is a way to take over what the eyes beheld? To transport someone's consciousness to be across the realm in a non-tangible form. Presented to someone as if they were immediately before them." Her face remained unreadable as she stared down at me from the top of the dais.

My mind wandered for a moment, unsure of where exactly she was leading with this. "Forgive me for asking, but how does projecting one's consciousness elsewhere assist us in a war we are already bound to win?"

"It ensures an early victory," Idina answered. "We shall corner her where she hides and cut off her sense of self. Forever making her wonder if we can see her every move, or when I will appear before her again. She is impulsive and childish. It will force her out of hiding to rush back into our war—where *we* will be ready. If she were prepared, she would've made it known by now, and you would've spotted her from the skies."

"*You* will be the one to appear before her, Your Majesty?" I asked, raising a brow.

"Indeed," she snarled. "Did you assume that it would be you?"

I couldn't admit to the bitch that I was indeed hoping for such power.

"It was just a question, my queen. I wasn't sure if it would be you or the High Witch," I lied.

"Well, what say you then, Adler? Do you have any thoughts regarding such an action?" Azenna demanded of me, trying to ensnare me in a trap of disagreement.

"I would say that...something of such power may come in great use to us," I answered, taming the growl that was working its way up my throat.

"Excellent," she snickered.

"Just to be sure that I have all knowledge of what this beholds...you indeed cannot sense where she is with the spell?" I wondered.

Azenna's eyes narrowed in on me, their crimson rings swirling. "Correct, but that is none of your concern."

"Well, I would argue that anything to do with what this war brings upon us is my concern. I will be leading our army to our victory, will I not?" I challenged.

One of her eyes twitched at my words, and a pulse of satisfaction rolled through me.

"Very well," she hissed. "To answer your otherwise *invasive* question, Captain, no. We would not be able to locate her exact whereabouts with the spell. It would simply transport your queen's consciousness to whoever she demands it land before. All that is necessary for the workings of this magic is that the two of them have once met."

"She is also *your* queen, though, no?" I tacked on with a smirk, and the queen's eyes flared at the small tidbit she didn't catch in the witch's explanation.

"Yes, of course," Azenna mustered through a fake smile that didn't meet her eyes. She turned to Idina. "Apologies, *my* queen."

Her eyes then flashed down to me, boring through me as if I were lower than the dirt that coated the dungeon's floor, but my stance remained confident.

"There is one more item we are to go over, Captain," the queen stated.

"Aye?"

"We are to send your wyvern beyond the Sylis Forest, for Sylvae will be able to lurk through its eyes. You have searched our side far and wide, and you are now needed here for the final touches of preparing our army. We want to fully understand what we are up against, and any settlement found in its pursuit will succumb to its flame, further weakening any chance Elianna has to build her own armies."

My eyes flared, and I bit my tongue as the mention of Silcrowe being rebuilt almost slipped through my teeth. The queen was still unaware of the entire first battle that occurred as we tried to draw Elianna out from the confines of the city.

"Do you have anything to add regarding this, Captain?" Azenna asked, knowing I had no room for argument.

"Let me accompany the beast." My voice was more demanding than I intended.

"Are you deaf? I stated what you're needed for currently, and you shall remain here in Isla," the queen interjected.

My stare darted between the two cunts before me. I blinked as I contemplated how to word what I needed to say without further exposing the knowledge I held.

"If you are to send my wyvern away without me, wasting time that *you* stated I needed to bond with the beast, then I want to be sure he does a full sweep of what lies on the other side of the wood. Be sure he covers the entire side of the Ezranian Mountains until they meet the sea."

"As you command, Captain," Azenna answered.

An odd feeling mimicking panic clogged my throat the moment the words left my mouth, but I was too deep beneath the witch's claws now to reevaluate the circumstances the queen's decisions had led us to.

The queen was coming for Elianna's blood, and she would make sure every last bit of it was spilled upon the realm's soil if it was the last thing she ever did.

FORTY-SEVEN

Elianna

IN THE MAIN BATHING chambers of the Cadoria Estate, Avery aided me in readying for mine and Jace's wedding day—a day I never thought would become a reality.

While turning toward the floor-length mirror, my sister's voice had me halting instantly.

"I told you not to look yet!" she scolded me as she rushed back into the room, balancing the rest of the beauty enhancers Lynelle provided us.

I huffed out a breath at her as I tightened the strings of my robe. "Avery, I need to see if I like it!"

"And you will do just that once I am *finished*," she stated as she pointed to the chair in the corner of the room where I was told to remain.

"Fine," I huffed as I sat back down, the force of my dramatic landing on its cushion making my body bounce.

"Excellent," Avery cooed as she spread all the items out on a small table.

Closing my eyes, I felt everything she did, from lining my lashes, dusting my cheeks, and painting my lips.

"How did you learn to do all of this, anyway?" I asked as my eyes remained closed.

"You learn quite a bit when things are forced upon you daily. Now hold still before I get this rouge on your teeth," she demanded.

I stifled a giggle at her bossiness while she finished her self-proclaimed masterpiece on my face.

"Open your eyes," she ordered. "How does it feel?"

I smirked. "As if I have paint on my face."

"Well, you essentially do," she said with a laugh. "Zaela, it's time for the dress!"

A figure appeared in the doorway a moment later, but it wasn't Zaela.

"Lynelle," I breathed, and she watched me with eyes that seemed to already be filling with tears as she stood beneath the door's arch, draping a cream-colored gown over her arms.

"The tailors have just finished it. I rushed to get it here since Zae had to help the boys get ready."

I smiled softly. "She's always looking out for those two."

"Indeed she is," Lynelle admitted as she took a single step in.

"I, um, I will go see if Veli needs anything downstairs," Avery announced as she rushed out the door.

I stood from the chair and sucked in a sharp breath as nerves worked their way through me. Lynelle then approached me.

"My dear, it's a custom in our mortal culture for a family member to escort the bride down the aisle, but I'm not sure if it's the same for the fae."

A smile tried to form on my lips, but it refused to meet my eyes. "It's the same for our culture as well," I answered.

She pressed her lips together as her eyes roamed over me slowly. "I am so very sorry for your loss, my dear. There has been so much of it on both sides of this."

"Indeed, there has been," I whispered. "And thank you. I'm forever sorry for yours as well, Lynelle."

She waved her hand at me to brush off my remark, as if my birth hadn't played a part in her own husband's death. She then carefully hung the dress on the wall beside her.

Lynelle gently placed each of her hands on either side of my arms and looked into my eyes. "That is neither here nor there, sweet girl. You have the weight of the realm on your shoulders, and you are now fighting *for* us instead of against us. You are our hope."

She caringly moved my body to twirl before her, so I now faced the wall that was at my back a moment before. Her hand reached out toward the table at our side, and she picked up the beautiful hairbrush that had been resting atop it. I nearly let out a sob as she pulled it gently through my hair.

"Are you alright, Lia?" she asked in a calm whisper.

My lungs released a shuddering breath that felt as if it rattled my entire body. "I just..." No words found me as I desperately tried to explain what I was feeling.

"You don't have to speak of it if it causes you pain." Another pull of the brush through my hair nearly had me ruining the work Avery had done to my face as tears threatened me.

"The scars that I bear on my back..." Memories of the day beneath the dungeon slammed into me. "Well, a few of the scars, that is...they are a result of wishing I had a mother to do just this with," I admitted, never realizing how pitiful it all sounded once spoken aloud.

The brushing faltered, but then continued a second later. "That's such a horrible thing to hear. I'm so very sorry. How old were you?"

"Thirteen," I whispered. "I had always watched the queen with her brushes and how I wished I had a mother to share one with. One day, I was caught sneaking into her chambers..."

"Oh my," Lynelle whispered nervously.

A sad laugh left me. "I combed it through my hair a single time, and when I looked up into the mirror, the queen was staring back at me in disgust. You would have thought the dirtiest peasant in her city's slums had ravaged through her finery."

"And you were punished for this? As a child?"

"She had her personal guard take a whip to my back three times. Let's just say the entire ordeal kept me in line for quite a few of the following years. My father never heard of its occurrence."

Silence blanketed the room for a few seconds. "I'm so sorry you were treated so horrendously, Elianna."

"It's quite alright. Her cruelty made me stronger. At least that's what I would like to believe."

"But it's something you shouldn't have had to endure, and for that, I am sorry."

"Thank you," I whispered.

Her hand then reached out toward a vase on the table that held freshly trimmed flowers and greenery from the estate's front garden. She plucked a few of the vines and subtle blooms from the vase and began intertwining them in my hair, lacing them into braids that she twisted back from my face.

"May I help you into your dress?"

"Of course." My voice was hoarse from trying to hold in all the emotions that threatened to flood me from her kindness.

The robe I wore fell to my feet as she moved to grab the gown that hung on the wall and then assisted me into it. Her movements paused as my scars became visible to her, and the weight of her stare made my stomach tighten, but I was grateful she didn't comment on them further. She carefully guided my arms through the flowing lace sleeves and then laced the back with a cream-colored ribbon that matched the gown itself.

When I turned to face her, a kind smile tilted her lips. "Please, Your Majesty, take a look." She gestured to the mirror.

"Please don't feel that it's necessary to call me that," I said with a small laugh as I turned to face the mirror once more.

My lips parted at the sight that I beheld in my own reflection. I thought I had felt beautiful during the disastrous night of Kai's wedding—when Lorelai had placed me in her finery gown and dusted my cheeks with rouge—but what I saw now held no comparison.

My hair pulled back from my face, with beautiful flowers woven between each braid as the rest of the curls fell down my back. The kohl that lined my eyes made their color flare beneath the candlelight, and the faint pink placed upon my lips made them more plump and pout-like.

The gown was breathtaking—its form-fitting bodice adorned with delicate embroidery in champagne thread, with a sweetheart neckline elegantly framed with a trim of tiny pearls. Its sleeves were long and tapered, fitting closely to my arms while extending into a slight flare. The gown's skirt flowed in cascading layers to the floor, with a train that extended several feet behind me.

I didn't recognize myself in the mirror—for the fierce, blood-soaked warrior was no longer who stared back at me, but a queen.

"I look..."

"You look as if you're the most beautiful bride and queen that the realm has ever seen. It will bring my nephew to his knees."

A choked laugh left me at her words, but when my eyes found hers once more in the mirror, I watched as she wiped a single tear away that had slipped down her cheek.

"Are you alright, Lynelle?"

"My nephew...he has always been a boy filled with so much anger. So much *rage* because of all he had been forced to hold knowledge of from such a young age."

"I know," I whispered, as my heart thudded at the reminder. "And I will forever love him with every breath."

"Yes, I know that, sweet girl. It is just...I never would have even dreamed of him loving someone else so deeply in return. He's a changed man because of you, and that is for the better. His mother would have been so proud and would have adored you to no end."

Tears finally escaped me and slid down my cheeks.

She caught them with the tip of her finger and smiled. "Neither of you have parents any longer, but my door will remain open for the rest of my days. That is a promise."

"Thank you, Lynelle," I choked out as she took a step back from me.

"There is one more thing," she admitted as she made her way to the door. "I will be right back."

My mind raced for an unbearably long minute before she appeared before me once more, holding a small box between her two hands.

I raised a single brow at her as a smirk formed on my face. "What is that?"

"Jace had this made for you. Now, I insisted that we could have expedited a finer one to be made, but he declared that you would have preferred this anyway, and well, he knows you best, I suppose," she answered.

She stepped up to me and lifted the top of the box. I let out a tiny gasp at what my eyes beheld—a dainty tiara, crafted from silver to mimic woven and twisted leaf-covered vines that met in its center at a point, where an emerald was fastened securely—a mirror to the one upon my mating ring.

"Oh my gods," I breathed as my eyes flashed up to meet hers.

She chuckled. "I have a feeling that he was correct in his notion of you loving this how it is."

A smile found my lips as my heart fluttered wildly. "It's perfect."

She moved to place the box on the table and carefully picked up the delicate crown, turning to me with pride beaming in her eyes. I slowly lowered my head toward her in a half bow, and she gently placed it atop my head.

Turning back to the mirror, I couldn't help but grin at the person staring back at me as the crown twinkled. A female who had undergone torture at the hands of those she should have been able to trust. A warrior who led armies and brought countless victories to the feet of the wicked beings who tricked her out of her own crown. A mate who would finally attain her happy ending she never knew that she so desperately desired. And lastly, a queen—one who would never again allow her realm to fall at the hands of such wickedness, and would rule with compassion, just as her father had.

My stare leisurely drifted to Lynelle's as she gazed at me through the mirror, standing off to the side. "I'm ready."

Her hand lifted toward the door as she inclined her head toward me. "After you, our queen."

FORTY-EIGHT

Jace

As I STOOD BENEATH the arch that was placed atop the valley's most scenic hill, I stared out at the small crowd as we all waited for Lia's arrival. I turned to face the lake resting behind us, the setting sun casting a fiery reflection off its surface as the breeze blew the tall grasses in the distance.

Gage stood at my side, puffing his chest out as if he were the proudest man alive.

"You do realize that you aren't the one getting married, correct?" I teased, and he scoffed at my words.

"Can a second-in-command not be happy for his commander? A best friend? A—"

"Brother," I finished for him while clapping him on the shoulder. "Thank you, Gage. For everything."

Surprise shone in his stare, and I had to turn from facing him before he managed to get me even more worked up than I already was.

Figures emerged over a smaller hill from where we stood, and I counted three of our women as Nyra trotted around their feet, but still no sign of Lia.

I blew out a nervous breath as my eyes peeled over each of them. "Where is she?"

391

"She will be here. Don't worry," Gage said softly.

My gaze roamed over the fields and snapped to Zaela from where she sat in the front row. "Where's Nox?! She would want him to be here."

She shrugged her shoulders as her lips turned down into a frown. "I couldn't find him in the yard or the skies."

"Gods-dammit," I breathed. Nox and Lia hated being apart from each other, and if he wasn't hovering over her in the fields or perched atop the war chamber, he was guarding the estate.

Once they arrived, Avery positioned herself on the opposite side of the arch, mirroring Gage, while Veli stood a few paces behind her as we waited for Lia.

My aunt approached me then.

"Handsome, nephew," she greeted as she cupped my cheek in her hand. "Thank the gods you combed your wild hair."

A laugh left me without permission, but ceased as we locked eyes. "Where is she?"

"She's coming. She just needed a minute alone. You must realize that she hasn't had much of that in quite some time. Lia has lost many loved ones who couldn't be here today, just as you."

I dove into our bond, searching for any sign of her, and I was thankful that there wasn't a single sign of hesitance from her.

Lynelle wrapped her arms around me and embraced me in a hug that I returned. She then whispered in my ear, "Your mother would be so proud."

She turned from me to head to her seat beside Leon, who greeted her with a beaming smile ear-to-ear. My throat tightened as the overwhelming feeling of wishing my mother could be here, wishing that she could have at least *met* my Lia, nearly consumed me.

My eyes collided with Finn, and he gave me a curt nod. Landon then did the same from his side as he reached down to scratch Nyra's ears as she sat between their legs.

The sound of beating wings then filtered through the air, and everyone turned in the direction from which the girls had arrived.

As if an answer from the gods themselves, Nox appeared on the horizon. My eyes remained locked on him as he landed halfway down the hill we stood upon. Intense palpitations made it feel as if my heart was about to beat out of my chest as the most stunning sight I had ever laid my eyes on peered out from the cover of the wyvern's shoulder.

Carefully lowering his body to one side, Nox allowed Lia to gracefully walk down his wing while lifting the front of her gown.

She placed her tiny hand on his snout in thanks before turning to face us, making my breath catch at the sight of her in her wedding gown and diadem—looking every bit the gorgeous queen she was and would always be to me.

And now here she was, standing before me at the end of the aisle, her eyes sparkling with anticipation as she took her first step towards the edge of our forever.

Elianna

As I took my first step down the aisle, the soft strums of the harp floated around me as the musician began to play. The gentle melody made it feel as if time had ceased and no one else existed in the world but the two of us.

My eyes fixated on the end of the aisle, catching a sweet glimpse of *him*, the greatest love I had ever known and my sworn enemy. His eyes locked on my own, and in his hazel stare, I saw the promise of several lifetimes together, the two of us sitting side by side on our thrones and fighting alongside one another in battle.

The echo of my footsteps filled my ears as time continued to slow. Memories flashed before my eyes—the shipwreck that brought us stranded together, the sneaky, shared laughter beneath the Sylis trees from euphoroot, and the night in Celan Village, when he had saved me from his own guards and made love to me hours later, locking our mating bond forever, unbeknownst to us both.

A single tear slipped down my cheek as the memories flooded me, realizing just how far the two of us had grown together in such a brief span of time.

More than anything, I wished for my father to be here—to see what I had become and who I was meant to be. His true heir, who he had always believed in and wished to rule his kingdom following his reign.

My breath caught as I reached my mate, but my eyes had drifted beyond him in the distance. The world around me blurred as my gaze narrowed in on the figure that materialized, emerging from between the trees at the edge of the lake—a black-coated stag.

The magnificent, rare creature was a near replica of the one that had been mounted on the wall of my father's chambers—the one I had always teased him for but secretly loved because I knew how much he had. A smile tilted my lips as a sob of bliss escaped me, realizing that he was here with me after all, always watching, even from the vale.

Jace's stare followed my own to where the stag lingered, its attention locked on us.

I stepped up to my mate as we continued to gaze down toward the beast. "Father," I whispered.

Jace's stare moved to me, and he smiled so radiantly it nearly made my heart stop. I then realized that everyone's attention had wandered to where ours had been. Avery's fingertips flew to cover her mouth as her cheeks flushed, and Finn wore a proud grin—each of them feeling his presence here with us, too.

My mate extended his hand to me, and as I placed mine in his, a surge of completeness washed over me, knowing that all of my loved ones were here with me—with *us*.

Veli stepped up behind us in the center of the arch. "Well, now that we are *all* here..." She winked at me. "It is time that we now begin both the ceremony and joining."

Embodying the role of a High Priestess, Veli spoke the words of the gods into the vast expanse of the sky, sealing our ceremony of marriage with their blessing, ensuring our lives together would be filled with love and longevity.

"Do you, Jace Cadoria, Commander of the Mortal Army, take Elianna Valderre to be not only your mate in this life but your gods-favored wedded spouse?"

He looked at me then, and the entire realm melted away as I stood beneath his unfaltering, blazing stare.

"There is not a moment, nor has there ever been one, where I have not loved you with every fiber of my being, even since the moment we met. I believe I had always known there was something about you that I wasn't able to shake. Even as your prisoner, I found myself staring at you, wanting to know you—*needing* to. And while I tried so hard to despise you, I knew I never could. My feelings for you, my *mating* to you, have melted away a hatred that cut so deep within me that it had consumed me since I was just a boy. You are everything to me. I vow to be your protector and shield, and any enemy that dares cross you will meet the edge of my blade—but that is, of course, if they don't meet your own first."

A prideful smile graced his face before he continued. "And as we stand here before our family and the eyes of the gods, my answer now and will always be that I do. I take you to be my wife, my mate, and my queen for eternity. From now until my very end."

My eyes never left his, and my lips parted at his words.

"And do you, Elianna Valderre, Rightful Heir and Queen of the Velyran Realm, take Jace Cadoria to be not only your mate in this life but your gods-favored wedded spouse?" Veli's voice broke the silence.

"I never thought I would find a love so great, one that flows so deeply in my veins that it has become the very essence of my existence. A man who was my mirror in our enemy's ranks had shown me a kindness that hadn't even been granted by those who had sworn themselves and their loyalty to me. Jace, you have gifted me a love that I never believed existed, and in turn, you have also gifted me the courage and support needed to reclaim what is rightfully mine by birth and blood. There will never be enough in this realm that I could provide that would feel worthy of repaying your constant love and aid, so I will start by offering you both my heart and soul forever. For they are yours—always have been, and always will be. And as we stand here beneath the eyes of the gods, I do, as well. I take you as my husband, my mate, and the king of both of our people. In this realm and beyond."

With these words, Veli's stare began to glow, their golden hue projecting onto us, mixing with the fiery shades of the setting sun cast in the distance. Ancient, forgotten words left her in a whisper, and with each syllable, the gold in her irises intensified as her spell draped us like an invisible cloak—its presence not seen but felt.

Lightning crackled through the clear sky, a phenomenon I never thought possible. A wind-like tunnel surrounded only the two of us, our hair swirling in its mix as we stood with our fingers intertwined and locked with one another's.

Suddenly, we each began to glow ourselves—our skin illuminating a golden, radiant light as the gods gifted us their blessing.

Faster than we could blink, the wind ceased, dropping from us instantly, and the lightning vanished as Veli's words halted.

I sucked in a breath through my nostrils, refusing to break our gazes, as everyone in the crowd remained eerily silent and still, watching the ancient ritual of merging mated souls.

"As a blessing bestowed from the Velyran gods above, I am honored to pronounce the two of you as not only husband and wife but fated mates of the soul. May your lives and love be everlasting. You must now seal your joining by kissing your bride."

"You will never have to tell me twice," Jace breathed as he cupped both of my cheeks in his calloused hands and pressed his lips firmly to mine.

My heart melted, and my knees buckled as his hands moved down my body—one supporting the arch of my back as the other was placed on my hip. He twirled me, gently guiding me into a dip beneath our wedding arch, his lips never leaving mine in a soul consuming kiss as everyone around us clapped and cheered.

"*Always.*"

His voice filled my mind as his mouth remained on me, stunning me as I was held in his arms.

He broke our kiss and gazed down at me with a knowing grin as he held me in the dip. A smile cracked my lips as I realized that the bridge-bonding to each other's minds had been successful, feeling him and his comforting presence so much more now than I ever had before.

"Always," I echoed in a whisper.

FORTY-NINE

Elianna

THE HOURS FOLLOWING THE ceremony were filled with booming laughter, the clinking of wine goblets, dancing, and kisses snuck beneath the shadows that Veli kindly cast upon us when she sensed privacy was needed.

After a while, we realized we weren't the only ones sneaking kisses when we thought everyone's eyes lurked elsewhere. Gage and Avery slowly danced beneath the lit torches in the estate's backyard, while Finn and Landon were often found roaming about the outskirts of the gathering, hand-in-hand. As for Veli and Zaela, on the off chance the witch's shadows weren't looming over us, it was safe to assume they were covering their maker and another sneaky blonde.

As the night died down, and everyone who had come to attend the celebration for us said their goodbyes, I watched as most of our family drunkenly wandered up to the estate to end the most perfect day.

Lynelle had left with Leon, considering they had been inseparable the entire evening.

Avery twirled gracefully toward me, her dress flowing around her, as Gage and Jace moved through the yard, extinguishing each torch while leaving behind a trail of fading light.

She threw her arms around my shoulders, and we both spun, our giggles echoing through the air as our gowns tangled at our feet.

"How does it feel to be a *married* female?" she asked through her laughter.

"Very surreal," I answered. "I never really considered myself to be the marrying type—Jace, either, for that matter."

Her smile beamed even more. "And the mind connection?"

I blew out a breath as my own laughter faded. "We've been too distracted to do much with it tonight, but I'm sure that will all come in time."

"*Imagine all the things I can say to you...all the plans I have for what I want to do to you, all while they remain oblivious.*"

My eyes widened as Jace's voice filtered through my mind with his promises of sweet taunting. My gaze shot to him from across the yard, and his wicked chuckle echoed through our bond as we made eye contact.

My eyes drifted back to my sister to find her staring at me with a knowing glare.

"Too distracted," she mocked while her eyebrows fluttered rapidly.

"It's the truth," I hissed, but my lips betrayed me with a slight curve of amusement. "Well, it was only a moment ago." A laugh left me as I shook my head.

The yard fell into complete darkness aside from the moonlight, and the boys made their way to us as we stood in its center.

"Are you ready for bed, *husband?*" I asked as I stretched my hand out to Jace.

"Yes, however, we won't be staying in the main house this evening."

My brows furrowed in confusion. "Where did you wish to stay?"

Gage cleared his throat before Jace could answer and put his arm around Avery's shoulder, pulling her close to his body. "We'll see you in the morning."

He inclined his head to us as he turned her on her heels and guided her up the small hill that led to the estate's back entrance.

"Wait, but where are they sleeping?" she asked curiously as she tried to look back at us, but he hushed her in response and kissed her forehead, silencing her.

I slowly pivoted to face my mate once more. "Where *are* we sleeping?" I asked with a laugh as I crossed my arms.

He spun me slowly, pulling my back against his chest as he wrapped his arms around me and placed his chin atop my head—facing his mother's cottage that was set back in the corner of the estate's land.

My eyes flared. We hadn't even spoken of his mother's home that Lynelle had offered to us. The pain in his eyes when we first arrived had been too great for me to ever force that on him, and we had been staying in the main house with the others ever since.

"We don't need to stay there. If it's privacy you want—"

"*You* are what I want, and I should have shown this to you on our first night here and every night since. It's a part of me, and forever will be, just as you are," he interjected.

His words continued in my mind as a whisper. "*I felt your father's presence with us today. I don't know how I felt that it was him, but I just knew. The look on your face and what I sensed from you. It was very special.*" His arms tightened around me.

Despite my initial fear of the mind-joining, I found it surprisingly easy and comforting to hear his voice as it echoed through the bond instead of just basing everything off of emotions felt.

I focused intently on answering him in the same manner—how he had already made it seem effortless was a mystery to me, but I could feel him there, constantly lingering in the background of my soul. It felt like another tether that my mind could travel over whenever I needed him.

I dove toward the bond, reaching for it, and spoke the words, willing them to float straight to him. "*Your mother was there with us, too. She watches over you and us, just as my father.*"

"Perhaps you're right, my sweet Lia." His voice was soft, gentle—one he only ever used with me.

Without warning, he swept down, scooping me up by cradling the middle of my back while his other arm lifted beneath my thighs. A roar of laughter escaped both of us as he pressed a quick kiss to my forehead and carried me all the way to the cottage's door.

Once at the entrance, my arm reached out and pushed the door open. The sound of its creaking echoed through the cool night air.

"Lynelle had it tidied up earlier this morning while everyone prepared for the wedding."

I tilted my neck to face him as he held me in the doorway. "You planned this the entire time?"

A smirk formed. "I may have."

He angled his body to walk through the doorway while I remained in his arms. Once inside, he kicked the door closed behind him. The only light provided was filtered in by the moon peeking through the windows.

My neck slowly pivoted as I peered around the room, my gaze lingering on the shadows from the furniture that was spread about the home he grew up in.

He gently placed me on my feet, and I picked up the front of my wedding gown and strolled about, my fingertips grazing over the décor as I passed by. The cottage was quaint and sweet, instantly portraying itself as a home made from love.

Jace watched me as I roamed curiously, his eyes moving with me, but down the bond, beneath his feeling of admiration, a sense of heartache lingered.

My steps halted as I came across a portrait that hung on the wall. My fingers lifted and brushed over the painting of a mother with her young son. Hazel eyes that matched my mate's stared back at me in two beautiful stares. Her arms were wrapped around him as if holding her little boy in place while the portrait was painted.

Footsteps sounded behind me and I felt his warm presence at my back.

"This is her?" I breathed.

"That's her."

I turned to face him. "She's beautiful."

He gave me a soft smile. "Indeed, she was, and she would have adored you. Mainly for managing to put me in my place from time to time."

I lifted a brow. "Oh, from time to time?"

"That's what I said." He grinned. "Let's not forget all the times the other half of us must be put in place herself," he whispered wickedly in my ear.

"How rude of you to remind me of such things on our wedding night," I teased.

Jace let out a breathy laugh, the one that made my knees weak. "There she is."

"How does it feel to be a Valderre?" I whispered. "Did you ever think this would be possible?"

"That I would marry my sworn enemy and take her last name to sit at her side upon her throne? Oh, of course," he teased.

"We will need a crest," I said as I leaned into him. "Tradition holds that it contains an element from our predecessor. My father's crest contained the antlers of a black stag in remembrance of his father. He grew to love the creatures just as much."

Jace met my stare and smiled. "We will create a crest that symbolizes both you and your ties to your father. I'll see that it will be branded on your army's armor and posted on our flags the day you reclaim your crown," he promised.

My heart galloped in my chest. How was it possible to love someone as much as I loved him?

After wandering about the rest of the living room, he gently gripped my hand and tugged me into him. I wrapped my arms around his neck as his hands rested on my hips and he placed a kiss on my nose.

"Now, to show you our room for the evening."

He led me to a room at the far end of the hall, and when the door was pushed open, a large bedroom materialized in the dim light. It was simple, with just a few bureaus and a large bed in its center.

Jace closed the door behind us—the click of its lock echoed off the walls. When I turned to him with a lifted brow, he said, "We know how much Gage loves to barge in once the sun rises."

"Very true," I said with a laugh.

He stepped up to me, gently taking my chin between his fingers, and lifted my gaze to his. His lips pressed against mine, and they parted for him as if commanded, deepening our kiss instantly as we explored each other for the first time as husband and wife.

Guiding me toward the bed in the middle of the room, his fingers worked their way up my spine, unlacing the back of my gown with ease. Once the back of my knees hit the edge of the mattress, he steadied me before I fell.

"The sight of you in this dress is nothing short of breathtaking, and as I watched you walk down the aisle wearing it, my heart nearly stopped. The gown is beautiful."

His calloused fingers brushed against the skin of my shoulder while he carefully pulled the laced sleeves of my dress down my arms. The fabric fell at my feet, leaving me standing before him entirely bare—aside from the crown that rested atop my head.

"But *you*, my Lia, are exquisite," he breathed, his voice tinged with desperation.

I lifted my arms to remove the diadem, but his hands reached out and halted them. "Leave it," he demanded. "For when I take you for the first time as my wife, I want you to feel just as the queen you are."

A shiver worked its way up my spine as he tenderly guided me down onto the bed.

Jace explored every inch of my body for hours, providing both a mixture of eager, loving kisses and greedy, insatiable ones, forever keeping me on my toes.

We made love as man and wife countless times into the night, surrendering ourselves to each other and realizing that no matter how deep our connection dove, it would never be enough.

FIFTY

Elianna

My eyes fluttered open to realize that darkness still blanketed the room. I pivoted under the covers to turn and face the window and noticed dawn wasn't far off, the moon's glow dimming.

I closed my eyes to fall back asleep once more, but couldn't shake the feeling that I was being watched. An overwhelming sense of having eyes on me sent my heart racing in my chest.

I pulled the blanket over my face to try to drift off to sleep, telling myself that I was being ridiculous and that no one would be foolish enough to break into our home—I also would have heard them.

Yet still, the feeling remained.

I shoved the covers off and looked at Jace, who remained sound asleep beside me, appearing as peaceful as ever.

Blowing out a breath, I rubbed my eyes before glancing around the room, but all I noticed was that the door was still closed, and everything else remained untouched.

I was about to tell myself I was losing my mind when my gaze caught on the corner of the room, where an otherworldly shadow lingered—one that I had grown accustomed to over these passing weeks.

"Veli," I grumbled, annoyance filling my tone. "Veli, what in the realm? This isn't funny at all."

Silence answered me, but the shadows swerved, as if working to cover something—or someone.

"Jace," I whispered nervously, but he didn't stir.

I leapt up from the bed, my gaze locked on the corner where the shadows swirled, their darkness appearing more smoke-like than they had a moment ago.

"Who are you?" I asked sternly as I clutched Jace's shirt to my front that I had worn to bed.

Nothing answered me aside from the mocking wisps of darkness.

"I am Elianna Valderre, Heir of the Realm, and I demand that you present yourself to me at once and state how and why you are in my home."

"*Jace*," I sent down the bond. "*Jace, wake up.*"

"Heir of the Realm?" A wicked, bone-chilling voice that I recognized all too well echoed, and my lips parted as it reached my ears.

Idina stepped out from the cover of the shadows, their remnants swirling around her figure like wraiths.

"It is a bit presumptuous to be declaring yourself as such with no proper declaration from the prior king. Do you not agree?" Her head tilted to the side in a predatory manner.

"How did you get here?" My lip curled back into a snarl as my eyes followed her movements.

"Ah, yes, well...you are not the only queen that has acquired witches and their use of magic."

"I have acquired no one and nothing. People stand by my side because of what they believe is right. I didn't obtain them as if they were objects to barter for. They are my *friends*."

A wicked cackle left her. "Friends." Her eyes drifted to my husband, who remained asleep in our bed. "Is that what this mortal filth is that you lay beside?"

My steps carried me to block her view, shielding him from anything she might try to do. "You will stay the fuck away from him."

She tsked and her eyes wandered around the room, taking in the sight of the space—her eyes caught on the gown that remained on the floor at the foot of the bed.

My heart was beating so fast I thought it would burst in my chest.

"*Jace, if you can hear me, do not move*," I warned.

Finally, a stir from him down the bond.

"*Lia?*" His voice sounded groggy with sleep, even as it filtered through my mind.

"*Do not move. Do not stir. Just remain as you are.*"

His eyes flew open, and I felt the panic that rumbled through him.

"*Close your eyes, Jace. Let me try to show you, but you can't react because I don't know how deep this magic goes.*"

I felt his body tense. "*Lia.*" His voice was stern. "*Who the fuck is in here?!*" he demanded, but I ignored him.

Putting in every ounce of effort possible, I focused as hard as I could to show him the room and who now stood in it, willing him to see it through my eyes.

409

The moment my vision overtook his own, Jace sat up instantly, ready to strike the queen down in his mother's cottage. The force of his movements startled me enough to drop the sight connection.

When my eyes flew to his, he was panting as he stood beside our bed and then looked at me. "I...I can't see her."

"What?" I breathed.

"Show yourself to me, you bitch!" he roared into the dark room.

"A queen does not concern herself with mortal filth," she hissed at him.

Idina was watching him intently now, and I willed my sight back into his, his eyes flaring as he saw her once again through my gaze.

"Now...is that what I think it is?" Idina asked with a malicious chuckle as her gaze returned to the dress. "You *married* one of them? Elianna...I knew you had always been a traitorous snake, but I never thought you would take it to such an extreme height."

"It was never I who was the traitorous snake, Idina. That title has always been yours alone to claim. And you wear it so well, I might add."

"You think that betraying your own race, and inter-breeding with lesser beings, is not treasonous? And you believe that you are fit to rule? While I despise your existence, you are the daughter of the late *fae* king, and I had not taken you to be quite so reckless."

"*Elianna*," Jace growled. I could feel his patience slipping as he frantically tried to watch through the bond's haze.

"*We don't have any weapons in here. And I can't even see her with my own eyes. I don't know what the fuck to do.*"

"*Stay where you are. That is an order.*"

"*If she fucking touches you...*"

"*An ORDER, Jace.*"

I felt him hold himself back at my command—his anger igniting our tether in searing flames.

Idina's stare drifted back to my mate, and my heart crept up my throat. "At least it appears that you keep your mortal pet in line as he stands in the corner with his tail between his legs."

"You will not speak of him." My nails dug into the palms of my hands as they balled into fists, shaking with rage. "And interesting for you to declare what deems an act treasonous...considering you *murdered* my father!" I barked, my voice rising with each passing word.

If my knowledge regarding the manner of the king's death surprised her, her face certainly didn't show it.

The corner of her lips tilted into a venomous, knowing smirk as she took a single step toward me, placing her hands behind her back.

"You were always such a good little youngling for your father, doing as he said and always making sure he was pleased with you and what you had accomplished...you and I are not so different in that sense, I suppose," Idina said.

My eyes flared. "You are implying that you murdered the King of Velyra over a century after your father's death. If that had been his wish, I'm sure many chances for that had presented itself when your father was still alive...or even shortly after his death."

411

Her eyes narrowed in on me, as if I had struck a nerve. "You know nothing, and I will not waste my breath in explaining what I have done for my kin. I know how you are with your own, and you would have been just as ruthless."

"If a threat presented itself! Not to steal the throne from the royal bloodline of the realm! And *you* are a threat, Idina," I hissed.

Anger-riddled pride radiated from Jace.

She took a step toward me, and I stood my ground at the edge of the bed.

"I am a threat?!" she seethed. "You stole my only children from me. Murdering one in cold blood for his claim to the throne you so desperately seek while poisoning the other two against me. I am their *mother*. Make no mistake, I *will* get my other children back from you, whether you hand them to me or I pry them from your grasp."

"Murder in cold blood? Claim to the throne?!" My fists were getting ready to strike her the second another word left her mouth. "Your son was just as malicious as you are, and he possessed as much claim to the throne as a peasant beggar in the slums that you look down upon so much."

Her eyes widened in shock as her jaw ticked with fury, its aura filling the room.

"As for Avery and Finnian, they hate you just as much as the rest of the realm does. Perhaps even more," I continued.

A huff of approval sounded in my mind from Jace as he impatiently watched through my eyes.

"I don't know what it is that you *think* you know, but—"

"It is not a matter of what I think to be true, but what is true by blood. And that is that Kai was not King Jameson's son," I stated.

"And how do you know of such things, little Elianna?" she hissed.

My lip curled into a snarl once more. "The realm always knows. Every vine that sways from a willow tree, every root that runs deep into the soil, and every creature that roams above it...possess the power of knowing."

Her eyes leisurely roamed up and down my body before meeting my stare again. "And who would father a child of the queen if not the king?"

My brow rose, and this time, it was my turn to smirk at the knowledge I held. "Perhaps the menacing, personal guard she kept so close all these years?"

She scoffed, pretending to be disgusted, but something resembling rage-induced hurt flashed across her eyes. "That is quite an accusation." Her voice was deceptively sweet.

"One that holds truth," I bit out.

"*Lia, her tone has changed,*" Jace warned, and I peeked over at him as the veins in his neck throbbed from continuing to hold himself back at my order.

"*I know. Don't move. The shadows are swirling at her feet and I don't know if they can harm us.*"

I could feel his temper slipping as he reluctantly obeyed.

"Well then, *Elianna*," she spoke my name with venom, one somehow more poisonous than she had my entire life. "Let me make this as clear as possible for you..."

My heartbeat quickened again as I watched her eyes dart back and forth between me and Jace.

She stepped up to me, putting her ruby-painted lips to my ear as she whispered her threats. "You will surrender your life to me, and I will forgive your merry little band of rebels for their treason."

"Lia!" Jace shouted, but I blocked it out, praying he remained where he stood. Pure agonizing panic rattled our tether from him.

"The humans, well, they will continue to be hunted into extinction. That is, unless they would prefer to offer themselves as slaves, declaring fae as the superior race of the realm once and for all."

An evil, breathy laugh left my husband. "Go to hell, you fae bitch."

Her face twisted into something horrific at his words, so I quickly brought her attention back to me.

"My people want freedom from your wickedness, not to offer themselves into a lifetime of servitude to you."

Idina laughed wickedly while shaking her head. She took a step back to get a better look at me, attempting to make me feel small beneath her stare. "Well, then, Elianna, when *your* people, as you have claimed them to be, all meet their end, you will have no one to blame but yourself. This includes the pet that warms your bed."

A growl rumbled through my chest as she threatened my mate, and I took a step to the side, blocking his body from her once more.

"Lia," Jace growled.

"*Stay back*," I ordered through my mind.

"Honestly, Elianna, what kind of ruler takes away the choices of her kingdom's people?" She winked at me. "Perhaps we are more alike than we wish to admit."

"We are *nothing* alike, and I know my people would rather fight for a chance at true freedom than be forced into slavery. Make no mistake, Idina, any chains you place upon their wrists...I will *shatter* them."

She watched my speech with a menacing grin. "You will do well to remember this when you discover what we have gifted you during our little chat this evening. It is a pity that it appears you're not there."

"*Lia, what does that mean?*"

She leaned into me once more, a shiver working its way up my spine at her proximity. "It poses the question...is one life worth more than another? Is your life worth more than the millions that will die?" She took a step back and then another, creating a short distance between us.

"I have made that choice now, not once, but twice," she admitted, and my eyes flared. "For the reckless decisions made by two foolish fae had threatened my family's plans for the realm and its superior race, so they had to be dealt with." She paused for a moment. "And my only regret is that you were not there when I slit your mother's throat, for I would have done the same to you."

My jaw dropped, heart nearly coming to a screeching halt in my chest as my surroundings evaporated. Time ceased as my vision skipped red and went straight to a blinding haze of black.

"That's it!" Jace boomed as he moved to charge toward her.

A scream of wrath tore through my throat as I surged toward her in unison, but the moment I thought we would collide, I was met with nothing but air. My body slammed into the floorboards where she had stood only a moment before as the vanishing shadows swirled.

"You made your choice, Elianna. Now, you must live with it." Idina's voice echoed through the room as if coming from every direction.

And then she was gone.

"Lia!" Jace bellowed as fell to his knees at my side. His arms wrapped around me as he heaved me to sit upright beside him.

"Why did you make me stay down, Lia? *Why*?! She was eyeing you like prey. I was bursting at the fucking seams. Please don't ever demand something like that of me again. *Ever*. Are you okay? Are you hurt?"

His eyes roamed over my body, pure worry radiating from him.

"I didn't know if she would harm you, and I wasn't willing to risk it. Especially with the sorcery that had brought her here." The words were barely audible as I tried to gather my thoughts.

My rage-hazed, unseeing eyes darted back and forth, refusing to land on any one thing as my entire body remained tense. I wanted to crawl out of my skin, feeling more violated than I ever had before.

I had endured chains, whips, and the hands of unwanted males on my body—but none of that had felt like *this*.

His eyes softened, and he bowed his head. "Gods, I'm so sorry. I was just terrified. Why the hell couldn't I see her too?! I could only see her through your eyes. It wasn't as if I was a bystander, but exactly where you stood beneath her stare. I saw it all...*felt* it all. Lia..." His tone teetered in desperation.

My lips parted as I worked to put my thoughts into words. "She killed my mother," I whispered.

"I know." His tone was more gentle than I had ever heard.

"Idina *murdered* my mother the day I was born...and she allowed everyone to believe that *I* had killed her from the birth. She lied to my father and told him that it was a birthing complication—that she bled out on the bed as she lay there alone." My voice rose with each word as tears of rage streamed down my cheeks.

"My Lia," he breathed. "Your father knows that it wasn't your fault." His thumbs worked to swipe the tears as they slipped.

"I'm going to fucking destroy her."

He nodded. "Yes, you will. And I will be right there with you as you set her world ablaze and watch it burn."

My gaze lifted to his—the golden flecks in his eyes illuminated as dawn filtered through the curtains. "We move our armies *now*."

FIFTY-ONE

Elianna

I BURST THROUGH THE front door of Jace's old home after putting my wedding dress back on, the only item of clothing I had since our surprise stay in the cottage, and stormed up the hill that led up to the estate's back door. Jace remained right on my tail as we passed Nox, whose golden gaze was locked on us while we ran past him.

With each step, I internally worked on the speech on how to convince my court that we needed to move our army sooner than anticipated. Not only that, but Idina's possession of the witches' dark magic had now been more than confirmed.

I stormed through the back door to find Zaela standing in the kitchen, looking every bit of hungover from the night prior.

"Is everything okay?" she asked as her eyes flared.

"No. We need the others," I stated as I stalked through the kitchen, aiming for the living area.

"You look like shit," Jace said to his cousin.

I peered over my shoulder in time to watch as she flipped him off in response. Normally, I would've laughed, but there was no room for that in our current situation.

"Family meeting!" I bellowed.

When no one answered, I stormed up the stairs and down the long hallway that held all the bedrooms, banging on each door I passed.

"Everybody up, now! Family meeting in the living room in five minutes."

Sleep-filled groans sounded on the opposite sides of the doors as I made my way back down the stairs. Jace sat in the chair next to the fireplace, rubbing the sleep from his eyes, and when he looked up at me, pure exhaustion was etched into his features. My heart lurched, realizing that this was truly only the beginning of the exhaustion that we were about to feel.

The stairs creaked from the weight of the small stampede that paraded down them as they all made their way to us.

"We couldn't have *one* day to sleep in?" Finn groaned as they took their seats around the room.

"I'm sorry, but something has happened," I admitted.

"Oh, gods, Elianna, you're still in your gown?" Veli asked.

"Thought that would have been torn to shreds by now," Gage joked, but when no laughter answered him from either Jace or myself, they all felt the seriousness of what was to come.

Veli let out a huff. "What has happened, Elianna? In a matter of hours."

I blinked a few times as I tried to form the words. "The queen appeared in our room just before dawn. It was as if she had materialized from shadows."

"What?!" The word echoed from everyone as they shouted in shock.

"She was physically in your room? You saw her?" Avery asked.

I nodded. "I woke up feeling uneasy, as if I had eyes on me, and when I noticed motion in the corner of the room, she emerged."

"Was her body present in the room, or was it a projection of herself?" Veli demanded.

"I'm not sure I know what you mean," I admitted. "I saw her, though her presence was certainly from sorcery. Shadows were whirling around her feet."

Swirling fuchsia eyes snapped to Jace. "You saw her as well, and she didn't move to harm you?"

"Aside from insulting me, she was focused on taunting Lia. I wasn't able to see her on my own, but I watched through her eyes."

"Through the bond?"

"Yes," I answered. "He saw everything as I did."

"And felt it," Jace growled, anger crawling through him.

"I knew the dress had to come off at some point," Gage whispered.

"Gage!" Jace and I yelled in unison.

"Okay, I'm sorry. In my defense, I think I might still be half drunk."

Avery reached up and smacked his cheek lightly a few times as she pressed her lips together in a flat line.

"Did she touch you? Did you feel her skin in any way? Her clothing, hair...anything tangible?" Veli asked.

"No. When I went to strike her, she vanished."

The witch's eyes flared. "You tried to hit her?"

"She taunted Lia to bring her to the edge. She was trying to get a rise out of her," Jace interjected.

"And it *worked*." Veli crossed her arms and raised a brow, a scowl working its way across her face. "Elianna, what have we talked about with the impulsivity? If she had been physically there and grabbed you, she could have pulled you through the portal back to where she came from!"

Panic erupted down the tether, and my eyes wandered to my husband. "I never thought of that," I whispered.

Jace placed his face in his hands. "Gods, Lia, that could have been a trap the entire time. And neither of us thought of it being a possibility."

"Well, it appears that Idina didn't think of that either, so we lucked out," I said.

"If she touched you..." His nostrils flared as his hands balled into shaking fists. "If she had been able to bring you back to Isla...you would have been put to death immediately or handed over to Kellan if he managed to survive. Lia..."

"I know, okay?! I realize that, too. We have to be more careful. But how are we supposed to look out for shit like this if she can now come and go as she pleases?!"

I was never going to be able to sleep again.

"What did she say to you that made you want to strike her?" Avery asked.

I forced myself to swallow. "That she killed my mother. She slit her throat the day I was born, and her only regret was that she wasn't patient enough to wait and do the same to me."

Avery's and Finnian's eyes widened in horror, exchanging a quick glance before looking away. My own eyes narrowed in on them as I watched beneath furrowing brows.

"Oh, gods, Lia..." Avery started.

My gaze moved back and forth between my two siblings.

"What is it, Avery?" My tone had more bite than I intended, but I had a sinking feeling in my gut as I watched their quick exchange.

She audibly swallowed. "We...we knew this. We found it out the same day we discovered she murdered Father. Lia, I—"

"You, *WHAT*?!" I shrieked as the feeling of betrayal violently slammed into me.

Jace reached out from where he stood and grabbed my wrist, stroking it with his thumb, but I wasn't naïve enough to think he wasn't also subtly trying to hold me back as he felt the agony of it all bubble through me.

Tears were streaming down Avery's cheeks, and Finnian looked too terrified to speak.

"Tell me it's not true," I demanded. "Tell me that you did not withhold information like this from me."

"We didn't *withhold* it from you." Avery's voice was on the verge of breaking into a sob. Gage stood then, carefully wrapping his arm around my sister's waist.

"Liar!" I screamed, and everyone averted their eyes from me as the tension in the room rose, except for my sister.

Her lips trembled, but she steadied it before she spoke. "So much has happened since we learned of this. This was back when you were still assumed dead after the shipwreck.

Before you were dragged back to Isla by Kellan and before your escape from the dungeons."

"It's true, Lia, it was a horrible bit of information that we had overheard months ago while learning about our own father's death as well," Finn chimed in. "It slipped from us, but we never planned to not tell you. *Everything* changed for us that day."

I sucked on my tongue as guilt loomed over me like a taunting shadow.

"I led a rebellion to you." Avery took a hesitant step toward me. "I have done everything you have asked of me since the night of the wedding massacre at the castle. You begged me to get us out and run... I did that. I brought Finn, Landon, Veli, *hundreds* of fae...Nyra! Our entire lives were uprooted in a single night. I had barely ever left the castle grounds, never mind the city. We risked our lives and committed treason against the crown to find you, not even knowing if there would be anything left to find."

I was clenching my teeth so hard I thought they would shatter as she looked at me with her doe-eyes filled with tears—tears that I put there in my fit of rage.

"So no, Elianna," Avery continued, and the use of my full name from her made me feel so small. "We did *not* withhold information from you. I will beg for your forgiveness for forgetting that we knew this, but you need to know that it never once crossed my mind that we held this knowledge while you didn't."

The room fell into an unbearable silence.

"Okay," I choked out after a few moments. "There will be no need to beg for forgiveness when you've done nothing wrong."

"Oh, I have done plenty that is wrong. My mother now has this dark magic at her disposal because of my fuck-up, but you must know where my loyalties lie. It is right where they have always been, and that is with you."

My eyes softened, and I tugged my wrist from Jace's hold. "I know, and I'm so, so sorry for assuming otherwise in this brief moment of insanity," I admitted.

She gave me a nod before she sat down on the settee, and we all blew out a breath as the tension in the air slowly fizzled out.

"Well, since that is now out of the way," Veli started. "I believe I now know how she materialized before you and evaporated when you moved to touch her."

"By all means, Veli, go on," I announced.

"It was not a portal spell they cast to make her appear in your room." Jace's relief was palpable at her words. "You would have seen her slip back through the rift. I believe that she had projected her conscious before you, appearing in a non-tangible form."

"Such a thing is possible?" I wondered aloud.

"As if she was a ghost?" Zaela asked from where she stood, leaning against the windowsill.

"Precisely," Veli answered. "Which means that she does not necessarily know where we are. If a portal had transported her there physically, the witch who cast the spell would have had to, at one point, physically be in the location that she opened it to. Now, it's impossible to say if they have ever stepped foot on this particular soil over the centuries, but given the circumstances of Idina appearing directly in your bedroom, it's safe to assume that is not the case."

"What does it entail to project one's consciousness before another? Are there rules or guidelines like the portals?" Jace asked.

"All it would take is for the person to have met the individual they wish to present themselves to. Once the spell is cast, it only takes merely a whisper and picturing them in their minds. Seconds later, they will appear wherever the person is located."

"That may be the most terrifying form of dark magic I've heard of to date," Landon said softly.

"It's not even classified as dark," the witch answered. "Though, since shadows were present, I'm assuming they were acting as an extra barrier of protection for the queen."

"That's even more terrifying," Finn echoed.

"So the good news is that she can't travel here by portal and she likely doesn't know that we lay hidden beyond the mountains. The bad news is that she may appear before us whenever she wishes, and depending on where we are at that time, she may discover our whereabouts."

I rubbed my temples as a migraine brewed from everything she was unloading on us. "Mother's tits, this is a gods-damn nightmare."

"That it is," Veli huffed.

"We need to move our armies, and we need to move them soon. Much sooner than we planned," I stated.

"How soon?" Gage asked, every bit the calculating second-in-command, and no longer the joking, half-drunk best friend.

Nyra trotted up to me and sat on my feet, tilting her head to the side as she looked up at me. I reached down and scratched her ears as I blew out a breath.

"I want us marching by the end of the week," I stated. "Can we make that happen?"

Gage's eyes darted to Zaela and then over my shoulder to Jace. "It won't be a simple task, but we can talk to Leon too, and get a better idea."

"Excellent. I want the ships prepared, too," I stated.

He gave me a curt nod. "We will do everything we can."

I aimed for the stairs set back from the living area. "I'll come with you to speak with him. Let me just change out of this first."

The sound of footsteps filled the room as everyone dispersed, following me up the stairs to prepare for the demanding day that awaited us.

FIFTY-TWO

Elianna

MY GAZE LINGERED ON my wedding gown sprawled across our bed as I pulled my fighting leathers up my thighs, wishing more than anything that I had time for a hot bath before the day ahead.

Jace approached me and placed a gentle kiss on my forehead as he finished buttoning his shirt. "You still feel guilty for what you said to Avery," he guessed.

"I don't know what came over me," I whispered before placing my hands on my hips.

"Lia, you have the weight of the realm on your shoulders and our wedding night was bombarded by the queen. You're angry and scared and *hurt*. You have every right to be each of those things and more. Nobody blames you for feeling this way. To be honest, they're probably shocked you've held it together this long."

"I have never lashed out at her before. Ever."

He shrugged as he took my chin between his fingers. "We often lash out at those closest to us. The gods know that I have too many times to count on both Gage and Zae before we met."

"You? Lash out in anger?"

427

The corners of his lips lifted. "There she is."

A soft smile formed on my face, but then the estate's front door slammed open, startling us both. We grabbed our weapons on instinct, fastening them to their belts and sheaths as we rushed out of the bedroom.

"Commander!" Leon's voice boomed through the house as we turned the corner of the stairs, everyone else shoving out of their own rooms behind us.

Jace raced down the stairs, taking two at a time as I remained at the top with the others.

"What is it, Leon?" I asked.

Lynelle came running through the door behind him. "Thank the gods they're here!" she yelled, out of breath.

"What's happening?" Jace demanded, his hands balling into fists.

Leon's eyes flew to my mate and then up to me, prompting me to slowly descend the steps.

"I fear for Ellecaster."

My eyes flared as my steps quickened until I was at Jace's side. "Did something happen?"

He blew out a breath through his nostrils. "You all need to come see this."

The general turned on his heel and marched back through the door, and everyone followed.

Racing into the front yard, we turned to face the mountains in the distance, and my jaw locked instantly at the sight beheld.

Thick, black smoke was lifting into the sky at an alarming rate on the opposite end of the peaks.

"No," Jace whispered as he turned back to face me, eyes filled with ruin.

I swallowed. "She said she left a gift for us to find."

"Gods fucking dammit!" Jace bellowed as he pivoted and stormed up to Gage. "Prepare a fleet to march back to Ellecaster, and—"

"No," I interrupted him, bringing everyone's attention to me. "We don't know what lies in wait there. It could be a trap." My eyes moved to Veli and then back to my mate. "You and I will take Nox and scope it out before we involve any soldier. With any luck, some of them may remain and they will meet their fate by fire. However, for all we know, a trap is set at the opposite end of that tunnel."

His nostrils flared as I felt his aggravation, pure enough to believe it was my own, but he answered me with a nod.

"I have reservations regarding it just being the two of you," the general admitted.

"The two of us and my wyvern," I reminded him, and he swallowed his retort as he stood frozen in my glare.

"In the least, we can prepare a small troop to await at our gates on this end, in case we need to storm the city at its opposite end immediately," Gage interjected.

"And if they have discovered the tunnel and are on their way now to Alaia?" Zaela questioned.

I turned to her. "Then we will scorch the passage. They'll have nowhere to run."

The dense smoke filled the skies ahead as it danced and swirled with the air currents. Nox raced through the clouds and between the peaks. Jace and I kept our eyes peeled, watching the passage down below for any intruders as we leaned over the sides of the saddle, but we hadn't seen a damn thing.

"We're nearing the city," Jace announced, and I turned to him, just as Nox's flight took us into the outskirts of the smoke.

"Gods," I said through coughs. "What could've done this?"

As our eyes adjusted, we looked down towards the city that we could catch glimpses of as the smoke passed.

There was...nothing left. No movement remained on the ground aside from that of the lingering flames. I gazed out in the distance to find that no retreating army remained in sight.

"Mother of the gods," I breathed.

"We're too late," Jace hissed. He wore the face of wrath incarnate as devastation emanated from him.

"Nox, take us below," I ordered, and on command, he tucked in his wings and sent us shooting down to the center of the once great, rebuilt city.

My lips parted in horror as I took in what was displayed before my very eyes.

Jace immediately jumped down from Nox, not even bothering to climb down the side of his saddle.

I watched him as he moved in circles, nervously scratching at his beard with widened eyes. My gaze wandered around once I climbed down to meet him.

The cobblestone streets that once shone brightly beneath the sun now bore black stains of ash. All that remained of the rebuilt structures from Velyra's timber were ember-coated planks scattered across the city.

"They're gone. All of them," Jace breathed, and I felt the agony creep into him. "Hundreds of people stayed behind, Lia."

"This isn't your fault. They knew the risk." I wondered if I was trying to convince him more than myself.

A guttural roar of anguish left him, bellowing through the smoke-filled air as he kicked a crumbled piece of stone among the debris.

"Does it matter?" he wondered aloud as he turned to face me. He looked every bit the grieving commander who bore the weight of his people's lives, just as he had the day I met him. "They didn't wish to uproot their lives and leave their homes, and we can't fault them for that."

"We can't fault them for it, but we also must recognize that we did everything we could without forcing them to flee," I reminded him as I stepped up to his side, making him meet my stare.

"This is just another fucking tragedy for us and our people, Lia," he stated.

"You think I don't know that? We need to be thankful for the lives we *did* save by evacuating, which are thousands."

A growl rumbled through the air, turning our attentions to Nox. We observed him as he strolled about the space, sniffing the crisped remnants of the buildings, flashing his teeth and growling each time.

My eyes drifted up to the crumbling watchtower that once held Ellecaster's gates. My feet carried me to it, and I climbed up the half-shattered steps to get a better look at everything.

Blocking out the sun's glare with my hand as the last bit of smoke faded away, I scanned what remained of the city. Bodies lay sprawled in the streets, their skin charred and melted from their bones, making my stomach roll with nausea.

"Hello?!" I yelled into the air. "Are there any survivors?" My voice echoed, bouncing off the cliffs that loomed at the edge of the city, but no responses came.

I met Jace back down where he stood, and we patrolled the ash-covered streets, desperately searching for anyone who survived or remained hidden from the attack.

We reached the back of the city, and my eyes flared as they locked on where the passage to Alaia had once been.

"Fuck," I whispered, and we both took off into a sprint in its direction.

The courthouse's eastern tower was destroyed. Massive boulders and fragmented pieces of its stone had collapsed and piled over the opening of where the passage had once been, completely blocking travel to and from the other side.

My eyes flew to my mate, and his shoulders sagged in defeat. "Well, it's safe to assume that our enemy hasn't discovered our haven. However, this proposes the issue of our armies being able to leave for war."

Dread crept through my veins. The passage was entirely blocked. Soldiers would ultimately be able to climb over the mountainous pile of boulders, but what of our horses and supply wagons? Our food? This was a death sentence for our already battered troops.

"*A new plan must be forged,*" I said into his mind, as I couldn't bring myself to speak the words.

"Is there even time for such things?"

"We don't have a choice, Jace."

A gasp of air erupted to our left, and our weapons were drawn on instinct.

"Who are you?" Jace demanded, his blade extended out toward where the sound came.

A gurgling cough answered his question, and he looked at me. "A survivor," I breathed, and ran toward the mountains of debris.

I combed through the pile of stones, desperately digging through as the coughing quieted beneath it. Finally, a dusty, bloody face appeared before me, and I inhaled sharply at the sight of one of our men.

"Soldier," Jace said calmly, but I could feel his concern.

My eyes drifted down to the rest of him—or what remained of him. The lower half of his body was completely crushed beneath the stone and judging by the blood that slipped from his lips and labored breathing, I knew he had little time left.

The man's eyes slowly lifted to Jace's, but they appeared cloudy and unseeing.

"What happened?" I had never heard my mate's voice so soft when speaking to someone who wasn't me. "To the city. Did an army attack?"

The man's voice was strained. "No," he said, the word ending in a cough. "It came from the sky."

My eyes widened, and my heart sank. "The sky?" I asked. "What do you mean?"

Dread flooded me, hoping that my hunch wasn't true.

"We thought it was you." He pointed his trembling chin in my direction, and my sinking heart cracked in two.

"Me?" The word left me in a whisper.

"*Nox*." The word traveled through my mind, and my eyes met Jace's.

"The beast came from the sky, screeching its warning with glowing eyes the color of blood." My jaw locked, my memory taking me back to when I stood under Azenna's stare. "Once it reached the city gates, it unleashed its flame in the streets. There was no time for escape."

I swallowed thickly. "I'm so sorry." I hated the words as they left me, knowing they held no weight to the situation—an apology to a dying man as he lay crushed beneath stone next to the corpses of his brothers in arms.

"It left as quick as it came, breathing its fire onto every street, and bashing its tail against the buildings that remained." His words left him at a sluggish pace, his voice diminishing with each passing syllable.

The man's eyes drifted to the sky before he continued. "I will get to see my family again soon."

A tear slipped from me as I tried to steady my voice, realizing that his family must have remained here with him and perished in the fires. "You will."

As if that was all the confirmation he needed, he took his final breath—his eyes remained open as they looked at the sky. Jace blew out a breath and gently closed the man's eyes with a hand.

"We must burn him," I reminded him, and he nodded in answer.

I called for Nox, and fallen stones crunched beneath his steps until he stood before us. I motioned to the wreckage, where the man's body remained beneath the boulders. "*Ignystae*," I commanded, voice hoarse with regret and brewing rage.

Nox's jaw opened wide, and I felt the scorching heat of his flames as they erupted from him. When the fire winked out, his vertical pupil narrowed in on me.

"That's why you were growling, isn't it?" I asked, and Jace curiously looked at us. "You could smell the other wyvern that had been here. The one that destroyed the city."

A purr-like rumble sounded to acknowledge my guess, and I took it as my answer.

"It appears that our worst fear has come true," I said to Jace.

"It does indeed," he answered. "Ellecaster is lost. We need to get back to the valley and regroup with everyone."

"Agreed. Everyone must be there." He nodded at my words. "And I do mean *everyone*."

FIFTY-THREE

The Queen

MY EYES BLINKED RAPIDLY as my vision focused on the room I stood in, morphing back into the throne room when my consciousness had just been wherever Elianna hid within the realm.

Locking eyes with Azenna, who stood only feet from me, I shot her a sinister smile. My stare then moved to the crone, who stood in a near trance beside her, eyes glowing as she used her magic to see through our wyvern's mind.

"It's done then?" I asked.

Her lips curled into a smile that I assumed mimicked my own. "It is done. The wyvern found a large city at the foot of the Ezranian Mountains."

"Silcrowe?" I wondered aloud. "We had destroyed it."

"It appears to have been remade," she answered. "But not to worry. It ceases to exist once more."

I stood from my throne and began to pace along the dais. "I don't believe she was there. She's hiding elsewhere; otherwise, I would have been able to hear the commotion or seen a reaction from her regarding it."

"What did you see?" Kellan asked as he leaned against the far wall, arms crossed.

436

I ignored the blatant disrespect in his stance. "She was sleeping when I emerged, which we had anticipated, as it was just before dawn. She was in bed with a human, a wedding gown on her floor."

Adler nearly threw himself from the wall and stalked toward the middle of the room—his eyes locked on me. "Wedding gown?! Surely your eyes—"

"My eyes can see quite fine, Captain," I cut him off, and a grin slid across my face. "We interrupted her wedding night."

His entire body stiffened, and his jaw locked as I gave him the news of his ex-claimed lover.

I tilted my head to the side. "Did *you* wish to marry a treasonous snake, Captain?"

"Absolutely not, Your Grace. I'm just not sure why she would seek a marriage alliance with human scum. I doubt there are mortal families left with ties to significant numbers of men."

"From what I gathered, she cares for him. Which is good to know that she has a weakness aside from my two remaining children."

Adler's eyes flared for a second, but I didn't miss it as his initial reaction to the news. "Aye," he answered.

He thought I didn't recognize the bite in his tone or how his eyes watched me in a calculating manner. Ideally, I would dispose of him when the time came, too, but as of now, I knew that Elianna either feared him or loathed his existence, and that could work to my advantage.

"Did you get any information regarding where her whereabouts might be?" Azenna asked, bringing my attention back to her.

"Considering I stated she was in a dark bedroom, the answer would be no," I snapped. "Perhaps I would have been able to get a better understanding if you could have transported my physical body there as well."

"As we have discussed before, Queen Idina,"—the High Witch's voice was slick with challenge—"we may not open portals to places we have never been, and considering we do not know where she is, that's not possible to do at this time. Even for the High Witch."

"I have scouts posted across the realm that send word daily. No one has seen her or any mortals in known areas as of late," Kellan chimed in.

My neck whipped in his direction. "Nor have they spotted my two living children?"

"Unfortunately, there has been no sign of Princess Avery nor Prince Finnian," he answered. "We are under the presumption that they are with her—wherever she may be. Forgive me for this next question, but do you not consider the acts of your children treasonous?"

My nostrils flared as I clenched my teeth. "Are you Captain or King?" His eyes narrowed in on me in response. "I do *not* answer to you, Kellan Adler. You will do well to remember that. Otherwise, the only traveling in your future is a walk to the gallows in the city square."

He stood perfectly still for a few moments as something resembling pure hatred slithered into his eyes. "Apologies, my queen."

I huffed out a breath of annoyance. "Now, back to why we are here. We weren't able to find her whereabouts. So, you will prepare to have our armies march north. You are bound to find her eventually, and I'm running out of patience."

"Of course," he answered sternly as his eyes drifted to the crone, who remained still as she steered the wyvern back to Isla. "Can I expect my mount back before you plan on having us leave?"

"Your mount?" Azenna tsked as she raised a brow in his direction. "Foolish male, you own nothing of magic."

Adler looked as if he would strike the witch—the skin of his neck flushed the moment the words left her.

"Yes, Captain, you will not depart until the wyvern returns from its journey, and we have a better idea of where Elianna and her army lay hidden. Now, go do something useful. Your presence here is no longer needed," I ordered.

He gave a poor excuse of a half bow and stalked out of the room. My eyes leisurely roamed to the two witches, who stood watching him with knowing smirks.

Adler wasn't fooling anyone.

Kellan

Storming through the streets of Isla, I searched for any familiar face that I thought I could trust. I desperately needed to form a new plan—everything had gone to shit since the High Witch and her crone had arrived in Isla, and while I was pleased with the newfound power that derived from their wyvern, they still left me at a significant disadvantage.

I no longer had my own fleet that obeyed my orders above that of the crown's—what we had journeyed back to Isla with from our last battle was a fraction of what had always been beneath me. The entire fucking Velyran army reported to me, but I couldn't trust a gods-damn one of them.

Perhaps killing Callius was a catastrophic mistake, for while he had become wary of me and my integrity when it came to the crown, if he were here, these witch bitches wouldn't be. That I was certain of.

Idina had welcomed them with open arms after witnessing a fraction of their power. I couldn't help but wonder if Callius was here, if he would have been able to steer her in a different direction.

While I eliminated one threat to my plans, I created an entirely new one—one that had significant strength and influence. The first threat that I had ever deemed viable against me.

I had foolishly underestimated the link between mates, thinking that Idina's grief would force her to latch onto me in a time she needed comfort. The plan was for her to either seek a husband and king out of me after falling for my false sympathy, or desiring a lord as her aide. Instead, what I received was being shut out entirely—the threat of my title and a trip to the gallows constantly looming.

But while Callius had warned me that the wrath of a female scorned could rival that of the gods, he forgot that the same could apply to a cornered, desperate male.

I would win this war for the vile queen and destroy Elianna as she desired. Then, once the victory was claimed, I would end her life as well—making me the realm's conqueror and newest heir.

FIFTY-FOUR

Elianna

AFTER OUR FLIGHT HOME, Nox perched himself atop the courthouse as we announced that a meeting was to be held immediately in the war chamber. Gage was ordered to collect the general, Lynelle, and his most trusted high-ranking soldiers, while I asked Veli to summon Empri and Madalae.

Jace and I occupied the seats at the head of the stone table, observing the realm etched onto its surface as everyone filed in and took their seats.

The twin witches appeared just outside the door as the last of everyone arrived, and they silently slipped into the room, Veli locking the door behind them.

Silence blanketed the room as Gage lit the scattered torches along the walls. I could feel everyone's stare on me, and it was evident that everyone in the war chamber sensed the impending news of Ellecaster's fate.

"What's your plan, Lia? Are we just telling them what we found and will work on a plan together? My concern is the witches," Jace admitted through the bond.

"I have an idea, but I will need everyone's cooperation," I answered.

"Thank you all for coming on such short notice," I greeted. "I regret to inform you all that Ellecaster has fallen."

Small gasps escaped a few of the attendees. Zaela's hand balled into a fist as it rested on the table, and Gage's usually kind eyes morphed into something murderous.

"Were there any survivors?" Lynelle asked after clearing her throat.

"None that we were able to find," Jace answered. "There was one man, but he has since been lost."

"He was able to tell us that it wasn't an army that attacked the city," I admitted.

Gage was rapidly shaking his head on Jace's opposite side, as if in denial. "If not an army, then..."

I sucked in a breath through my nostrils as I prepared to confirm the news they feared. "A wyvern."

"Fuck," Zaela hissed.

"So, they do have one then," Landon chimed in.

Finnian ran his fingers through his hair as he sat beside him. "How are we supposed to fight against a wyvern, Lia? One aided by magic."

They all began to voice their fears at the same moment. Tempers quickly flared, and the table descended into bickering—the air grew thick with skepticism and defeat.

"*They're losing hope...if this information is brought before the armies...*" Jace warned.

"Silence, please," I demanded, and the arguments ceased. "With the news of Ellecaster being destroyed, we also must bring the news that the passage linking the valley to the rest of the realm has been blocked by demolished buildings and stone."

"Mother of the gods," Gage whispered. "Without that passage, we aren't able to move the troops. We don't have enough ships to transport us across the sea."

"I know." I let out a sigh as I faced Veli once again, and she shrank in her seat.

"Why do I feel as if I'm not going to agree with this next part?" she asked with a sigh.

"Before we traveled to the isles, you stated that a single witch couldn't open a portal for an entire army on her own and that it would require multiple."

Her jaw ticked as she crossed her arms again, but this time, her stance was anything but relaxed. "Aye."

"Well, I now count three witches in the war chamber."

"To conjure a portal wide enough for your army to pass through would require an immense amount of magic, Heir of the Realm," Madalae stated, her annoyance evident.

"Are you declaring that you're not powerful enough to do so?" I challenged while cocking my head to the side.

Jace's chuckle echoed down the tether, and I had to suppress my smirk.

Two crimson stares glared at me. "No," they said in tandem, tones full of disgust.

My eyes darted over to Avery, who had to turn away from them to hide her giggle.

"It is a lot of power to hold for that amount of time and could exhaust our bodies when needed in battle," Empri continued. "Mortals are not as agile as fae."

"We have horses for most soldiers," Jace interjected.

"Elianna, I haven't opened a true portal in centuries. And where would you even have us open the rift in the realm? Where do you plan to meet the queen's armies?"

My heart pounded in my chest as I braced myself to say the final part of my plan, knowing chaos would erupt the moment it reached their ears.

"Right at the foot of the Islan gates."

FIFTY-FIVE

Elianna

"ARE YOU OUT OF your gods-damn mind?!" Veli's screech set off a chain reaction, with everyone talking over each other in a flurry of arguments.

"Lia..." Jace spoke softly, concern radiating from him. "The city of Isla?"

"*Just trust me, okay?*" I spoke into his mind, keeping the mask of menace on my face, but it didn't ease any of his concern.

We watched as everyone bickered and argued over how my idea was a death sentence, not only for our soldiers, but for Isla's citizens as well.

"*This is madness.*" His voice was a whisper in my head.

"*And it's why I loathe politics,*" I answered.

I cleared my throat and interlocked my fingers, resting them on the table. Their arguments slowly transformed into soft murmurs until finally, silence filled the chamber.

"This would ensure that they're caught off guard, without the opportunity to gather more soldiers in other cities and barracks as they marched towards us, potentially discovering more of our hidden villages and towns."

"It also ensures death to your citizens," Veli hissed.

I flinched, Idina's words echoing in my mind of dooming my people—but I had a plan. My gaze slowly moved toward her, our eyes locking in a silent battle, both of us unwilling to back down.

"Have you ever considered I have also thought of that? It will also give you the practice needed for the portal gateway."

My gaze moved around the chamber, and I could tell by their faces that none of them agreed with me.

"I understand the hesitance that you're all feeling. However, I have thought this through, and I believe it could work if you're all willing to listen."

Their faces softened slightly, but the air remained tense.

"You once allowed many to escape by casting a whisper spell that entered the minds of my supporters," I started, and she gave a curt nod in response. "If we open a small, hidden portal within Isla, we could evacuate people through it, allowing them to escape and also minimizing casualties."

"You're bringing a war to its gates. Casualties will be inevitable, Elianna," Veli hissed.

"*I am inclined to agree with her.*" A lump formed in my throat from Jace's thoughts, but I was thankful he didn't vocalize them.

"I don't plan to bring the battle within the streets of the city, just beyond its borders. This will be an extra precaution, one that makes me feel better about following through with this. We blindside them and bring it straight to the bitch, while her army is unprepared."

"And we will what? Wait for them to line up as they prepare to slaughter us on their soil?" the general asked, his tone more stern than I appreciated to be questioned in, but I understood that these were his people before they were mine.

"I'm hoping it won't come to that, and that we're able to force their hand into surrender, but time will tell. If they choose to fight, then it begins the moment the first soldier steps in our direction, and then we unleash *everything* on them."

"She will never surrender," Avery said, sounding defeated.

"I know. And I'm counting on it." She looked at me, confused. "Why would her armies fight for her when she won't even consider coming to their defense? I plan to remind every ear that will listen that she is a tyrant murderer, and that the realm will respond for as long as a Valderre heir breathes."

"She'll just work to have you killed," Finnian said, and Jace's anger flared beside me.

I nodded. "She will try, but there are two others that come after me. And while Idina is many things, I don't see her risking her remaining children. Her desire to have you back with her is stronger than we originally believed—she spoke of this when she appeared in our room."

"Our mother won't risk her throne, and she knows you'd never harm us, even if false threats are given," Avery said with a sigh.

"Yes, but as long as you each remain alive as well, she cannot be the true queen. If it *appears* that she's willing to risk her own children, the city will turn on her. I'm sure of it. They know of your kindness and they loved our father until he met his end. If we can turn her terrorized supporters on her and all band together, we have a chance at winning."

"This is a great risk, Lia," Gage stated as his eyes moved back and forth between me and his new love.

"If we're not willing to take risks, we have already lost," I answered. "We get everyone out of the city that we can, maybe even bring them among the ranks to fight, and then we end this."

"If a portal is opened within the city, Azenna will be alerted of magic at work. She will sense it," Veli stated.

"Then we have to be quick," Jace responded, and a corner of my lips lifted at his support.

I looked at Leon as he watched both Jace and me intently. "Prepare our forces, General. I want them ready at a moment's notice."

"You will *not* be going into the city alone, and I honestly advise against you going at all. However, I can see your mind has been made up, so I know you won't listen to that. Also, the humans may not enter. Any fae or witch would be able to sniff them out immediately," Veli stated.

A growl rumbled from my mate.

"*She's right*," I reminded him.

"What other options do we have?" I asked her.

Her stare moved to the twins. "A portal large enough for two or three to move through at a time...you can handle that, no?"

The twins exchanged a glance. "Should be no issue. We haven't been to Isla in centuries, but have set foot on its soil," Empri answered.

"Very well." Veli's attention moved back to me. "I will be coming with you. You will need shadows to help with concealment." As she spoke of them, tiny, dark wisps began to dance around the sides of her face, as if they had been hiding beneath her hair this whole time, listening.

"Do you not need the practice, then? For opening a portal?"

"It's more regarding the power needed to be generated between the three of us," Empri answered for Veli. "We have the experience. As long as she lends her power when we open it for the army, it should work."

"As I said, you will not be going alone, and we're out of other options. This is what I ask, as your aide," Veli stated. "And I may regret this next bit, but may I suggest your sister comes along with us?"

"Me?!" Avery gasped. "I assumed I would never be welcome on another trip again."

"Don't remind me." Veli rolled her eyes. "However, the people seem to listen to her. Whether that's because she is Jameson's known daughter and they trust her stance on her own mother or that she is just bossy, I am not entirely sure."

"Well, what say you, Avery?" I winked.

"You want me there?" she whispered.

"Only if you wish to be. It will be dangerous, but I've learned that trying to shield you from every danger in the realm hasn't benefited us. As a member of this court, you're able to make the decision for yourself."

"Don't worry about me," Finn chimed in. "I wasn't much help the first time." Chuckles filtered through the space.

"You held your own with Zae in combat training. You will do great," Gage said to Avery sweetly, as he picked up her hand and pressed his lips to the back of it.

Her cheeks flushed instantly before she answered, "Count me in."

"It's settled then," I declared. "Empri and Madalae will cast the portal spell, and Avery, Veli, and I will run through to escort as many through as possible." My stare moved back to my aide. "Can you cast the whisper tonight?"

"Aye," she spoke softly. "But if I say we retreat, you will do so. I need your word, Elianna. As your aide, I am begging you to not break this trust."

My jaw locked, and I blinked a few times as I contemplated how to respond.

"*Please listen to her.*" My gaze moved to Jace, and the only emotion his face wore was the calculating stare of the commander as his eyes wandered over the table. "*I once again cannot be with you, and you know what happened the last time we were forced to be separated. Don't make me go through that portal to drag your ass back here.*"

My jaw ticked. "I will do as you wish," I assured Veli. "There will be no room for error and we must be quick. You have my word. I promise."

She gave me a look that seemed as if she wanted to smile. "Then I shall cast the whisper and we will leave this evening."

"Well, then," I started as I stood from the table. "Let's go reclaim our kingdom."

FIFTY-SIX

Elianna

ONCE THE MEETING IN the war chamber ceased, everyone scattered. Leon, Gage, and Zae left to prepare the troops, letting Jace and I know that it may take a few days, which we granted. The twin witches were ordered to stay close while we prepared to enter Isla unseen. Everyone else retreated back to the estate to get some rest before the madness persisted.

Jace and I stayed behind at our headquarters with Veli as she prepared to cast the whisper spell.

We stood across the room from her as she remained seated at the stone table. Closing her golden fuchsia eyes that we were barely used to, she set her focus on those who sat in Isla under the queen's grasp.

"*Venifikas sussorae,*" she spoke, and the otherworldliness of her voice sent a shiver up my spine.

We watched as her mind worked, her eyes darting beneath closed lids as if under the trance of her own spell. Her head twitched in each direction, appearing as if she was looking around wherever her mind had drifted.

"*Is that supposed to happen?*" Jace asked silently, not wanting to disrupt the spell.

"*I'm not entirely sure,*" I answered.

Her eyes snapped open, the glow from them flashing through the room as it slowly diminished. Her breathing became erratic, as if she had to work to catch her breath.

"Veli," I said as I moved toward the table. "Are you alright?"

"There is magic at work in Isla. Azenna's presence is everywhere."

Jace and I exchanged a glance as he pressed his lips together into a firm line.

"But you were able to reach them?" he asked.

"Yes," she whispered.

I tilted my head to the side. "You don't seem sure."

"No, I did. I have just never had to navigate around another's magic. It must be because of the book. Her power grows, and she was felt in every inch of the city." Veli stood from the table. "But perhaps this is not the best idea, Elianna. There is a high possibility that Azenna sensed that magic."

I crossed my arms. "Well, would she be able to tell what kind of magic was used?"

"No, just sense its power and presence."

"Then we proceed as scheduled. Worst-case scenario is that she senses another witch is present in the city, not necessarily who. It could be others from your coven looking to aid her cause to Idina. Lines are being drawn, sides are being chosen at every end of the realm. We aren't even giving them enough of a chance to prepare for a possible attack—we leave in hours."

"Perhaps you're right," she answered.

"Besides, she won't think we would be, in your words, *foolish enough* to barge into the city and start escorting people out. They would never guess that was coming. What did you say to those who received the whisper?"

"They were instructed to remain in their homes until the moon is set highest in the sky this evening," she stated. "We are to rift walk through so I can knock the guards unconscious with magic...or kill them. Whichever you would prefer."

I considered it for a moment. "We don't know where their true loyalties lie. It may, at the moment, just be with survival. Let them live."

"You are too kind sometimes, my Lia," Jace growled.

"She has that in common with her father," Veli stated, and I half rolled my eyes. "Let's get some rest. We have a long night ahead of us."

Our court and generals gathered a few miles outside of the city to transport in anyone who flees with us. This also ensured our citizens were protected in case someone undesirable managed to sneak through the portal's rift.

Veli, Avery and I stood at its front, dressed in all black leathers, to better blend within the shadows. I smirked as my eyes roamed over my sister and the weapons strapped to her body as a precaution.

"You all know the plan. No one who rushes through the gateway is to be harmed. They will likely be frightened and untrusting until we return. We will run through last in order to make sure that everyone who risks treason against the false queen finds sanctuary."

"Understood," Leon said with a nod as he stood off to the side, a small troop behind him, waiting to assist the newcomers.

Jace approached me and pressed his lips to my forehead. Mocking coos sounded from all the surrounding men, forcing a quiet scoff from him.

His eyes bore into mine, soft smiles adorning both of our faces.

"*Come back to me, okay?*" His voice echoed in my mind as he held my hand in his, toying with my wedding ring.

"Always," I answered aloud, and he slowly backed away from me.

I turned to the right, where Gage was giving Avery words of encouragement. "You're going to be great, and I will be waiting right here for you when you return."

"Thank you," she answered, her cheeks blushing.

"Give them hell, my little rebel princess," he teased, before turning to stand with Jace.

I gave her a thumbs up as I winked at her. "Rebel princess!" I whisper-shouted, and she giggled.

"That's enough, you two," Veli hushed us. "They're about to open the rift."

Empri and Madalae held each other's hand, interlocking their taloned fingers together while they simultaneously held out their opposite ones towards the fields that lay before us.

A scarlet glow cast beyond them as their magic brewed. "*Odium Embulae*," their voices echoed in tandem, and the air instantly changed.

The wind picked up, sending my braided hair whipping around as the grass beneath our feet lashed out in all directions. Lightning erupted from thin air only several feet before us, forming a tiny crack in the realm. In seconds, it shattered into several more until a hole appeared—a darkened alleyway of Isla awaiting on its other side.

"*We will keep this open until you're back, but you must go. I feel the presence you spoke of when you cast the whisper. I believe there is a shield at work,*" Empri's voice sounded, as if she spoke it into our minds.

Avery looked terrified as she realized that Empri hadn't spoken aloud. The twins each remained frozen in their stance as they held the rift open.

"We must go. Now!" Veli announced as she stalked toward the gateway that mimicked a mirage of flowing, opaque swirls.

"Is it going to hurt?" Avery asked as we stepped up to it.

"A bit of a tingle, but no pain," she answered as she led the way and stepped through the rift.

My sister turned to me, and I gave her a gentle nod. "Stay close."

And then we stepped through to Isla.

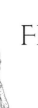

FIFTY-SEVEN

Elianna

AN ODD BUZZING SENSATION glided over my skin as we walked through the portal and into the Islan street. The grey cobblestones we stood on shone in the moonlight. The familiar sounds of the city I loved were absent, leaving an eerie silence to its aura.

"That's strange," I whispered as I faced Veli. "Usually, it's still lively in some areas at this time of night. I can't hear anyone or anything."

"Perhaps the queen has issued curfews," she stated.

"To an entire city?"

"I wouldn't put it past her," Avery chimed in.

I crept up to the corner of the alleyway and peered around to get a better look. "There's...no one here. Not a single soul in the streets."

"Elianna, get away from there!" she hissed. As I turned to her, shadows like I had never seen burst from the confines of her silver hair and straight at me, shielding me in their darkness.

My aide stepped up to me and let out a huff. "There is magic at work here. I can feel it all around us. We should turn back."

"And what of the people who risk everything for our aid and meet at the city's center? What will become of them when we don't show and Idina's guards see a gathering?"

She let out a huff as her fuchsia eyes radiated concern. "We must stay close to the sides of the buildings for the shadows to remain convincing. And since the portal is emanating power, we are already running out of time."

Relief flooded me that she didn't fight me on risking the rebels. Their lives would be threatened if we didn't come to sneak them out of the city as promised.

Veli broke into a run, leaving no room for arguments and forcing us to follow her lead.

With only occasional flickering torches, the city became a labyrinth of shadows as the moon moved to hide behind shifting clouds. We moved swiftly through the deserted streets, our steps silent on the stones, as we navigated to the city's heart through its narrow alleys.

My eyes flared as the fountain that stood in the city's center came into view. Still, not a single person in sight. At any time of day or night, people could be seen around the fountain, whether it was younglings during the day, or the occasional drunken fool in the late hours of the evening.

"Something isn't right," Avery whispered as we halted, all of us peering around where we stood.

"I need to get a feel for the guards...it's bothersome that we haven't come across any yet," Veli admitted.

"Is there a chance they may have become aware?" I dreaded the answer.

"Let's hope to all the gods that's not the case, for all of our sakes."

Hidden within the shadows of a looming building, Veli dropped her own—the power that radiated from them instantly ceased as they disappeared.

"*Impyrum Kortyus.*" The ancient words left her mouth, and we waited as she searched for the minds of lingering guards.

My eyes wandered to a small alleyway a street away, where a small figure sat on the ground beneath a hood. My heart began racing in my chest until I realized that, by its shape, it had to have been a youngling.

A shuddered breath left me. Everything about this felt wrong. The empty streets, not a single soul in sight, but I would never be able to live with myself if I left a child behind—a child alone in the cruel streets of the relentless queen.

Where would I have wound up in the world if I didn't have Lukas while growing up beneath her? The message sent out was to rescue any lingering rebels and those who sought refuge. If the only one brave enough to bear the consequences of betraying the crown was a youngling, then I would be damned to leave them behind.

"Stay here," I whispered to Avery as my eyes remained on the figure.

"Lia, no! We need to stay together."

"I will just be right here. I think there's a youngling over here waiting for us," I said over my shoulder.

As a precaution, my fingertips drifted to the hilt of my dagger sheathed on my thigh, but I tried to conceal the movement to avoid frightening the little one. The closer my steps brought me, the more apparent it became that the figure was indeed that of a small child.

"Hi, friend." My voice was gentle, causing the hood to stir slightly. "Are you here for help?"

I was answered with a nod beneath the cloak.

I squatted before the youngling, trying to get a better look under the hood. "Are your parents here, or are you a Solus? I also bore the name growing up, and there's no shame in it." My hand reached out as a peace offer. "I'm not going to hurt you."

At the same moment my hand reached out, I was frozen where I stood from the next thing that reached my ears. "Elianna, no!" Veli's voice echoed in a near scream that startled me. "They know!"

Before I had time to react, my gaze whipped back to the child, or what I thought was one. An aged, withered hand shot out from the cloak and gripped my wrist, just as its hood lifted to reveal crimson eyes beneath them and a bone chilling cackle from the crone.

"Fuck!" I hissed as her grip on my wrist tightened, and she tried to pull me to her.

Damn this soft heart of mine.

On instinct, my opposite hand unsheathed my dagger and ripped it through the skin atop her arm, forcing her to release me with a screech of pain.

I nearly tripped over my own feet as I hurried back to Veli and Avery. Soldiers flooded the streets then, coming out from every alley and corner. Kellan was at the front of them, a cruel grin on his face.

"Evening, Princess," he greeted with a wicked grin, and a growl rumbled through me at the sight of him still alive. "Did you really think we wouldn't know?"

"We need to run. Now!" Veli screamed as she tugged on our arms, propelling us into a sprint back towards the portal.

"Get them!" he boomed and his soldiers funneled around him, chasing after us as he remained in the square.

"How did they find us?! How did they know?!" I shouted, trying to breathe through the desperate run we were in.

"Azenna must've created a shield around the city. You know I have not explored the magic of that book. It could be anything!"

The echoes of armored boots reverberated through the streets as the army of soldiers closed in. Moving swiftly, we darted around corners and deftly weaved through the shadows cast by the towering buildings. We only had a few more blocks until we reached the portal.

"*Foolish little heir of the realm.*" Azenna's all-powerful, malevolent voice filled my head. "*Did you truly think we would allow you all to just come here and waltz out with our people? The only one who heard your whisper was me. And, my dear, you will never be leaving this city again.*"

"Get out of my head, witch!"

"Don't listen to her, Lia!" Avery boomed.

I let out a scream of frustration as I forced my body to move faster, and out of the periphery of my vision, power lashed out from the side of us.

"Avery, look out!" I tugged her into me, but we both lost our footing and tumbled to the ground.

461

Veli's magic lashed out back toward the source of the attack as I pulled Avery to her feet, and we were on the move once more.

"Come on!" I screamed as a volley of arrows soared through the air, narrowly missing us.

As we turned the last corner, the portal appeared, and tears were streaming down my face at the sight of it. We were close. We were so gods-damn close. Veli continued to have her magic attack the soldiers behind us, sending her shadows to devour and choke them the closer they loomed at our backs.

"Don't look!" she demanded. "Just keep going!"

My steps quickened as we neared the rift, but somehow, time slowed all around me. A figure of swirling, lashing darkness formed at my side, moving along with me in tandem. My eyes whipped in its direction mid run, and what I saw gazing back at me made my heart nearly stop.

The shadows revealed Azenna's face, an ear-to-ear grin adorning it. "I told you, you will not be leaving the city, *Heir of the Realm*."

"No!" Veli boomed from behind me, and suddenly, my body felt as if it would collapse as power slammed into me on all sides.

"Lia!" Avery's desperate, heart-wrenching scream filled my ears as she reached out for my hand, but it slipped from her grasp.

Azenna's shadows reached for me, threatening to consume me whole as a burning blast erupted at my back from Veli, sending my body violently soaring through the air and blasting through the opposite side of the portal that was twenty feet before us.

The portal's essence sizzled my skin, and then my body slammed into the unforgiving terrain of Alaia. The force of Veli's power sent me tumbling halfway to where our soldiers awaited.

"Lia!" my mate screamed in horror.

He was at my side in an instant, but my head whipped up to the closing rift, ignoring the agony tearing through my body.

"No!" I demanded in a guttural scream. "Leave it open!"

My arms and legs pushed me to crawl toward the hazy, swirling gateway, and my eyes never left Avery as she and Veli raced towards us—two wicked sorceresses and an army at their backs.

We all watched on in terror as Veli reached out for Avery's hand and raced for the portal that Empri and Madalae held open just wide enough for the two of them.

"Weapons up!" Jace boomed, and the sound of metal unsheathing filled the air.

"They're going to make it!" Zaela yelled from behind us as Veli's first foot emerged through the rift, but at that same moment, we watched as Azenna's shadows lashed out once more.

"*NO!*" I cried as I forced myself to my feet.

"Lia, *stop!*" Jace roared as he threw his arms around my chest and tugged me into him. I vigorously tried to shove him away, but he dropped to his knees, forcing me back down to the ground with him.

Veli's second foot was through the portal, and as she turned to tug Avery with her, Azenna's magic wrapped around her ankle and yanked my sister back down the alleyway, a fading scream of terror echoing from her.

My aide's jaw dropped, and just as she was about to run back through the rift, the twins closed it on her as the guards were about to reach it and blast through to the valley.

"*AVERY!*" My scream tore through my throat as tears rushed down my face, uncontrollable sobs leaving me as Jace held me down.

Gage rushed past us and Veli as if he could run through the portal that no longer remained before us and go get her himself. He silently fell to his knees where he stood, his head hanging below his shoulders as his hands balled into fists at his sides.

A booming, guttural yell of heartache left him that echoed through the fields.

I shoved out of Jace's hold as he tried to keep me still and comfort me, but I would never be able to find comfort again—not while they had my sister.

My breaths were rapid—my lungs feeling as if they were on fire, and I couldn't get enough air. Whipping around to face the others, my eyes locked on them as they watched me with absolute devastation written on each of their faces.

Finn was sobbing in Landon's arms, who held him back, just as my husband had with me, only gentler. Zaela had tears slipping from her lashes, one hand covering her mouth in disbelief as the other clutched Veli's wrist.

Everyone else watched on in horror, unknowing of what to do or say.

I stormed up to Veli, towering over her small figure, hoping that she would cower beneath me. "Why did that happen? How did you not sense them?!" I yelled in her face, knowing that as the words left me, my anger was misplaced.

"It wasn't her presence I originally felt. It was a shield..." she started as her eyes darted back and forth. "More powerful than anything I've encountered, with other spells woven into its inner workings. I had no way of knowing!" She was yelling, but her voice wobbled, as if she was fighting back tears herself.

My breathing remained heavy as I took a step back from her. "This is my fault." My nails dug into my palms so hard they began to bleed.

Veli shook her head. "You are not the only one to hold blame for this."

"You tried to warn me, and I made us press on."

The rest of my court made their way towards us while Leon sent the soldiers away to give us privacy.

"Lia, what happened?" Jace asked.

"I didn't listen," I whispered.

Gage's eyes met mine, and all I saw was disappointment—in me. My heart somehow shattered into more pieces.

"No," Veli interjected. "We didn't know that Azenna was the only one who heard the whisper. I warned you that I felt their power, but we had no way of knowing that would happen. You pressed on to save the lives of those citizens, not because you were being reckless. I didn't motion to talk you out of it further because you were right."

"We knew there would be risks. You said so yourself," Zaela said softly from behind us.

I turned to face her, my lip curling back. "Not at the cost of my sister!"

"We're going to get her back," Jace said.

"The city is on complete lockdown, and now they know we are coming one way or another. Our plan of surprising them at their gates may be ruined now that they know we have used portals to enter the city."

"The good news is that we know Mother won't hurt Avery physically. If it were you or Veli, you would be lost to us, and everything would've been for nothing. Worst-case scenario is that she is held up in the dungeons, just as you had been," Finn stated.

I huffed out a breath. "She will use this against me. She will use Avery against *us*, and you know it. Whether it's telling the realm a lie that her daughter once again supports her and that I'm a tyrant, or dangling her life in front of us."

"Avery won't break. She won't give up our secrets. I know it," Gage said, a lingering anger in his tone.

My eyes lifted to his and softened. "I know," I whispered. "Gage, I'm so sorry."

He held up a hand at me. "Forgive me, Elianna, for I know you're our queen, but I don't wish to hear your apology right now." He paused for a moment as the veins in his neck throbbed, as if he were holding himself back from lashing out at me.

"Gage. *Easy*," Jace growled before stepping in front of me.

Gage's jaw ticked. "We're going to get her back."

"We are," I whispered as I nodded slowly.

"*I've never seen him this upset,*" Jace said down the tether.

I couldn't bear it—couldn't even swallow with the sickening lump in my throat. "Even if I have to burn the castle to the fucking ground. I promise you, we will get her back," I vowed.

My eyes drifted over the six of them. This was no longer a game for the throne. This was a matter of life and death for the realm, for my people, and for everyone who called Velyra home.

"Preparation is over. We move out in five days' time and not a moment more. Bring everyone," I ordered.

My feet moved me past them, and I began the walk back to the city. Alone.

PART THREE

RETRIBUTION

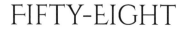

FIFTY-EIGHT

Avery

MY EYES FLUTTERED OPEN, my body aching as I lay on the cold, dirt-covered ground. My vision was hazy, but I sat up as it cleared and noticed I was being held within the castle's dungeons like some kind of criminal.

What the hell happened? I remembered running for the portal and Veli's hand grabbing my own, and then everything went dark. Had they captured Lia and Veli, too? Would they even still be alive if they had? I was going to be sick.

A figure appeared before the cell door, and as I blinked, I realized it was Kellan. He stood there, unspeaking, watching me through the bars as if I were a caged animal.

"What do you want?" I managed to choke out as I stood from the floor.

The captain whistled at me, as if I were a whore in one of those brothels he loved so much. "The pretty little princess is out of her gowns and in fighting leathers now? Your mother will be most displeased."

I stormed up to the bars. "And where is my dearest mother? She had me locked up in her dungeons as if I was a criminal?"

"Avery, that is exactly what you are to the crown. A treasonous criminal who vowed herself to the queen's sworn enemy. Honestly, tsk tsk, little princess. Do you have anything to say for yourself?" he taunted.

My eyes bore into his. "Only that I would do it again."

He let out a laugh. "I can't wait to hear you say that to her," he admitted as he unlocked the cell door and swung it open.

My body instinctively shifted into a fighting position.

"I hate to be the bearer of bad news there, little love, but you are not your sister. Don't put up a fight. You will only embarrass yourself."

He stepped up to me, his arm extending to grab my own, when my opposite fist swung out and punched him straight in the side of his face. It caught him off guard, making him stumble back.

My fist was on fire from the impact, causing me to hiss. Despite the pain, a smirk slowly formed on my face, knowing I had landed at least one solid hit.

Kellan whipped toward me, the side of his face swollen and red. "You will regret that."

He stormed up to me, clasped my arms behind my back faster than I could react, and clicked the heavy metal cuffs around my wrists.

"We're so eager to learn what you know, Princess Avery. Let's not keep your mother waiting any longer."

Kellan dragged me into the throne room, where my mother sat upon my father's old throne. The evil witch that had taken the forbidden book from me stood at her side on the dais. The sight of it was nauseating—how had everything come to this?

Once I was at the room's center, my mother stood as her eyes drifted to Kellan. "Why is my daughter in cuffs, Adler?" she demanded.

"It was a bit difficult to get her here. It seems she has had some...training since you've last seen her, Your Grace."

My stare wandered up to his cheek, that still had a pink tinge to it, and I grinned.

"Take the cuffs off of her. Now." My mother's voice echoed through the room.

Without a second of hesitance, Kellan took a step behind me and unlocked the metal bindings. I pulled my arms to my front and rubbed the bruising, aching skin of my wrists.

"My darling daughter, I am so glad to have you back home where you belong." She was staring down at me, wearing an obviously forced smile on her face.

"This is not my home. It hasn't been in a long time," I said, and her fake smile dropped.

I knew I should keep this next part to myself, but seeing her in person again made every bit of anger I felt toward my own flesh and blood rise to the very surface. "Not since you *murdered* our father."

The queen's lips parted, and she sucked in a breath. "I don't know what it is that you *think* you know, Avery, but—"

"But nothing, Mother. Finnian and I heard you that day in your chambers speaking with Kai and Callius. *You* killed the king. You killed the father of two of your children. All so you could take the throne for yourself!"

She took a single step down from the dais, fury swirling in her amber eyes. Kellan took a few steps out to the side of me, steering clear of her wrath.

"Do you mean the father of all of my children?" She cocked her head to the side.

"I do not." I held my ground, even though fear was slipping its way into me beneath her blazing stare.

"And what exactly do you mean by this, my daughter?"

"Kai was not King Jameson's son, but your personal guard's. He was not the rightful heir, and Elianna Valderre is. That's why you hated her all these years. That's why Father kept her so close. And *that* is why you killed him."

"I don't know why you would ever think that Kai is not the kin of your father, Avery..."

"I have my suspicions." My lips snarled.

She clasped her arms behind her back as she descended the rest of the dais and made her way toward me.

"Your loyalty remains with the bastard heir, it still seems," she said. "Yes, you and Elianna share the blood of Jameson, but what of your brother? The one that she *murdered!*"

"Kai received the fate he deserved. He was a tyrant, just as you are, who would have doomed the realm."

She stormed up to me then and smacked me across the face so hard that it sent me stumbling back. I lifted my stare back to her, my cheek feeling as if flames were dancing on it.

"He was your brother!"

"And King Jameson was my father!"

Her jaw locked as she stared at me and took a few steps back.

"Your half-sister is not as bright as she pretends to be. She thought she could waltz in here and steal more of my citizens, turning them into treasonous traitors against their own queen? A pathetic attempt, really. Azenna shielded the city the moment we became allies."

My eyes drifted over my mother's shoulder and to the witch that remained standing atop the dais, staring down at us.

"You speak of your citizens as if they are cattle that belong to you," I stated as my gaze wandered back to the queen.

"They may as well be. They are here to serve those who sit upon the throne."

"You are a horrible ruler. They will never love you as they had Father."

She reached out and took my chin between her fingers as she took a step toward me. "It has never been their love or admiration that I desired. While that may gift you loyalty in their hearts, it does not give you their support in war. Do you know what does?" She released my chin and stepped back once more. "*Fear.* Fear is the heart of what keeps them loyal to me now. Betray the crown, and your life is forfeit."

"I have never been more embarrassed to call you my mother," I whispered as my heart raced at the words she spoke so freely.

"Embarrassment aside, it's something you cannot change. I am a part of you, my dear, and you would not be here without me."

The room went silent for a few moments as the tension escalated.

"Now, where were we before this all took a turn?" my mother asked the room.

"You were to have her tell you all that Elianna has planned, Your Majesty," Kellan answered from where he now stood at the bottom of the dais.

My teeth clenched as my eyes locked on him.

"Ah, yes, tell us, Avery. What does little Elianna have planned for her extravagant reclaim of her throne?"

"I will never," I spat. "There is nothing you can ever do or say that will make me betray her. I would sooner die!"

"Enough with the dramatics, Avery." She rolled her eyes. "Now, I will give you one more chance to speak it freely, and if you do, you will no longer be considered a prisoner of the crown. Make us force it out of you and back to the dungeons you go."

"What makes you think you could force such things from me?" I took a step toward her, and I was surprised when she matched it by taking one back. I leaned into her. "Are you going to have Callius take a whip to my back like you had with her?" I whispered viciously.

Her lip curled at her lover's name, and hurt flashed across her eyes. "Well, she made sure to claim her revenge on him, didn't she?"

I tilted my head to the side in confusion. Lia hadn't told me that Callius was killed in their attack. Not that I would care, but it was odd it wasn't mentioned unless he succumbed to Nox's flames like many others.

Kellan took a few rapid steps forward. "My queen, let's get the information out of her before she can distract you further. She's only prolonging giving us the information."

I glared at him beneath furrowed brows—the sudden change in direction from him made me think he was hiding something.

My mother's eyes roamed over me. "Very well. You wish to do this the hard way, it seems." She turned and stalked to the throne. "Azenna, do what you must."

The High Witch's eyes instantly began to glow their deadly crimson hue. "*Meritsas Lokoi.*"

The words she hissed slammed into me, filling my veins with ice, freezing my body where I stood as her eyes bore into me. I sucked in a sharp breath as it felt as if my body was turning into stone. My breathing quickened as fear worked its way through me, but I began struggling as the rapid movements of my chest were even forced to slow.

"Is it ready?" my mother asked her, and she received a subtle nod in response as Azenna locked me beneath her spell.

"My darling daughter, I have been informed that this spell works by forcing the truth out of you. You no longer have the ability to run from me or withhold information regarding my enemies. You will spill their secrets bare before us, and you will not have a choice."

My panic started to suffocate me.

"Don't fight it," my mother pleaded. "I don't wish to cause harm to my only daughter."

I tried to roll my eyes, but they remained frozen in place, staring directly at her.

"Now tell me, does Elianna have a plan of attack?"

I remained silent. The ice in my veins somehow grew colder at my lack of response, working its way through me. My body betrayed me and forced a small squeal of pain from my lips.

"I told you not to fight it. It will force its way out of you."

She was right; the words were at the edge of my tongue, and I bit down on it to keep them in.

"Your daughter is strong-willed," Azenna spoke from where she remained.

"Then break her spirit," my mother demanded, and my eyes flared in horror.

Azenna's eyes glowed even brighter, and my body felt as if it would shatter.

"Yes." I cursed myself as she forced the word from me.

"Very good, my darling. Now, where does she plan to attack us?" she asked.

My body was thrashing, desperately trying to escape the spell's suffocating hold, but in reality, I remained motionless before them. An ear-shattering, internal scream threatened to deafen me, but the only ears it fell upon were my own, having never left my lips.

"Gates," I answered, and a single tear slipped from my lower lashes at the betrayal I couldn't help.

A cackle left my mother, accompanied by a wicked, beaming smile. "Here? The Islan gates? Surely you're joking." Then her smile dropped as her eyes darted back and forth. "But you cannot lie. So it must be the truth," she whispered. "And Elianna thinks she is better than me, bringing a war straight to its citizens."

The queen turned to Kellan. "I want every fucking soldier here immediately guarding the city. I want ships stationed in the harbor and an army guarding the gates at all times. Am I understood? Call for aid from other cities. Any army that can march here as soon as possible. Send all the falcons we have. Their queen demands this."

My mother then looked at the witch. "You may release her."

My body dropped to the floor the moment Azenna's hold on me lifted, and I broke out into a fury-filled sob.

Kellan approached the queen. "Her plan may change now that we have her." He motioned toward me while I remained on the marble floor.

My mother contemplated his words before saying, "Do as I commanded, Adler. Her plans won't change. She will come for my daughter."

The High Witch aimed for my mother, her movements so smooth she appeared to be floating. "May I suggest a gathering of your citizens?"

"For what?"

"This would be the perfect opportunity for you to turn any of her lingering supporters against her. Show them your daughter has willingly returned to you and that Elianna is the true usurper. She desires to bring the war straight to their city's gates." She paused for a moment and took another step toward the queen. "They will not take that lightly. This is their home."

My eyes flared, and I pushed myself to stand. "I will *never* turn the citizens against her. There is nothing you can do to me that will make me."

The High Witch lifted a single brow at me, the corner of her lip tilting up into a challenging smirk. "My dear, little red one. Was my last demonstration of power not enough to convince you? You have no idea what I can make you do."

I forced myself to swallow as I stood beneath her crimson gaze, a shiver running up my spine.

My mother observed us all as the tension in the throne room escalated. "Adler, be sure she is locked up. I don't need her wandering off again. We will need her to convince the citizens."

Kellan approached me then. "Don't put up a fight. We know how well that went for you the last time."

And I didn't. Without another word from my mother, he forcefully clasped my hands behind my back and escorted me back down to the dungeons.

FIFTY-NINE

Elianna

I STARED AT THE map carved upon the stone table in our war chamber and was instantly overwhelmed by the sense that we were about to be vastly outnumbered. Our expected numbers and allies were quickly diminishing as we lost the troops in Ellecaster and the possibility of bringing other soldiers from our small villages hidden throughout the realm.

The door creaked open, revealing Jace, Gage, Veli, and Zaela standing beneath its arch.

"It's late. You should all be sleeping."

"And so should you," Veli answered.

I turned from them and faced the window, crossing my arms as I looked out at the moon. All I could think about was how I snapped at my sister, screaming in her face as I let my rage consume me when all she had ever done was support my claim. My throat clogged, realizing I never had the chance to apologize properly.

"I don't think I will be getting much sleep for the foreseeable future," I finally answered.

They all entered the room and took their seats at the table.

"We're here to help you with a plan. We're going to get Avery back," Jace assured me.

"Lia, I'm sorry for blaming you earlier," Gage said, pure sorrow radiating in his deep brown eyes.

"Gage," I whispered as I walked over to him and placed my hand on his shoulder. "You had every right to be upset. I know you care for my sister."

He blinked and gave a small, slow nod in understanding.

"How fast can our ships sail to Isla?" I asked.

"From here?" Zaela asked. "It would take nearly two weeks, and that's if the tide is on our side."

I blew out a breath. "That won't do, and we can't waste any more days. All of our soldiers will have to remain with the land fleet." Rubbing at my temples, I tried to think of a plan.

"Is it bad for our entire army to remain on land? Wouldn't it be better to all be together at the foot of the gates?" Zaela asked.

"I want them surrounded on all sides, including the harbor," I answered, and then my eyes widened. "Wait a second."

My mate looked at me with a raised brow as I stormed across the chamber and opened a wooden chest we kept on the side table. I reached in, my fingers closing around the smooth, iridescent conch shell I had stolen from the sirens all those weeks ago.

"I think it's time to call in my favor," I announced as I made my way back to the stone table and took my seat at its head.

"Favor." Zaela snorted. "I think you mean bribe?"

I shrugged with a lazy smile. "Semantics. Regardless, they know that if they want this back, they must aid me somehow in the war. And I think I know just what that would be now."

"What are you thinking, then?" Veli asked.

"We will have the sirens in Isla's harbor. If there are ships there, then perfect, we have one of our secret weapons ready to attack. If no ships lay in the harbor, then we didn't waste precious time sending our own fleet there."

"And how do you wish to alert them?"

"You will rift walk back to Elora and tell them the plan. If they show up and fight for me, they get their sister's conch back. If they don't, it will be destroyed."

"That is a bold threat, Elianna," Veli hissed.

"If they had legs, I would have them take a knee before me, but they do not. This is how they will show their loyalty to the true heir of the realm."

She grinned at me wickedly, shadows dancing around her face. "Very well."

"I have one last plan to obtain more allies."

"Lia," Zaela breathed. "There's no one left. We have our armies ready for war, but it won't be enough. Not against the fae *and* dark magic."

"I have made friends along the way," I exaggerated. "They may help us."

"Who are these so-called friends, Elianna?" Veli demanded from my opposite side.

I winked at her, earning a huff of disapproval. "The realm itself works to support the true heir and Valderre bloodline."

"Yes, but vines on trees won't—"

"Let her finish, Veli." Jace's voice radiated authority.

I cleared my throat. "After I escaped the Islan dungeons, Nox and I spent time in the Sylis Forest. We were attacked by a herd of centaurs, and when my skin bled into the soil, the forest reacted. The herd no longer worked to attack me and, in fact, let us go a moment later. As the witches stated to us in the isles, the creatures of the wood don't wish to upset the balance of the realm."

"And you believe these centaurs will help us?" Zaela asked.

"I believe we have a chance of many creatures coming to our aid. All it will take is a bit of convincing."

"Lia," Jace breathed as he placed his hand atop my own on the table. "We don't have the time or resources to wander around the Sylis Forest looking for them. Not to mention, it's dangerous."

I dipped my chin before turning to Veli. "I know. And that's why I need my aide to transport my conscious before them, wherever they may lie in the wood, so I can try to convince them myself."

"What?!" Jace gasped with a half laugh.

I turned to him. "It's good to know I can still surprise you."

He scratched the back of his neck. "Yeah, that's the word for it."

Veli remained silent as she watched us.

"Let's hear it, Veli. Where does the foolishness lie in this plan? And what will it take for me to convince you? I need to get my sister back. The time has come for me to save my kingdom."

Her stare roamed over me, and my eyes flared as the corner of her lips tilted up. She crossed her arms as she leaned back in her chair. "I actually believe that there's no harm in this attempt."

"Wait, what?" My eyes widened in disbelief.

"I'm just as surprised as you are," she admitted.

Jace's back stiffened. "And they won't be able to harm her, right?"

"Correct, for her physical body will not be presented to them. She would be just as Idina appeared to you."

"Can anyone accompany her?" he asked.

"If you have not met them, then no."

Irritation rattled the bond.

"*I will be okay*," I said, trying to calm him.

"Bruhn is the leader of the centaurs, and I believe I can convince him to help," I spoke aloud to everyone.

"While your plan may work, you should know that centaurs are stubborn, savage creatures that have always hidden within their forest. Do not think just because they know you, that they will help," Veli stated.

"I believe, aside from this, we're out of options. Would you not agree?" I challenged her. "Aside from ships and rift walking, we are essentially stuck in Alaia. Our only known passage out on foot has been barricaded by stone. There are no more allies to seek. This is it. They are our last hope."

"I just don't want you getting your hopes up," she said as she clicked her talons on the table.

"Have no fear in that," I stated, and the room turned solemn.

"*My Lia.*" Jace's voice rattled through me, and my eyes closed tightly as I desperately tried to keep myself together.

"What I am certain of is that Idina will now use Avery as a shield. She wants me to come there and get her. Whether they guess I'll bring my entire army is unknown. She may think it's just me coming, but make no mistake, she knows something will be. And I'm sure she is already preparing, so we must do our best to as well."

Veli gave me a curt nod. "Very well. I will do as you asked and send you to your centaurs."

"Thank you," I whispered.

"What do you need us to do?" my mate asked.

"Just make sure our armies are ready to leave within the next few days. Weapons, armor, everything...I want every capable, able-bodied soldier in formation."

I looked to the window. "Dawn isn't far off. What will you need for this to work?"

"Nothing is needed aside from you thinking of who you wish to appear before," Veli answered.

"Finnian was right. Magic is terrifying." A huff of a laugh left me.

A knowing grin crept over her face. "It is."

"Well, I see no better time than the present, no?" I said as I stood from the chair.

"Sit down then," she demanded.

I raised a brow at her.

"Your body will be limp as your conscious leaves it. It is better if you are sitting." She tilted her head to the side in a challenge, and I nearly laughed.

"You're doing this now?" Jace growled.

"We're running out of time, handsome." I sent him a wave of love down the bond, and a tiny sense of calm washed over him.

He turned to Veli. "How does she come back?"

"For her to return, she must have the will and desire to come back to her body."

I leaned back in the chair, and my stare met Veli's. "Do your worst, witch." I gave her a wink.

She shook her head at me. "Always causing trouble."

Her once violet eyes glowed in their new hue of pink as she mumbled ancient words from the gods, aiming her taloned finger in my direction. The force of the power draped over me instantly.

As the magic took over, I thought of the day in the forest when Nox and I had been under attack by the centaurs—how they freed us when they watched the willow tree protect me as my blood spilled into its soil.

My mind was no longer my own, and the vision of the war chamber melted away into a twisting, morphing haze of the haunted woods.

I stood deep within the Sylis Forest. The tree's canopy above blocked out the moonlight, and the area was cast in a foggy mist. Moss covered the twisted roots of the trees from where they protruded from the ground, and the sound of buzzing insects filled the air.

I lifted my hands to my face, surprise taking over me as it appeared as if I was wholly there, just as Idina had when she appeared in my room.

I followed the sound of conversations, carefully navigating my way through the forest, stepping over the twisted roots, scattered rocks, and crunchy fallen leaves, only to find that no sound came from my steps. It was as if I were a ghost.

I peered around the corner of a large oak tree to see the herd of centaurs gathered among huts and a small fire. My eyes wandered over each of them, first immediately recognizing Agdronis, the centaur who had tried to kill me, and then finally, my gaze landed on Bruhn.

I steadied my breathing as I forced myself to walk up to the herd, fully aware that they wouldn't take something like this lightly.

Agdronis immediately spotted me and nocked an arrow into his bow, alerting the others. They all scattered and turned to face me as I calmly continued to approach them.

I put my hands up. "I'm not here to harm you. You know me."

The centaurs were chirping their alerting calls, as Bruhn's gaze locked on mine. My steps halted as my hands remained up in surrender. A scowl crawled across his face and he moved to gallop toward me.

The others followed, all with arrows nocked. If I was truly here...I might've actually been nervous, but the comforting thought that they couldn't harm me in this form made me nearly crack a grin.

"What are you doing back here?" he demanded.

"I come to you weaponless and seek your aid."

"Have we not helped you enough by allowing you to leave my forest once, Elianna Valderre?"

A wicked smirk crept up my face. "Seeing how you know my name, then you also must know that this is truly *my* forest, not yours, Bruhn."

"But do you sit upon the Islan throne? Last we heard, you do not."

"And that's why I'm here," I admitted as I gradually lowered my arms to my sides. The other centaurs pulled their arrows back tighter, and I slowed my movements.

He laughed at me. Not even a chuckle, but a full-on laugh, which only aggravated me. "And why would we do such a thing? This is not our war."

"It has become a war of the realm. For a Valderre no longer sits on that throne, and she seeks to destroy the very last of the bloodline." I paused for a moment as his eyes roamed over me, somewhat softening.

"I come here seeking your aid. Help me win this war, and I will see to it that you are officially named Lord of the Wood and that the title is recognized under the crown."

He scoffed. "And I am to just take your word for it? A throneless queen. Besides, I am already considered a ruler of the forest."

"Considered and what is the truth are two very different things. Now, I am asking for your help, and that of the creatures that reside here. I am the true heir—you know this from before. I shouldn't have to spill my blood here before you to prove it once more. You saw it with your very stubborn eyes."

The eyes I spoke of roamed over me once again. "Ah, but could you if I even asked?"

Agdronis released his arrow, and before I had time to react, the weapon flew through my body and slammed into the trunk of a tree several feet behind me.

My hands flew to my center as shock took over me, looking for a wound that I was thankful wasn't there. My breathing turned heavy as my eyes bulged.

My gaze lifted back to theirs, anger flooding me. "That was fucking uncalled for!"

"And so is your witch magic," he spat. "Did you think I could not smell it on you? It seems as if you have enough aid already, Heir of the Realm. Why should my herd risk anything for you?"

"Because even with our witch magic, we may not win. I have an army full of mortals. They are brave, skilled fighters, but they are fragile. We are fighting against an army of fae. For everything that I have, Idina has one to match."

"So you are saying it is an evenly matched war, and you seek our help to win."

"It is hardly even," I growled.

He trotted up to me, circling my body. My neck craned up toward him and our eyes locked on each other.

"You come to my home and demand that we fight for you, creatures that the fae have exiled for centuries. All creatures of these ancient woods live here because of this, and you think that they owe you and your bloodline. Just because the realm itself may fight for you does not mean all of its creatures owe you a damn thing, Valderre."

"First of all, I was asking...*pleading*. Begging, even." I huffed out a breath as I tried to calm myself. "Under my reign, all creatures would be equal. Everyone may live the way they wish as long as it abides by Velyran law. I give you my word."

He chuckled and shook his head at me. "The last fae to seek an alliance with us ended up with a chest full of arrows dipped in velaeno berries. You're lucky that you are not truly here, and that I somewhat enjoy your spirit."

My mind spun the moment he said velaeno berries. "What?" I breathed. "What did you just say about velaeno berries?"

"The last fae that—"

"Sought an alliance with you, yes. That part I got. Who was it?" I demanded.

"He claimed to be a lord and demanded we aid his armies to destroy the humans that lived in Velyra. Promised us all the gold and riches we could desire. A centaur has no need for such nonsense. When we told them this, they got angry and moved to draw their weapons."

"And then?"

"Let's just say the arrows were released before their blades were fully withdrawn from their sheaths," Bruhn said with a chuckle.

A chuckle left me that matched his, and then another, and another after that. A burst of wicked, cackling laughter escaped me, my back arching from the force of it, and the sound echoed in the misty forest air. They all watched me—each with a raised brow.

"Please tell me you're fucking joking," I said once my manic laughter finally settled. "By chance, did this happen to be in the forest directly north of Ceto Bay?"

"How did you know of that?" he barked. "It was one of the few times we ventured beyond into a different forest. There is only a mile's distance from Sylis' end and the forest surrounding the bay. We haven't since, and it was because of our run-in with *your* kind."

"That's why humans were blamed," I whispered to myself.

"Excuse me?" he snapped.

I took a step toward him, and the herd pulled back on their bows. "Oh, for fuck's sake, you know I cannot harm him like this!"

My attention returned to Bruhn. "You started this war! The lord that you killed was the queen's father, and one of the other men was his son. You killed the queen's kin, and it was believed that humans had done it outside of Ceto Bay. All this time. More than a century, humans have been slaughtered for a crime they didn't commit."

Bruhn's eyes narrowed in on me. "Do not blame your war on us when they sought to destroy humans before their deaths."

"It had been the ultimate tipping point against the humans. The fae thought the lord and his son were murdered by mortals. That is why this war began! It has cost *thousands* of lives!" My voice rose with each word as fury took over me.

All this time...the humans had been completely innocent. Jace hadn't even known about velaeno berries when we were lost in the forest—he even wondered how information could have become lost to humans over the years. I should've known then.

His animalistic ears pointed backward as a scowl worked its way up his face. "Do not blame us for protecting our herd against a threat and for your kind's lack of investigation against the deaths of their own people."

My teeth were clenched so hard I thought they would crack as my eyes bore into his. "The queen has my sister. She holds my people hostage in the city she occupies, and she stole my throne. I'm asking for your aid in a war you accidentally began. More innocents will die. Who is to say that Idina will stop there and not raid the forest next? Without a Valderre on the throne, you know very well that the realm, as we know it, will cease to exist. It is against Mother Goddess Terra's wishes. The Valderres are her only true heirs—*I* am her true heir."

His eyes roamed over me, but he said nothing. It was then I knew I would never get through to him.

"My army will be in Isla in four days' time to fight for what is right. They are fighting to reclaim their lives against the evil that has sunken its claws into the crown by murdering their way there. Bruhn, I'm not demanding you assist in eliminating a race. I'm asking you to do what is right."

The creaking sound of shifting bows filled the forest air as the centaurs all lowered their weapons.

I huffed at them as the entire herd's stares were fixated on me.

Bruhn's gaze continued to roam over me multiple times as I stood beneath him and his colossal form. "Goodbye, Elianna Valderre," he dismissed me and then turned away in a gallop, his herd moving to follow his lead.

I remained at the edge of their deserted camp in defeat until the sounds of their hooves faded away, and then I willed myself back to my body.

SIXTY

Veli

ELIANNA LET OUT A gasp for breath as she returned to her physical body. Her arms flew out as if reaching for something until they met the stone table.

"Lia, Lia!" Jace boomed. "It's okay, you're back. You're alright."

Zaela's eyes kept flashing back and forth to Elianna and myself, as if I had any answers for her.

Once Elianna finally caught her breath, she looked around the room at each of us, a sadness in her eyes that told me all I needed to know—her last resort for allies had refused.

"What happened?" her mate asked in a whisper.

Her deep breaths caught my attention, and I raised a brow.

"They will not be fighting for us in the war," she stated, and everyone's shoulders sagged in defeat. "But I did learn something of value."

"And what might that be?" I asked.

Elianna had been unraveling at the seams for some time now, and this certainly wouldn't help on top of losing Avery. I knew centaurs were the most stubborn of creatures, but even I had hoped they would prove me wrong—and I *loathed* being wrong.

She told us everything the leader of the herd said about how they had ventured beyond the Sylis Foret over a century ago and murdered the queen's father and brother.

My eyes flared at what she had uncovered—these moronic half-horse beasts started a war they had no intention of fighting in. I had half a thought to break into their minds and force them to finish what they accidentally began, but that would go against everything I stood for.

Jace placed his head in his hands as his elbows rested on the table. "I can't believe this."

"I know," Elianna whispered.

"And they won't even help us end what they started," Gage growled.

"It appears that way," she answered.

"Can this information be used in any way for us? Could we use this against that bitch queen by letting the realm know she started all of this on false accusations? Fae have died, not just humans. Your people will be upset that they have lost family members for her failed revenge," Zaela stated.

I truly liked this blonde girl. Quite a bit.

"I'm not sure that we have the time, but if we could somehow get this information to them, it could cause a revolt in the city," Elianna said.

"What about that witch whispering spell? Could we try that again?" Gage asked.

"Azenna is shielding the city. No one would hear it but her," I reminded him.

"Not if we kill her first," Elianna stated, and all our eyes shifted to her. The heir's face was void of all emotion—nothing but calculation in her stare.

"Kill Azenna? The High Witch? We would have to remove her heart from her body, or find a way to get it to stop beating. Do you know how difficult that would be?" She opened her mouth to speak, but I cut her off. "Actually, do not answer that. I know you are clueless as usual."

She rolled her eyes at me, but I ignored her tantrum.

"Then, if we manage to kill her, the spell will be broken, and you will cast the whisper. Idina's city will come undone beneath her," Elianna said.

"We could take the city easily without their magic at work. We wouldn't even need the citizens to revolt," Jace said.

"They deserve to know," his mate answered. "Everyone deserves to know the truth about what happened over a century ago."

"Agreed," I chimed in, and she gave me a nod.

Elianna cleared her throat. "This was our last chance at obtaining more allies. We're out of time, and we need to move out. We've done all we can, and I want you all to know how sorry I am that this is what our reality has become. I truly thought we would have more on our side. More time, more allies...more *hope*."

"We haven't lost hope yet, Lia," Zaela said.

The commander put his hand on top of his mate's, and her shoulders visibly relaxed at his touch.

Elianna then turned to me. "You will need to rift walk to Elora and alert the sirens of their task. They will need to swim fast."

"That will not be an issue for them. It is part of their magic," I stated as I stood from my seat.

"You're going now?!" Zaela nearly screeched at me, and everyone looked at her with a raised brow.

"Well, it is what your queen wishes. And as we have stated, we are running out of time."

Her eyes quickly averted my own. "Right, well...be careful."

I smiled at her. I never smile, but her concern for an all-powerful sorceress was...cute.

"Aye, Zaela. I will be careful."

Her cheeks flushed a bright pink as everyone else stood from their seats.

"Now that dawn has risen, we will check in with the general in the meantime," Elianna alerted me.

"I will meet you once I return."

And with that, the four of them left me alone in the war chamber.

I sucked in a sharp breath and held out my hand, focusing all of my attention on the isles. "*Odium Embulae.*" I cast the spell and a small gateway appeared that held The Elora Isles on its other side.

I stepped through the portal and was instantly transported back to the marsh where we had met the sirens.

I walked to the riverbank's edge and rested my hands atop the water, sending a pulse of magic out toward the sea, calling for the wicked creatures that roamed the deep.

Within minutes, multiple heads emerged from the seawater several feet in front of me. I counted at least nine at a quick glance.

I recognized the two that Elianna had set her barter with. They hissed at me the second we locked eyes.

"Wonderful to see you, too," I greeted them as I crossed my arms. "It is time for your debt to be paid."

"We have no *debt*," one of them hissed. "Your queen stole something from us, and we want it back. She stole our sister."

"Ah yes, just how you tried to steal her mate." I paused for a moment. "And *eat* him, I might add."

Feral grins crept up their faces, as if they didn't regret it for a second. "He was a handsome one," the other cooed.

"I am here to give you orders. You will receive your sister's conch back so long as you swim for Isla's harbor and rid the males on the ships, if there are any, in four days' time."

"You think we can swim to *Isla* in four days?"

"I have no doubt in it. You forget I know of your abilities, *siren*."

Her tail lashed out of the water and splashed the murky water at me, but I threw up a shield just in time for it to bounce off and slam back down into the swamp.

"Your orders have been given." All of their eyes narrowed in on me as their mouths remained beneath the surface of the water. "Fight for Elianna Valderre in Isla's harbor and you will receive your sister's conch. It is quite a simple bargain."

I cast the portal spell back open behind me and slowly marched backward towards it. "I would just hate to see our queen crush her shell and punch one of you in your pretty little faces again."

With that parting threat, I was back through the portal in the valley, and they disappeared beneath the tides once more.

SIXTY-ONE

Elianna

SITTING ON THE OUTSKIRTS of the training fields with Nox, I hugged my knees tightly to my chest as I gazed up at the night sky. The stars twinkled as if it were any other beautiful night in the valley—only it now felt empty and cold.

"Nox, what have I done?" My words were barely audible as I leaned into his scale-covered body. He lifted his enormous head and nuzzled his chin on my shoulder, trying to comfort me. I couldn't bring myself to confess that I had lost faith in finding solace in anything.

We had sent the soldiers home to enjoy any time they could with their families before our inevitable departure, but I couldn't bring myself to see my own. How could I look them in the eyes, knowing I had doomed us all? My aide and co-seconds spoke words of comfort and forgiveness, but how could I believe them when I couldn't even forgive myself?

I had done the unthinkable—I had lost my sister and a member of my court, and now she sits in the hands of the enemy. Not only that, but nearly every attempt to collect more allies ended in defeat or ruin, only aiding the wicked queen's victory.

Time was up. There was nothing, and no one else left. My throat felt as if it was being crushed beneath the weight of Idina's heel, knowing she was winning the great war as we neared its end.

Footsteps sounded behind us, but I didn't have to turn to know who it was as I remained hugging my body, tucked beneath Nox's wing.

Jace sat down at my side and leaned against the wyvern. I felt his stare boring into my cheek, but I couldn't bring myself to face him—couldn't bring myself to even speak.

"*Do you want to talk about it?*" he spoke into my mind.

A huff left me. "*No.*"

His hand wrapped around my own as it fell to the ground. "*Okay, then let me rephrase. I need you to talk about it, and tell me what is churning in that head of yours, Lia. I can't help you otherwise. And I refuse to let you simmer in it on your own.*"

I turned to face him then. "I fucked everything up. Not a single thing I've done has worked or aided us. She's always one step ahead of me. No matter how smart I pretend or try to be, she slithers through the cracks and rips everything out from beneath me! Beneath all of us. She's never set foot in battle, yet she sits on my throne and has seized my kingdom."

My fingernails dug into the palms of my hands.

"She clawed her way there through deception and murder. There isn't a single part of her that has demonstrated battle intellect, Elianna."

I huffed out a grunt as I shoved to my feet, and he mimicked the movement. Nox went on high alert then, his head lifting from the ground as his golden eyes narrowed in on us intently. Jace and I now stood chest to chest.

"No?! Explain then, Jace, please! Everything I have been able to provide for our armies, she has matched. We are cornered in the realm, with nowhere else to go. I was a captain, Jace! Yet she has continued to outsmart me in this war."

"You've done everything right! Broken oaths and malicious lies don't define *you* and the kind of leader you are, Elianna. The world is not kind, nor is it fair. It's horrible and wicked and deadly, but we must work to fight against it, or all of this was for nothing!" he bellowed. His stare roamed over me. "So, go on. Let it all out. What else? Whatever else is eating you alive, tell me here and now." His tone was authoritative—one he never used with me.

Nox let out a low growl. I placed my hand on his side to ease him, and the rumbling ceased. I knew this conversation with Jace was long overdue, but Nox couldn't be here with the tension in our voices—he would work to protect me against my mate, and that was the last thing I needed. What I truly needed was to be protected from myself. And Jace... Jace knew that.

I looked into my wyvern's stare and said, "I will be okay. Go back to the estate. We'll find you once we return."

He let out a huff through his nostrils, and his stare narrowed in on Jace.

"She is safe with me. You know that," my mate assured him. And after a grumble of annoyance, Nox shot into the sky.

Suffocating silence wrapped around us, and I swallowed thickly as I stood beneath my husband's piercing stare.

"My actions and methods have doomed us, Jace. Can't you see that? My own sister is captured, stuck in the hands of the enemy across the continent. We had Nox and Veli on our side. That was it! We went to the isles for allies, and all it did was present our enemy with their own witches and wyvern. We are evenly matched in numbers and magic; only our men are significantly weaker. I'm the descendant of the first of the fae, and I can't even get the realm to answer my call. Idina is right, and I'm a fuckup. The prophecy is bullshit."

He took a step closer to me, his breath warm on my nose. "Speak that way about my wife one more time, and you will regret those words." A growl rumbled through him.

My lips parted. "Jace, this isn't a game. I'm being serious." A single tear slipped and rolled down my cheek.

"And so am I. Don't speak of my queen that way." He took my chin between his fingers and forced my stare to meet his. "Tell me what you need."

A hate-filled laugh left me. "I need to hit something. I need to scream and erupt and get my fucking kingdom back, Jace." My voice cracked.

"Then do everything you just said." His head tilted as his eyes remained locked on mine.

My hands lifted to rub my temples. "I'm working on it."

His hand shot out then and gripped my wrist, making my eyes flare. "No, you aren't." He released his hold on me and took a single step back, his arms stretched out low at his sides. "Hit me. Scream. Erupt. And *then* we will take your fucking kingdom back. It's not going to work until you start with what you need first, sweetheart."

I let out a bewildered huff, feeling my breath catch in my throat. "Hit you? I'm not going to hurt you, Jace. You're the last person I would do that to." My eyes narrowed in on him in confusion.

A smirk played on the edge of his lips. "You're not going to hurt me, baby."

He moved to strike then, his fist coming for my side in a slower movement that I easily side-stepped, trying to provoke me.

"What are you doing?!" I spat, and then we moved to circle each other. "I'm not going to fight you."

"I'm not fighting you—I'm sparring with you. Training you. We all need reminders sometimes, Lia. Get just enough of your anger out to be levelheaded and then release the rest on the queen once we arrive at her gates." Without warning, his foot hooked under my ankle, and he sent my body crashing down to the terrain.

My gaze whipped to him, my lip curling back. "That's *my* move." I jumped up to my feet then.

"Do you not like when your own tactics are used against you, my queen?"

An annoyed cackle left me as we moved around each other in a predator-like dance. "And tell me, husband, why is it *now* that you choose to go full commander on me?"

"You didn't need it before, but I see now that you've lost hope, and it's not something I'm willing to accept for you. It's not just you in this, Lia. It's both of us and our court that's waiting for us to come home. When one of us falters, the other provides strength."

"I can't show them I'm feeling this way. They're relying on me to lead them into war! They can't see me unraveling like this."

"You're not showing them, Lia. You're showing *me*. I feel everything you feel. Every burst of joy, fear, and heartache. I've told you before, and I will say it again—you are the crown, and I am your sword. I will fight any battle for you that I can, so long as you let me. So share this with me, Lia. It shouldn't only be your burden to bear."

My breathing quickened at his words, and what he said next was spoken into my mind. "*Now, be a good girl and do as you're told. You'll never get out of your own head without the release you need. This is life or death, and you're not going into battle without being as levelheaded as possible.*"

I let his words seep into me, and my lips tilted into a grin. "As you wish."

Without another thought, I lunged at him. Jace expertly blocked every blow I threw at him. His maneuvers were effortless and composed, yet he didn't counterattack.

My throat tightened as my body unveiled all the built-up tension, devastation, and wrath that festered within it.

Visions of the queen flashed through my memory with every strike I made. Of her staring at me with pure hatred in her eyes when she caught me using her hairbrush as a youngling. The look on her face when I watched her emerge from my father's chambers with his wine the last night I saw him alive. How she appeared in our room on our gods-damn wedding night and threatened me, my mate, and people.

"Come on, Lia. Harder," Jace urged, his voice steady and strong, yet soothing.

Frustration seeped into every punch and kick I threw at him, causing them to become more forceful, yet all he did was continue to block. "Why won't you fight back?!" I shouted, my voice breaking with emotion.

Jace finally grabbed my wrist mid-punch and pulled me close, our chests heaving as they pressed together. "Because this isn't about me. It's about *you*. Let it out, Elianna."

I nearly broke down right there as my husband confessed he only wanted to let me unleash the storm brewing within myself—even if it was at his expense.

In a burst of raw emotion, I let out a primal scream that echoed through the valley and wrenched my wrist free. Jace dropped his arms and purposefully absorbed a hit, my fist hitting his chest as if it were a solid wall.

A grunt left him at the impact. A mixture of tears and sweat streamed down my cheeks as the weight of my actions sunk in, but when my eyes met his, I was met with nothing but pride and satisfaction.

My body faltered. Panting heavily with trembling hands, I nearly dropped to my knees. Jace caught me then, his own breaths ragged, as he wrapped his arms around my body and fell to the terrain with me. I collapsed against him, burying my face in his shoulder as he held me tightly to his chest.

"It's okay, Lia. I'm here," he whispered softly.

My body shook with silent sobs, the rage and frustration slowly fading away, replaced by the comfort of *him*.

"Thank you," I said, voice hoarse.

He cupped my face in his calloused hands, brushing away a tear with his thumb. "Always."

With a deep, shuddering breath, I leaned in and kissed him softly, savoring the way our lips met tenderly. I was thankful for the moment of shared vulnerability. When he broke the kiss, he brought his forehead to mine as our breaths mingled.

"We're going to save Velyra. We're going to get Avery and your kingdom back. We'll get through this, my Lia. Just as we always have," Jace whispered. "Together."

I nodded, a small smile breaking through the remnants of my fury and heartache. "Together."

SIXTY-TWO

Kellan

MESSENGER FALCONS HAD BEEN sent to all armed cities and towns south of the Sylis Forest seeking their assistance in the war. Nearly all the lords in power responded to the queen's demands in search of payment. They desired gold to give up their armies and a substantial amount of it. The lords expressed that the mortal army could potentially conquer their unguarded cities, much to the queen's discontent. So, she did what any ruler would do and offered her daughter's hand in marriage to the lord who provided the largest army to our own forces.

Days later, thousands of soldiers were knocking at the Islan gates.

The armies worked in shifts. One lord's fleet kept watch beyond the gate during the day and the next in the evening, all of them rotating through the cycle to be sure that eyes were kept on the task at hand. Ships had also arrived and positioned themselves in the harbor, ready with cannons to destroy any enemy vessels that approached the city from the sea.

Isla now resembled an enormous war camp, where the only souls who filled the streets were that of patrolling soldiers. The air was thick with tension as we awaited the looming attack from Elianna's army. Personally, I couldn't fucking wait.

I kept a close eye on everyone to ensure they were at their assigned posts and focused on their tasks. Soldiers, draped in armor adorned with Velyra's emblem, moved with practiced precision in their march up the cobblestone streets.

The citizens huddled in the corners of their homes and shops like frightened animals and cowered on the street beneath my stare as I passed. Their wide, terrified eyes revealed the fear that the queen had instilled in them.

The distant echoes of a blacksmith's hammer added to the eeriness of the near-silent city as weapons continued to be forged. The sharp clinks and metallic clangs resonated through the air, matching that of the armor of the parading guards.

My mind delved into the tactics of battle, but I considered it to be already won. There would never be a way for Elianna to win her throne from the queen with everything we had stacked against her. At the very least, not as long as the High Witch remained in the queen's ear.

I strolled back up to the castle, where my wyvern mount remained perched upon its battlement, watching every person who walked by. Its glowing, all-knowing eyes meant it was currently under the control of the crone, which irritated me. Mostly because we shared a bond connecting our minds, thanks to the cuffs permanently on each of us. I didn't know how deeply the witch magic reached and if, by breaking into the wyvern's mind, they could also see into my own.

The unknown of it only pissed me off—an oversight I never thought of in the dungeons when they forged the blood bond with me and the beast.

When the wyvern wasn't in use with me, it was used as the only castle guard, ready to ignite anyone unwelcome who strolled too close. I gave it a curt nod, and the beast rolled its shoulders as it moved its attention back to the streets.

Tugging open the castle's doors, I was surprised when I came face-to-face with the queen and was even more aggravated when I saw Azenna silently standing at her side.

"Captain," she greeted.

"Get *off* of me!" Avery's voice echoed throughout the hall, making me peer over the queen's shoulder as I watched two of my guards forcefully drag her towards us.

"You are just in time," the queen continued. "We are about to make an announcement to the realm."

The queen, princess, and High Witch stood upon the stage before the quivering masses in the city square. I sat atop my mount; the beast perched on the top of the center stone fountain, the structure groaning at the weight of him. Thousands of pairs of eyes were locked on the stage, refusing to meet the stare of my wyvern as soldiers loomed on the outskirts of Isla.

Azenna had placed the princess under a spell to incite cooperation, which kept her frozen in obedience. The queen's hands were clasped in front of her as she stood next to them, her ruby gown flowing behind her from the wind rolling off the sea.

"Thank you for gathering here today for your queen." Silence answered her. "My sincerest apologies, for I know I do not venture out here often, but threats have been made against our city. Against all of you."

Wide eyes frantically glanced in all different directions in the crowd as murmurs echoed from them all.

"Now, I know you all adored my late husband and king and that some of you believe in the false claim that the treasonous Lukas Salvinae declared regarding the proper ascension of the throne. I am here to put an end to your blind allegiance to her because of some statement screamed by a traitorous guard. Where is Elianna Solus now? Do any of you see her among you?"

The crowd's occupants turned from side to side, looking at one another as if they were attempting to search for her within the masses.

"No, and you will not. Would you like to know why? Because she has turned her back on the Kingdom of Velyra. She turned her back on the crown and the family of the king that she declared to love so much...all so she could build up the armies of our own enemy. And what did she do with this army? She murdered your heir and rightful king! Kai Valderre's life was brutally taken by her in cold blood.

Your prince and future king, dead! All because she believes she has laid claim to the throne. A bastard daughter. An unwanted burden of your late king."

Shouts of agreement rang out all around, and my eyes flashed back down to the princess, whose neck was straining as if she was internally screaming, begging for the words to come out of her.

I swallowed thickly at the sight, remembering what it felt like to be caught under the witch's talons.

"Yes, you heard me correctly. Elianna Solus now leads an army of mortals straight to our city. My own daughter,"—the queen turned and pointed to the princess—"barely escaped with her life as she came back to warn us of Elianna's treachery and can still barely speak of the acts she has witnessed. My Finnian is still a prisoner to the mortals. Only the gods know what is happening to my only living son."

My eyes remained on Avery as her stare of burning hatred bore into the back of the queen's head.

"Now, I know you have not always had a love for me as you had for Jameson. You fear the company I keep and the wyvern that soars above the city, but these are all for your protection. Every choice made by your queen has been in your best interest."

I smirked to myself, knowing damn well that these were strictly to incite obedience—it had nothing to do with protection.

"The lords of Velyra have graciously sent us their soldiers to protect their realm's capital and its citizens. They will be led by your fearless captain, Kellan Adler, and we will put an end to the treasonous usurper once and for all!"

Cheering roars of agreement came, but echoing from the outskirts of the crowd—from the soldiers she spoke of. Not a single cheer came from the masses of citizens, who still looked mortified at everything occurring before their eyes.

The queen held up a hand to silence the troops. "The streets may be quiet and empty now, but soon they will be filled with the clashing of steel. Remember who brought it to you when that day arrives. Consider who tried to protect you and who brought blood and flame to our gates."

The queen lifted her stare to me and gave me a nod, signaling our show of power.

I dug my boot into the wyvern's side and willed it to launch into the air. With a deafening screech and a crouch from its powerful legs, the beast shot up into the sky, soaring over the crowd below as they ducked and tried to run for cover.

I peered down as we circled Isla from above and watched as the civilians dispersed and were ordered back to their homes. Azenna then grabbed the arms of the royals and pulled them through a rift she had conjured to return to the castle.

SIXTY-THREE

Elianna

OUR DAYS GIVEN FOR preparation were over, and it was now time to storm Velyra's capital and end Idina's reign over the realm once and for all.

I stood in front of the vast window of the war chamber that overlooked Alaia's great city. My eyes wandered over each building, civilian, and alleyway in sight. My mind raced, realizing that this could be the last time I saw this beautiful sanctuary that Jace had helped build. There was a large chance that many of us would never see it again, and it left a gaping wound in my heart.

Walking up to the center table, I picked my dagger up from where it sat. I admired the way the early morning sunlight glistened off the obsidian blade. A small smile formed as my gaze moved to the wyvern wings adorning its hilt and the antler carving of Nyra.

I thought of everything it represented and how this blade was the true beginning of the rebellion. How my father gifted it to me as a surprise when he declared he wished to have named me his heir.

This blade protected me from Kellan's crew on his ship, opening my eyes to the male he truly was and would always be. It had then been taken from me and used against Jace before being shattered. The scream that tore from my throat when I witnessed Kellan's attempt to kill him will forever haunt my mind, as will the heartbreaking sight of it being destroyed. But much like myself, the blade rose from the ashes of what it had been dealt—and I had my mate to thank for that.

My fingers tightened around the hilt, fueled by the burning desire to exact vengeance on the usurpers who had ravaged my kingdom, stolen my crown, and mercilessly ended the lives of my parents, Lukas, and countless others.

I strapped the last of my weapons to my leathers and blew out a breath as the door to the chamber opened. Turning to the doorway, I came face-to-face with my mate, who wore his full suit of armor—a sword strapped on each of his sides, daggers hidden beneath metal flaps, and the commander's helmet held in his hand.

Our eyes were locked on each other as love radiated down the bond, bringing me a sense of comfort.

He placed his helmet on the stone table and took my face in his hands, pressing his lips to mine.

When our eyes met once more, he spoke. "We're ready for you, my Lia."

I opened my mouth to speak but couldn't find the words—consumed by the fear of what lay ahead.

As we planned, Veli, Empri, and Madalae would open the rift directly beyond the Islan gates. Jace would lead our armies through the portal on the ground while Nox and I took to the skies. Zaela, Gage, Leon, and Landon were the pointed leaders of designated battalions. And then, once everyone was on the other side of the rift, the witches would join us in our fight.

My plan was to try to convince Idina to surrender before the battle, but I knew she would never yield—it didn't matter, though, I *had* to try. If only to convince myself I did absolutely everything possible to avoid bloodshed. So, once the fighting ensued, my task was to find Avery and get her to safety before returning to the battlefield to join my mate, court, and kingdom in one last fight for freedom.

I knew deep within me that if we didn't win and their lives were lost, I wouldn't be able to live without them—I wouldn't be able to live without *him*.

Jace clearly sensed where my mind had wandered. "*No matter the outcome, I am so proud of you. Wherever this battle leads, I will never regret a single choice made since the moment I laid eyes on you. No amount of time with you will be enough, but if we meet our end in this, just know that it was the honor of my life.*" His soothing voice wrapped around me like a warm embrace as it flowed down our tether.

"The honor has been mine," I answered.

He took my hand in his and escorted me from the war chamber, out into the city streets where the citizens cheered in awe of our bravery, and straight to the fields where our soldiers awaited.

Matthias galloped alongside Jace's stallion as we approached our troops. The lines were forming beautifully as thousands of our men prepared to march into Isla.

Stretching as far as the eye could see, our soldiers stood in disciplined order. Their armor gleamed vibrantly beneath the sun's rays as emerald banners whipped in the wind on our catapults.

The air was filled with the resonating sound of armored boots and hooves hitting the ground. Nearly matching their rhythm was the beat of Nox's wings as he soared overhead, circling the army.

My eyes focused in on the banners as they fluttered in the breeze, displaying an insignia I didn't recognize. Adorning the center of the emerald, flowing fabric was a crest that beheld a design of my original dagger with giant wyvern wings wrapping around it as the Valderre name perfectly flowed through the design.

As the wind tousled my hair, my gaze flew to Jace, his horse thundering beside mine as we approached the back of our army.

"*I told you we would have a new crest for you, my queen.*" His voice filled my head, and an excited, booming laugh left me in answer as we raced up through the center of the lines.

As we approached the front, my court came into view. I owed everything to my loyal friends, who constantly risked their lives by leading a rebellion in my name and claim to power.

The general, Gage, Zaela, and Lynelle all stood front and center before the army, my Nyra girl sitting at their feet. My gaze drifted to where Veli stood off to the side, accompanying the twin witches. Lastly, my eyes fell upon the healers' wagons posted separately from the troops of soldiers—Finnian stood at their front, his stance beaming with pride.

I tugged on Matthias' reins, and his galloping slowed into a trot until his steps completely ceased before the masses.

I dismounted my horse and led him to Landon, who was in the center of the first lines. His hand reached out for the reins, his face hard as stone as he focused on the task of leading this side of the battalion.

"I will trust my horse with no one else. A stable hand turned troop leader...I am so very proud of you," I said to him softly. A curt nod was given to me as the tiniest smile cracked his lips.

As I turned around to meet the others, Jace, ever the commander, rode his steed along the front lines, his voice carrying over the assembly as he brought their full attention to us.

Veli met me in the center as I faced the army while my mate finished his rounds. Our gazes remained looking out towards the troops.

"What you have done will be written into history, regardless of what becomes of the realm. You have made a difference without the crown properly adorned atop your head. And while I still think that you are a foolish, reckless girl..." Her whispering paused, and a grin formed on my lips. "I am honored to hold the title that you gifted to me. Thank you for trusting me in being your aide."

I blinked as my eyes flashed down to her while she stood at my side, her face wearing a wicked smile I rarely saw. Her once violet eyes met mine as her shadows danced around her face. "Thank you for guiding a foolish, reckless—"

"A brave, loyal, and noble queen," she cut me off. "It has been an honor."

A smile formed without my permission from her praise—something I never thought I would hear.

Jace brought his horse to a halt at our side and looked down at me. "They are ready to hear from their queen."

My feet carried me forward, separating me from my court as my eyes drifted over everyone—their stares boring into me.

I lifted my hand and let out a sharp whistle into the sky, and a moment later, the ground beneath our boots rumbled as Nox landed directly behind me. His horn-covered head hovered over my shoulder only a moment later, acting as my usual guardian.

Soldiers that once cowered at the sight of my wyvern now stood proudly before us both. Not a single flinch caught my eye as he faced them all.

The tiniest smirk tilted my lips as I turned on my heel and climbed onto Nox's back. I stood on his shoulder, my arm reaching for his neck for extra balance.

"My fearless warriors," my voice rang out, cutting through the silent valley like a blade. "The day is upon us when we must end the brutal slaughter of the mortal race. Our enemy remains tireless and insatiable, seeking to destroy everything you have rebuilt."

I paused, letting my gaze linger on the faces of each soldier on the front lines.

"Now, I understand that I have never had the pleasure of fighting side by side with most of you on the battlefield, and I am thankful for you giving me that opportunity today. Not only to be alongside you but trusting me to lead you there. Many of you have fought by my mate's side for years—facing the horrors dealt from the fae that would break the spirit of lesser men. You have bled, you have suffered, and yet you stand here unbroken and unyielding."

My gaze drifted down to Jace, who remained in the saddle of his horse directly next to Nox. "*Your words mean a great deal to them...and to me.*" His voice filtered to me.

"I will never be able to take back the part that I played in this war before your commander opened my eyes to the true horror of it all, but you must know that where my heart lies now and for the remainder of my existence is with *you*. The innocents of it all. Both the innocent mortals and fae that have been roped into a gruesome war of power and greed."

"We do not fight for glory graced from the gods or for unfathomable riches. The fight we wage is for the very essence of our existence, the lands that have nurtured our hopes, and the people we hold close to our hearts. We fight because we are the last line of defense against the cruel, malicious beings that usurped my throne through treason and murder." My words were a battle cry that echoed through the sky.

My hand clenched into a fist at the mention of the queen and all she had done.

"This battle will not be easy. There will be bloodshed, and our spirits will be tested like never before. The enemy may outnumber us, but we have something that they do not—hope. The false queen rules and leads by inflicting fear on anyone beneath her. That is not who I am, nor who I will ever be. Her soldiers fight you because of her greed. Our soldiers are fighting back for their *freedom!*"

Cheers and shouts of agreement erupted down the lines, their echoes resonating through the valley.

The burning intensity in my eyes mirrored Nox's flames. "Battles and lives have been lost over the last century, but today, you do not fight alone. We fight as one, both mortals and fae—a formidable force that will shatter the darkness lingering in the realm and ignite a new dawn for our people. A people united together as one under my reign!"

The air reverberated with the echoing roar of the assembled warriors, the clash of swords against shields filling the space with harmonious chaos. I unsheathed the sword from my hip and raised the blade high above my head as I remained balancing on Nox's shoulder.

"Today, we march not towards death but towards the triumph of light over darkness. Now, let's make our enemies tremble as they hear the thunder of our march and our roars for battle. For a better realm!" I screamed.

As if commanded, Nox let out a booming roar of triumph into the air. I leapt down onto my saddle and he turned to face my court, who remained behind us, smiles beaming on each of their faces.

"*I love you,*" I whispered down the bond as I met Jace's stare.

"Don't whisper that as if it's a goodbye. I will see you on the other side." His eyes radiated concern. *"I love you more than anything in this world and beyond. The realm needs its queen."*

"Remember, we don't want to distract one another, so we must only use this in a time of true need," I reminded him, and he nodded as his eyes remained on me.

I looked to Nox's opposite side, where Nyra sat, and then my eyes met Lynelle's. "Take care of her until we return?"

"Of course," she answered while guiding my wolf off to the side of the lines. My heart ached as my stare followed her walking away, but this would be too dangerous for her.

My eyes found Jace, Gage, Zaela, and Veli as they all stood before Nox. "Remember, no fighting within the city. It must be prevented at all costs, and we will stay beyond the gates unless Jace or I state otherwise. That is essential. If Idina or Kellan don't come to negotiate a surrender before the battle begins, I will ride Nox above the city and try to get to Avery or the queen, whichever comes first."

The veins in Gage's neck strained at the mention of my sister. "We will get her back." His voice was low, with the promise of revenge evident.

I gave him a curt nod. "That I promise you." My eyes moved to Veli. "It's time."

"Aye, and just in time. The sirens have arrived at their destination," she announced to me with a wink.

Her eyes radiated their golden, fuchsia glow as a wicked grin formed, and she turned from me, facing the distant fields that awaited our army. Empri and Madalae met her on either side, the three of them interlocking their taloned fingers to further combine their power.

The twins raised their outer hands and lifted them towards the open valley, Veli's hands bound to theirs as their grounding power.

Whispers carried on the wind, and then I heard the barely familiar words, "*Odium Embulae*." A crack splintered through the realm, mimicking a bolt of lightning crashing from the sky above. In a display of immense power, the three witches worked together to create a rift large enough to accommodate an entire army, their veins and muscles visibly straining against the force of it.

I shielded my eyes from the blinding sun as the thundering stomps of hooves and armored boots echoed from behind me. A growl of anticipation rumbled from Nox's chest as his wings shot out from his sides, readying himself.

My heart was galloping in my chest while my eyes were fixated on the power exploding before us all.

And then Isla appeared through the rift.

SIXTY-FOUR

Kellan

DAWN WAS ON THE horizon of the Vayr Sea as I inspected some of our vessels and their crews that awaited in the Islan harbor. We made sure to be prepared for the imminent arrival of Elianna's fleet, which we expected any day now.

I gazed out at the sea, the only thing I would ever truly love, and a grin formed on my face as I imagined what it would be like to finally end this pointless fucking war and make my move to sit upon the throne.

Once the battle was won, and the witches exited Isla and took what they had bargained from the queen, the opening to force my way into the crown would be vast once again. Even I couldn't stomach the thought of sleeping with that cold-hearted cunt to get there anymore—no, I would rip the crown right from the top of her fucking head.

My eyes glazed over as I imagined it all, my fingertips brushing over the wood of the ship's wheel.

"Captain," William's voice carried to me from across the ship's deck, snapping me out of my trance. "We weren't expecting you here this morning."

William had been reassigned once more and took charge of ensuring that the sea fleet was in pristine condition while I terrorized the queen's citizens from my wyvern's back.

"Aye, but does a captain need to announce his arrival for inspections?" I challenged.

"Of course not." He took a few steps closer and met me at the helm. "It's just that, lately, you take to the skies, not the sea."

A growl slipped from me. "It's not by choice, William." I gave him a vicious smile. "The things we do for what we desire most."

He lifted a single brow at me. "And that would be?"

Baring my teeth, I was about to lash out at him when my ears picked up a melodic sound that carried in from the waves.

Both of our gazes drifted to the deep sea, where the tide was rolling in. The rising sun reflected off the waves as an enchanting chorus flowed in, drawing us towards it.

My steps brought me to the bow of the ship, and I placed my hands on the railing as my stare focused out toward the haunting call. I stuffed my pinky in my ear and twisted, making sure that I was hearing correctly. I had never been a male who feared many things, but growing up as a son of the sea, I quickly learned that sirens were among the few creatures worth fearing.

Call it a gut feeling, but I was nearly certain that call was exactly what I heard. The melody grew louder and surrounded the ships in the harbor, as if coming at us from all sides while a mist drifted in on the waves.

"William?" My voice was just above a whisper as he stood next to me at the bow, but I went unanswered.

My eyes whipped toward him and flared as they beheld what his own looked like—glazed over with a cloudy haze. My steps sent me stumbling backwards, and my arms caught the rail, stopping me from falling overboard.

"William!" I barked, but his stare remained unseeing as he peered out at the water. I jogged to the center of the ship, where the troops were lined across the deck, and was horrified when I noticed that every single pair of eyes matched William's. From what I could tell, everyone aboard the surrounding ships in the harbor was stuck in the same trance.

"Fuck," I muttered under my breath, and then my gaze flashed down to my wrist—to the cuff that linked my mind to the wyvern's.

It will serve as a barrier for exterior magic, Azenna had said that day she bound this cuff in our blood, and I had never been more fucking thankful for something in my gods-damn life.

I peered back out towards the sea, where the sun had nearly completely risen, and my stomach dropped as hundreds of slick-haired heads emerged from the surface of the water, stark white eyes glowing from them.

Fog continued to roll in with the tide, but I knew it wasn't of nature. The haunting melody grew louder, and then a subtle splash caught my attention from the front of the ship.

I stalked back up to the bow, where William had been, to find he was gone. "Holy gods," I whispered, and my quickened steps brought me to the very tip of the bow.

I leaned over the edge of the rail to see bubbles emerging from the water where his body fell, and then a long, scaled onyx tail lashed out from the surface. Thick, swirling crimson then flooded the waves.

"FUCK!" I bellowed as I unsheathed my sword. The fog had already crept its way aboard the deck of the ship, swirling around my feet as I ran back toward those who remained standing.

"Wake up, you morons! Everybody, snap out of it. Now!" I screamed. Some of their eyes began to blink, but not enough to rid them of their milky hue.

As if I had commanded them, they all started walking towards the ship's edges, where webbed fingers curled over the railings.

Sirens heaved themselves onto the ships in the harbor. My eyes flashed in all directions as they climbed up the sides of the wooden vessels and sat upon their rails.

I frantically ran around the deck, swearing and grunting at the situation as I shoved sailors to the ground while their steps moved to carry them to their doom.

Then, a voice broke through the sirens' song.

"Handsome captain, why do you stop them?" My steps halted, and I whipped in the direction of the voice, where a siren held herself up on the ship's side. Ice-colored hair that matched her piercing eyes clung to her skin.

I took a step toward her, and my lip curled back in a snarl. "Why do I stop my soldiers from running blindly into their death? A bit of a foolish question. Wouldn't you agree, *sea-witch?*"

Her unseeing gaze narrowed in on me beneath furrowed brows as a smirk tilted her sharp lips. "And why does the captain not answer our call?"

I held up my arm that the cuff was clasped around and waved my fingers through the air as if in a mocking greeting.

She hissed in response, and before I could blink, her oil-hued tail whipped out at me, its razor-sharp fin slicing through the skin of my forearm.

I roared in pain, and it ignited the harbor into full fucking chaos.

Sirens leapt onto the ship from all sides, their tails wrapping around my sailors, shoving them overboard into the water—their talons and rows of fangs sinking into their flesh.

Screaming ensued from all ships, echoing throughout the harbor. Blood splattered from all directions, soaking me and the floorboards of the ship.

Sailors were snapping out of their stupors as the roars of agony continued, but not in time to save themselves.

With supernatural speed and strength, the sirens continued to maul my sailors, their claws easily tearing through flesh and bone.

The wails of anguish and torment blended with the lingering echoes of the sirens' song. The ship's deck became stained with the deep red of their spilled blood. Sailors, who fell from their trance, desperately swung their blades and any makeshift weapons they could get a hold of, but the sirens moved with a grace that defied even that of the fae.

I cut through any fin or reaching claws that swiped too close to me—the shrieks of pain that tore through the conch embedded in their throats was true music to my ears. However, I was surrounded by those who weren't as lucky, still half under the trance of the sea-witches' calls.

Some succumbed to the sirens' seductive allure, their vacant eyes betraying a surrender. Faces of those who resisted the trance were overcome with a mix of fear, rage, and despair as they tried to flee, while the sirens were lost in their bloodlust.

Everything was happening so fucking fast—too fast. I couldn't keep up, and I watched as countless crew members met their fate at the hands of the wicked sea creatures. I swiped my blade in the air as quickly as I could, but rarely did I meet my target.

I wiped the back of my hand across my face, only smearing the blood of my crew around my eyes more when I meant to clear it from them.

A distant roar thundered through the air from my wyvern mount, snapping my gaze to the castle in the far distance.

My hands held my blade out before me as I backed myself against the ship's mainmast. I tapped into my wyvern's sight, hoping to the gods that I was quick enough to not get mauled by one of these cunts from the sea.

My jaw locked as my vision focused in through his red-stained gaze to see that a crack had splintered through the sky beyond the city gates. It was then that I knew. This siren attack was Elianna's doing, and she was using it as a distraction to make her grand fucking entrance.

I willed my mind back into my own body, just in time to slice through the torso of an oncoming attacker as she lunged at me. Her severed body fell to my feet with a loud thud as black gore poured from her.

A deep growl rumbled through my chest as I tapped my bonded blood cuff three times, alerting the beast to come to me immediately. With a bloodcurdling battle cry, I unleashed all my wrath on the sirens that remained on the deck as I plunged my blade through them. However, I quickly found that I was outnumbered, as their claws sunk into my skin and shredded anything they could grab hold of.

Growls of disgust and rage continued to flow through me, and I imagined how fucking glorious it would feel to wrap my hands around Elianna's throat and choke the life out of her for somehow catching us off guard.

Avery

The sound of my cell door creaking open woke me from the little sleep I had managed to get since I had been locked in this gods-forsaken dungeon. When I wasn't wallowing in self-pity, I was violently trying to shake the bars of my prison, hoping that the minimal strength I had would somehow break the ancient rusted door from its hinges. But if Lia wasn't able to break free from this place, then I knew I was doomed.

My eyes snapped to the door as the creaking ceased, and I was met with the hideous crone. I let out a hiss at the sight of her, and my legs moved to push me further up against the far back wall.

"We do not have time for your stupid games, traitor princess," she murmured. A second later, she appeared directly before me and wrapped her shriveled, taloned hand around my forearm without permission.

An evil, toothy grin was flashed in my direction. Suddenly, it felt as if all the air was ripped from my lungs while the realm soared around me in a tunnel of rushing wind.

When I reopened my eyes, I was in the throne room, standing before my mother and the High Witch. The moment I found my balance after the wisp-travel, I dry heaved and vomited onto the floor from the dizziness.

Veli was right—it certainly wasn't safe for non-witches to travel that way.

"Thank you, Sylvae," Azenna said, and then her gaze flashed to mine. "It appears that your little court of rebels has come for you, Princess. Magic bursts beyond the gates."

My eyes widened as I stood beneath her and my mother's stares.

"Sylvae, go to one of the towers and place a shield around the city's battlement. None of the heir's soldiers are to breach the gates. Am I understood?" Azenna ordered.

"Yes, of course," the crone's bone-chilling voice answered right before she vanished.

531

My heart was racing—they came for me, but they were unknowingly falling into a trap.

"You will not use me against her!" I screamed.

Ignoring my outburst, both Azenna and the queen took steps towards me until they flanked me on either side. My lips curled back in disgust as I returned their hate-filled stares.

"Anything you'd like to say before we greet your sister?" the High Witch taunted.

My eyes darted back and forth between each of theirs, and a sinister smile leisurely spread across my face. "Only that I hope she kills you all."

My mother's lips parted in horror as Azenna scoffed in annoyance while she grabbed both mine and the queen's arms. The rushing, shadow-filled winds took over, threatening to make me sick once more.

This time, when I opened my eyes, we were atop the east tower of the Islan gates. Countless rows of armored soldiers stood at the foot of it, sprawling forward for nearly half a mile.

The sky before us in the distance was splintering into severed cracks, forming a rift in the realm that made my heart race with anticipation.

And then a wyvern burst through it.

SIXTY-FIVE

Elianna

THE MOMENT THE OPENING in the sky was large enough to fit through, with a thunderous beat of his wings, Nox soared through the rift, breaking through what remained before us of the valley and into that of Isla, Velyra.

With a raging battle cry, we burst through to the other side of the realm. A journey that would have taken us over a month on foot took only seconds through the power of our witches' sorcery.

Endless rows of perfectly lined soldiers were at the foot of the gates, guarding the city at their backs as we flew towards them with a galloping stampede of war horses and foot soldiers trailing behind us. My gaze swiftly turned towards my brave soldiers, and a smile spread across my face at the sight of Jace leading them all.

As I faced forward once more, my eyes flared as I caught sight of three figures standing atop the gates. My heart nearly stopped as I realized the witches had already sensed our arrival, and standing with the High Witch was the queen and my sister.

My mind was racing, questioning how they sensed our arrival was coming and swiftly gathered such a large army. My hands balled into fists, thinking about what they must've done to Avery for them to gain knowledge of our plan.

I ordered Nox to a halt, and his wings caught the wind as he kept us level in the sky, directly above the warriors guarding the city gates. My army came to a halt behind us.

As the last of our men stepped through the portal, my gaze drifted backward once more, just in time to catch Veli, Empri, and Madalae emerge through the rift themselves. My throat tightened as I caught the sight of them already looking disheveled and out of breath from holding it open. Within moments, the phantom doorway dissipated, granting a view of Isla's sprawling terrain.

I faced the city, my eyes locking on my sister, who, despite being captured, wore a knowing grin on her face as if my presence here was all she needed in answer.

The queen's eyes bore into me, and somehow, her stare appeared even more malevolent than that of the crimson-eyed witch that stood at her side.

"Idina!" My voice echoed through the sky. "The war you relentlessly pursue has resulted in an unimaginable amount of bloodshed. Show your people that you value their lives. If nothing, let your last act as queen of the realm be that you spared them from slaughter. The men standing below me...they are not to be considered disposable. Show them that you have an ounce of decency left within you and that they are not just faceless blade wielders."

Her blazing eyes narrowed in on me as I went unanswered. The sound of shifting armor rattled from her soldiers that stood beneath my mount.

"The men you see behind me...the bravest soldiers I have ever met, even comparable to your troops that aim to destroy the very person who once led them, are not disposable. Not to me—*never* to me or my mate that the gods had placed among them for this very reason. To *unite* us! Fae and mortals living together in harmony throughout the realm."

The instant I declared that I had a mate, her eyes flared wide, and a lethal blend of shock and fury flashed across her face.

A growl rumbled through Nox. Idina's lips curled back, and my head tilted to the side as I stared down at her, waiting to see if she would even deem my declaration worthy of a response.

"You come to the Islan gates not only as an escaped treasonous prisoner but now as a self-declared usurper of the crown. The people of Velyra know of your treachery, Elianna. They know of the lies you speak regarding your false entitlement to the throne, and they know that you now fight for the enemy, as you have made clear before them all just now by leading them right to their homes in a time of war." Idina extended her arm before her and gestured to my army of mortals.

"My men will not enter the city, and if they do, not a single blade is to be swung unless they are under attack by one of your own. They are here strictly as a precaution and to prove that fae and mortals are able to live in harmony with one another as they stand side by side among my ranks! You have the opportunity to end this before it truly begins. Throw down your crown, Idina. For the only female among us that is false and treasonous is *you*. You hold your own daughter captive as a use of leverage against someone who truly loves her."

"I love my children!" she snapped. Avery's gaze shot to her, but I noticed that her body remained frozen where she stood, as if being held in place. "And you murdered the only heir of the realm they had known. You cannot expect them to blindly follow a known, murderous queen."

Her smile turned vicious and deadly, and in that moment I knew what the outcome of this would be, but I would not be silenced as I had been my entire life.

"The only murderous queen is the one that currently holds the throne in the castle that looms over their city. Spare your people, soldiers, and the citizens of Isla, and I will grant you a merciful death that you certainly do not deserve. This is your final warning."

As Idina's eyes flicked over my shoulder, she took in the sight of my silent, awaiting army and then brought her attention back to me.

"Enjoy your death and the death of your people, Elianna," she called. Her voice carried to me on a breeze, sending a surge of pure, all-consuming rage through me.

A vision flashed in my mind of ordering Nox to send his flames upon them as they stood on their high tower, ending this once and for all before the blood of my people would be spilled at the foot of the gates. But the cowards knowingly used my sister as a shield.

I looked to Azenna, whose bone-chilling stare remained on the far reaches of the battlefield—no doubt remaining on three witches from her own coven that accompanied us.

She snarled in disgust, her top lip curling at the sight of them.

With the queen's parting words, the High Witch flashed her glowing eyes in my direction as she grabbed hold of both the queen's and Avery's arms.

Nerves sank into the pit of my stomach, watching pure fear take over Avery's features at Azenna's touch. I blinked, and a moment later, the three of them vanished before my eyes.

My wrath, infinite and blinding, wrapped itself around the mating bond, humming down our tether.

"*A cowardly bitch.*" My mate's voice filtered to me, his rage mimicking my own as a growl lingered in his words. "*I can't wait to watch you be the end of her. We're ready for you. On your word, my queen.*"

Just as I was about to give Nox the order, a piercing screech echoed through the air, causing my eyes to widen, realizing it hadn't come from my own wyvern.

My gaze moved beyond the gates and toward the Vayr Sea, where the echoes of screaming could be heard when I focused in on it. My lip curled in a menacing smile to see that the sirens kept their word. Then my eyes locked in on the wyvern that Azenna had sent to destroy Ellecaster, soaring directly towards us at an unfathomable speed. As it rapidly approached, a sight I never considered appeared, causing my throat to tighten in panic.

"*Lia! What is it?!*" Jace's voice boomed.

I closed my eyes tightly and willed our bond open for him to behold what I was witnessing through his own eyes.

"*That cannot be what I think—*"

"*It is,*" I cut him off. "*Kellan is on the back of the wyvern. He's headed straight for us.*"

"*Lia...*" His pleading whisper filled my head.

"Forward!" A soldier's voice sounded from below in our enemy's army, and the thundering sound of marching boots filled the sky.

As my eyes remained fixed on the threat hurtling towards us, my breathing became increasingly heavy. My jaw locked, and my neck strained as a vision of everything I had been forced to endure at the hands of both Kellan and Idina took over me.

Decades of mental and physical abuse from those I should have been able to trust. The murder of both my mother and father, and then the only parental figure I had left once they were gone. The treasonous lies whispered in my name to turn the realm against what it needed most—the rightful heir. Above all, what haunted me was the ever-present threat that hung over the ones I loved and the heartless attempt at the eradication of my people's existence by those who believed themselves superior.

They clawed their way to the throne through lies, manipulation, and deception. And now, I would take it all back by blade, blood, and flame.

Kellan's eyes were fixated on me. His wyvern was closing in on where Nox kept us level in the air as Idina's forces marched toward my own. An evil grin was plastered across my ex-lover's face as he raced towards us, assuming to finally take what he desired most—my life and that of my army.

But I wouldn't let that happen.

"*Lia!*" Jace's guttural voice screamed.

"*Give them hell, handsome,*" I whispered through the bond.

"*IGNYSTAE!*" The command tore through my throat as a battle cry.

Nox responded instantly as he sent a blistering blaze directly at Kellan and his ferocious mount—right before they violently slammed into us.

SIXTY-SIX

Jace

WITH LIA AND NOX at the front, our armed forces had marched through the portal on the opposite end of the realm with ease. Gage and Zaela had flanked both of my sides, with Landon close behind the three of us. The rush of racing through the realm's rift as we led thousands of our warriors to the end of a century-long war was beyond words.

Only weeks ago, I had thought the most magnificent sight my eyes would ever behold was the day of our wedding when my wife agreed to bind herself to me before the gods, but I had never been more wrong. The greatest sight was when she defiantly stood at our enemy's gates, at a city she once called home, and pleaded for peace among our peoples.

However, the vision was quickly overturned by gut-wrenching fear as I watched my mate's ex-lover barrel into her and her mount with his own—fire bursting from each wyvern as their bodies collided in the air.

I cursed every god above as I was forced to tear my gaze from her and Nox as Idina's army raced towards us on the ground below.

Time slowed, and my gaze twisted to each of my sides, where Gage and Zaela watched for my word.

"It has been an honor to serve next to you both," I said, a deep growl slipping from me as chaos ensued in the sky, where Lia was already waging her own battle.

"The honor has been mine, brother," Gage said, voice lethal.

"And mine," Zaela echoed.

I sucked in a breath as I straightened my spine, unsheathing my sword from its case.

"NOW!" I bellowed while raising my blade high in the air above.

My warhorse lifted us up onto his hind legs as a roar of triumph erupted from our forces while they raced forward, past me and my horse, and straight into the enemy's front lines.

Our armies clashed, slamming into each other with weapons and fists. The air was pierced with horrifying screams as lives were abruptly ended at the very start of the battle. We were at a major disadvantage against the fae army, who were stronger, faster, and more lethal. While they could easily heal their wounds, we had to compensate by staying united and relying on our extensive training.

While galloping through the masses, enemy soldiers flanked me on all sides. I swung my blade in every direction, ending their lives short, just as they already had with my own men.

I desperately willed myself to focus on the chaos ensuing on the terrain and not on the giant blazes of raging flames that continuously erupted in the sky above.

The once serene meadows at the foot of Isla's towering gates were now a deadly battleground, the air reverberating with the sound of clashing steel and the metallic scent of spilled blood.

The enemy forces launched their assault with a deadly ferocity. It made me wonder if they truly fought for Idina's cause or if they feared that *not* fighting for it would doom them even further with her once this was over. No soldier wanted to fight on the losing side of a war—I would know...I'd been fucking leading it for years.

Our catapults groaned and roared as they launched volleys of boulders toward the city walls, but when we expected stone blocks to rain down upon the back of their lines, our enormous rocks *shattered* instead.

My eyes flared as they remained fixated on where the boulders had struck the city's battlement. Sparks of crackling power were left in their wake as if a physical shield was forged around the city.

"Fuck," I breathed as I jumped down from my mount.

Shouts of horror sounded from the gate, and my gaze whipped to the center of the madness unfolding. My eyes landed on the three witches.

Shadows erupted from each of them, and those wearing Islan armor within their proximity dropped to the terrain they stood on, blood seeping from their eyes.

"Holy gods," I breathed through swipes of my sword.

My gaze landed on them once more as one of the twins, Madalae, formed a ball of lightning in her hand—the force of its crackling power was felt even down the battlefield.

My eyes followed it as she launched it straight at the battlement.

I expected the force of her power to shatter the shield, or at the least crack it—but nothing could have prepared me for what occurred next.

The force field around the city absorbed that power she unleashed and shot it directly back at her. The glowing ball of lightning flames soared over the battlefield, the roar of its crackling power even louder than the sound of clashing steel, and slammed right back into Madalae's chest.

No, not into her chest—*through* her chest.

My jaw dropped, and I blinked over and over again, praying to Terra herself that what I beheld was a lie. However, no matter how many times I blinked, the sight held true.

Where the ball of power struck the witch, a gaping hole remained in the center of her chest, where her heart had once been. Her eyes were wide and unseeing, Veli and her sister's matching as they were frozen in pure horror at her side.

Madalae's body began to char, starting where the power struck her, and quickly took over her entire being until she withered away into nothing but flaking ash on the wind.

A gut-wrenching scream of what could only be described as pure agony left her twin. Empri's eyes were glowing a blinding red as she sent out a blast of rage-induced power around herself, destroying all within thirty feet of them—including *my* fucking men.

"EMPRI!" I roared, and her ravenous eyes locked on me.

Veli snapped out of her trance and screamed at Empri to stand down.

The remaining twin's breath was heaving, and I was forced to catch quick glimpses as I swung my blade at more oncoming soldiers.

A moment later, my horrified eyes watched as Empri vanished, leaving the battlefield and abandoning us to our doom.

Veli's face was a mixture of pure devastation and fury. Her long silver hair glinted in the pale light of the waning sun as her body began levitating high in the air, her robes flowing around her like an otherworldly dark goddess.

The sorceress' eyes exuded their pink-tinged golden glow as shadows erupted from the palms of her hands, shooting towards the Islan troops. Bodies dropped the moment they came in contact with her mischievous darkness, and I was thankful that, for the time being, Idina's witches weren't placed among us within the battlefield.

"Yes!" Zaela roared a few feet away from me as she struck down soldier after soldier, her eyes repeatedly flashing in Veli's direction as she admired the use of her shadows put to work.

Archers appeared then and lined the parapets, releasing their arrows through the air and finding their marks among our ranks.

My eyes widened in horror as an arrow found purchase through one of Veli's palms, immediately cutting off her shadows and forcing her body to drop to the ground. Her shriek of pain radiated over all the surrounding sounds of war.

"VELI!" Zaela screeched as she was forced to fight her way through the onslaught of enemy soldiers.

"Fuck!" I roared at the same moment as I swiped my sword alongside her.

My mind raced as I desperately tried to come up with a plan. The surrounding men became distracted by the outburst and eruption from Veli, and I immediately was forced to start shouting out orders to get their minds focused once more. If they thought our witches were already defeated, it wouldn't be long before they all lost hope.

My mate had endured too much—and so much of it I wasn't even able to help her with, feeling entirely gods-damn useless. I couldn't step foot on the haunted isles. I couldn't enter Isla when we tried to evacuate her people. And the worst of all was that no matter how hard I tried, I couldn't take the weight of the realm off her shoulders. But what I could do was lead our armies in her absence and do everything in my fucking power to ensure our victory. And I intended to do just that.

"Hold your fucking ground!" I screamed over and over. "Do *not* forget your training! Everything we've done our entire lives has led to this moment!"

The massive Islan gates held firm against our relentless catapult attacks, and Lia and Nox were still raging through the sky.

I forced my way to my queen's aide and heaved her body up from the ground, mortified to see that the arrow was still protruding through her palm.

My hand reached to help her pull it out, but her eyes flashed, not the pink color that we had grown used to, but pure, blinding scarlet—a red as deep as the rage that was exuding from her.

The arrow ignited in flames beneath her stare and burned to ash within seconds, the flurries of it fluttering down to the blood-soaked terrain.

Through deep breaths, I placed my hand on her shoulder, and she flashed her terrifying stare at me. "Are you alright?!" I shouted over the chaos.

"Yes." The word barely left her in a whisper as her eyes roamed over the insanity unleashing around us at every angle.

Screams of terror sounded as the roaring beat of wings erupted from directly above us, sending storm-like winds through the field.

"*Look out!*" Veli screamed, the sound blood-curdling, as she lifted her uninjured hand above us and towards the sky.

A bright golden light burst from it right before Adler's wyvern sent a roaring blaze directly down at my troops, not even giving a damn that his own men were deeply mingled among us all.

A roar of horror left me at the sight of the blinding, all-consuming flames that were unleashed upon us, just barely blocked by the force of power Veli shot out to meet it.

The flames poured over the far ends of the shield she conjured, scalding the unfortunate souls that were fighting just beyond its reach.

Lia and Nox were directly behind him, her mount snapping at the tail of his as she desperately tried to distract him from raining more hellfire down on our troops.

Veli's force field dropped, and she nearly collapsed into my side, drained from exerting herself while already injured.

"I'm alright!" she snapped as she shoved out of my protection.

I struck down a soldier that barreled toward us.

"No, you aren't!" I barked. "Go to the healers' tent! Check on Finn!"

A rage-filled retort was working its way up her throat, but I cut her off before she had the chance to say it. "That is a fucking order, Veli!"

She watched me beneath furrowed brows as her breathing quickened, but a moment later, she vanished. An enemy soldier immediately took the place where she stood, who aimed to strike her down, but I met his attack just in time, killing him instantly.

We were already surrounded. It barely took any time at all for absolute chaos to ensue. My men were scattered, some troops no longer working as a unit as they desperately fought for their lives.

"Hold the line! Hold the line, damn it!" I bellowed, my voice straining to rise above the madness. "Archers, cover the left flank! Hold your fucking ground!"

The archers, positioned towards the back of our lines, released a volley of arrows instantly. Below them, infantrymen locked shields and braced against the oncoming soldiers who charged toward our arrows as if they were nothing.

Leon found me then, his face smeared with dirt and blood, panting heavily. "Commander, the eastern troop is under heavy assault with Landon. They're aiming for our healers' tent to take them out. We were relying too much on the witches. We need reinforcements!"

"There are no fucking reinforcements! Send the reserve units to the eastern troop. Tell them to hold it at all costs! Finnian is in there! If too many are injured, have them fall back to the second line if you must, but do *not* let them get to the healers' tent!"

Leon gave me a curt nod as his gaze swept across the battlefield before taking off in their direction, swinging his blade with each step.

More than anything, I wanted to reach down into the bond and check on Lia, but I knew that any distraction could cost each of us our lives. So, I forced myself to stay true to our promise to one another and kept my focus on cutting down the enemy fleet.

Yet, I knew that this was only the beginning.

SIXTY-SEVEN

Elianna

KELLAN'S WYVERN HAD SLAMMED into Nox head-on, bursting through the wall of flames he shot at them, completely unfazed.

My eyes flared as they met his, a menacing grin adorning the rest of his features as he greeted me in a yell over the madness. "Hello, Princess."

He winked and blew me a kiss, right before ordering his wyvern to lash out again at Nox.

The sky above the battlefield morphed into a chaotic dance of flame and scales as our mounts repeatedly slammed into each other, clawing, thrashing, and snapping at anything they could get a hold of.

I commanded Nox to soar upwards, to lure Kellan and his wyvern away from the battle below. Racing through the clouds, their enormous, stretched wings eclipsed the sun, casting shadows on the blood-stained earth below.

The skin beneath my armor burned as the wyverns repeatedly shot an eruption of flames at one another. Their roars echoed like thunder across the sky, and my own matched theirs as I desperately clutched my saddle to keep atop my mount. And I had never been more thankful for it.

My eyes roamed over the conjured wyvern, who looked nearly identical to my Nox. Scales the color of obsidian, only they reflected ruby beneath the blinding sun instead of his amethyst—all that differed aside from that were their eyes. While Nox's gaze had always been a blazing gold, this beast's eyes were similar to its creator.

Nox's tail whipped towards them, cutting into the other creature's hind leg, a shriek of pain echoing from it at the contact of it. With a flash of speed, Kellan's mount disappeared within the cover of the clouds.

Nox leveled us as we hovered in the sky, slowly beating his wings to keep us steady. Working to catch my breath, I unbuckled myself from the strap of the saddle to get a better look at Nox.

I peered over his shoulder to see a small bit of blood leaking from between his scales, but I was thankful it was minimal compared to the damage we had just done to Kellan's mount.

"Shit. Nox, are you okay?" My eyes darted back and forth from his face to the wound. A continuous growl rumbled from him. "I can't touch it," I whispered. "It will burn me."

He let out a sad whimper, and my eyes softened, lips parting as sorrow overcame me at the sight of him being in pain, and there was nothing I could do to help.

I sat back in the saddle while my gaze moved through the clouds, and only an eerie silence accompanied us. My once settling heartbeat picked back up again after realizing Kellan had truly disappeared—the fucking *coward*.

"Nox, we need to—"

My order was cut off by a scream that tore through my throat as Kellan's mount came barreling at us from the side, emerging from the cover of the thick clouds. Jaw gaping open, the beast unleashed torrents of flame from its maw, scorching Nox's side and the straps of my saddle with searing heat.

A deafening screech left my wyvern, and my heart cracked, knowing how much pain he must've been in to make such a guttural sound.

"Fuck, fuck, fuck, Nox!" I screamed as one of my hands had a death grip on his back fin and the other on my saddle that was barely holding on by a scorched thread.

He leveled out his wings as Kellan's mount circled through the clouds—both of their lethal stares locked on us.

A snarl crept up my lips, and I positioned myself as quickly as I could, waiting for the attack I knew was coming.

"Come on, you vicious fuck!" I bellowed. "This is what you've been waiting for, is it not?!"

He wore a sly smirk as he winked at me the moment I finished uttering the words. Without even being commanded, his mount took a nosedive toward the ground, jaw snapping as its red gaze was locked on the battle that raged beneath us.

My heart instantly sank. "Nox! Dive!" I ordered, and he obeyed.

The wind stung my eyes as we raced to catch up to them, descending toward the unforgiving terrain. We were nearly directly behind him, but still not close enough as Nox's maw snapped at the other wyvern's tail while it lashed out at us.

As the ground came into view, the armies fought relentlessly at the foot of the gates. My eyes locked on Kellan as he lifted a single arm and then pointed it at the ground, where both of our armies fought.

"No!" I cried, my voice desperate and breaking. "Nox, faster!"

My wyvern tucked his wings in closer to his sides, sending us shooting toward the ground at terrifying speeds, but we were too late to stop Kellan's ordered attack.

The red-gazed wyvern unleashed a fiery blaze down toward the land, right atop our soldiers.

I was screaming. Words weren't coming out of me, but only sounds and cries of fury and horror as I watched the flames fan out over a quarter of the battlefield.

Assuming my own screams were drowning out those of the ones being burned alive, tears streamed down my soot-covered cheeks. But as the flames cleared, my eyes flared.

The blaze was met with power—pure, blinding sorcery, as a golden light slipped back into a silver-haired witch that watched us from the ground below, my mate standing next to her.

"*YES!*" I roared as I pumped my fist in the air, causing the saddle to slip further off of Nox from accidentally releasing my hold on it.

Both Kellan's mount and Nox pulled up right before slamming into the terrain, our beasts racing only feet above the chaos of battle.

He turned back to face me, our eyes meeting once more, and I could have sworn I heard his scoff of annoyance over the rushing winds.

My vision was fixated on him. A pure obsidian haze blocked out everything else that surrounded us, and I knew it wasn't from the smoke from our wyverns' flames—but from my wrath.

My mate was down there. My *husband* was right where Kellan placed the attack. He would've been consumed by the blaze that was unleashed upon them if it wasn't for Veli and her shield of power.

As if ordered, Nox sped through the skies as Kellan's mount pulled upwards, sending us soaring toward the sea that rested at Isla's opposite end.

Nox snapped at the beast's tail, his countless rows of dagger-sharp teeth sinking into the flesh beneath its scales. The shriek of pain it let out echoed over the city, but my only reaction was to hit them while we could.

"*Ignystae!*" I bellowed, and Nox answered by sending a helix of flames licking up the wyvern's tail and scorching Kellan's back.

His anguished screams filled the air, and my eyes remained locked on him, burning with fury. A twisted grin tugged at the corners of my lips as the sound reached my ears.

He swatted at his back, desperately trying to put out the embers that continued to burn.

My mind raced as we continued to chase them, knowing that at some point, Nox's flames would run out. It wasn't a matter of if but of when. And the knowledge of that was both terrifying and valuable. If I ordered him to unleash everything he had, and they escaped the blaze, we would be left vulnerable, and it would doom us.

Keep your wits about you. Lukas' old warning played in my mind. They threatened to paralyze me, but I had to listen to them. I had to be smart if I was to be deserving of my crown.

I growled as his mount made it over the sea, dipping its tail that had remained ablaze into the water, extinguishing what had remained of our attack.

Our wyverns weaved through the empty, blood-stained ships, where my eyes caught the sirens lingering beneath some of the vessels and in the distance perched on jagged rocks.

As we glided out over the sea, he circled back to the city, aiming for the castle. We caught up by cutting across the open sky beneath them.

"What's the matter, Kellan?" I called over the winds, and his furious gaze snapped to mine. "Crew caught in a siren song?" I taunted him with a wink.

He chuckled. The psychopath *chuckled* at my words right before reaching into his boot and whipping a dagger in my direction. His beast veered left, gliding away from us as I barely dodged the blade by slamming my chest down onto Nox's back.

"Mother*fucker*." I growled. "Get him!" Nox took off as commanded, barreling after them over the city.

We rapidly flew around Castle Isla as we weaved between its stone towers, high in the sky. The wind howled around us, carrying the scent of burning embers and spilled blood. The other beast twisted and looped, attempting to evade the oncoming barrage of flame Nox sent without my permission.

"Nox, no!" I screeched.

Kellan's mount circled up one of the east towers, and we followed in a relentless dance. His wyvern's jaw snapped at me, and I foolishly released my hold on Nox's fin—our saddle began sliding down his body, bringing me with it.

Shit. Shit. Shit.

I gasped in horror as the saddle completely slid over his side, Kellan's beast still snapping at me and my own, as the booming beat of several wings threatened to make me deaf. One of the clawed tips of Nox's wings sank into the other's chest, and he used the forceful momentum to shoot us higher in the sky and our enemy back down to the ground, hundreds of feet below.

Finally, I released my hold on the ruined saddle and used all the force of my body to heave myself back up onto Nox's back, but my grip slipped. Suddenly, I was free-falling in the open air.

Nox let out a high-pitched shriek of terror as he moved to dive back down, watching me fall to what would be my death, while a scream tore through my throat.

My breath caught as time slowed. The red-gazed wyvern finally leveled out below us as his wings shot out, slowing their fall—directly beneath me.

A grin grew on my face as I reached to unsheathe my dagger from my thigh. The second my blade was free, Kellan glanced up, eyes flaring as they made contact with mine—but he was too late as he reached to unsheathe his sword.

With a battle cry, I dropped down onto his mount and slammed into him—repeatedly stabbing anything I could with my dagger as I ferociously swiped my blade in every direction, feeling each time it found purchase in his flesh.

Kellan's blood sprayed, covering me, but I couldn't stop as he roared in pain—his mount too, as if I was stabbing the beast and not its rider.

His hands reached out and grabbed my throat as he tried to suffocate me while we both worked to not fall to our deaths. Each time he aimed to squeeze, the slipperiness of his own blood loosened his hold, and I head-butted him the second he brought me close enough.

He yelped as he threw me, aiming for over the side of his wyvern, but I landed halfway down its back instead, grabbing hold of its scales as the rushing winds nearly swept me off.

My gaze shot to the side at the sound of a violent roar as Nox burst out from the clouds and collided with us. The second the force of their bodies met, I pushed myself to my feet and ran up his wyvern's back, desperately leaping out toward my own.

My body was mid-air as Kellan's mount slammed into the castle tower closest to us. Large bricks of stone shattered from the structure, raining down into the courtyard at the terrifying depth below.

With a desperate reach, I willed my body toward Nox as the tower's pieces flew all around us, slicing into my skin. The second I sensed his wing beneath me, my legs mimicked a run through the air, touching down on his powerful wing and had me racing up it until I reached his back.

"Holy gods!" I screamed as I settled back into my seat at the nape of his neck.

Chest heaving, my gaze whipped back in the direction of the collapsing tower, and I watched as Kellan fled, guiding his wyvern far beyond the reaches of the castle.

"Fucking coward," I whispered, shaking my head as Nox hovered in the air.

I glanced down at the front of myself and watched the blood of my enemy dry onto my skin and armor. My body ached from the attack, but we were alive, and I doubted Kellan would be within the next few minutes after everything we had just unleashed on him.

I reached down into the bond, sensing Jace there, his heart racing with adrenaline just as mine was—but he was alive, and that was what mattered. I didn't dare risk full communication, worried my voice could distract him from defending himself or our people.

My eyes drifted to the city streets that were shockingly empty. I expected the citizens to be trying to get glimpses of the battle occurring just beyond their gates, but they appeared to be hiding in their homes. Then my gaze found the castle, leisurely moving over the crumbling tower and across the other sky-high spires.

I reached down as my breathing finally slowed, patting the scales of Nox's shoulder. "I need to find Avery," I admitted.

He twisted his neck to look at me, a golden eye narrowing in distrust for those inside the palace.

"I know," I whispered, forcing a soft smile at him. "But she needs us. She needs our help."

He let out a groan, sounding as exasperated as my mate did when I was up to my usual mischief. A moment later, he swooped down and hovered above one of the east balconies, allowing me to jump down from him.

I landed on the platform and twisted back to meet him; he nuzzled his scale-covered snout into my chest. I reached out to rub his own, careful to avoid any of his fiery blood that dribbled from between his scales.

My eyes found his. "Go find Jace," I whispered. "Protect them. I will find you."

Nox then took off toward the fields beyond the city gates, where the sound of clashing swords persisted. I blew out a breath before peering around the balcony entrance, creeping low to the floor to say hidden.

Once deemed empty, I pulled off my armor to avoid causing any extra noise, revealing my fighting leathers underneath. Rushing out on silent feet, I made my way to the throne room, where I was certain the queen was hiding with my sister in her wicked grasp.

SIXTY-EIGHT

Avery

AZENNA HAD THROWN ME into my old bedroom chambers at my mother's orders, stating that it was too risky to keep me locked beneath the castle in the dungeons, saying it would be the first place Lia would look if she breached the gates. So, naturally, the only suitable place was in the tallest tower of the gods-damn castle. My door was locked and bound with witchcraft, leaving no room for escape.

It didn't matter how hard I banged on the door or slammed my shoulder into it—the damn thing wouldn't budge an inch. I had even tried to pick the lock with one of my old hair pins that was in my dresser drawer.

Storming into the bathing chambers connected to my room, my eyes locked on the intricate steel robe rack, where I would hang my dresses before bathing for the day when this was my home. I rushed up to it and ripped everything hanging from its hooks down, throwing them carelessly onto the floor. Wrapping my hands around the rack, I dragged it out into the center of the bedchamber.

My arms struggled to lift the rack, and using every ounce of my weakened strength, I swung it at the door.

The moment the metal touched the enchanted wooden door, a golden flash of power lashed out, causing the pole to violently reverberate while throwing my body across the room.

"Mother's tits of the stupid gods," I huffed as I worked to catch my breath and threw the rack down to the ground.

Ugh. What the hell was I going to do?

I shoved the dresser from the wall and ripped the old tapestry down that Nyra and I had used to escape when we led the rebellion from the city.

My jaw dropped at the sight I beheld—cemented bricks had replaced the ancient wooden door that led to the tunnels within the castle walls. I placed my hand on the cold stone that blocked my only way out of my new prison, and my lip instantly trembled.

My body turned, back resting against the wall as I slid to the floor against it and wept.

The sounds of war echoed from my tower's window as the battle raged on beyond the city gates, and there was nothing I could do to get out of here or help my family who could already be injured, or...I wasn't even able to bring my thoughts to the other option.

A deafening, shriek-like roar boomed from beyond my window, making me jump up from the floor. I used the sleeve of my filthy gown to wipe away the tears that slipped down my cheeks—which I had been wearing since the queen forced me to stand before the masses and placed the label of tyrant on my sister's name.

I hated everything the gown represented—what I had been and believed before Lia opened my eyes to the truth of our war and family. My body no longer felt comfortable in the soft, flowing fabric. It craved the fighting leathers and *pants* that I had come to love, because it meant I was a warrior. Like my sister and Zaela.

I ran to the window and instantly ducked down to the floor as two wyverns and their riders whizzed past me, their teeth and tails lashing out at each other continuously. Pulling myself up on the windowsill just enough to peer out of it, I watched as both Lia and Kellan attacked one another atop the flying beasts.

"Oh gods," I whispered, my eyes darting back and forth between each rider as their mounts aimed to kill the other.

The sight of the wyverns vanished, replaced by the sound of a thunderous blast that rumbled the floor beneath me and shook the walls of my chambers.

"Shit!" I gasped as I tried to lean out the window and peer around the side of the castle, but it was no use. All my eyes took in was thick, black smoke from their blast of flames and a mingling gray dust that had erupted from the boom.

My lips parted as terror consumed me. "Lia!" I screamed.

My neck twisted back and forth, searching the sky for any sign of her. My gaze drifted down the side of my bedroom's tower to where a thin lip of stone wrapped itself around the structure—the same lip I deemed impossible to use for escaping all that time ago in my original escape of this room.

"I must be out of my gods-damn mind." I sighed.

Taking in a shuddering breath, I lifted myself onto the windowsill, carefully swinging my feet over the opposite end of its ledge. My stare shot down to the ground that was hundreds of feet below, and my stomach dropped. Slamming my eyes shut, I worked to talk my nerves down, but it was no use—my heart wouldn't stop racing in my chest.

I had to do this. Lia may be depending on me right now, and being a coward, locked in the same tower I had been my entire life, wouldn't help her or anyone else for that matter.

My eyes narrowed in on the tiny ledge, and my fingers tightly gripped the edge of the windowsill as I wiggled myself down onto the lip. The moment my feet touched the stone, I bit the inside of my cheek as I worked to concentrate on not slipping to what surely would be my death.

My red locks of hair fluttered around my face, dancing like fire in the smoke with the wind. I pressed my back flush against the cool stone of the castle's tower and carefully slid my foot along the ledge—and then again, and once more, until I was scaling around the side of it.

My lungs forced me to breathe as I slowly made my way, my heart sinking every time it acknowledged the height of the tower.

Finally, a bridge appeared to the next spire over on the east side—where the castle's library was. The smoke leisurely cleared the air, carrying away toward the sea on the wind, and my eyes glimpsed Nox in the far distance, headed straight for the battlefield—Kellan's wyvern nowhere in sight.

"Thank the gods," I breathed.

Once I stood before the bridge, body still pressed against the tower, I whimpered, slamming my eyes shut and turning my face away from the situation I had trapped myself in.

"Well, Avery," I said to myself. "You've already come this far."

Without lifting my foot completely from the ledge, I carefully slid it forward until I felt comfortable enough to put my weight on it. My back lifted from the wall's barrier as I carefully took my first step along the unrailed bridge, clearly never designed for walking upon. My eyes drifted along the path over to the next tower, where a window was placed only feet from where the bridge met the structure.

"You can do this. You can do this," I worked to convince myself.

My feet moved, taking step after step, gaining confidence in each one as my arm shot out at my sides for balance. The dress I wore fluttered in the wind, threatening to rip me from where I stood. The connecting bridge was barely a foot in width, leaving no room for error in where I placed my steps.

My left foot slipped off the side, and my body dropped down into a crouch, my fingers' grip on the bridge sending broken pieces of stone down to the ground below. Pure fear took over me, racing up my spine like a lick of ice as my gaze narrowed in on the remaining distance that stood between me and the next window—the distance between life and death.

I blew out a breath and slowly rose to stand, balancing my arms out at my sides once more. With furrowed brows, I quickened my pace across the aerial walkway until I finally reached the opposite side.

"Yes!" I cried when I made it, and wrapped my arms along the curve of the tower's structure, nearly kissing its stone in thanks.

Not daring to turn around, I moved my feet along the new ledge until I reached the library's window and climbed through.

My body hit the marble floor of the seemingly abandoned section of the castle, and a wicked cackle forced its way out of me from pride.

"Gods, I can't believe I just did that," I whispered to myself as I lay there, staring up at the arched ceilings and towering, ancient bookshelves.

Pushing myself to my feet, my eyes roamed over the dark chamber, where clearly the only thing that had accompanied the books since my departure had been dust.

On silent feet, I rushed toward the door, but then realized that while I had freed myself, I was without any means of protection.

My eyes flashed back to the abyss of books, roaming over anything that could be used as a weapon when my stare landed on two mounted, curved daggers that were hung above the fireplace.

Those would have to do.

I raced across the room, dragging one of the table's chairs with me to the fireplace and climbed on it. My hands wrapped around each of the daggers' hilts, and I was thankful they easily slid out from their mount. I carefully climbed down from the chair and admired the blades in the light that shone in from the window before tucking one beneath the belt of my dress as I kept the other in hand.

The next moment, I was racing through the library's door and down the halls, carefully peering around each corner before thrusting myself forward.

I had no idea where to go, or how I would even get outside without finding a tunnel I could navigate—and that was even if they hadn't all been boarded up like the one in my chambers.

All I knew was that I had to find Lia. I had to help all of them, even if it was the last thing I did.

SIXTY-NINE

Veli

THE HEALER'S TENT STOOD at the edge of the violent battleground. What would normally be a haven amidst chaos had turned into absolute madness itself. Sounds of the injured and dying erupted through the air, coming from all directions.

Horror and pure anguish clogged my throat as the scene of Madalae bursting into ash replayed in my mind, along with the sounds of devastation from her twin—who had abandoned us a moment later after blasting everyone near her into nothing.

Anger originally fueled me as I watched her flee, but I couldn't blame her. Empri fled before she mistakenly erupted her entire rage on Elianna's supporters, so it may have been better off this way. Even though we now had significantly less magic on our side, with only me and my already injured body to wield the sorcery.

I burst through the flaps of the tent, the scent of medicinal herbs and the tang of spilled blood stuffing my nostrils. A low table stood at its center, various vials, jars, and instruments sprawled out in disorder as the healers frantically grabbed items needed to save any of the lives they could.

Wounded soldiers lay on crimson-stained cots, their armor removed to expose injuries ranging from third-degree burns to severe stab wounds and missing limbs. The healers moved desperately from patient to patient, some stitching lacerations while others lathered salve atop raw, charred skin.

My breathing quickened as my eyes shot around in every direction, absorbing the overwhelming energy the others exuded as they flashed by me on all sides.

My eyes locked with Finnian from across the tent as he worked to stitch a soldier, and I raced toward him.

His stare held nothing but panic and sorrow.

"What can I do?" I asked.

"Go back out there, Veli!" he snapped, and my eyes flared, never hearing the boy lose his temper before. "We have this handled."

"I was sent here, boy. Use me while you can!" I ordered. "I am here to help while I heal myself." I raised my palm before him, the hole from the arrow slowly stitching itself closed before our eyes.

His eyes flared as they landed on mine while he worked to stitch up a gaping wound in a soldier's side, his needle holding firm in his grasp. Something resembling pride flared in me at the sight of the boy finding his mark.

I knelt next to the cot beside him, where another man was taking what seemed to be some of his last breaths as blood poured from his wounds and trickled from his lips. My focus narrowed in on the soldier's injuries, and my eyes cast their glow as I willed the injuries to heal from the inside out.

"Veli, should you be doing that as your body tries to heal itself?" Finnian asked warily.

"Hush, boy," I quieted him. "There is much to do, but if I am to leave here and go back out there and fight, I need to leave you all here in a good place as well."

He gave me a curt nod in response.

The man I was working on suddenly took in a shuddering breath—his last, making me realize I was too late.

My teeth were clenched in both sadness and anger at what our reality had become. My magic was already draining, and I could barely focus enough to heal others as I worked to do the same for myself. And there was still an entire gods-damn war raging outside.

I stepped away from the cot and fixed my face into neutrality. When I turned to the other healers behind us, all I found were desperate eyes locked on me, pleading for help without the words.

"I have this side of the tent," Finnian stated. "Do what you can."

Injured soldiers and unconscious bodies were piling in with each passing second. "Mother of the gods," I breathed, then I went to work.

SEVENTY

Elianna

As I ʀᴀᴄᴇᴅ ᴅᴏᴡɴ the several halls and staircases of Castle Isla, it became abundantly clear that Idina had exasperated nearly all of her armed guards within the city to aid her in the war, likely using Azenna and the crone as her only source of protection.

It didn't matter, though; I would get my sister out of here, even if I had to trade her capture for my own. I would think of a way out of it—I always did. Her safety was what mattered, and after watching Idina use her own daughter as a shield, I no longer trusted her not to harm my sister.

It wasn't until I came barreling around the corner of the main staircase that I came face-to-face with two patrolling guards, eating my own words.

"Shit," I said under my breath as I unsheathed my sword.

"You!" one of them yelled in my direction as they both withdrew their own weapons.

"Come on, gentleman, we all know this won't end well for you," I taunted them.

They glanced at each other and laughed. "Solus, you look beat to shit. Save yourself the trouble of healing more and

come with us. The queen will be delighted to see you."
The male's smile was malicious, earning a snarl from me.

"If you're afraid...you could've just said that." I winked
and then charged.

I ran at them full force, one of their blades instantly
clashing with my own. As the other moved to attack, I
pivoted my body and kicked him in the chest, sending
him flying backwards into the wall.

Twisting back to the other, I lunged forward, slicing my
sword through the air with precision, and our blades met
the other's each time. The guard reacted swiftly, parrying
each strike, working to corner me. The clang of metal
echoed through the corridor as our swords collided.

The next moment, the other guard was at my back,
ready to strike. I dodged his attack, weaving between
each of their swinging blades.

I disarmed one of them with a swift maneuver, sending
his sword clattering to the marble tile beneath our feet,
and didn't waste a single second before plunging my own
blade through his gut. His eyes flared in shock as blood
trickled from his lips, beading down his chin.

A whipping sound of the other's swinging sword
echoed through my ears—*fuck*. I quickly lifted my boot,
pressing it against the dying guard's torso, and ripped
my blade free from his body. I pivoted just in time
to send my sword straight through the other's chest.
The momentum of his swinging blade faltered, and it
dropped to his feet.

I held my weapon in his chest and watched the light leave
his eyes as I worked to catch my breath. His body dropped

to the floor with a thud, his blood pooling around both of them.

"Gods," I breathed, chest heaving, as I glanced around the halls, making sure no one else had come from the commotion. Re-sheathing my sword on my hip, I took off in a run down the main staircase, leaving their bodies in my wake.

My once silent steps now echoed off the marble floors as I neared the closed doors of the throne room. I abruptly halted before them, and the sound of my blood droplets hitting the tile filled the otherwise quiet halls as they fell from my wounds.

As I stood there, I realized that everything in my life had built up to this very moment, and now it was finally here. Where I would make my final stand against the wicked queen for all she had done to me and my people. In this moment, I felt no sorrow or ache in the name of what I had lost. All I felt was fury-driven determination.

Gaze fixated on the elaborate door handles, one of my hands reached out for it as the other reached for the hilt of my dagger. I pulled the door open with all my might, my anger nearly pulling the heavy door from its hinges right before it slammed into the wall.

I stormed through the arched doorway, covered in the blood of those guards, and was met with two pairs of malicious eyes. The queen sat on my father's throne, glaring at me through knitted brows as the High Witch stood before the dais, arms crossed, while giving me a knowing grin.

My feet continued to carry me through the throne room until I stopped in its center, breath heaving at the sight of her, sitting where my father once had. Our eyes remained locked on each other.

"How dare you," I seethed, lip curling back ferociously. "How fucking dare you sit where he once did? Where the rightful Valderre ruler should be!"

My voice bounced off the walls of the room, and I was answered with a cruel smile from the false queen.

"How lovely to see you somehow made it past our wards, Elianna," Azenna greeted.

"And how did she do that, *witch?*" Idina hissed at her back, eyes never leaving mine. "Have our wards fallen?"

"They have not," Azenna stated. "The shields remain intact."

"Next time, try warding the skies." I gave them a menacing wink accompanied by a mocking bow.

"Her mount," Azenna growled.

"And Adler?" Idina barked.

"Dead," I answered with a smile, tilting my head to the side as I imagined what it would feel like to finally send her to the depths of hell along with him.

My gaze snapped to the High Witch as a grin reemerged on her face. "She lies. He lives."

Gods fucking dammit. He just wouldn't die.

I huffed out a breath through my nostrils as my jaw locked. "Where is she? What have you done with Avery?"

"My daughter's whereabouts are not, nor have they ever been, your concern, Elianna."

"You have kidnapped a member of my court and hold her as prisoner against her will. That is every bit of my concern," I growled.

A vicious smile tilted the queen's lips. "Brave of you to come here. And alone, I might add."

"Gutless of you to hide behind your battlement as your armies fight for your treasonous cause," I countered.

"A queen needn't fight her own battles when she has the resources to do so for her."

A rage-filled, breathy laugh slipped from me as I observed her and took another step forward. "And that is where I am most proud—for our differences will always set us apart. My soldiers find peace in knowing I would never ask them to fight a battle that I wouldn't fight alongside them myself."

"You have led your soldiers to their deaths in a false hope that you will win this, Elianna. If you were a true queen that cared for them as much as you claim, you would have spared them their lives today by lying hidden until we sniffed them out throughout the realm. You have not granted them hope. All you have provided them is an early grave."

"My people would rather fight for a life worth living than remain in hiding for the remainder of their existence. They have something worth fighting for. Their freedom!"

She stood from the throne, looking down at me from the dais. "Is that what you plan to give them? You believe that after all this time...fae and mortals will be able to just live in harmony? You foolish girl."

A spiteful laugh left me. "I have been called that many times by both friend and foe, and while it may still hold some truth to it, I believe in my cause. I know it's possible to live in harmony because I have *seen* it."

My eyes darted back and forth between the two of them. "The mortals welcomed our kind when they fled your reign. A race that had been slaughtered by our own for multiple generations...they accepted them because they finally realized that one individual's actions do not define that of its race."

"Laughable," Idina spat.

My eyes narrowed in on her. "The only thing that's laughable is that you started a century-long war with a race that had nothing to do with the death of your kin!"

Her jaw locked, and she stormed down the dais. "And what does that mean, Elianna?!"

I unsheathed the sword from my hip, but magic ripped it from my grasp a moment later, sending the blade flying across the room. My eyes followed it until it clattered to the floor. When my gaze found Azenna, she shook her head and tsked at me.

I took a step up to Idina. "Mortals were not responsible for the deaths of your father and brother! They tried to barter with centaurs and it went awry, because they were just as wicked and vile as you are! They were murdered by creatures of the forest, not humans!"

"Liar!" she screeched. "Your time has come, Elianna."

She snapped her fingers, and Azenna's arm shot out toward me, her power slamming into me and working its way through my veins.

My blood caught fire, sending my body ablaze as Azenna's magic slithered through me—the blood magic Veli had warned me of taking effect and ruining me from the inside out.

My mind instantly flashed to Jace, knowing he would sense something was happening, and then I remembered Veli's words, *if there is ever a time where you need to block the bridge, you may build a wall in your mind if you concentrate hard enough.*

So that's what I did—I imagined a wall between our bond and minds and built it brick by brick, throwing everything I had into it to protect him from this.

Pure agony took over me, blurring my vision as my body was lifted from the floor, the High Witch guiding me upwards as she raised her hand toward the ceiling.

A scream tore from my throat as my body remained stiff as a board, levitating twenty feet above them in the center of the throne room. The witch was slowing the movement of the blood within my veins by slipping her magic through my bleeding wounds.

A banging rattled the bond as Jace slammed his mental fists on the shield. I desperately fought to keep it up as I heard the distant echo of his voice in my mind, begging me to let him in.

"Ah, and who might that be, Heir of the Realm?" Azenna asked, forcing my gaze down to where she remained on the floor beneath me.

I tried to lash out, but the grasp that her magic held me in kept me utterly still.

"Who whispers into your mind, Elianna Valderre?"

Even through my blurry vision, I saw Idina take a step toward the High Witch. "What are you talking about? Surely her false speech of a *mate* was to distract us," she snapped.

"A bond," she answered as her eyes remained on me. "Someone calls to her through it, but she won't let them in."

"That is impossible," Idina whispered, but then her voice rose. "She married a human. I saw it with my own eyes. I saw *them* the night of their wedding."

A laugh left me through the pain, but it was filled with nothing but rage. "That's right, Idina. My husband and *mate* is a halfling. And until he met me, he acknowledged only the parts of him that are human because of being sired by one of your vile soldiers. He wanted nothing more than to see every last fae head on a spike...until he met me. Until he *loved* me!"

"Once again, that is not possible," she hissed. "Why would the gods grant someone of lesser blood a mate? And what makes you or Jameson *think* themselves worthy of such a bond?!"

Her tone was a swirling mix of wrath and heartache, making my brows furrow. My entire body was screaming in anguish as Jace continued to tear his way through the wall that I desperately clung to. I tried to force words out but couldn't bring myself to move as Azenna continued to make my blood work against my own body.

"A mate," the queen scoffed, crossing her arms as she glared up at me. "You are not worthy of such a bond, and neither was your father. It is beautiful, ancient, and all-knowing. Not only is a bastard born not worthy of such, but a halfling is even less. So, why would the gods place such beings together?" She paused as her lips curled back. "They wouldn't! So you are a *liar*, Elianna."

My lips parted as I gave her a blood-stained smile. "The malevolent gods wouldn't have granted such a bond, but their mother goddess, Terra, would. For I am her heir and she has always wished for peace among her children."

I chuckled at the look of disgust on her face, the ache of it rattling my body. A thought hit me then.

My eyes darted back and forth, all over the throne room as quickly as the pain would allow, realizing that Callius wasn't here with her—nor was he atop the city gates when we had first arrived. He would never be on that battlefield with it being this close to the castle, no. Callius would be right here at her side, as he had always been.

The queen was getting emotional—an ache in her voice I had never heard. A defensive notion against mates, saying we weren't worthy of such a thing. That my father wasn't worthy of such a thing when he claimed to have found that with my mother.

I forced my eyes back down to her. "Where is Callius, Idina?"

Her jaw locked; the veins in her neck were pulsating beneath her skin—amber eyes radiating a blaze as if they would burn a hole through me.

"Release her," she demanded of Azenna.

"Your Majesty?" the High Witch asked, half turning to her as she held me in the air.

"Now!" she roared.

Azenna dropped her hand, releasing me from the despair of the blood spell, but also from her hold in the air. My body violently slammed onto the floor, the tile beneath me cracking from the force of it. My ribs fractured from the impact, and every open wound I had from the wyvern attack was pouring blood even worse than before as its natural flow in my veins returned.

My shield dropped as the pain of everything overwhelmed me, letting Jace's voice through.

"*Lia!*" My name was desperate from his lips, pleading for an answer, but I could barely focus enough to respond. "*Lia, please, are you alright? I will come and find you. Just tell me where you are! Nox is here and you're not with him! Sweetheart, please.*"

I groaned from the agony tearing through me as I moved to push myself up to sit. My eyes locked with Idina, who was standing not even two feet before me, waiting to end me here and now herself.

"*I love you,*" was all I was able to push through to him before I put the wall back into place, his fists beating into it once more. I knew he could still sense my pain with the shield, but neither of us could afford the distraction of each other's voice.

My thoughts were consumed by the thought that the bitch was this close to me. All I had to do was reach for my dagger quick enough to cut her throat, and this would be over.

"Keep her still," she ordered Azenna, and I lost all use of my limbs.

My body fell to the floor as the arm I used to hold myself up slid out from beneath me—my skull felt as if it had cracked as it slammed into the marble. Idina approached me then. She reached down and grabbed my face, squeezing my cheeks tightly between her fingers, pulling me closer to her as her eyes bore into mine.

"You have the fucking audacity to ask me about *my* mate when you are the one who plunged a blade into his heart?!" she screeched in my face, her fury-filled words rattling the throne room.

Shock took over me, eyes flaring wide at her declaration of Callius being her mate, but also that she believed *I* had killed him—and so specifically.

"You killed my mate, and now claim to have one of your own. Well, little Elianna, I have now changed my mind. You will live through this day, just long enough to watch me rip your own mate's heart from his chest with my bare fucking hands. And then you will die, but not before you know what it feels like to have the other half of your soul ripped from you."

I thrashed against the hold the witch had on me while a smirk crept up her face. On the inside, I was flailing, scratching, clawing, and biting at anything I could to tear the bitch's eyes out and watch her bleed out on the floor—but on the outside, my body remained perfectly still within her hold.

"Your father thought that your birth mother was his mate, but I knew better. I knew what that bond was like—what it smelled like. It's what I had with Callius since we were barely older than younglings. I had a duty to uphold for my family, and your father did as well..."

Her nostrils flared, eyes glazing over as if she had transported back to a distant memory.

"One of us held that bargain...and it was not the king." Her breathing turned heavy as her focus returned. "I did everything I was told, Elianna, *everything*! Including making my mate suffer. He suffered every time I was forced to bed your father for an heir. And then he gets that stupid bitch healer pregnant before he did me, claiming that he loves her and you!"

I was screaming. Internally, I was screaming a raging battle cry at the top of my lungs, choking the life out of her as she spoke of my father and mother. However, every time I tried to lash out, Azenna sensed it against her magic and sent a shockwave of icy flames through me, rippling through my veins—but I still wouldn't stop.

Idina chuckled wickedly. "Did I expect a few bastard children? Of course. Did I hope the male would occupy himself in the bed of another female? *Obviously*," she hissed. "But not the first child. Not his heir. And certainly not one he loved."

Idina released her hold on my cheeks, and my head fell to the floor once more, causing me to wince in pain as my entire skull ached.

"That's why your mother had to disappear. And your father, well, he outlived our plans by decades. Plans change as years pass—they evolve into something greater. But do not worry, darling Elianna." Her hand reached down and gently brushed over my cheek, as if it were from a loving mother's touch. "You will be with your parents again soon."

She stood tall and turned to Azenna. "Break her."

An eruption of power slammed into me once more, making my body soar through the air and into the back wall of the throne room—and then all I knew was agony.

SEVENTY-ONE

Jace

LIA WAS HURT.

I could feel it with every fiber of my being that she was suffering at the hands of our enemies, and there was nothing I could fucking do about it.

A guttural scream left me. Grunts escaped through desperate breaths with every heave of my blade as I plunged it through enemy soldiers.

I called out to her. Begged for her to answer me as I slammed my fists against her mental shield she placed so I couldn't reach her, and all that managed to slip through was her saying *I love you*.

I heard it for what it was—a goodbye.

I wouldn't fucking accept that. Lia was wounded and terrified—likely alone, too, since Nox was here. I felt it. I felt fucking all of it, and I couldn't bear it.

In that moment I decided I would get her my gods-damn self, and started pushing through the enemy's army, aiming for the city's gates.

My eyes lifted to the castle on the eastern side of Isla. They had my queen in there, and they were *torturing* her. I would climb the city's battlement with my bare fucking hands if I had to—I would make it to her before it was too late. I didn't care what it took, even if it was offering myself over in her place.

It was as if something else had taken over my body entirely—a beast that wouldn't be satisfied until he had his mate in his grasp once more. My strikes into enemy soldiers were fueled by pure adrenaline and rage.

A male stepped in my path then. The look on his face made it known he didn't plan for me to take a single step further. He certainly wasn't expecting me to throw myself at him, sending my sword deep into his neck.

The air was thick with the metallic scent of blood as chaos raged on in every direction I turned. My eyes flashed to Gage, watching him cut down everyone in his path, but I hadn't seen Zaela in only the gods knew how long, making me panic. I forced myself to push forward, aiming for the gates to get to Lia.

Suddenly, a scream sounded through the air. My gaze whipped in its direction from farther down the battlefield. I watched as my cousin tripped over a body and fell to the terrain, swiping her blade desperately as multiple males pursued her in an attack.

"Fuck. Zaela!" I screamed, hating that I had to turn away from my pursuit of Lia, knowing I could never live with myself if something happened to Zae because I didn't turn back.

My scream caught the attention of Leon, who, thank the gods, was significantly closer to her. His eyes locked on his lover's daughter, and he took off in a sprint in her direction.

Blood sprayed, and screams sounded, but I worked to get to my cousin, who continued to scoot back on the ground, unable to push to her feet as they relentlessly cornered her.

Leon arrived then, swinging his blade in the air at them as he leapt over her, landing before her feet. Zaela's eyes widened as she looked up at General Vern while he worked to protect her.

One soldier succumbed to one of the swipes of his blade, falling to the ground with a scream cut short—the other two backed up a step as they beheld him.

"Not her daughter! You will *not* harm her." He lunged then, his words leaving him in a triumphant bellow.

Then two more arrived, and then another...and another. A moment later, Leon was surrounded by endless enemy soldiers as he continued to push them as far away from her as possible.

When I reached Zaela, I hauled her to her feet—my gaze meeting Leon's as he turned towards us, still engaged in the fight now thirty feet away.

My lips parted as our eyes remained on one another while everything around me slowed, knowing—*dreading*—what I knew in my gut would happen next.

Zaela lashed around in my hold, her screams filling my ears as she watched Leon lead them away from us.

Leon was a proud man and a strong warrior. He had lived the life of a combat general who was forced to watch all of his friends perish on the battlefield, dying with honor. Yet, he was also a man who lived long enough to know the love of a good woman—a woman whose daughter he now knowingly sacrificed himself for so she could live.

"No!" Zaela cried in my arms, snapping me from my stupor as we watched our enemy's blades plunge into his flesh.

"Get her out of here!" he roared at me right before he fell to his knees in the dirt.

Blinding rage consumed me. My hold on Zaela fell, and her wrath mirrored my own as I locked eyes with Gage as he crept up on Leon's murderers from behind them.

With a mirrored battle cry, the three of us lifted our blades and charged at those who had just killed our general.

And we ended them all.

Kellan

I stood atop the cliffs beyond Castle Isla, and my entire body was riddled with stab wounds, making it difficult to breathe. My injuries weren't healing nearly as quickly as I needed them to, and it pissed me the fuck off.

I let out a roar of fury into the smoke-filled sky. How the fuck had I let her get the upper hand on me *again*? And this time, she nearly killed me.

The bitch *jumped* onto my wyvern—she free-fell through the air and landed on top of us, blade out. I hated that I had to give her credit for the brave stupidity that worked in her favor.

My gaze moved from the sea, still riddled with blood-stained warships, to the battlefield that raged on beyond the gates and then to my beast.

My hand went to above my right lung, where the worst of the stab wounds were. When I lifted my hand, it was drenched in my own blood.

"*Fuck*!" I bellowed into the sky.

I felt the piercing stare of my wyvern's red gaze as it eagerly waited for my command. "Let's fucking end this."

I pushed through the agony of my wounds as I stormed up to him and climbed onto his back. Once ordered, the beast took off into the sky, barreling towards the armies that continued to fight for their lives.

Bodies were piling everywhere, their outlines clear even from the sky. "Let's have a little fun, shall we?" I said to myself and then ordered the wyvern to send a blaze of hellfire down to the terrain.

Screams sounded from all sides, bodies flailing as they ran in all directions, engulfed in flames.

We landed in the center of the chaos; the roar of the other wyvern sounded in the far distance, from where it was defending the healers' tent. That's what I should've blown up from the sky when I had the chance, if only just to piss her off.

"Adler!" My name was called to me over the deafening sounds of war, and my gaze snapped in its direction—only to land on the most perfect fucking gift I could have imagined. Elianna's *husband*.

A growl rumbled through my chest as my nostrils flared. The moronic man was sizing up my wyvern, blade held high, as I sat upon its back, staring down at him.

The man was bloodied and beaten, covered in the gore of my soldiers. My lip snarled as my mount dug the tipped claws of its wings into the terrain and let out a deafening screech at him—the force of it blowing his hair back and causing his steps to falter. However, the fucker continued to move toward me, unphased.

"How about you fucking come down here and fight me, man to man?" he taunted me with a blood-stained grin.

I smiled down at him, giving him one that matched. "How about I just turn you to ash where you stand and then find your wife and do the same to her?"

His grin morphed into a hate-filled scowl that promised death. The veins in his neck looked as if they would burst, and his grip on his sword tightened.

He took a step in my direction. "You will not touch her. However, it appears she's already gotten you pretty good herself, asshole."

My face dropped at his words, but as my eyes looked him over, my smirk returned. "Oh, Commander. What makes you think she even still lives?"

"I sense everything about her, Adler. I feel her in every fiber of my being because not only is she my wife and queen..."

My gaze narrowed in on him through furrowed brows. There was no way in any hell this fuck was about to say what I thought he was going to...

"Elianna Valderre, rightful heir and queen of the realm, is my *mate!*" he roared triumphantly. "And now, for all you have put her through—*you* will suffer *me*."

An all-consuming rage overcame me at his words, and then I commanded the beast to release its fiery blaze upon him.

SEVENTY-TWO

Avery

THE CASTLE HALLS WERE dimly lit by torchlight as I navigated through its shadowy corridors. My dress flowed behind me as I darted down the halls, my steps barely making a whisper against the cold stone floor.

My race came to a skidding halt as the bloodied bodies of two guards were laid out across the corridor. My eyes flared, and I quietly went to move past them, stepping over their ruined corpses that someone had left behind.

Nausea threatened to consume me at the sight of them, but an overwhelming sense of hope crashed into me, realizing that someone from Lia's court or army must've been the one to have killed them.

My heart sang at the thought of Gage coming to rescue me if they had breached the castle, but knowing the possibility of him running into the vile witches or my mother made me panic.

I reached the grand staircase leading to the lower levels, where the main entrance and throne room awaited. My steps halted at the top of them, contemplating the best way to sneak out of the castle, but my thoughts were interrupted when a wicked cackle from the western tower staircase caught my attention. Chills ravaged my body at the sound, but something in my gut was telling me that was where I needed to go.

I blew out a breath and took back off into a run, gliding up the spiral stairs of the tower. As I ascended the upper level, I sought refuge in the shadows as I spotted one of the staff's rooms—where the crone's sinister chuckles echoed from.

My eyes scanned the dimly lit hall for any sign of movement. As I approached the door, a sliver of hope surged within me, masking the danger that lurked in the room's depths.

I could make a difference. I could fix everything that I had accidentally destroyed for my sister, Gage, and our friends. Not only that, but the kingdom we desperately wished to rebuild.

I stepped into the sunlight that peered in through the room's window, where the crone's back was to me while she gazed out at the scenes of war. Her arm reached through the window while she weaved a powerful spell of wards, fortifying the city against Lia's army.

My mind raced, and I wasn't even sure if I was breathing as I tiptoed silently toward her—pleading to all the gods that she didn't hear me enter or sense me behind her.

I glanced down at my hand, where one of the curved daggers remained, and my grip tightened around its hilt. My hand trembled as I realized how insane what I was about to do was, but this was my chance.

Once at her back, I lifted my arm high above my head. The shadow of the curved blade cast off the wall next to her, and I sensed her awareness a moment too late.

My arm moved to plunge the dagger down into her back, but in the same breath, she whipped toward me, her glowing crimson eyes blasting a pulsating fear through my entire body as they narrowed in on me.

While she looked ancient and decrepit, she was entirely too fast for even me to react to and *strong*. Her taloned, withered hand shot out at me, grabbing me by the throat.

The crone's sharp nails dug into the skin of my neck, and I felt my blood slip from the wounds. My breath caught, gasping for air as she lifted me up by my throat. My arm was still frozen above me in the same stance I had been in when I went to kill her—but now she was going to kill me.

"*I see inside this heart of yours, Princess.*" Her ancient voice echoed through me before she spoke aloud. "You will never be like the heir. You believe yourself to be brave, but it is stupidity that runs you, making you think you could sneak up on an all-powerful sorceress."

A whimper left me, but it wasn't sadness that I felt—it was anger. I had been trapped my entire life. In the castle, in Isla, beneath my mother's manipulation, and now here, trapped within the clutches of a witch. When would it end? Certainly not this way. I had plans. I had a kingdom to deliver to my sister, and a man that I promised I would come back to.

"I could smell you the second you took the first step onto the spiral stairs, hear you the second you slipped that blade from the library. And now, you will die. All because you just couldn't listen. Once I am through with you, I will send your body through this window behind me. It will be such a shame that you fell to your death trying to sneak from your bedchamber. The queen...she will be so very sad. Her only daughter."

Her talons dug further into my flesh and I tried to gasp for air as she held me above her, but my vision was darkening.

My eyes drifted upwards to my hand that still levitated high above us both with the dagger in its grasp, unable to move.

I glanced down to my hip, where the second dagger remained tucked in the belt of my dress, and slowly placed my other hand on its hilt. Carefully slipping it out from its makeshift sheath, I prayed to every god imaginable that she didn't notice the movement as she continued her speech on my impending death.

It was now or never. Once I knew I had a firm hold, my lip curled, revealing my canines, as my gaze narrowed in on the crone's withered face.

With a suffocating battle cry tearing from my throat that remained in her talons, I used all my strength and plunged the curved blade into the witch's heart, *twisting* it within her chest.

Black blood sprayed me as her grip remained, but pure horror carved itself into her features as she glanced down at the dagger that now protruded from her ruined heart.

The crone's eyes glowed brighter than ever, threatening to blind me as I remained before her, screaming an ear-shattering screech of death. A moment later, she burst open—her body vanishing before me and replaced by swirling shadows of malicious smoke and slick, onyx gore.

My body dropped to the ground as she exploded, the blade I killed her with clattering on the tile next to me. The

592

floor, walls, and my clothes were covered in what remained of the crone, and I stared up at the window she had just stood in front of in disbelief.

And then a laugh left me—it started as a giggle and morphed into a full eruption of manic, disbelieving laughter as I sat there in shock at what I had just done.

I killed the crone—*me*, Avery Valderre. The princess, whose only purpose in life was to be sold to a far-off lord as a bartering chip, just destroyed an all-powerful sorceress.

Pushing myself to my feet, ignoring the aches in my bones and pain from the puncture wounds in my neck, I brought myself to the window and peered out.

Black smoke still filled the air, the battle continuing on the ground below—but the wards were down. The spell the crone had been casting, shielding the gates of the city, had dropped. Which meant that our armies could now breach the gates.

"Holy shit," I breathed.

A scream echoed in the distance, snapping my attention back to the spiral stairs.

"Mother of the gods." My voice was a whisper. "Lia."

I didn't waste a second. I crouched down, picking up the curved blade I had just used on the crone, and rushed through the door. Sprinting down the staircase, I aimed for the throne room, where my sister's screams continued to erupt from.

SEVENTY-THREE

Jace

STARING DOWN THE GAPING maw of Adler's wyvern, Lia's pain and fear repeatedly slammed into me. Her last words that she let slip through—*I love you*—replayed in my head over and over. My heart was shattering, but I poured all my focus into my rage, ready to kill this vicious prick once and for all so I could find my queen.

Adler had tried to taunt me, telling me that Lia was dead, unknowing of the fact that not only was she my wife but also my mate. The look on his face once he heard those words may be the last thing I ever saw, and the only view that I wish could have replaced it was her.

Nox raced towards us from where he was guarding the healer's tent, but I knew he wouldn't make it in time. The fire building in the back of the red-gazed wyvern's throat was already blinding me, and I lifted my sword high, ready to die swinging.

A roar erupted from me as I took my first step, the fire blasting through the creature's throat, when suddenly, the beast erupted into nothing but smoke and gore, sending my body soaring violently down the field.

I crashed into the terrain nearly fifty feet from where I had stood before them, agony slamming into me at the forceful contact with the ground as my body rolled even further.

My name was being called, but I couldn't tell if it was from near or far. I blinked as I looked up at the blazing sky—a once sunny day now consumed by smoke and shadows. And then Zaela appeared above me, followed by Gage.

"Jace!" she screamed, but it was muffled in my ears as my hearing and vision worked to return from the blast.

Gage lifted me up by my back, having me sit up in the middle of the battlefield, surrounded by the bloodied corpses of both man and fae.

"Brother!" he yelled, and I slowly turned to face him, blinking the dirt and haze from my eyes. "You're okay, you're okay!" he was screaming as he frantically looked my body over.

The veins in my neck bulged as I tried to stand, but they caught me, slamming me back down onto the ground. "Let me go!" I barked at them. "Where is Adler?!"

All three of our gazes flew to where he had been perched atop his mount only moments ago. The wyvern he rode was gone, nowhere to be seen, and he was covered in what remained of it. Pushing himself to his feet in visible pain from the explosion, his eyes were locked on us, absolute fury radiating from them.

My eyes moved across the battlefield, where soldiers from both armies continued to fall to their demise with each passing second.

I swallowed as I pushed myself to stand, reaching down and grabbing two swords at my feet from fallen warriors. "I don't know where Lia is. She won't let me in, but something's wrong. All I know is that she's alive."

"They have our girls," Gage breathed, chest heaving.

"Adler is coming," Zaela warned, as she positioned herself in a fighting stance.

We were losing. Even with Kellan's wyvern gone, we had no sight on the witches or the queen, and they likely still had Avery and now Lia.

Our men were falling, their bodies giving into exhaustion. One of the twin witches erupted into ash, and the other abandoned us. Landon was still swinging his blade halfway across the field, but he was moving slower than before. Veli was injured, and the healers' tent was overflowing. Leon had fallen in battle, and Nox was out of his flame and visibly wounded.

Everything we worked and aimed for was bursting into flames before our eyes, and I saw the knowledge of it in their stares. My two best friends positioned themselves next to me as we prepared to face our final moments, ready to die for everything Lia needed to bring the realm peace.

Suddenly, a horn sounded in the distance, echoing through the skies and fields, projecting from our backs.

We all whipped around, the clashing of steel halting as everyone's focus turned to the noise that filtered in from the distance.

I squinted through the sun's rays as it peered through the clouds and smoke, and my jaw dropped at what my sight took in.

Endless rows of beastly warriors lined the tops of the hills in the distance, taking all forms of shapes and sizes. A leader stood on four hooves at its center—an enormous centaur, lifting itself on its hind legs as it continued to blow into the enormous, bone-carved horn.

"What in the name of the gods..." I breathed.

Knowing laughter left Zaela as she shook her head, stepping back up to my side. "She did it. They're here for her!"

Pride burst within me, and I shot it down our bond, hoping that it reached her as I watched thousands of creatures from the Sylis Forest stampede down the distant hills and aim for us. Battle cries erupted from them as their march rumbled the ground beneath our feet.

It wasn't just centaurs in our added army, but also trolls and giants that towered over even them. Sylis bears appeared after the first wave of warriors, dwarves saddled on their backs, riding towards us with sharpened axes held high in the air.

They slammed into the outskirts of the battle with ferocious ease, eliminating the enemy forces faster than we ever could. The Islan soldiers scattered and ran for their lives, terrified as the beasts of legends charged at them.

A laugh left me as I shook my head. *My Lia did it.*

Veli wisped herself before us as we turned back to face Adler, who had shaken himself from his trance at what now stampeded towards what remained of his men, and he aimed for me once more.

I lifted my double swords as both Zaela and Gage took off to rejoin the battle.

"Something has happened. The wards of the city have been shattered," the sorceress declared in a near yell. A look resembling hope lingered in her stare.

Veli was about to send her shadows out when I took a step up to her, forcing her to look back up at me as Adler drew closer.

More than anything, I wanted to find Lia, but I knew I wouldn't necessarily be the fastest—I didn't know Isla or its castle, and she could be anywhere. I also knew that there was no way in any fucking realm I would let Kellan walk away from this battlefield.

"We have this handled. Adler is mine," I declared. "Go find our queen. Bring her back to us. Please."

Her fuchsia-hued eyes flared but then softened in understanding. She gave me a curt nod right before she vanished, wisping herself to our queen's aid.

Kellan was feet from me now, and a growl erupted in my chest. Head twisting to the side in a predatory manner, I said, "Not going to run away this time and take the coward's way out, Adler?"

"I am no coward." His voice was as lethal as my own.

A feral grin crept up my face, knowing that my words clawed their way under his skin. "Twice now you've evaded the consequences of touching what's mine."

The muscles in his neck strained as his jaw visibly locked.

"First, you needed your men to bind my limbs and hold me back for you to maim me with a poisoned blade, leaving me to rot in the dirt. Then, you fled a battle, running away like the pathetic pussy you are after my wife plunged that very same dagger into your flesh."

He lifted his sword into the air, getting ready to strike as he bellowed, "You know nothing of me, mortal cunt."

"Oh, I know enough." I took a step toward him. "You find yourself superior to females and women. However, I must say, every single one that I have had the pleasure of knowing has shown *far* more courage than you."

A moment later, Adler's blade met mine.

SEVENTY-FOUR

Elianna

PURE AGONY PULSED THROUGH me in a violent haze, as if every bone in my body had shattered a thousand times over while the queen's puppet tormented me. Both of their gazes remained on me, enjoying every bit of pain they witnessed at their disposal.

The only thing keeping me going was knowing that Jace was alive, feeling him on the other end of the bond that I desperately yearned to let him through—but I knew him sensing all of this, *feeling* the full extent of it, would only put him at greater risk.

He would hate me for shutting him out, but I wouldn't risk him—just as he wouldn't risk me in the battle at Ellecaster.

"Be sure that her heart is still beating. I don't want her dead yet," Idina stated.

Azenna smirked as she slammed my body into yet another wall—a grunt left me at the force of it. "It beats. She is strong-willed. Defiant."

Idina snarled. "She always has been."

I flashed a blood-stained smile at them in response, ignoring my body as every inch felt like it was bursting into flames.

Azenna's eyes flared as panic took over her features. She started glancing frantically in every direction—her torture attempts at me ceasing from whatever suddenly distracted her.

"Something is wrong!" she bellowed. The High Witch turned to the queen. "The wards are down! Something has happened to Sylvae."

Mother of the gods. Hope surged through me at her words as Idina looked as if she would kill Azenna right there for something going awry with her plans.

Everyone's attention moved to the throne room doors as they burst open, slamming into the walls at their sides as my sister leapt through them.

Her eyes met mine, and my heart was ready to burst from both pride and nerves for her being here.

"Mother!" she barked. "Release her!"

Idina laughed at her daughter's demand but then shot Azenna another vengeful look. "How did you get out?!"

"You have always underestimated me and what I'm capable of," she hissed while storming towards them.

She shot me a sympathetic look, but I had never been more fucking proud in my life. That was my girl—*defiant*, just like her sister. A grin stretched across my face as I remained under the witch's faltering hold.

Azenna took a threatening step in Avery's direction and I lashed out at her sorcery, writhing beneath it to get to her. "Where is Sylvae?!" she barked.

Avery's hands balled into fists at her sides. "Dead," she answered proudly.

My eyes flared. "Holy gods," I managed to breathe.

"And I would be in her place if I hadn't stabbed her in the heart first!" Avery ripped a curved dagger from the belt of her dress and showed it to the High Witch.

Idina's head snapped to Azenna. "Your crone tried to kill my daughter?!"

Chaos ensued in the throne room as arguments lashed out from everyone—and then all the windows *burst*. Glass shattered from all sides and angles of the giant room as they rained down from the high ceilings.

Everyone moved to shield themselves from the sudden blast, including Azenna, causing her to release the spell she held me in. My body fell to the floor, but I blocked the hard contact by tucking and rolling the best I could.

Glass cut into my skin as I landed while it continued to rain down on us. My hand flew to the hilt of my dagger, ready to strike as I lay in a non-threatening position, trying not to draw too much attention as everyone remained distracted from the blast.

Shadows erupted through one of the windows, swarming through the room like a haze of death—and then Veli appeared above us. My aide levitated in the air as she leisurely lowered herself to the ground, eyes illuminating with pure, surging power.

Complete awe took over me at the sight of her, and the pure fear that slithered into Idina's eyes.

Azenna took a step up to Veli, eyes glowing with her blinding power. "Fool of a witch, deserting your kind, as always."

"Fools flock to fools, I presume. And I will choose *them* every time," Veli answered with a menacing smirk that mirrored my own as I watched through the curtain of my hair.

"Witch, don't you dare leave my side!" the queen roared at Azenna's back, but it was too late.

The High Witch shot out in a rush of shadows at Veli, whose own flew to cover her instantly. I worked to push myself up as the two witches soared around the chamber, their magic lashing out at each other in deadly strides.

The air crackled with untapped power as their sorcery was unleashed. The throne room's tapestries fluttered, and some were ripped from the walls as a tornado-like wind formed in the space.

A swirl of inky darkness enveloped Veli, coiling around her like a living serpent. Azenna unleashed bolts of the same shadowy energy across the room, but Veli's own countered them, acting as a barrier.

Shockwaves reverberated through the room as their forces clashed, causing everything around us to rattle. A clicking sound echoed, drawing my attention up to the swaying crystal chandelier as it fell from the ceiling. It was aiming right for where Avery stood, stuck in a daze of watching the witches fight one another.

"Avery!" I screamed as I leapt up, ignoring the pain tearing through every one of my muscles from Azenna's torments, and dove for her. I tackled her to the ground just in time, our bodies rolling along the glass-covered floor. The chandelier exploded into millions of tiny shards the second it came in contact with the marble.

Veli's eyes flashed to mine in horror, and then gave me a nod. She reached out for Azenna, wrapping her shadows around the screaming witch, and sent both of them blasting back out through the windows and into the air above the city.

The throne room turned eerily silent as their battle took to the skies. The only sounds were our deep breaths and the crunching of glass beneath us as we slowly began to move.

"Avery, darling." Idina's voice sounded from the dais, where she now stood in front of my father's throne—*my* throne. "Come with me, darling. Come with your mother. We must leave. It isn't safe." Her words were frantic and full of nerves.

Avery scoffed and then sat up next to me. As I worked to push myself up alongside her, I reached down toward my sheath, only to find that my dagger was gone.

Fuck.

"I will never go with you," she breathed.

Idina's mouth twisted into a scowl as she stormed up to us, aiming for Avery. My eyes landed on my dagger, only feet away, hidden beneath the piles of glass that littered the floor. The obsidian blade glistened in the light that shone through the shattered windows.

The queen reached us then, her attention flashing between me and my sister cautiously as she stretched her arm out and grabbed Avery's wrist. She tugged at her daughter's arm violently, sliding her body through the glass, leaving a trail of blood in her wake as Avery screamed and clawed at her mother's grasp. Crescent-shaped blood pooled on the queen's arms from Avery's fingernails digging into her skin.

Idina's attention was fully on forcing Avery to escape with her. I used the distraction to push my body through the searing pain and reached through the pile of glass, wrapping my fingers around my dagger's hilt.

Avery kicked and screamed at Idina, but she was injured from our fall, and the queen's grasp on her was like a death grip as she dragged her body up the steps of the dais.

I pushed myself to my feet, my eyes narrowing in on the female who had taken everything from me—my life, parents, crown, and siblings. All because of hatred in her heart from what her own family had done to her, and jealousy of not being able to be with who she loved when my father only desired the same. They were each prisoners of a contract they had nothing to do with. It cost my father and mother their lives—and now the queen's actions would have the same deadly consequences for herself.

They say the wrath of a female scorned could rival that of the gods, but what of two queens? Each willing to burn the realm down for those they loved—one benevolent, like her father, and the other even more cruel than her own.

I positioned myself into a fighting stance and held my dagger tight in my grasp—the blade my father had created for me, and that my mate had reforged. The dagger that meant everything to me and reminded me of those I loved most would now take the life of the person who had worked to take theirs.

Idina's amber eyes widened in horror as they met mine. I took my first step toward her and then another. Before I knew it, I was storming up to the queen, the corners of my lips tipping up at the sight of fear in her eyes—mimicking the fear she had placed upon so many others.

It was satisfying to know I was the one who put it there.

Avery finally shoved out of her mother's hold once I reached the dais. Idina stumbled backwards, clutching her chest as she watched me approach in slow, taunting movements.

"Elianna, I—" She sounded as if she was about to burst into tears, and one of my own slipped, but mine wasn't out of fear or sadness. The single tear I let slip was that of relief as my fingertips ached with the need for vengeance, sensing that it was about to be within their grasp.

I forcefully grabbed the false queen by her hair, slamming her against the unforgiving brick wall and silencing the plea for mercy that tried to escape her lips. "You do not speak here. Anything you say will fall on deaf ears."

Pulling her hair down, I brought the tip of my dagger's blade to her throat as it became fully exposed.

"If you would just let me try to explain!"

I brought my lips to her ear, and I felt a shiver of terror roll through her body. "Such a terrible listener, as you have been for the last century. Idina, it's my turn to speak—*my turn* for revenge."

A retort was working its way up her throat, but I pressed the sharpened tip further into her skin, a bead of her blood rolling down its blade.

My face was now positioned directly in front of her own, making sure she was looking into my eyes for what I was about to say. "You are a tyrant, usurper, murderous cunt. Everything that you did was to exact vengeance on innocent beings, all because you believed yourself to be superior to them."

"Your father—"

"My father was many things. Yes, a fool was one of them, but it was heartache that drove him there, caused by *you*. The male was terrified of you, for what he feared you would do to me, and he let his entire kingdom suffer for it."

"He never even gained knowledge of the scars my body still bears because of you. You state that neither he nor I are worthy of having mates, but it is *you*, Idina, who is undeserving of one." I huffed out a hateful laugh. "Or perhaps you and Callius just truly deserved each other."

Avery pulled herself to her feet, watching us with wide, disbelieving eyes.

"I just wanted to love freely." Idina's words were hoarse, barely above a whisper.

A wicked grin crept up my face. "Always such a liar. You wanted *power*. You wanted to take back what was ripped from you by males your entire life, and in turn, did just that to another female—one whose birthright was that power. To rule over the realm and protect *all* of its creatures. You never protected anyone but yourself."

Tears slipped from her lower lashes then, but nothing but pure fury-filled hate lingered in her stare as she watched me, trapped between the wall and my blade.

Her gaze moved to Avery. "Why?" she croaked out. "You support her and her claim, yet I am your mother."

For a moment, I felt awful that my sister had to see this—until she spoke.

Avery's eyes darted back and forth between me and Idina. "And she is my sister," she answered. "And Jameson was my father. I share just as much blood with them as I do with you. You took my father away from not only us and your other children, but the Kingdom of Velyra."

My heart was ready to burst as I listened to her condemn her own mother in my honor.

"This is what you deserve," she whispered ruthlessly.

My eyes locked with Avery's then, and she gave me a subtle dip of her chin.

Another plea of terror was working its way through the queen, but never had time to escape her as I lodged the blade in her throat. Her eyes flared before they turned lifeless as I held her in my grasp, her blood pouring down her front. Once I released her, I sent her body tumbling down the steps of the dais, leaving a trail of crimson behind her.

The only sounds now were mine and Avery's labored breathing, and my stare slowly lifted to hers as it filled with tears, slipping down her cheeks.

"I thought they were going to kill you," she whispered.

"Me too." I gave her a soft, tight-lipped smile.

A moment later, we lunged at one another in tandem, crashing into each other's open arms, and tightened our embrace. We hugged each other so firmly I thought our bones would snap.

The day began with so many unknowns, one of them being that I wasn't sure I would ever see my sister again, and I was thankful to Terra and every wretched god above that wasn't the case.

"I'm so sorry," I whispered.

She pulled back from me then. "For what? You just saved me."

"Everything. For this." I gestured to Idina's body. "And for accusing you of keeping the nature of my mother's death from me—I regretted it the moment it left my lips. I know you would never do that, and you didn't deserve what I did and said following it. I'm just so sorry, and since you were taken, I didn't know if I would ever get the chance to tell you that. It's been killing me." The last words left me in a whisper.

She smiled at me softly. "Lia, you were forgiven the moment it happened. I knew your anger was misplaced. I can't even fathom how you've dealt with everything. Let it go down in history as our first sister fight."

A snort left me at that.

My eyes then roamed over her body—her dress was covered in onyx gore, while her skin was littered with bleeding cuts and bruises. "Are you okay?"

"Yes," she breathed. "Gage? Is he alright?"

My lips pressed together in a thin line. "I'm not sure. We have to go out there and help the others," I said.

I took her hand in mine and guided her towards the throne room doors, picking up my sword that I had lost when Azenna first attacked me and sheathed it on my hip as we left her mother's body behind.

"*Jace*," I breathed down the bond, praying to the gods that he was okay, but I felt him there—his heart beating rapidly.

"*Lia!*" His scream echoed through my mind, and my pace quickened, feeling the sense of urgency in his tone.

"*I'm okay, and I'm coming to find you.*"

His sight took over my own, and the castle walls morphed into a hazy battlefield, where males and men raged on in their fight for victory, but they weren't alone. Centaurs, giants, and countless other creatures of the forest were sprawled throughout the battlefield, aiding the mortals in their fight for survival.

My steps faltered and a booming laugh left me, stunning Avery, whose stride halted with mine.

"Those lying bastards." I chuckled out loud as relief worked its way through my aching veins.

Three swords flew in front of my vision, two held by my mate, crossing as a shield in front of him, as another blade worked to push through them—through *him*.

A growl, deep and ferocious, worked its way out of me as the sight of Kellan came into view, holding the other blade.

"*Hold on, handsome. I'm coming.*"

I turned to my sister and reached for her hand. "Help has arrived. I'll explain everything later, but I had one more trick up my sleeve before we came to get you. We need to get out there."

We both took off in a desperate run, through the castle's main entrance and down the streets of Isla, aiming for the city's gate.

SEVENTY-FIVE

Veli

ABOVE THE SPRAWLING CITY, the late afternoon sky became a battlefield of its own as I put every ounce of myself and power into defeating Azenna. Our onyx robes billowed around us like raven wings as we soared through the air.

I sent blasts of power at her every chance I could, unleashing a torrent of shadowy tendrils, each pulsating with the ominous energy that I had come to love, feeling as if they were part of my very being. The shadows of darkness snaked through the air, aiming to ensnare Azenna in their suffocating grip.

The High Witch countered with a burst of flaming light, as if it had come from her conjured wyvern, not the palm of her hand. The heat of her blaze forced my shadows to disperse and singed my robes, the tails of it catching fire from the blast.

"Veli, Veli, oh foolish Veli," she hissed through the air. "Did you truly think you would win? Did you think that your power could defeat that of your High Witch?"

"You are *not* my High Witch," I roared back at her, sending a blast of shadows back in her face, but she blocked it by putting up a wall of flames.

As the blaze dissipated, her gaze locked on me, lip curling back in disgust. "Yes, well, you made sure of that yourself when you turned your back on the only real family you'll ever have."

I grabbed her by the throat, surprising each of us, and her skin caught fire, burning my flesh and taloned nails, but my grip didn't falter.

"I have found a family of my own," I announced, not expecting the words to ring so true. "Admit it, Azenna. You lost. You finally lost after all these centuries." My eyes roamed over her while I ignored the blisters forming on my hand as I gripped her throat tighter. "Or perhaps you lost a long time ago when I took the only thing from you that you desired. More power."

Azenna conjured gusts of wind, sending turbulent currents spiraling around us, shooting my shadows outward and distracting me enough to loosen my hold.

I forcefully waved my sizzling hand in the air, urging my skin to mend quickly. Yet, the strain from my earlier injury and the exertion of using my powers made the healing process significantly slower—and I couldn't afford it.

Azenna took the opportunity of distraction and retaliated by conjuring beams of otherworldly fire, shooting them directly at me. However, my shadows responded with a swift, swirling barrier of darkness that consumed and snuffed out her flames, leaving behind only a fleeting trail of smoke.

Our personal battle raged on, weaving a tapestry of light and shadow high above Isla and its citizens, who were now funneling into the streets. They stared up at us in fear and awe, their screams echoing and mixing with those of the true battle that lay just beyond their gates.

My body was faltering, the power I had used to get me here draining me nearly entirely.

"It's over for you, Veli. I sense your magic failing, little witchling." Azenna cackled at her own words.

I knew this was the last chance I would get, and I would give my entire self over to the darkness if it meant defeating her and giving Elianna and the others a chance at survival. For what is The Queen's Aide if not an unfaltering line of defense?

Sinister shadows exuded from me, conjured in a swirling vortex of wrath. "No, Azenna. The only witch it's over for is y*ou*." Her crimson eyes flared at my declaration, and with a booming, rebel yell, my summoned darkness erupted, threatening to consume everything in its path, including the High Witch.

The collision of our final, devastating force of power created an explosion of uncapped energy that threatened to consume the both of us—and then my shadows snuffed everything of hers out.

They wrapped around her limbs like prisoners' chains, forcing themselves down her throat through her lips and nostrils. The dark tendrils were relentless, choking and blinding her as they worked to save me—their maker.

My body levitated toward her as the ethereal swirls of darkness lingered around me, guarding me as fiercely as Elianna's wyvern did for her.

Azenna's skin repeatedly tried to ignite itself in flames to remove the shadow's grasp on her, but it was no use. She was finally trapped as I desperately held onto the thread of power I had left, keeping her held in place, high above the city.

"*Veli*," she croaked out through her mind as her body lashed in all directions, trying to free herself. "*Please, it was the dark magic! Not me. Spare me, and I will leave all of Velyra. I won't return to the isles. Please.*"

The High Witch feared death.

A smirk tilted my lips, knowing that the dark sorcery only responded to that of the mind of the witch it was summoned with. My shadows were proof of that.

"Go to hell, Azenna." My words were that of the most soul-freeing wrath.

Her jaw locked in response, the false plea for mercy in her eyes vanishing.

Power surged from her, ready to break her free. I appeared in front of her then, taking my taloned hand and digging it into her chest, pushing through cloth, flesh, and then bone, until my fingers wrapped around her beating heart.

She screeched in agony, lashing around frantically as I held the life of the all-powerful High Witch in my hand and then ripped it from her chest.

Azenna's body instantly burst into flames and plumes of smoke. Ferocious cracks of all-consuming lightning erupted from the immense power she possessed as High Witch. Midnight-slick gore rained down on the city below, her screams still echoing through the wind.

However, the power from her eruption crashed into me, and the lightning struck my chest, ripping my breath from my lungs. The force of it had my shadows seeking shelter back into my palms, and my body began free-falling, descending rapidly toward the ground below.

My power was depleted, exhausted from the efforts of everything I had done.

The rushing wind threatened to deafen me while my body plummeted to the unforgiving terrain. My gaze locked on my hand, drenched in slick, onyx blood—and between my taloned fingers, the High Witch's heart remained, still beating.

And then—as the lightning fizzled out in my veins—my own heart was reduced to ash.

SEVENTY-SIX

Elianna

CITIZENS WERE EMERGING FROM their homes as blasts of shadows erupted in the sky—where Veli and Azenna unleashed their powers on one another.

Avery and I shoved through the crowds, begging them to return to safety, not knowing what would happen between the witches that fought in the sky and the blazing battle just outside of the city.

I turned to my sister. "They listen to you, try to get them at least under some form of cover. Don't let them know the queen is dead yet. We need to handle everything carefully."

She grabbed both of my hands in hers. "Be careful."

"You too," I whispered, and then we both took off into a run in opposite directions—me toward the city's gates, and her to its center.

The tall gates of Isla were chained and barred, as if they were never meant to be opened again. I looked up at it through furrowed brows, annoyance sizzling through me. "Gods-dammit."

With a grunt, I raced to the steps of the tower. Unsheathing my sword, I climbed the tall stone stairs.

Guards stood atop it, and they noticed me the moment my foot was placed on the steps.

"It's Solus!" the one closest to me on the tower roared as he descended the staircase, aiming straight for me.

Our blades collided, sparks flying from the clash of steel on steel. I wrapped my foot around one of his ankles and maneuvered my body around his, sending him tumbling over the railing and down to the cobblestone streets below.

His scream echoed through the air until his body slammed into the ground, cutting it short.

"Actually, it's Valderre!" I called over the rail as I raced up the rest of the high steps.

At the top of the tower, I encountered three soldiers who were once under my command, a memory from what felt like a different lifetime.

Their gazes were fixated on me, and I blew out a breath as I lifted my sword back into a fighting stance.

What happened next surprised me.

They exchanged quick, nervous glances and threw their weapons to their feet. My brows creased in confusion as they all leisurely lifted their hands in surrender. I warily lowered my own blade as my eyes wandered over the three of them.

"Does she live?" one of them asked.

I swallowed, my grip tightening on the hilt of my weapon. "You're going to need to be more specific."

"The queen," a different one answered, bringing my gaze to him.

"No," I said on a breath, the word barely audible. I prepared to lift my blade once more, considering that they could attack me for murdering their queen, but instead, they looked relieved.

"Thank the gods," the middle one murmured. "It's over."

"Not yet," I reminded him. "Almost, though. If I put this blade down..."

"Don't worry, we won't do anything. We always liked you far better than Adler." He paused. "And your army is destroying us."

"What?!" I gasped before running past them to the tower's opposite edge that overlooked the battlefield.

It was true, and we had the creatures of the forest to thank. I couldn't believe what my eyes beheld, but now I needed to find a way to stop it.

My eyes landed on Jace, who was still engaged in an intense duel with Kellan, both of them looking exhausted and ready to drop—I had to make sure the one to fall wasn't my mate.

A roar sounded, and my eyes snapped to Nox, who was halfway across the battlefield, tearing into enemy soldiers with his teeth and clawed wings. They weren't even moving to attack him anymore; they were just getting caught in the crosshairs of his rage.

Lifting my fingers to my lips, I let out a shrieking whistle in his direction. "*NOX!*" I bellowed, and my wyvern's attention snapped to the tower. His wings instantly lifted him into the air and had him hurtling towards me.

I turned to the soldiers I had mistakenly turned my back to, but they kept their word. My eyes landed on a bow that was leaned against the side rail with a cluster of arrows.

I nodded in its direction. "Can I borrow that?" The words sounded foolish the second they left my mouth, but I didn't have time to care.

"By all means," one said as he picked it up and practically shoved it at me.

Looping the bow around my back, I prepared myself to leap onto Nox as he came racing towards us. I looked back at them over my shoulder to find they were watching me intently. "Don't kill any more of my men, or it's *me* you will face. Understood?"

"Yes, Captain," they answered in unison, and it made me pause for a moment, blinking in confusion. A smirk cracked my lips at their use of my old title.

"Are you going to have your beast harm us?" one of them asked as Nox was almost at the tower.

I heaved myself onto the rail, balancing on the thin bricks of stone. "Who, Noxy? He wouldn't hurt a fly." I shot them a menacing grin, and their eyes flared.

A second later, the beat of his wings sent wind flying in our direction as he soared next to the tower, and I ran along the rail in tandem with him, until I leapt off its ledge. Touching down on the nape of Nox's neck, I grabbed his fin for support, and we effortlessly resumed his high-speed flight.

We soared through the smoke-clearing skies while my eyes were locked on the fight raging between Jace and Kellan.

My mate stumbled backward, leaving his body wide open and vulnerable to Kellan's strike. My heart stopped painfully while everything around me ceased to exist.

"Nox, now!" I screamed at the top of my lungs as I ripped the bow from over my shoulder and nocked an arrow in place. Tucking his wings into his sides, my wyvern spiraled down toward the terrain, aiming for them.

Jace

The battlefield stretched out like a canvas of chaos. So many had fallen on each side, lives and good soldiers lost, but all I could focus on was Adler as he relentlessly came at me with his weapon.

The air was thick with tension as we frantically swung at each other, sworn enemies with histories written in blood and vengeance.

"Give it the fuck up!" Kellan screamed at me as I blocked his attack by crossing my two blades once more and shoved him back.

"You're dying," I breathed, a growl rumbling through me as we each grunted through our counterattacks. "It won't be long now until your body gives out."

My body ached, but I could tell he was significantly worse. He was riddled with stab wounds that continued to ooze blood from Lia's assault on him in the air, and truthfully, I couldn't believe the bastard was still standing.

A roar erupted overhead from Nox, and my gaze flew up to him, pride beaming from me at the sight of my queen on his back.

Adler's battle cry echoed through the air as I countered each of his strikes. He was driven by his desire for power, while I was fueled solely by my desire for revenge—for what his fleet had done to my people, for what he had done to my face, and for touching what was *mine*.

My eyes swept the field. Zaela, and Gage were each in fierce battles of their own. Centaurs galloped alongside riderless warhorses, striking down our enemy that surely would have defeated us by now if they hadn't shown up. Landon and his group struck down any enemies that tried to access the healer's tent, protecting Finnian and the others who remained helpless inside in place of Nox.

Countering one of his attacks, my boots slipped in the thick mud that overtook the ground beneath our feet, sending my body stumbling back right as Adler moved to strike.

My gaze lifted over his shoulder to see Nox and Lia barreling towards us, an arrow nocked in her bow, aimed at Adler's back.

One of the swords I held slipped from my hands, and I moved to block his blow with the other, but didn't fully make it in time. His weapon collided with mine, but the force of his assault was stronger than what I was prepared for. The blade of his sword slid down my own, slipping over the edge of mine—what was aimed for my heart now steered in the direction of my shoulder.

The moment his sword pierced my flesh, agony overwhelmed me, but what I felt above all else was hers over my own as she sensed my pain.

"*JACE!*" Her voice flooded me, as if she were standing beside me.

My eyes locked with hers as she stood atop Nox's back midair and released the arrow. She sent it spiraling towards Adler as he loomed over me, still pushing his blade into me, just above my heart.

Baring my teeth from the pain, I let out a roar of retribution—if I was going to die, I was bringing this fucker with me.

But then Lia's arrow met its mark and shot through his back, protruding from his chest.

Blood splattered as it erupted through his flesh, and his nostrils flared before roaring out in pain and fury. Adler moved to strike his fatal blow, and he yanked his blade out of me, triggering a piercing howl of anguish to reverberate from deep within me—but he was slower, weaker.

With all my remaining strength, I raised the hand clutching my other sword and brought it down on his arm, completely severing it from his body. His eyes flared in shock as he watched it fall to the terrain, his sword still in its grasp. Blood poured from his missing limb as his gaze lifted back to mine in disbelief, right before I plunged my blade straight through his gut.

He fell to his knees with my sword still protruding from him, eyes bulging in horror while blood trickled from his lips.

As Nox landed amidst the chaos, the ground shook beneath his weight. Onlooking soldiers ceased in their attacks, clutching their blood-stained weapons as they watched in fear.

Lia dismounted by running and leaping off of Nox's shoulder. The moment her boots touched the soil, she ripped her dagger from its sheath and tossed her bow aside.

My queen stormed toward us—nothing but pure vengeful wrath written into her features as I felt it pulsating down the bond.

It was the most ferociously beautiful sight I had ever laid my eyes on.

As I glanced down at my wound, terror surged through me, causing my vision to blur. However, I managed to catch the sight of the light slowly leaving Adler's eyes while he watched me from where he remained on his knees.

My jaw locked. "It wouldn't be fair to my wife if I took the entire claim of your life. For all that you have done to her and all you still planned to do."

Appearing as if he was unable to speak, his body moved to fall completely forward. She appeared behind him then.

Lia reached out and grabbed him by the back of his blood-crusted hair, ripping his body back into her. Her gaze fell to him, boring into his as her lip curled back in disgust, revealing her canines.

She brought her lips to his ear, and he coughed out a whimper beneath her as I watched in awe. "You will *never* touch *anything* that is mine, ever again."

In a swift movement, she released his hair and ripped the protruding arrow from his chest while simultaneously taking the dagger in her opposite hand and plunged it into his heart.

He let out a grunt as it pierced his chest, staring up at her face as if longing for her, and then his body sagged. The moment she yanked her dagger from his flesh, he dropped to the ground at her feet, unmoving.

And then we were surrounded.

SEVENTY-SEVEN

Elianna

"Jace," I breathed. A gut-wrenching sob escaped me as his name left my lips at the sight of him, blood drenching the front of his armor—*his* blood, I realized.

But there was no time to react, for we each felt the enemy's presence surrounding us on all sides.

Our eyes were locked on each other as we became encircled. My lip curled back as his nostrils flared, both of us ready to fight side by side out here until our very end.

We each let out triumphant screams as we leapt around, turning from one another as we pressed our backs together, guarding each other. Our blades were outstretched, breaths synchronized as our hearts pounded in unison, the two of us becoming a singular entity of fury and lethal grace.

Only, as my eyes adjusted through the smoky haze, they flared as they took in the sight of what *truly* surrounded us.

All fighting had ceased as nearby eyes were fixated on me and my mate. Soldiers were strewn across the disrupted ground, their exhaustion draining them from the brutality of the battle.

"*Jace*," I whispered down the bond as my gaze swept across the terrain.

A field that was once full of life now lay in ruins, painted in scarlet red, and littered with the fallen and remnants of war. The ground was adorned with protruding spears and swords, while banners lay trampled in the mud.

"Holy gods," he spoke aloud as the feeling of his back left my own, and he took a step up to my side.

In every direction I turned, the Islan soldiers were throwing down their weapons in surrender and defeat, their eyes cast to the ground.

Were they aware the queen had perished? Or was Kellan's death enough to cause this?

As relief and shock swirled within me, I felt Jace's adrenaline falter, feeling the true weight of his wound.

My gaze slowly lifted to meet his as he bowed his head, the last reserves of his strength slipping away. He sucked in a sharp breath right before he collapsed to the ground beside me, too fast for me to catch him, his breathing ragged and shallow.

"Jace!" His name left me in a guttural scream as I positioned myself protectively over him.

"The commander has fallen!" Someone shouted over the crackling embers, and I let out a growl.

"Oh, gods, Jace!" Zaela's voice carried from the distance, and my eyes shot to her as she shoved people out of the way to get to us as Gage did the same, not far behind her.

Our soldiers rallied, forming a protective ring around us—their loyalty unwavering. The enemy soldiers continued to watch, frozen where they stood, not willing to take the chance to attack.

My attention returned to my husband, whose eyes were fluttering shut from the agony of the wound that pierced the flesh directly above his heart. "*Handsome, I need you to keep your eyes open.*"

A lump formed in my throat as my nerves threatened to consume me.

"I'm okay, my Lia." His voice was raspy and barely audible.

"Do *not* lie to me! I can feel it, Jace. I can feel you, and you're not okay." My gaze swept my surroundings once more. "Where the fuck are the healers?!" I screamed.

I could barely catch my breath.

Gage and Zaela dropped to his opposite side then, eyes searching both of us for what to do. My breathing quickened, making me feel faint.

"Jace..." My voice cracked. Tears streamed down my face in a flood of waves, dripping onto his own as I hovered over him. "Please, I can't do this without you. What is the fucking point in this if you're not here with me?" I broke out into a gut-wrenching sob and could no longer vocalize what I needed to. "*I am nothing if you aren't here with me. The kingdom needs its king. I need my husband. I need my mate.*"

"Help me lift him up," Gage said to Zaela, and when they both went to move, I stopped them.

"Don't touch him," I ordered, and they instantly froze.

I bellowed a cry of desperation into the air as fear consumed me and then put my face next to his ear. "Jace, the queen is dead. *Kellan* is dead. It's over—we won."

A breathy, pained laugh left him as he looked up at me through cloudy eyes. "We won."

"We did." I swallowed thickly as I sniffled. "But not if you leave me for the vale."

The sound of galloping hooves approached us and the slightest bit of relief hit me to see it was Landon and Finn. They each jumped down from Matthias and ran to us.

"Finn," I nearly gasped.

"I'm not as quick as Veli," he warned warily. "He's lost a lot of blood, Lia."

"Just hurry, please!" I begged as I looked to the sky, where Veli had chased after Azenna, but they were nowhere to be seen.

"I'll be fine," Jace said through his teeth, but winced as he voiced the words.

I felt his worry—it was palpable, but he was still trying to put on a brave face for the rest of us.

"You lie to me so beautifully," I whispered his own words that he used when we first met. Something in him relaxed at hearing them.

"Do your worst, Finn," he rasped, trying to lighten the mood, but I still couldn't catch my breath.

Once Gage carefully removed Jace's shoulder armor, Finn dropped to his knees on his other side. He then pulled out vials of herb-infused liquids and salves, pouring and smearing them onto his gaping wound. I watched silently, barely breathing, as my brother went to work to save my mate's life. His fingers worked quickly as he stitched the wound close, the once-flowing blood ceasing.

Jace let out a hiss at the contact.

"He needs to drink this—it will help with the pain and loss of blood. It was extracted from sedaeyo leaves."

My husband gave me a subtle nod, finally admitting he needed help.

I took the vial from my brother and carefully lifted Jace's head into my lap. Bringing the vial to his lips, I slowly poured it into his mouth. His cloudy eyes remained on me as they gradually started to clear—his fading heartbeat growing stronger with each beat.

"My Lia," he rasped as a small smile leisurely tilted the edge of his lips.

Zaela and Gage let out shuddering breaths of relief as they remained at our side.

Sobs escaped me as I wrapped my arms around him tighter. "Thank the gods," I whispered. "I thought I was going to lose you." My tears formed a puddle on his skin.

"Never," he answered, and a smile tilted my lips as the tears continued to rush down my cheeks.

One of the promises we had always kept to one another. That we would *never* leave each other, and *always* find a way back to the other. In this realm and the next.

I lifted myself from him and hovered over his face. His hand moved to wipe the tears from my cheeks. A quiet laugh escaped me as I stared into his hazel eyes, never being more thankful in my life to still have him with me.

"Are you okay?" I asked in a whisper.

He gave me a knowing look with a half-smirk as he tried to hide his pain. "It's just a flesh wound."

I barked out a huff of a laugh. "Gods, that is *not* a flesh wound."

Jace pressed his lips firmly to my forehead, and I felt his touch tremble as relief settled into the both of us.

When he released me, I turned to the others. "Okay, now you can help get him up."

They didn't waste a second as they each aided him by lifting his back, being careful of his wounded shoulder.

"Gods, that's fucking brutal. I thought he pushed it straight through me." Jace let out a hiss as they moved him, but his eyes remained on my face the entire time. "Is it really over?"

"It is," I answered and then looked over my shoulder, across the battlefield. The gates caught my attention as they started to open, causing my eyes to widen.

Soldiers, both mortal and fae, watched from a distance, waiting to see the final command I would make. My eyes drifted over our enemy fleet, whose weapons remained laid down in surrender at their feet.

Then hooves sounded from our opposite side.

I turned to face Bruhn and crossed my arms, a single brow lifting at the sight of him. "Nice of you to show," I taunted him.

Jace's amusement tiptoed down the tether as he stood a pace behind me.

The centaur scoffed. "Watch it...Heir of the Realm." He paused for a moment. "Or should I now call you Queen?"

A smile curved my lips. "Lia will do."

I took in the sight of his powerful body, covered in lacerations. My people weren't the only ones who suffered loss today, but he came for me. The creatures of the realm came to aid their rightful queen.

"Thank you," I whispered as my eyes softened.

He huffed at me as if thanking him was a waste of time. "Do you have orders?"

I blinked at him. Shoving down the confusion of him being so cooperative, I cleared my throat. "Gather those who remain and bring them into the city. They will be given a choice. I will not slaughter those who surrendered." My words paused for a moment. "I'm not her."

Bruhn gave me a curt nod and took off, galloping towards those waiting in the field.

Turning back to face everyone, I nearly did a double take as I took in the sight of my family. They were all covered in ash and blood, their skin littered with wounds, exhaustion seeping into their faces, but they each had a glow about them.

My mate's stare met mine. "*You did it.*"

"*No. We all did.*"

A prideful smile answered me, and a caress of love warmed our bond.

Gage caught my attention then, his gaze peering over my shoulder toward the city at my back as he took a step in its direction. His lips parted, wearing a look that could only be described as pure relief.

Turning on my heels, I followed his line of sight, landing right at the center of the gates, where Avery stood in front of an enormous crowd of Isla's citizens.

"You did it," he whispered as his steps moved him past me.

A second later, he took off into a run, leaping over the leftover carnage of war to get to my sister.

Avery met his pace and raced toward him in the same breath, her torn gown flowing behind her in the wind, and when they met, she leapt into his arms. She wrapped her own around his neck and embraced him, her fiery locks cascading over his shoulder.

She lifted her gaze to mine as I stood in the distance with the others and gave me a soft smile that I returned.

An arm then wrapped around my waist, and Jace worked to stand tall at my side. Our eyes collided, and I looked him over. The arm with his injured shoulder was laced through a makeshift sling that looked as if it had been ripped from one of their shirts, but the bleeding had ceased, thanks to Finn's quick stitching.

"What are your plans if those who surrendered refuse to take a knee to your claim, Lia?" he asked as his gaze remained on me. A subtle growl lingered beneath his words.

"I'm hoping it doesn't come to that."

Zaela stepped up to my opposite side on near-silent feet, her stare locked on Avery and Gage as they approached us. "Has anyone seen Veli?" she asked in a whisper.

My eyes flared and instantly lifted to the sky. "Oh, gods..." I whipped back to Jace. "She saved us! She saved me and Avery. We never would have been able to get out without her."

His jaw locked, and his stare lifted back to the gates, where the centaurs and forest creatures lined up the Islan soldiers and guided the gazing citizens back inside.

"There was an eruption in the sky toward the far edges of the city. I saw it briefly and assumed it was Nox...but he's been out of flame since he returned to us down here."

"Oh, gods..." I whispered.

Avery and Gage came to a halt before us. I looked into my sister's honey-hued eyes, so similar to her mother's, yet entirely different. "Veli?" I asked warily.

She bit her lower lip, sucking it in through her teeth. "There was so much going on. I was just trying to get everyone to listen to me and get to safety, but then the guards on the tower shouted the fighting had ceased, and everyone rushed back to the gates."

Bruhn appeared once more, galloping up to us. "There is something you need to see," he announced to me. "My herd hurried into the city the second the gates opened. It was just reported to me that your silver-haired witch has been found in the castle gardens."

My eyes widened. "And?"

He pressed his lips together and shook his head.

"No," I breathed and took off in a run toward Nox, who waited in the center of the ruined field.

Jace rapidly caught up with me and extended his good arm, allowing me to assist him in getting onto the wyvern.

Everyone else raced towards the gates.

SEVENTY-EIGHT

Elianna

THE ONCE-CALM WINDS BECAME a storm from booming wyvern wings, rustling the leaves and tousling the flowers as Nox's immense shadow eclipsed the castle garden.

His landing shook the ground, but I was up and running before he had settled. The echo of Jace calling my name from our mount carried to me on the breeze, but all I could focus on was finding my aide.

"Veli!" I called, but my voice only echoed through the floral tunnels.

I raced to the garden's center, hoping to climb its fountain and get a better look over the area, but my steps faltered the moment the stone structure came into view.

"Oh no," I whispered, my fingertips flying to cover my lips.

"Jace, over here!" I frantically screamed as I ran toward the sorceress.

Once I reached her, I fell to my knees beside her lifeless body. My gaze shot to the sky, then whipped in every direction of the garden, searching for any sign of Azenna.

Jace caught up to me then as the sound of the others' racing footsteps funneled into the garden. He called to them as I gently placed my hands on either side of her shoulders.

Her body was broken, as if it had been shattered as it collided with the garden's floor. Veli's chest didn't move with steady breaths, and her skin was white as porcelain, icy to the touch.

My stare met Jace's, and all I saw in his eyes was sorrow.

"She's *not* dead," I said, voice cracking.

"Lia..."

"NO!" I roared. "I didn't accept it with you, and I will not accept it with her either."

"Lia...she isn't breathing." His voice was barely above a whisper, and I shot him a look as silver lined my vision.

The others finally reached us, and Finnian rushed over, dropping to the ground. Checking Veli's pulse, he shook his head as he sniffled and slowly stood back up, confirming the unthinkable. Avery's hands flew to cover her mouth as tears welled in her eyes. Zaela looked...devastated. There was no other word.

I wouldn't accept this—I refused.

"Veli. Your stupid, reckless, *foolish* girl is here demanding that you come back to us. You saved us. Don't you *dare* fucking die on us!" My voice rose with each word.

My jaw locked, veins bulging from my neck in anger. It wasn't fair—nothing about this was.

Zaela fell to her knees beside me, and I lifted my stare to hers. Something rarely seen lay in her eyes—tears.

"She's truly gone," she whispered.

A sniffle left me, and I looked up to the sky that was falling into twilight. "You said there was an eruption?"

"Yes, but it could have been anything," Jace answered softly.

My eyes drifted around once more and then back down to Veli's body, halting on her hand. Gaze narrowing in on her taloned fingers, I noticed she clutched something between them—and then the sound of it carried to my ears.

"It could have been anything," I mimicked him. "Even a witch."

"What?" Zaela gasped, her stare boring into the side of my face as I stared down at Veli's broken body.

I took hold of Veli's wrist and placed her fist in my lap. Swallowing thickly, I carefully unraveled her fingers from what was held between them, and my eyes flared when they were met with a black, beating heart.

"Holy gods," Zaela breathed. "Is that...?"

"I believe so," I answered softly, sitting in just as much disbelief.

"Witches are immortal," Avery whispered from behind us, forcing us all to turn.

"Well, apparently not, Avery," Zaela snapped.

"They are," she shot back, just as viciously. "Aside from their hearts. They can't live without the essence of a beating heart."

My own heart raced as I realized what she was trying to say.

"I can't place the heart inside of her, Avery," I said, and the words hurt more than I was willing to admit. "There isn't a hole where her heart would be. Her body was likely crushed at the impact, and her bones were shattered. For all we know, they could have impaled her heart." My voice cracked on the last word.

"Magic is will and intention," Avery whispered. "And the heart still beats."

Zaela's breath caught at my sister's words, and she reached for Veli's hand, which lifelessly rested on my lap, and gently lifted it.

Carefully wrapping her hands around Veli's talons that clutched the heart, she guided it to the sorceress' chest, directly above where her own once beat.

"Listen here, witch," I started, a false laugh leaving me. "I refuse to let you die. We have lost too many today and every day for a century. You're not like those other witches. You are *good*."

Zae looked at me and then back down at Veli's body before she spoke. "Our queen needs her aide...if you leave us, you are leaving one of the rest of us to be that for her, and only the gods know where that will bring the realm. So stop being so damn selfish and come back to us," she demanded. "Come back to me." Her last words were spoken so softly I barely heard them.

Zaela's hand trembled as she held Veli's in place.

"Zae," I started, but she shot me a look, so I sat back on my heels in defeat. Her head fell, sagging between her shoulders as the loss slammed into her, too.

"Oh my gods," Avery breathed from behind us, and both of our stares snapped back to Veli.

Right there before us, beneath Zaela's hand that clutched her lover's, shadows appeared—leisurely emerging from between the witch's talons, dancing and swirling as if carried by a faint wind.

"Mother of the gods..." Zae gasped softly.

"Don't move your hand," I ordered.

She flashed her hazel eyes at me, nerves filtering through them, but she obeyed.

The heart emitted an unnatural, scarlet glow, casting an ominous light that shone through both her and Veli's intertwined fingers.

With a sudden surge, the heart in the witch's hand pulsed a brighter red as more darkness emerged from its depths until it burst into nothing but shadows. As if made of smoke, the dark tendrils glided and danced in the air, draping themselves over her lifeless body, cloaking her like a second skin.

Zaela's hand snapped back toward herself, clutching it close to her chest as her eyes remained on Veli.

"How did you kill the crone, Avery?" I asked warily, half turning to face her.

"I stabbed her in the heart and twisted the blade," she answered. "She erupted a second later."

"Essence," I breathed after a moment. "What she spoke of was literal—it truly is the *essence* of a beating heart that a witch needs to survive."

Veli's body twitched as her bones snapped back into place. A flicker of movement stirred beneath her closed eyelids, and my lips parted as we all watched in awed silence. Everyone behind us rushed forward, looming over our backs as we all held our breaths.

The shadows enveloped Veli's entire body and seeped into her as if they were a phantom. My aide's eyes snapped open, now aglow with their usual otherworldly radiance, except now they were a full scarlet hue.

Life surged back into her veins, causing her to take a sudden intake of breath. Her gaze, now sharp and piercing, surveyed all of us who stood over her.

"Veli?" I whispered in shock.

"What have you done?" she asked. "I was gone...no longer in my body, floating to the vale of the afterworld alongside my wretched sisters, and then I was called back..." Her eyes drifted between me and Zaela. "You called me back—willed it."

Zae's cheeks flushed a vibrant pink. "I don't know how," she answered, and suddenly it felt as if we were all intruding on a very intimate moment between the two. "This is impossible. We don't possess magic."

Veli slowly sat upright, both of us reaching out to catch her in case she fell. Her red gaze then drifted down to her hand, the one that had clutched the High Witch's heart. "The realm itself is magic, Zaela. It has been woven into its soil since the day the gods conjured us all from it," she stated. "It is why the land answers to the descendants of the first of the fae, and it is why the beating heart of a sorceress listened to her sheer, stubborn will."

She paused. "Although, being bright enough to place it atop my corpse did help its essence sense where it was needed."

A few nervous chuckles left me. Placing my hand on Veli's shoulder, I said, "I have never been more thankful for stubborn will." And she smiled—a genuine, beaming smile that I had never seen the witch bear.

She was different, though. An intense, ancient otherworldliness radiated from her like never before, and I had a feeling it wasn't just because of her eyes morphing to that of a dark sorceress.

Zaela pulled Veli to her feet, but her gaze flared as their skin touched. She eyed her as if trying to understand what she felt from her, just as I was.

Their stares were locked on each other, and while Zae looked skeptical, Veli was giving her an almost mocking, knowing look.

"You're different," Zae announced.

Jace came up to my side then and wrapped his uninjured arm around my waist as if he would need to move to protect me from my own aide. I shot him a look with a raised brow.

"I am," Veli answered her.

Shadows came out from beneath her silver hair, dancing around her face as if in answer. "They are the same, though. The shadows will not harm you unless I will them to." Her grin was wicked.

The realization of it all hit me then. "You're..." I started.

"I am High Witch," she finished for me. "The coven, even when dissipated, needs balance, and the power transferred to me upon Azenna's death."

My mouth popped open and a nervous giggle left me as I remained beneath her stare. Despite being nearly half a foot shorter than me, Veli always had a presence that made her seem significantly taller—even more so now.

"Wow," Finn let out from behind us all, where he stood with the others as they watched. "Well, isn't that just the most terrifying thing I've heard all day..." We all gave him a look. "And we went to *war*," he added with a half laugh.

Avery slapped her hand over her mouth to hide her own giggle.

"Heir of the Realm," Bruhn's voice broke the brief span of silence after his joke, and we all turned towards its echo. "Your prisoners have been taken and are lined up throughout the city. We await your orders."

I blew out a breath and turned to my mate.

"Are you ready?" he asked, and I looked to my court, whose bodies were bloodied and half-broken, but I couldn't have been more thankful that we had made it through.

I looked up into the sky, where the sun had been setting, slipping the realm into darkness.

"It's time. They will be given a choice to take a knee to my claim or meet their end in Nox's blaze," I answered, and then turned back to Bruhn. "Bring them to the battlement gates."

SEVENTY-NINE

Elianna

NOX SAT PERCHED ATOP the castle's stone battlement, overlooking the soldiers that waged war against us only hours ago. Thousands of soldiers stood before me, their faces dimly lit by only the light of the moon, and torches that lined the cobblestone streets.

The Islan army stood in disciplined rows, looking terrified and full of exhaustion, just as my own men had.

I held my chin high as I stood before them, commanding the attention that some of them had refused to give even when I was their appointed captain.

Choosing my words carefully, I made sure they conveyed a sense of authority. "I stand before you not as a tyrant, but as the rightful queen who seeks unity for all creatures under her reign."

My eyes drifted over them, surveying their faces as their eyes flickered with a blend of dishonor and curiosity. An intense silence filtered through the air, and while I craved acceptance from them, I was determined to show that if they were not willing to abide by my law; they had no place in Velyra.

"You have known me for decades—the *real* me, not the usurper the false queen whispered lies about into the tips of your ears. You knew my father and who he was as your king. It is important that you know you stand here not as prisoners but as subjects of a new reign. For a better realm," I declared.

Pride flowed down the bond from my mate as he stood off to the side along with the others. Each of them wore faces of pure steel, letting any wandering eyes know that, while benevolent, we were not a court to be fucked with.

A growl rumbled from Nox as his head levitated directly above my own—showing his approval to me and his deadly temper to those who stood before us.

As I spoke, the soldiers' expressions shifted. Any lingering defiance waned into hesitant acceptance.

"Every soldier standing before me now faces a choice," I continued, my tone more assertive. "You can resist the inevitable change of reign, clinging to the remnants of what had once been...or you can choose to kneel before your new queen, whose birthright is to rule over that of your realm. And if you refuse, well...my wyvern stands behind me for a reason."

There was a tense silence as the soldiers before me exchanged wary glances. I unsheathed my sword from my hip and placed the tip onto the ground before my feet, standing tall and proud before them. Not only would I be their queen, but I remained one of them—a fighter, a warrior by choice. It was who I was and always would be.

The weight of their decision hung in the air around us like an invisible force. My stare locked onto theirs, gaze unwavering in a challenge to them to defy me—but then my eyes softened.

"I cannot stand here before you and state that everything will be simple and easy. In fact, I'm willing to bet that we will face challenges never before seen. How does one undo over a century of hatred and vengeance? How does a queen seek the confidence of her people when they have been at odds for more than triple the lifetime of one of its races?"

Silence answered me, and I took it all in, standing beneath the weight of their stares.

"*My sweet Lia.*" Jace's voice filtered through me, gentle and reassuring.

My gaze flickered over to him then, and my eyes met the fierce commander, staring down potential enemies before they swore an oath to his mate and queen. Eyes narrowing in on him, I forced myself to halt my smirk, knowing that he would slaughter them all himself without hesitation if they defied me.

After a tense moment, the first among them, a battered warrior with fatigue etched across his face, stepped forward. "Solus," he started, and my husband aggressively cleared his throat from where he remained, startling the soldier.

"Captain...Valderre," he continued. "I cannot say I speak for *every* individual here, but I will confidently say that this is for most of the masses that had been trapped under Idina's control. We will gladly follow you and your reign. You had my sword as my captain, and now you will have it as my queen." He slowly sank to one knee on his last word.

My eyes flared as I willed the rest of my features to remain emotionless. "And what say the rest of you?" My voice was stern.

Suddenly, his surrender rippled through the ranks like a quiet wave. My lips parted at the sight I never thought I'd see.

The clinking of armor was the only sound to be heard through the darkened streets as, one by one, the Islan army knelt.

EIGHTY

Jace

IT HAD BEEN a month since the battle decimated the land directly beyond the Islan Gates—a full turn of the moon since we defeated the malevolent beasts that usurped their way to my mate's throne, and since their people chose to bow before her, pledging their allegiance to the rightful queen.

The city itself had been partially destroyed thanks to the battles of witches and wyverns that took to the skies. Entire towers of the castle had crumbled to the ground, and their lashing tails and power had slammed into the terracotta roofs spread throughout Isla, bringing buildings down with them. Thankfully, the civilian casualties were minimal from inside the city walls, but any loss was too great for my Lia.

She had desperately tried to prevent the fighting and destruction from entering the city, but an aerial war was unavoidable upon arrival.

She had spent every moment of the following days out in the streets with her people, getting to know them further. And for every life lost, she personally visited the homes of their families, offering condolences from the crown, and aid if needed.

Every moment I thought to myself that I couldn't possibly ever love her more, she proved me wrong—which, of course, was her favorite thing to do.

The sirens had lingered in Isla's harbor the following days as we worked to clean the disaster created. None of the soldiers would even near the docks, fearful that they might catch the sea-witches' attention and fall into a lulling song.

Lia had confidently swaggered down the longest dock that sat in the bay, twirling the conch shell she had stolen from them between her fingertips as I watched from the port. Of course, she taunted them with it before handing it over, making them swear to only feast upon the flesh of the wicked that sailed the sea, but she took it for what it was—a battle for another day. In that moment, the sirens were allies, and that was what mattered.

Veli's ascension to High Witch was both terrifying and relieving, though it was clear she mourned her old self. She originally expressed her nerves regarding the power she now exuded, but quickly learned it didn't change who she was—for magic was merely a reflection of its wielder's nature. And she now kept the book, *Tinaebris Malifisc,* under lock and key, hidden away from the rest of the realm.

The witches who remained hidden all this time were still nowhere to be found. Even Empri was missing, who vanished from the battlefield after her sister's death. We didn't blame her for her reaction, but she caused casualties on our side from her explosion of fury, and it was unacceptable. Veli searched for them throughout the realm with her newfound power, but they were now hiding the use of their magic, just as she had for centuries.

Whenever they were brought up, Lia and Veli both wore menacing grins, stating that they couldn't hide forever—and may the gods help those traitor witches if they were found.

If there were ever two females that I would never want to be on the receiving end of their wrath, it would be those two—and where they went, Zaela followed, which made them even more terrifying.

Now that Veli held the nearly untapped power of High Witch, she was able to summon portal rifts effortlessly and opened a bridge from Isla to beyond the mountains, where Alaia Valley awaited. Our mortal soldiers were able to return home to their loved ones and heal in comfort. However, there had been one reunion that held nothing but shattering pain and sorrow.

Lynelle was the first to walk through the rift, Nyra trotting at her side. The wolf's eyes landed on Lia, pushing her into a sprint across the short distance between them and tackling her to the ground. She planted kisses all over Lia's face as she whimpered in happy excitement.

Zaela had stepped up beside me, her face etched with grief as her mother approached. The moment Lynelle's steps faltered, it revealed that she had pieced together Leon's fate. We told her of the sacrifice he made and that her daughter stood before her now because of him. *That is the price of loving a warrior*, she had said once she caught her breath.

My heart lurched for her as my gaze drifted to my own warrior queen while she stepped up next to me to give her condolences and support to Lynelle.

Now, a month after the Battle of Isla, I stood off to the side of the dais with Finnian, Gage, and Landon as the newly appointed castle guards funneled the realm's lords and the families of noble houses to their seats, awaiting our queen's coronation.

The throne room was decorated intricately, all of Avery's doing, who couldn't wait to direct the staff to the gardens to handpick her sister's favorite flowers.

The once blood-stained room now sparkled with an ethereal glow, the afternoon sunlight filtering through the high, reforged stained-glass windows that depicted the scenery of Velyra.

At the center of the dais stood the throne of her father, though there was one change made to the royal seat. Wyvern wings, crafted from steel by the city's finest blacksmiths, were fastened to its back, protruding out at its sides.

The walls were draped in luxurious evergreen tapestries, woven with threads of champagne and silver, depicting the new Valderre crest. A series of tall pillars lined the sides of the room, holding Avery's chosen florals, while torches bathed the shadow-draped parts of the room in their flickering light.

The atmosphere crackled with excitement as Avery, Veli and Zaela appeared, walking along the sides of the room, to their place on the opposite side of the dais from where us men stood.

"Are you ready to see your queen, brother?" Gage whispered from behind me.

I couldn't help my smile. "Always."

Music sounded from the small orchestras set off in the throne room's corner, and as if on cue, the great doors swung open. The opened, arched entrance revealed the most beautiful sight I had ever witnessed—my Lia standing before us all, Nyra at her side as a guardian. The crowd collectively held its breath as we watched her take the first steps toward her throne.

She moved at an elegant pace, at such odds with her usual swaggering facade, while her gown flowed behind her like a river of ivory silk.

The fabric of her gown cascaded around her in layers of pearl, and when it caught the light with each step, it showed a hidden luster of green—a testament to her house and kingdom. My warrior queen had never been accustomed to dresses and was sure to have that reflected in her coronation gown, as its shoulders bore silver embellishments that resembled both wyvern scales and armor atop her shoulders.

Her long, dark hair was unbound in curls as beautifully wild as she was, while those stunning green eyes were locked on me, threatening to bring me to my knees before the masses.

As Lia advanced with Nyra at her side, the crowd gazed at her, eyes wide with admiration. Lords bowed as she passed, their wives curtsying beside them. The air buzzed with murmured praises and gasps as they took in the sight of her.

Nearing the dais, her eyes remained on me, and mine on hers, and then the corner of her lips tilted in a menacing lilt. Her steps halted as she stood directly before us all, the wolf taking her place at her sister's feet. Avery quickly wiped tears as they slid down her cheeks, and Zae's lower lip trembled at the sight of the soon-to-be crowned queen. Then Veli stepped forward.

The sorceress was not in her usual attire of onyx, flowing robes, but now instead was adorned in an ethereal gown of violet that would have once matched her eyes. Her scarlet gaze looked over my mate and then drifted over her shoulder to the crowd at her back.

"You may all be seated," she announced, and the sound of groaning chairs echoed through the room as the orchestra softened their music.

She exchanged a glance with Lia, and then my wife gave her a subtle nod to continue.

"Elianna Valderre has lived a life of secret, riddled with hidden torment, torture, and betrayal. Her throne and crown stolen from her the moment her soul entered the realm. Both of her parents, our late king, and his love, murdered in cold blood, all because of a tyrant. She bore the last name Solus, disguised as an orphan of the realm, all while living a lie within the castle walls."

My heart cracked at the witch's words as she retold Lia's story to all in the room.

"*It's old news,*" she whispered in my mind.

"*That will never make it any more bearable to hear, my Lia,*" I answered, and she sent a loving caress through our tethered souls.

Veli continued her speech. "She fought her usurper's war blindly and found the means to end it, uniting enemy races that had been at odds for over a century. Elianna now fights for that of her people, and all creatures of the realm, who call Velyra their home. Her skin bears her earned scars and will for the remainder of her life. Let the markings upon your queen's skin be a reminder to you all of everything she has done for the realm, and what she has sacrificed to get you here."

The queen's aide lifted her taloned hands from her sides, hovering them palm open before her. Then, a crown manifested within her grasp, but not just any crown. The one she wore on our wedding day—and all she wore that night.

"Do you, Elianna Valderre, swear to justly govern and defend the Kingdom of Velyra as its rightful queen, protecting the sacredness of all the gods' creatures who call it home?"

Lia's lips curved subtly, as if in mockery of what her aide had asked—for everything that she had asked of her, the realm's rightful queen had always done just that.

Veli lifted a brow in her direction, and a breathy chuckle slipped from my mate, earning a grin from me as I remained at the side of the dais.

"From now until my dying breath," Lia answered.

"Then bow," she demanded, and our queen carefully lowered her head.

Veli took the silver tiara of twisted, leafy vines and placed it atop my mate's hair. The emerald sparkled in its center, mimicking Lia's eyes.

"I now pronounce you, Elianna Valderre, first of her name, Heir of the Mother Goddess and Realm, as Queen of Velyra."

With a dignified poise, Lia turned to the masses, bearing the weight of the realm's crown, representing the blend of both tradition and the promise of a new era.

The thunderous cheers of the crowd filled the grand throne room, their echoes bouncing off the walls. "Long live Queen Elianna Valderre!" they chanted in unison, bringing tears to all of our eyes.

I watched Lia as she clasped her hands in front of her, her stare remaining on the masses as they celebrated her ascension. After a few moments of allowing it to continue, she wordlessly raised one of her hands, halting their cheers, and placing the throne room into near silence.

"I am honored to be here before you all today, and even more so that you are proud to call me your queen, but there is one other to be crowned before you today," she started, and my heart nearly stopped in my chest.

She extended her arm toward me, beckoning me to join her in the center of the dais. Gage lightly kicked my foot, trying to get me to move, but it felt as if I was bolted to the floor.

"Go, you idiot," Gage whispered in a room full of fae, causing chuckles to escape the first few rows of seats.

I shot him a quick look over my shoulder, and then my eyes met the queen's. A beautiful, delicate smile adorned her face as she held her hand out to me, waiting for me to join her.

I took the few steps up to where she stood before her throne as Veli took a few silent steps back to her place in line with Avery and Zaela.

"*This wasn't part of our plan, my queen.*"

My fingers interlocked with hers, and then her voice filtered to me. "*I love you, and it was* always *part of mine.*"

The corners of my lips lifted at that.

"This man," she spoke aloud as her eyes remained on me before slowly drifting to the hundreds of pairs on us. "You know this man as the great commander of the mortal armies, who was once believed to be our enemy. The man who helped us win this war, who has protected his people since he swore an oath to them at a young age, just as I had...a *very* long time ago," she said with a small giggle, and the crowd echoed it.

"Jace is much more than that, though, for you see...he is everything to me. He stands before you today not only as a commander of war and protector of the realm...but also as my husband and mate." She paused for a moment, and the crowd remained still and silent. "And your king consort."

Small murmurs erupted, and she lifted her opposite hand that held mine to silence them again.

"You'll have to excuse me, for you should all know by now that I'm not one to follow rules or traditions, and I much prefer to make things up as I go along..." Brief laughter echoed once more, and a smirk found my lips. "A private wedding was held. It was special and beautiful, and when we truly didn't know if we would make it out of the great war alive. So today, I ask one more thing of the realm—to accept my husband and mate..." She turned to me and gave me a quick wink. "Jace Cadoria-Valderre, as Velyra's King Consort."

Veli appeared at my side a second later, a silver crown fit for a king in her grasp that I had never seen before. She motioned for me to bow, and I obeyed. The witch placed the crown atop my head, and my eyes flared in disbelief at what was happening before everyone. She vanished once more, appearing back at Avery's side.

Lia's eyes watched me intently, a smile adorning her perfect face, with eyes radiating love as she stared up at my crown. Her gaze then scanned over the quiet room. "So, Velyra...what say you?!" she bellowed, every bit the former captain.

The masses of Velyra's lords, mercenaries, and countrymen, both of fae and mortal heritage, erupted into a booming cheer for her—for *us*.

I turned to face the queen of the realm. My heart, once so cold and ruthless, beamed with pride and love for the goddess that stood before me atop her dais.

"And what say you, Commander?" she asked softly.

"Long live the queen," I answered, and then my arms wrapped around her waist, twirling her in a dip before pressing my lips to hers for the realm to see.

If I thought the crowd had been cheering before, it didn't even compare to the sound erupting from them now. When I opened my eyes, I found hers staring up at me.

"And you, my Lia?"

"Long live the king," she breathed.

EIGHTY-ONE

Elianna

AFTER THE CEREMONY, I waltzed down the aisle, arm in arm with my mate, husband, and now king, as our court leisurely followed behind us. We walked through the throne room doors and out the front entrance of the castle, my Nyra girl trotting playfully around our feet as we made our way to Isla's streets.

Nox sat atop the stone battlement, his favorite spot to perch in recent weeks, and chirped into the air at the sight of us approaching. Horses were at our sides, preparing to take my court through the awaiting crowds, as I was to be shown to the rest of the city as queen for the first time.

I looked up at Nox, who stared down at me, waiting for the command to descend to the ground, but I gave a slight shake of my head instead.

"As if you have never flown in a gown," Jace teased from my side.

My stare moved back to the horses, where Matthias waited with the others. "I won't be seen by the city from the skies. They will have plenty of chances to watch me wreak havoc through the clouds." A smile formed on my face. "Landon," I called over my shoulder. "Will you please bring Matthias to me?"

The castle's former stable hand looked as if he would burst with joy as he ran up to my old mount and brought him to me, placing his reins in my hands.

"Hi, boy," I greeted my warhorse and pressed my nose to his snout. "What do you say we have some fun, like old times, huh?"

More horses were brought for my entire court, and they mounted their steeds in unison with me. Veli used her magic to drape my gown gracefully along Matthias' back while I sat upon my horse as I always had—a warrior.

Peering over my shoulder, I was met with the gazes of our dearest friends—my rebellion-leading sister and kind-hearted brother, a stable hand turned soldier, my aide, who was now High Witch, and my mate's two fearless co-seconds. The Velyran Rebels turned the noble court of the rightful queen.

My stare lifted to Nox a final time, where his golden eyes were locked on me intensely. My usual smirk tipped my lips, right before I menacingly whispered, "*Ignystae.*"

Without hesitation, my wyvern shot a blast of flames high into the sky above, earning awe-like noises from those surrounding us. And then, with a powerful roar, Nox shot into the sky, launching himself off the battlement.

The castle's gates opened toward the city, and we all began the walk to our new beginning as my wyvern's shadow loomed over us from above.

The celebrations for the new queen and king of Velyra lasted days, with endless parties, food, and mischief of all sorts—my favorite things.

When the festivities came to a close, and the lords returned to their cities and ports, life in Isla resumed to how it had always been under my father's reign. However, the time had come for decisions regarding the rest of the realm.

Although we understood that changing everyone's beliefs and habits would take time, we started by spreading word throughout Velyra, emphasizing the importance of diversity and developing a sense of community between humans and fae in every city, port, and village. This started with the joining of our armies.

Standing in the living room of our new chambers, I looked over my court—where half of them would now live in the Valley as we remained in Isla.

I caught tears slipping from Avery's lower lashes with the tip of my finger while she stared at me beneath Gage's shadow as he hovered close to her—a constant guardian of the former princess and her now fiancé.

A giggle slipped from me at her expense, and she rolled her eyes at me, swatting at my fingers as she tried to wipe her tears.

"You *do* know that I can see you tomorrow, Avery." I leaned in closer to her. "That's why I keep the High Witch happy." I winked.

Veli scoffed and crossed her arms from beside us. "I heard that."

I shrugged. "Among other reasons."

"I know," my sister answered with a laugh. "I will just miss you."

"Shh," Gage said. "We need to get out of here before they realize placing us in charge of Alaia was a grave mistake."

"You think you're the only one in charge?" Zaela taunted from across the room. "You're not the *only* newly appointed commander, Gage."

Two bickering co-seconds turned co-commanders of Velyra's northern armies. We wanted more than anything for them to remain right here at our sides with us, but someone had to oversee the north—and it was their true home.

They would, once again, work to rebuild Ellecaster and clear the passage that was blocked to the valley from its devastation. Bruhn had even offered the assistance of the Sylis creatures, provided I *officially* named him Lord of the Wood, as he had introduced himself so long ago, and as I had promised when seeking his aid.

Finn and Landon would stay here in Isla, where they had always been. Jace planned to appoint Landon as a general in the king's army and couldn't wait to surprise him with the promotion. And Finnian, with Veli's assistance, planned to reopen the House of Healers in the city.

My brother had even promised to build a monument to the once great healer, Ophelia, who had birthed the queen of the realm and sacrificed her life for it. My heart swelled to the point where I thought it would burst when he told me his plan.

Memorials for both the fallen king and his loyal guard were also planned to be built within the city square, right where the rebellion began.

Avery hugged our brother tightly, swinging him as she held him in a death grip. "Avery, I will see you next Wednesday!" he screeched, trying to pull from her grasp.

The night we had chosen for family dinner and game night—where wine would be drank and responsibilities put on hold.

"Well, excuse me for already missing the one person who has been attached to my hip since his birth, Finnian," Avery scolded, and my hand flew to my lips to cover my laugh.

Gage clapped Finn and Landon on their shoulders and then practically shoved them out of the way as he barreled across the short distance to Jace, nearly tackling him to the ground.

He placed the king of the realm in a headlock and playfully punched him in the gut. "I'm going to miss you, you not-so-boring-anymore bastard."

Jace's laugh echoed through the room, his joy and slight annoyance thrumming down the bond as he swatted at his best friend.

Gage released him with a classic shove toward the ground and then stormed in my direction, wrapping me in a bear hug. "Queen of the Realm!" He swung me around in his arms.

Once he settled and loosened his grip, I looked up at him and pinched his cheek. "And soon-to-be sister-in-law." I winked.

"Cadoria!" he shouted over his shoulder at Jace. "You are no longer the luckiest man in the realm." He turned to him. "It is I who gets to not only marry a Valderre but also be the queen's in-law."

"You do realize that also makes Jace your in-law, too, right?" Zaela sassed him from where she stood in the corner near Veli.

"This is the best day ever," Gage breathed, and we all burst into laughter.

While everyone was distracted, my eyes drifted to the two blondes hidden within shadows as their whispers traveled through the chamber softly.

"It appears that our time together has come to an end, witch," Zaela taunted.

Veli offered her a closed-lip smile as she looked Zaela up and down. "I will be just a rift-walk away."

With a wave of her hand, a portal appeared on the balcony of the chamber we were in, where Alaia Valley sat at its opposite end.

After everyone finished their goodbyes, I finally allowed tears to slide down my cheeks, but it helped to know that, with the help of Veli's magic, it wasn't as if they would *truly* be across the realm. A wave of my aide's talons and I could appear right back at the Cadoria Estate or the war chamber, where all these plans that we never thought would come true were made.

One by one, our court stepped through, leaving Isla and entering the northern valleys beyond the Ezranian Mountains, where only a year ago, I thought was a barren wasteland. However, there were a lot of things I believed a year ago that held little truth.

Once they were gone, Landon and Finnian left the chamber to head into the city for dinner. Veli sensed the change in the atmosphere with it just being the three of us, and vanished before our eyes, bursting into her shadows that she now adored to no end—the only dark magic she allowed herself to use.

And then it was just the two of us—the queen and king of the realm. Husband and wife, and mates fated by the gods, standing alone in their castle's chamber as our wyvern circled the skies just beyond its balcony.

"Any plans for us this evening, my queen?" he asked. "Before the realm seeks our services."

I closed the distance between us and lifted myself on my tiptoes, pressing my lips to his.

When our kiss broke, I gazed into the hazel eyes that had me fall for him that night in the forest, when we thought our attraction was just the euphoroot clouding our better judgment. And, holy mother of the gods, how far had we come since then...

It all felt as if it were a lifetime ago now.

He took my hand in his and led me out to the balcony to summon Nox. We watched as he banked left in the sky and soared towards us until he halted to hover just beyond the rail.

A smile beamed from me, and I climbed over the stone railing and leapt onto my mount. Extending my hand back toward my mate, I said, "Care for another wyvern ride, handsome? I promise this one won't end in raining hellfire." I winked, giving him the most innocent smile.

He gave me a knowing smirk right before he let out my favorite breathy laugh of his. "I would be honored, my Lia," he answered as he climbed atop a saddleless Nox.

Our wyvern shot off into the sky, where the sun was ablaze with the fiery hues of sundown, our laughter echoing through the clouds.

Jace and I had done it. We had created a better realm for all of its creatures, just as we had always hoped and wished for—with him and I at the center of it.

THE END.

Acknowledgements

THANK YOU SO MUCH to every single person who has believed in me, and my story, from the very start.

Thank you to my love and family for supporting this and cheering me on the whole way. Your words of encouragement when I doubted myself kept me going.

Celia and Tory, as always, your constant support has meant everything to me, and this never would've been possible without the two of you cheering me on since this idea came to this little brain of mine.

Oh, coven, my coven. Who knew that joining a discord server would lead to such beautiful friendships? Thank you for *everything*. For keeping me going, cheering me on, crying with me, celebrating me, and so much more. I can't imagine a more supportive and inspiring group of women to learn and grow alongside with.

Tabs, my girl. This book wouldn't be what it is without you. I'm thankful for everything you've done not only for me, but for this series. And mainly, I'm thankful for your friendship.

And last, but certainly not least, thank you to my fans and the friends I've made along the way of this crazy, beautiful journey. Whether you're another author, are on my Street Team, have sent me words of encouragement, or have been a helping, supportive hand, I am eternally grateful.

Thank you for sticking here with me as I learn and grow as an author.

This is only the beginning.

To the moon!

Made in the USA
Middletown, DE
13 December 2024

66872691R00399